AF574380

South African Literature after the Truth Commission

South African Literature after the Truth Commission

Mapping Loss

Shane Graham

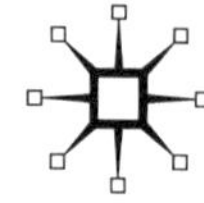

SOUTH AFRICAN LITERATURE AFTER THE TRUTH COMMISSION

Copyright © Shane Graham, 2009.

All rights reserved.

First published in 2009 by
PALGRAVE MACMILLAN®
in the United States—a division of St. Martin's Press LLC,
175 Fifth Avenue, New York, NY 10010.

Where this book is distributed in the UK, Europe and the rest of the world, this is by Palgrave Macmillan, a division of Macmillan Publishers Limited, registered in England, company number 785998, of Houndmills, Basingstoke, Hampshire RG21 6XS.

Palgrave Macmillan is the global academic imprint of the above companies and has companies and representatives throughout the world.

Palgrave® and Macmillan® are registered trademarks in the United States, the United Kingdom, Europe and other countries.

ISBN-13: 978–0–230–61537–3
ISBN-10: 0–230–61537–6

Library of Congress Cataloging-in-Publication Data

Graham, Shane (Shane Dwight)
South African literature after the Truth Commission : mapping loss / by Shane Graham.
p. cm.
Includes bibliographical references and index.
ISBN 0–230–61537–6
1. South African literature—History and criticism. I. Title.

PL8014.S6G73 2008
809′.8968—dc22 2008042812

A catalogue record of the book is available from the British Library.

Design by Newgen Imaging Systems (P) Ltd., Chennai, India.

First edition: May 2009

10 9 8 7 6 5 4 3 2 1

Printed in the United States of America.

Contents

Acknowledgments

This book has been many years in the making, and along the way I have accumulated innumerable debts of opportunity, kindness, hospitality, advice, feedback, and intellectual stimulation. To begin with: much of this book was researched and written with the help of a Postdoctoral Fellowship from the Andrew W. Mellon Foundation, sponsored by the English Studies Department at the University of the Witwatersrand in Johannesburg in 2004–05. I am deeply grateful both to the Mellon Foundation and to the Wits School of Literature and Language Studies for the chance to spend a year working and living in the city that looms so large in the narratives I study herein.

Certain sections of this book began life as part of my doctoral dissertation at Indiana University, which was supported by a Dissertation-Year Fellowship from the IU Graduate School. This support allowed me to spend several months in Cape Town, Johannesburg, and Pretoria in 2000, when the Amnesty Hearings were still taking place weekly, and when plays such as *The Story I Am about to Tell* were actively touring the country.

Several libraries, archives, and organizations have been exceedingly helpful: the National English Literary Museum in Grahamstown; the Historical Papers collections at Wits; the Centre for the Study of Violence and Reconciliation in Johannesburg; the National Archives in Cape Town; the District Six Museum staff; and the Mayibuye Centre at the University of the Western Cape, co-operated with the Robben Island Museum. I am grateful to all for their assistance.

Many good friends and mentors have helped me think through my ideas, have read various sections of the book, and have given me incisive and thought-provoking feedback at various stages. I would especially like to thank the following: David Attwell; Todd Avery; Jessica Baldanzi; Rita Barnard; Pat Brantlinger; Eva Cherniavsky; Stef Craps; Hermione Cronje; Christie Fox; Pier Paolo Frassinelli; Ronit Frenkel; Wendy Hesford; Eileen Julien; Valmont Layne; Andrew Libby; David Medalie; Sarah Nuttall; Pallavi Rastogi; Michael Titlestad; Natasha Vaubel; David Watson; and Al Wertheim. I owe a special debt to Pallavi, who read the entire manuscript start to finish—some parts multiple times—and always brought fresh insight to her readings.

I would like to thank the students in my World Writers course on Coetzee, Mda, Wicomb, and Magona during the Spring semester of 2006, and those in my Period Studies summer workshop on the South African transition in Summer 2007. Both groups of Utah State University students made me reevaluate my interpretation of texts I thought I long before had "solved," and made me appreciate the books anew for the stimulating discussions they provoked.

On my earliest trips to South Africa in 1999 and 2000, Stephen Gray and Nhlanhla Thwala extended their hospitality and made me feel welcome in what for me was a brave new world. They have my gratitude.

Thanks to my father for supporting me through everything.

Thanks to my mother for her endless support and for always believing in me.

And thanks to Christie—my *inamorata*, my partner in life and mind, and my best reader—for all the late-night walks.

* * *

I gratefully acknowledge permission to reprint, in partial or revised form, portions of the following articles:

"Apartheid Prison Narratives, the Truth and Reconciliation Commission, and the Construction of National (Traumatic) Memory." In *Colonial and Post-Colonial Incarceration*, ed. Graeme Harper. New York: Continuum Books, 2001. 223–39. © 2001, Continuum International Publishing Group.

"The Truth Commission and Post-Apartheid Literature in South Africa." *Research in African Literatures* 34.1 (Spring 2003): 11–30. © 2003, Indiana University Press.

"Layers of Permanence: Towards a Spatial-Materialist Reading of Ivan Vladislavić's *The Exploded View*." *Scrutiny2: Issues in English Studies in Southern Africa* 11.2 (2006): 48–61. © 2006, University of South Africa Press.

"Remembering to Forget: Monumental vs. Peripatetic Archiving in Achmat Dangor's *Bitter Fruit*." *Safundi: The Journal of South African and American Studies* 9.1 (2008): 39–52. © 2008, Taylor & Francis.

"'This Text Deletes Itself': Traumatic Memory and Space-Time in Wicomb's *David's Story*." *Studies in the Novel* 40.1–2 (2008): 127–145. © 2008, University of North Texas.

* * *

I thank Ingrid de Kok for her kind permission to quote her poems from *Seasonal Fires: New and Selected Poems* (Seven Stories, 2006). In addition, the publishers and authors of the following books have kindly allowed me to quote significant portions of the texts listed. Other quoted material in this book falls within legal standards of academic fair use.

Achmat Dangor, *Bitter Fruit*. Copyright, Achmat Dangor, 2001.
Aziz Hassim, *The Lotus People*. STE Publishers (Pty) Ltd., 2003.
Antjie Krog, *Country of My Skull*. Copyright Random House, 1998.
Anne Landsman, *The Devil's Chimney*. Published by Granta Books, 1999, and by Jonathan Ball Publishers, 1999.
Sindiwe Magona, *Mother to Mother*. Published by David Philip Publishers, 1998, an imprint of New Africa Books (Pvt.) Ltd.
Phaswane Mpe, *Welcome to Our Hillbrow*. Published by University of Natal Press, 2001.
Jane Taylor, *Ubu and the Truth Commission*. Published by University of Cape Town Press, 1998.
Ivan Vladislavić, *The Exploded View*. Copyright Random House, 2004.

Abbreviations

AC	Amnesty Committee of the TRC
ANC	African National Congress
DLA	Department of Land Affairs
HRV / HRVC	Human Rights Violation / Human Rights Violation Committee of the TRC
LRAD	Land Reform for Agricultural Development
MK	Umkhonto we Sizwe—armed wing of the ANC/SACP alliance
NP	National Party (white, Afrikaner-led party; instituted apartheid)
PAC	Pan Africanist Congress
RRC	Reparation and Rehabilitation Committee of the TRC
SABC	South African Broadcasting Corporation
SACP	South African Communist Party
SB	Security Branch
TRC	Truth and Reconciliation Commission
UDF	United Democratic Front

Introduction: Mapping Loss

"There are a lot of things that I may tell you, but I don't know where to start. I think I would stop there" (D. Khumalo). With this curiously circular statement, Duma Kumalo[1] ends his testimony to the Special Hearing on Prisons held by the Truth and Reconciliation Commission (TRC) of South Africa. Kumalo had been wrongfully convicted as one of the "Sharpeville Six" for a high-profile murder in 1984; he spent four years on death row before his execution was stayed, mere hours before his scheduled death. As we can see in those closing words, the experiences of facing his own demise and hearing fellow death row inmates being executed have played havoc with his sense of a self located in time and space. Cathy Caruth says that the traumatic ordeal is "a break in the mind's experience of time" (61); that fits Kumalo's situation, but his disorientation is simultaneously a more literal, spatial feeling of being lost, as well. Indeed, one source of his trauma is his former confinement within the enclosed space of the prison cell. As he tells a commissioner during his hearing, "I dream that I am still in prison, those are my dreams. Most of my dreams pertain to life in prison."

As I discuss in part 1 Kumalo has plenty of further opportunities after his two TRC hearings to tell his story in a public venue: he goes on to coauthor and star in two plays, and is interviewed for a documentary film about his life and incarceration. Yet up until his death in 2006, Kumalo never seems to escape the sense of being lost in time and space, as if a crucial part of himself were still back in that prison cell, and needed a "map" to escape. As he tells the commission, "I do not know how to put it quite clearly, I think if I could go back to that prison and assure myself that I have been released, maybe this psychological effect it had on me, might subside." In this sense, Kumalo's testimony and his dramatic work share much in common with South African culture and literature at large in the aftermath of apartheid and the Truth and Reconciliation Commission: it exhibits a collective sense of loss, mourning, and elegy, as well as a sense of disorientation amid rapid changes in the physical and social landscape. These changes necessitate new forms of literal and figurative "mapping" of space, place, and memory—hence the notion of "mapping loss" that gives this book its subtitle. Implicit in this idea is the assumption of complex interconnections between the body, memory, and social space. Ideally, memory acts as the connecting tissue between the body and the physical places it has occupied, providing at least the perception of a stable basis for identity and a sense of community.

Yet the whole history of colonization, modernization, and apartheid has served to rupture the connections between people and places in South Africa. The land, already long contested and fought over before European settlers arrived, has in the course of the last 200 years been systematically laid claim to, partitioned, fenced, developed, and farmed with unusual intensity. The indigenous black majority was forced from arable rural land onto arid reservations that later evolved into the "Bantustans" or homelands. Similarly, fearing a permanently urbanized African population that could pose a threat to white dominance, the colonial and apartheid governments forcibly removed blacks, coloureds,[2] Indians, and other nonwhite racial groups from most city spaces and relocated them to distant townships. In this context, memory bears witness not to any straightforward, cogent sense of collective identity, but to a pervasive sensation of loss, dispossession, and bewilderment.

In the post-apartheid era, many of the aforementioned policies of spatial regimentation have collapsed, and the sense of collective disorientation has only intensified. For example, the inner cities of Johannesburg, Durban, and Port Elizabeth (and to a lesser extent Pretoria and Cape Town) have been reclaimed and transformed by returning black, coloured, and Indian residents. Yet the racial legacy of apartheid is perpetuated by the remains of its built environments and by conservative elements in the society that struggle to limit wealth and privilege to those (white and black, now) who already possess it. Moreover, the production of space and the inscription of social memory on that space is problematized and contested by the forces of economic globalization and neoliberalism. My thinking proceeds from the assumption that in the last ten to fifteen years South Africa has been subject to the global flows of late capitalism to an extent that was never possible while apartheid made the country an international pariah. The newly intensified postmodern phenomena of technological change, hypermobility, planned obsolescence, consumerism, commodification, and time-space compression all act to thwart the inscription of memory onto urban spaces and exert a general amnesiac effect. Jameson describes this as a "crisis of historicity": he identifies a key feature of the postmodern as "a new depthlessness [and]...a consequent weakening of historicity, both in our relationship to public History and in the new forms of our private temporality" (6). In the face of disparate attempts to regiment, monitor, and control public space and memory, ordinary South Africans struggle to achieve autonomy and the capacity to determine their own spaces; in the process, they develop new modes (both aesthetic and lived) of mapping social space and registering their narratives of the past in shared social memory.

Many of these newly emergent modes of cognitive mapping have arisen at least in part through the processes and procedures of the Truth and Reconciliation Commission (referred to interchangeably hereafter as the TRC or Truth Commission). Paul Gready claims that the TRC "epitomized the newly found capacity to traverse space. By holding hearings throughout the country, the TRC declared a new ownership of and sense of being at home within and moving across the national space" (285). To this observation, I would add that the TRC broke down the fundamental divides between public and private spaces and narratives, and between the scales of the familial, the local, the national, and the international: that is, stories that were previously considered private and personal were told in a public forum, registered in collective consciousness, and mediated for a global audience.

In short, by staging a public drama about private traumas, and by inventing new rituals and modes of representation, the Truth Commission began a long and sometimes painful process of renegotiating South Africans' relationship to their social and physical spaces. But it was only a beginning; indeed, I argue that the TRC must be read as merely the opening chapter in the vast, ongoing process of transformation—a transformation of political structures, yes, but also of larger spatial schemas and of narrative frameworks for understanding the past. Charles Villa-Vicencio argues that the TRC's greatest contribution to the search for the truth about the past is not the Final Report but "a well-stocked archive to be located in the National Archives. The Commission's Report is largely *an annotated road map* into the archive" (24; emphasis added). To use a different metaphor: rather than allowing South Africa to "close the book on the past," as many of the commission's proponents suggested would follow from its work, the TRC helped make possible the continual writing and rewriting of that book.

The work of the Truth Commission, then, should be seen as only one part of a massive national project of transforming the ways social spaces are produced, used, and occupied, and the ways that social memory is encoded in those spaces. We can see this project manifest in the country's many remarkable museums and monuments to the past, such as the Apartheid Museum, the Hector Pieterson Memorial and Museum, the District Six Museum, the Robben Island Museum, and Constitution Hill. The latter example, which I discuss later, is particularly noteworthy in that it preserves the traces of the past inscribed on the site of the Old Fort prison, while transforming the space in the service of the new democratic principles of the constitution. We can also see the national project of remapping collective memory at work in post-apartheid literature, especially the texts I study in this book. Struggles over memorialization are the particular subject of part 1, which treats the literature of memory and trauma, much of it taking the Truth Commission as content and/or inspiration. These works explore the psychological challenges of trying to memorialize and preserve the traumatic past without freezing it into ossified formulae that may be easily forgotten precisely because they become so familiar.

The contested remapping of social space is likewise manifest in the recent decision to officially rename Pretoria Tshwane and to similarly change the names of municipalities, streets, and public spaces that once celebrated the legacy of past oppressors; it is also visible in the increasing fortification of the South African cityscape. I focus on these facets of national transformation in part 2: there I study a few examples of a rapidly burgeoning new urban fiction, in which representation and narrative are frustrated and distorted when it comes to depicting not just traumatic episodes in the past but even the labyrinthine, almost hallucinatory, cityscapes of the present. The authors of these texts thus struggle to develop new cognitive maps of the post-apartheid, postmodern city, where the amnesiac impulses of globalization are most in evidence. Those new modes of social cartography, I suggest, bear much in common with, and perhaps borrow from, the narrative and performative strategies used by artists in trying to come to terms with the horror unveiled by the TRC.

South Africa's national project of socio-spatial transformation is visible in the agonizingly slow and controversial procedures of the Land Claims Court, with its mandate to redistribute land whose rightful owners were dispossessed during the colonial and apartheid eras; it is visible in the national trends toward privatization and tourist-oriented development; it is visible, moreover, in the rise of various social movements that struggle for social justice and the preservation of public spaces and resources. Part 3, accordingly, turns from the city to the rural landscape, where these struggles are most immediately apparent. It focuses on literature that excavates forgotten traces of the past, and which must also develop new modes of mapping space and archiving the past and present; these texts must find new surfaces on the landscape for the inscription of memory and identity, and they must come to terms with the collective loss of land—a loss that lay outside the purview of the TRC.

When I talk about "South African literature after the Truth Commission," then, I mean much more than literary or dramatic texts that explicitly grapple with the TRC as content. Rather, the texts I have in mind are those that have taken full advantage of the new narrative and dramatic possibilities generated in part by the Commission's processes. Throughout this book I identify and analyze some characteristic features of post-TRC literature: narrative forms such as confession and second-person direct address; representational strategies utilizing displacement and condensation; recurring tropes involving mapping, archiving, and curating; the symbolic conflation of bodies and landscapes; excavations and holes; and palimpsests. Considered as a whole, these techniques, strategies, and motifs teach us about the multilayered complexity and ephemerality of memory, about the intangible importance of spatial relations, and about the ways in which generating and sustaining social memory is tied up with questions of time, space, place, and public memorialization. They teach us to be suspicious of fixed, immutable narratives of historical truth, and to query the motives and interests of those who most insistently proffer their narratives. Perhaps most importantly but also most elusively, these texts teach us that learning the truth about the past is like digging a hole and uncovering an empty pouch, as in Wicomb's *David's Story* (3.2). A hole being "a thing of absence" (Wicomb 55), the significance of this metaphor is that narrating the past must always be an inductive enterprise, one of decoding meaning through absence, loss, and rupture.

* * *

The National Party (NP) government, and the British Union administration before it, refused to accept the ephemerality of collective or national memory, and instead tried tirelessly to impose their own narratives onto the landscapes and people around them. The central segregationist strategy was to construct spatial divisions along racial and linguistic lines as an instrument of social control. The crucial moment in this project came in 1913 with the passage of the Natives Land Act, which expropriated most of the country's arable land for white farmers and forced the black majority onto arid reservations. There, poverty and the threat of starvation compelled the men to seek work in the mines and urban factories, thus creating a virtually inexhaustible supply of cheap, desperate labor.[3]

This process of racial segregation and "difference-making" only intensified following the National Party's victory in the whites-only election of 1948, when the government began to pass a series of laws that codified and standardized racial segregation. The bedrock of these laws was laid by the Population Registration Act (1950), which assigned a racial category to every individual in the country, and by the Group Areas Act (1950), which designated residential areas for each racial group. The Bantu Education Act (1953) mandated a separate and inferior education for black Africans, and the state-run school system thus became a tool for reshaping the narrative of South Africa's past and present. Enforcement of these laws required a slate of accompanying policies such as the odious pass laws, which required blacks to have proper documentation to live and work in certain areas; moreover, "petty apartheid" legislation, especially the Reservation of Separate Amenities Act (1953), designated public spaces such as parks and beaches as "whites only" areas, with the black townships regarded as mere temporary repositories for labor. Subsequent years saw the creation of the Bantustans, which nominally made the rural African reservations independent countries, and freed the apartheid government (they hoped) from responsibility for the actions and negligence of the puppet rulers of the homelands. A series of repressive "security laws" such as the Suppression of Communism Act (1950), the "Sabotage" Act (1962), the Terrorism Act (1967), and the Internal Security Act (1982) effectively criminalized dissent in every form and empowered the state to detain its opponents without trial and/or place them under "banning orders" and house arrest.

This hastily drawn history of segregation and apartheid in twentieth-century South Africa both confirms and complicates the claims of cultural geographers about the political dimensions of the production of space. In *South African Literature after the Truth Commission* I have attempted to reconcile these views into a spatial-materialist framework that is in harmony with what post-apartheid literature itself has to teach us, and yet usefully extends our readings of that literature to help us see more clearly the operation of global and national forces on local spatial configurations and cultural expression.

As a foundation for such a spatial-materialist reading, I turn to the work of French philosopher Henri Lefebvre, who argues that "every society—and hence every mode of production . . . produces a space, its own space" (31).[4] David Harvey too relies on a notion of space as deriving from and shaped by processes of economic production: The disorientation that characterizes the postmodern condition, Harvey says, results from such interrelated phenomena as air travel, the Internet and other information technologies, cellular phone networks, post-Fordist production methods, and the global decline of the nation-state.[5] Harvey's observation is seemingly confirmed in Ivan Vladislavić's novel *The Exploded View* (discussed in section 2.2), when Gordon Duffy loses his cell phone and finds himself disoriented and almost unable to function without tapping into the networks he has come to take for granted.

Another way to formulate this argument is to ascribe the sense of disorientation—nearly to the point of intoxication—of much recent South African literature (and of postmodern culture more generally) to the dissolution of previous modes of organizing and conceiving of social space.

In *The Production of Space*, Lefebvre, expanding on his central claim that "*(Social) space is a (social) product*" (26; his emphasis), argues that "the space thus produced also serves as a tool of thought and of action;...in addition to being a means of production it is also a means of control, and hence of domination, of power" (26). Perhaps nowhere provides a better example of space used as a tool of domination and control than apartheid and colonial South Africa, a case study which confirms Smith and Katz's claim that "the power to map can be closely entwined with the power of conquest and social control" (70).[6] For turn-of-the-century South African literature, though, these older methods of confinement and segregation have collapsed, and the struggle now is to refigure spatial relationships for the people's benefit before new mechanisms of division and control spring up to fill the void.

To discuss space as simultaneously a construct of modes of production and a means of social control, Lefebvre formulates a "conceptual triad"—which Harvey summarizes as "the experienced, the perceived, and the imagined" (*Condition* 219).[7] As I argue throughout this book, literature engages with space on all three levels simultaneously—representing both the spaces occupied by characters and their spatial practices, but also engaging with and transforming the spatial codes that determine people's use and experience of space. What a spatial-materialist reading of contemporary literature helps make visible, then, is the material conditions within which cultural production happens, and the potential contributions of literary and dramatic artists to popular understandings of public policy, social memory, and memorialization.

My cultural materialist reading of post-apartheid literature avoids the economic determinism of a base-and-superstructure model[8] by focusing on how the people themselves resist and challenge capitalist determinations of space. One goal of such a critical methodology is to discover through literature new models of class consciousness, including new models of economic and spatial organization. The first decade or so after the official end of apartheid was a particularly fruitful period for seeing this reorganization of social space take shape: arguably, the characteristic symptoms of late capitalism or postmodernism have only recently begun to manifest themselves in South Africa, coinciding with the collapse of the spatial regimes of apartheid, which partly explains why so much post-apartheid narrative reflects a particularly acute case of spatial disorientation.[9] Furthermore, the production of space and memory in post-apartheid South Africa is a process contested on several fronts simultaneously: What Gillian Hart has called the "disabling" rhetoric of globalization has partly transformed the socio-spatial divisions of apartheid into structures ideally suited for the demands of capital; at the same time, factions within the white communities still struggle to maintain the racial divisions of apartheid, and fear of crime (and probably of "the other") has led to white flight abroad and into gated communities and exclusive residential developments. Meanwhile, challenging all these influences on the production, organization, and use of space are the practices of the working class and unemployed black majority.

Literature and drama are two fairly rarefied avenues through which South Africans are contesting the conceptualization and organization of space. Anthony O'Brien argues that South African writers of the 1980s and 1990s were trying to imagine "radical democracy," which he defines as an openness in advance to the new and unexpected results of a fully democratic process—cultural and economic as well as political. I argue that this project of imagining new democratic forms and practices must necessarily tackle the interrelated problems of memory and the spatial legacy of apartheid. Hart explicitly and usefully links the necessity of challenging the disabling, "there is no alternative" rhetoric of globalization to the necessity of challenging the amnesiac impulses of the post-Truth Commission era: "our efforts to remake the future depend crucially on how we remember—and forget—the past, and... it has taken a huge dose of official amnesia to render the neoliberal project palatable. By reconstructing dimensions of local histories and translocal connections, we were disrupting elements of this amnesia" (9). This disruption is a key component of my project—and, I argue, it merges organically with the project of a whole body of post-apartheid literature: registering memories of the past so as not to remain trapped in that past but to use it to build new identities in the post-apartheid future. The memories that are recuperated or reconstructed, and the flexible and provisional new identities that are forged, can be used to challenge those who would create new myths about the past and new spatial regimes of power.

This national project has struggled, however, in the face of amnesiac pressures from numerous fronts. Throughout the negotiated settlement process, the National Party called for blanket indemnity of its agents and a convenient official amnesia about their actions (as did certain elements within the resistance movements). Even Nelson Mandela, at his inauguration and elsewhere, asked his compatriots to forget the past. Granted, the Truth Commission was ostensibly an effort to preserve and enshrine memory: the Minister of Justice Dullah Omar declared before the commission began its work that it would constitute "a commitment to break with the past, to heal the wounds of the past, to forgive but not to forget, and to build a future based on respect for human rights" (3). Yet much of the rhetoric employed by Omar, Commission Chair Desmond Tutu, Deputy Chair Alex Boraine, and other advocates for the TRC's work emphasized that it would be a remembering in order to forget.[10] It is worth remembering in this regard that the word "amnesty" comes from the same Greek root as "amnesia"—both words imply forgetfulness or oblivion.[11]

Two cartoons from early on in the TRC process by South Africa's premier political cartoonist Zapiro clearly reveal this rhetoric of catharsis and "burying the past." One (figure 0.1) shows Omar approaching "SA's Past," drawn as a haunted house on a hill, carrying the lantern of the "Truth Commission," and declaring, "If we don't find out what's in there, it will keep on haunting us forever." The second (figure 0.2) shows Tutu and Boraine as surgeons, explaining to a badly battered South Africa that "[w]e have to open up those festering wounds to cleanse them—it'll hurt, but you'll feel much better afterwards!" Zapiro explains in an interview that

> When the TRC was formed and I saw this project as beginning and needing to be explained to the public and also being resisted by certain people . . . I suppose that thrust of wanting to see this body working in some ways took over. I then did some of those cartoons about which I am perhaps a bit embarrassed now, because some of them are for me pretty naïve. (Verwoerd and Mabizela 155)

Certainly these early cartoons saw Zapiro adopting the rhetoric of the TRC's proponents, a rhetoric declaring that the book of the past has to be

Figure 0.1 Zapiro, 23 May 1995, *Sowetan* (courtesy of Jonathan Shapiro).

Figure 0.2 Zapiro, 1 December 1995, *Sowetan* (courtesy of Jonathan Shapiro).

written before it can be closed—and by implication, before it can be "put past us" and forgotten.

In addition to the various political motivations to forget the past, attempts at memorialization must contend with the "weakening of historicity" under late capitalism (Jameson 6). Andreas Huyssen argues that older models of collective memory that depend on stable formations of social and group identities are no longer adequate, and he notes the apparent irony of our turn-of-the-century obsession with memory (embodied most obviously in the explosive growth of the "Holocaust industry") in light of the postmodern tendency to produce dehistoricized, empty signifiers.[12] This paradox is apparent in the advertising slogan for Johannesburg's Apartheid Museum: "Apartheid is where it belongs—in a museum" (*Understanding*). While condemning apartheid, the slogan also implies that it is safely tucked away in the confines of a museum and can thus be largely forgotten in day-to-day life. In this sense, the museum and the archive—and, perhaps, the Truth Commission—are sites of relegation and consignment: official remembrances that enable a general forgetting.[13]

* * *

I have been suggesting that rewriting the history of South Africa's past and constructing new social memories—key components of the country's true democratic transformation—require a reconceptualization of social space and of what is thinkable. Jonathan Boyarin says that in forming the "imagined community" of the nation, "geographical boundaries of memory" are forged, which "may need shoring up from time to time" ("Space" 19). But this "shoring up" can be a fraught and controversial process, involving the renegotiation of the central myths of national identity.

Such a contest over the mapping of history and memory is taking place in South Africa today, and the process is especially tense because apartheid ended through negotiation rather than through a clear victory of one side over the other. One battleground that has emerged is over the construction of public memorials, and the fate of older apartheid- and colonial-era monuments. For example, the enormous Voortrekker Monument in Pretoria/Tshwane was built in 1940 to commemorate the Boer victory over the amaZulu at Blood River in 1838. Surrounding the monument is a wall representing a *laager*, or circled wagon train, an image that instantly evokes images of the "black peril" of spear-wielding savages. Inside the immense granite monument, a bas-relief mural along the wall tells a romanticized narrative of the valorous Voortrekkers, and of the treachery of the African "savages" and their eventual defeat. In constructing this nationalist representation of Afrikaner history—God's chosen people struggling righteously against a wilderness of black barbarians—the Voortrekker Monument literally and figuratively exiles blacks to the margins of South African history.[14]

Clearly one goal of post-apartheid monuments and memorials must be to counter and revise such right-wing nationalist visions of the past, a project that the TRC Report describes as "symbolic reparations" (Truth and Reconciliation Commission V: 175).[15] It is important to remember, though, that the new myths and symbols of liberation are no less subject to political appropriation than were the iconic images of the Afrikaner "Great Trek."[16] This fact is readily evident in the mythology surrounding Robben Island, which for decades served as a prison for political convicts, and in the museum that now occupies the former prison site. To stand in the tiny cell where Nelson Mandela spent many of his twenty-seven years of imprisonment in isolation remains profoundly moving. As Annie Coombes says, the museums that were developed after the first democratic elections in 1994 to commemorate such sites as Robben Island and District Six "share the need to reanimate particular spaces—the empty prison and the empty city center" (120). Yet the narrative the museum tells of Robben Island University, where the ANC's intellectual discipline and rigor were forged, far from being "reanimated," is a romanticized, even commodified, narrative that glorifies the new ruling party at the expense of, for example, its rival organization the Pan Africanist Congress (PAC), which also played an important role in the struggle against apartheid.

Tim Woods notes that "[n]ational myth petrified in stone is always a sculpture of deterioration. Monuments anchor official memory, by acting as material embodiments of versions of the past, which in time become institutionalised as public memory" (207–08). Memorial sites such as the Robben Island Museum, the Freedom Park in Pretoria/Tshwane, and even Constitution Hill fall prey to the same easy tendency to invite the populace "to view and narrate its history through the biography of great leaders" (Rassool et al. 123). Yet sites such as the District Six Museum, Constitution Hill, the Hector Pieterson Museum, and the Apartheid Museum partly or mostly avoid this pitfall (though each has blind spots of its own) by giving equal focus to stories of everyday lives under and against apartheid. Moreover, the sites that avoid the petrification of memory, Woods claims, are those that succeed in "destabilising the fixity of history and memory" (209), and he cites the District Six Museum as a successful example.

This site in Cape Town is located in the old Methodist Mission on Buitenkant Street at the edge of the formerly mixed-race District Six.[17] The first thing one notices on entering the museum is a sort of hanging ladder formed of street signs with the old names of streets (figure 0.3); the foreman of the construction crew charged with demolishing the neighborhood saved the signs, and donated them to the museum on its founding. A series of storyboards around the outer walls of the ground floor tells the history of the city, from precolonial times through colonialism, slavery, apartheid, and liberation. On the floor in the center of the museum is an enormous map of District Six (figure 0.4) covered in clear plastic; on this map, former residents of the area have written their names over the apartments and houses where they lived, and also the names of businesses, friends, and other remembered information. Ingrid de Kok describes the exhibition's strategy as an attempt to "reverse [apartheid's] fascist pattern of controlled disappearance, simultaneously re-establishing the street names and places, reconstructing the names of the inhabitants, and restoring a sense of the work and community roles people occupied. The official script is thus thrown off, and replaced with a denser, fuller account" ("Cracked Heirlooms" 65).

What makes the museum's map effective in countering the "official script" is, first, that it is ever-evolving, with anyone connected to the district free to make new contributions; and second, that the people themselves have, in McEachern's words, written "themselves into the map; they rendered social the map's physical representation.... Through the map, District Sixers make visible the histories which they have carried with them but which were rendered invisible in the destruction of the area" (230–31). In other words, the map's value lies in its power to reveal not only spatial structures and relations, but also temporal movement and change; it paints

Figure 0.3 District Six Museum, Cape Town; street signs removed before the demolition of the district (courtesy of Paul Grendon [photographer] and the District Six Museum).

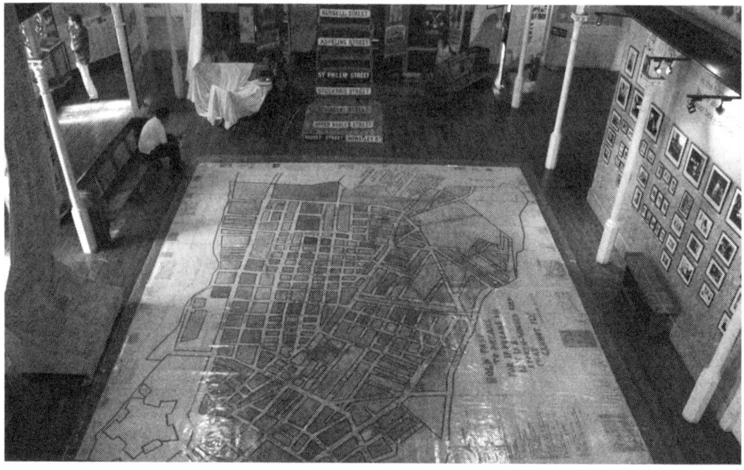

Figure 0.4 District Six Museum, Cape Town; floor map of the old district (courtesy of Paul Grendon [photographer] and the District Six Museum).

the now-erased inner city as a deeply layered palimpsest. Further preventing the museum's slide into an inert display of an apparently static past is its ongoing engagement with public education and issues of land claims and redevelopment in the district. The museum building also serves as a community hall for meetings, and the staff members act as community advocates in many issues involving District Six and its former residents.

Constitution Hill provides similar evidence that effective memorialization in the post-apartheid era requires attention to the palimpsestic elements of the spaces of memory, as well as a participatory aspect that can keep those elements alive and relevant. Indeed, the media firm Ochre Communication, which was part of the consortium that submitted the winning design for the site to the Johannesburg Development Agency, explicitly made the notion of a palimpsest central to their proposal: "Constitution Hill is a palimpsest. A palimpsest is a surface on which the original writing has been erased to make way for new writing, but upon which traces of the old writing remain visible. The site is—and must remain—a place where the layers of history contained within it remain visible" (in *Number Four* 116).

The designers and architects have followed the principle of the palimpsest in transforming the site of the Old Fort, a prison predating the Anglo-Boer War, into the site of the new Constitutional Court Building, where the nation's highest judicial body sits. Rather than simply bulldozing the old prison structures, the architects kept many of them intact and incorporated them into the new buildings, while keeping the infamous Number Four cell block, formerly used to house black prisoners, as a prison museum (see cover image of a cell door). Thus the site strives to preserve and make visible the traces of the past, while reclaiming and transforming the physical space in the service of the new democratic dispensation. To mention only one example of this, the photograph on the cover of this book makes that layering of history visible: the Judas Eye or peephole for guards to monitor the cells has not only been kept intact in the prison museum portion of the Constitution Hill site, but it still retains the graffiti carved into the paint by years of prisoners—many of the lives that passed through the walls of the Old Fort prison, it seems, left small but abiding marks of their passage, still visible today.

From its beginnings, the Old Fort was conceived as a mechanism of social control. It was constructed as a prison by the government of Paul Kruger's Zuid-Afrikaansche Republiek in the Transvaal region in 1893, with the ramparts of the fort added three years later. According to one of the information signs posted at the museum, the ramparts were "used by the Boers to intimidate and keep watch over the uitlanders (foreigners) mining for gold in the village below." When the British army seized Johannesburg in 1900, they garrisoned the fort, and used the prison cells to house those arrested under martial law. After the Anglo-Boer War ended in 1902, until the prison was closed in 1983, the ramparts continued to function "as prison walls. They hid what was happening inside the Old Fort and blocked criminal and political prisoners off from the rest of society." Indeed, the ramparts look from the street outside like a natural hillside; one must enter into the walls of the prison-cum-museum before one sees the main entrance to the court building itself. But today the museum claims that the ramparts form, not a barrier, but a "bridge between the past and the future."[18] This is another instance of city space as palimpsest: the true use of the Fort was formerly obscured by the ramparts, but the new museum draws attention to this very function, making visitors to the Court conscious of the lengths the apartheid government went to disguise its true character.

The Court building itself—in contrast to the imposing, magisterial court buildings in London, for instance—is unassuming, incorporating parts of the original graffiti-covered red-brick prison structure into its own design.[19] It is built where the Awaiting Trial Block once stood; today all that remains of the original structure is the four stairwells (the description that follows is from a sign at Constitution Hill): "Two serve as beacons on Constitution Square. The other two have been incorporated in the Constitutional Court building. The bricks of the demolished block have been re-used in the building of the Court chamber and the Great African steps." Thus, while parts of the prison have been kept virtually intact, other parts have been radically transformed even as traces of their original form remain visible; see, for instance, figure 0.5, which shows the rear wall of the courtroom, made from the bricks saved when the Awaiting Trial Block of the Old Fort Prison was torn down on this very spot.

The doorway to the court building consists of two enormous wooden blocks hand-carved with the words "Human Dignity, Equality, Freedom" appearing in all eleven official languages as well as in Braille. The windows along the west wall of the building are covered by metal shutters consisting of plaques illustrating stories told by people in neighboring Hillbrow. Moreover, while parts of the prison museum highlight the famous inmates

Figure 0.5 The Constitutional Court in session; the wall behind the justices is made from the bricks saved from the Awaiting Trial Block of the Old Fort Prison (courtesy of Guto Bussab [photographer]).

who were incarcerated in the Old Fort, including Nelson Mandela and Mohandas Gandhi, the facade of the court building itself emphasizes the role of ordinary people in the struggle for freedom—an aspect of the story that the Robben Island Museum has often been criticized for downplaying—and the participatory nature of the new democracy.

The main steps leading to the lobby and visitor's center approach the building not from the front, but from the side; one must step back into the courtyard some distance to get a perspective on the main entrance to the court building. Thus, in its rejection of monumentalism, the design of the building and its site avoid one danger that Huyssen identifies in the building of monuments to the past.[20] It remains to be seen, though, whether the memory industry in South Africa will succumb to another danger that Huyssen notes in the postmodern obsession with "musealization"—that is, with constructing monuments, museums, databases, and archives—as "a bulwark against obsolescence and disappearance" (23). Coombes gives us an example of this phenomenon in the "gargantuan dimensions" of the bust of early apartheid Prime Minister J.G. Strijdom that formerly stood in Pretoria, which "render it completely invisible to the passing crowds. Disinterest is the order of the day" (112). Post-apartheid South Africa's attempts to render particular versions of historical memory in virtually living form risk succumbing to this ironic amnesia of musealization—as Huyssen puts it, "any monument will always run the risk of becoming just another testimony to forgetting, a cipher of invisibility" (80–81).[21] For those authors interested and invested in carrying the democratic revolution through to its conclusion, the challenge is to generate maps that can make crucial narratives of the past real and present in social memory without casting them in bronze or consigning them to the archive or the museum.

My claims for the importance of literature's role within this larger project are modest. South Africa is a country with a low rate of functional literacy and an even lower percentage of population that reads literature or attends the theater. Moreover, while I have limited my discussion to texts written in English, English is in fact the first language of a very small percentage of South Africans. Thus the popular cultural impact of English-language literature and theater must be recognized as limited. Given the recent success of South African films in both the local market and in international film festivals, movies may prove to be the popular medium through which South Africa most fully engages with the past.[22]

Nevertheless, keeping in mind Verne Harris's claim that any archival record is at best "a sliver of a sliver of a sliver of a window into process" ("The Archival Sliver" 151), I hope to gain some insight by looking in depth at the sliver provided by literary and theatrical production in English. The model of archival discourse that Harris proposes, which aims at "a releasing of meanings" rather than "the closing down of meanings" (149), informs my own reading of post-apartheid novels, plays, memoirs, and poems: rather than validating and fixing particular versions of the past constructed by various authors, I read those authors as engaging in an ongoing contest over the interpretation of archival fragments and over the production of meaning, memory, and space in contemporary South Africa.

These remappings are crucial to negotiating what Njabulo Ndebele calls the "constant ebb and flow of shifting identities in South African history, which constantly subvert any tendency towards simplification" (146). Such an understanding of memory and the processes of transformation demands a continual, ongoing engagement with the past in ways that emphasize these multiplicitous, loosely aligned aspects of post-apartheid identity. Literature can help provide precisely such engagement. Not only is it capable of changing spaces, urban and otherwise, it is also capable (unlike, say, the TRC Final Report, which of necessity is accompanied by an aura of finality and authority) of continually revisiting the past and creating new narratives to meet the "needs of present consciousness" (Eakin 56).

* * *

I have organized my discussion of fifteen works of post-apartheid literature into three broad parts. In part 1, I study what I am calling "literatures of memory"—works that deal directly with the Truth Commission at the level of setting and content, including Ingrid de Kok's poetry (1.4), and Sindiwe Magona's *Mother to Mother* (1.5), and those that incorporate testimony from TRC hearings directly into their own texts, including Antjie Krog's *Country of My Skull* (1.3) and the collaborative theater pieces *The Story I Am about to Tell* (1.1) and *Ubu and the Truth Commission* (1.2). These texts together confront larger questions of truth, memory, the archive, and coming to terms with the recent past, questions that linger over the texts in parts 2 and 3 as well.

In the latter two parts of the book, I study the ways that social memory is inscribed in and intertwined with social space at different scales of development. Part 2 deals with the post-apartheid urban novel, and with the difficulties involved in mapping even the lived present. The authors of and characters in Achmat Dangor's *Bitter Fruit* (2.1), Ivan Vladislavić's *The Exploded View* (2.2), Phaswane Mpe's *Welcome to Our Hillbrow* (2.3), K. Sello Duiker's *The Quiet Violence of Dreams* (2.4), and Aziz Hassim's *The Lotus People* (2.5) all engage in peripatetic archiving and narrative mapping that can both decode and obscure spatial inscriptions of memory.

This project seems especially urgent in the context of the rapidly changing, disorientating urban landscapes described by these authors.

Finally, in part 3 I analyze a handful of novels that attempt to map an understanding of the present through genealogies, however twisted, and through the lost histories of the land itself: Anne Landsman's *The Devil's Chimney* (3.1), Zoe Wicomb's *David's Story* (3.2), and Zakes Mda's *The Heart of Redness* (3.3). All three texts follow two or more parallel time frames, one of which is set in the pre-apartheid past. And all three novels traffic in metaphors of excavation, exhumation, and digging. Ultimately, though, they all lead us to conclude that simplistic notions of a past that can readily be recovered wholesale are inadequate to account for the complex intersections of landscapes, bodies, and memories.

Roughly speaking, then, the three parts of this book contain, respectively, the literature of the Truth Commission; the new urban literature; and the literature of rural landscapes. They also correspond to three temporal groupings—commemorating the recent past; mapping the bewildering geographies of the present moment; and excavating long-forgotten pre-apartheid pasts—with all of the texts implicitly or overtly concerned with mapping the continuities between remembered pasts and imagined futures. The borders between these groupings are admittedly hazy: *David's Story* and *Bitter Fruit*, for example, both deal with traumatic events of the apartheid era, and could just as readily fit with the literatures of memory and the TRC in part 1. Likewise, similar motifs and representational strategies recur throughout all the texts. But my tripartite organization does effectively bring certain common themes and qualities of the individual works into focus: although the trope of "archival walking" appears in novels that are discussed in all three parts of this book, it recurs with conspicuous frequency in the urban fiction of part 2. Similarly, the works I discuss in part 1 are particularly noteworthy in their use of narrative and performative strategies borrowed directly from the drama of the Truth Commission hearings, even while those strategies are clearly evident in the novels of parts 2 and 3 as well.

Many of these techniques are essentially dramatizations of the twin phenomena of *displacement* and *condensation*. Both processes can be attributed to what Ato Quayson calls the "symbolization compulsion," or "a term for the sublimation of the effects of trauma" (82). We can see such sublimation at work, for instance, in text after text when bodies, landscapes, and memories of the past symbolically collapse into one another. We can also see it in the tropes of *ghosts* and *hauntings*—ubiquitous in post-apartheid literature—and in the frequent use of apostrophe and second-person narration directed at a dead or missing loved one. I frequently use the phrase "present absence" to describe these traumatic phantoms. Mark Sanders similarly notes this structure in many testimonial writings, and regards it as fundamental to the way that bearing witness (legal and otherwise) can serve the interests of justice: These apostrophic testimonies, Sanders argues, are "addressed not only to a transcriber and/or implied reader but at the same time to a figure who is dead. Such writings are, as it were, works of mourning.... Having named the addressee as the dead one, we perceive in such testimony... the instantiation of justice as exceeding, in a relation to the nonliving, the calculus of law" (*Ambiguities* 74). Such tropes and devices of displacement, haunting, and apostrophe all indicate the present absence of a past that has been erased from the landscape, but which leaves marks of its erasure. Over and over again, critics of South African literature turn to the trope of the palimpsest to explain these features of contemporary texts.[23] Clearly, what is called for in interpreting these works is a palimpsestic understanding of history as characterized by gaps, ruptures, and phantom traces.

Such an understanding of history is often at odds with "common sense" assumptions, and many archives and museums cultivate the opposite view: that artifacts from the past bear witness to a history that, with enough time and enough fragments, can be reconstructed wholesale and thereby safely quarantined and consigned to historical oblivion. Fittingly, then, another central motif in post-apartheid literature has been *excavation*. The imagery this motif evokes contains psychic echoes of the Truth Commission process, which included the exhumation of dozens of bodies whose whereabouts had been a mystery until information about their murders by security forces emerged in amnesty applications. Such findings were seen in some quarters as a major success of South Africa's unique amnesty proceedings, and, perhaps because exhumations offer a telegenic level of drama, these moments became iconic of the TRC and more generally of South Africa's efforts to grapple with the past.

Not surprisingly, then, South African literature after the TRC frequently contains tropes involving digging and excavation, tropes that become particularly significant in part 3. But post-apartheid writers have largely called into question the notion that the Truth about the Past, monolithic and final, is buried somewhere out there just beneath the surface, waiting to be recuperated, and if we only dig it out it will be revealed to us in all its totalizing explanatory power. Recent South African literature teaches us, instead, that the tapestry of history must be read as a palimpsest, by paying careful attention to that which has been erased as well as that which is inscribed on the surface.

Finally, if there is a common consensus among post-apartheid writers about *why* narratives of the past must be kept alive in collective memory, it is because these narratives contain forgotten modes of social existence that might enable the birth of true radical democracy—which demands autonomy and self-determination on the part of all South African people. This includes enabling people to seize control over both the construction of social memory about the past, and the production of space. In an article on Phaswane Mpe's *Welcome to Our Hillbrow*, Michael Green writes that

> movements like the Treatment Action Campaign, the National Association of People Living with HIV/AIDS, the Education Rights Project, and the Concerned Citizens Forum, quite specifically try to give ordinary people a voice and some control over their daily lives without calling upon a nationalized sense of the political. If we are to read *Welcome to our Hillbrow* seriously in terms of an attempt to "regain a capacity to act and struggle" in the post-nationalist political world of post-apartheid, then it is for some sort of alignment with these social movements that we could most profitably look. (12)

To Green's list I would add the more radical Anti-Privatisation Forum, as well as the activists who have organized recent protests against failures in service delivery throughout the country.

At any rate, Green is exactly right in identifying what is valuable about these movements: namely, they emphasize autonomy and self-determination for the poor. Moreover, his reading displays the cognizance of class issues that I find lacking in so much contemporary scholarship on South African literature and culture. And he addresses Arjun Appadurai's call for a theory that pays closer attention to "grassroots globalization" (3). Part of my aim in this book, then, is to analyze the ways in which post-apartheid literature remaps multiple flows and vectors: the movements of global capitalism and of the global grassroots; the regulation and resistance of space and place, as well as of memory; and figurations of loss, but also of future possibility. The TRC made a valiant beginning to this enormous project of social cartography, but it is in literature and the other arts that this project is being carried on most powerfully.

Part 1

Spaces of Truth-Telling: The TRC and Post-Apartheid Literatures of Memory

Introduction

I begin part 1 by considering the case of Captain Jeffrey Benzien of the South African Police, who applied to the Truth and Reconciliation Commission for amnesty for his actions as a member of the Terrorist Detection Unit from 1986 to 1990. His demonstration of his signature "wet bag" torture technique with a live volunteer during his hearing immediately became an iconic moment, with pictures splashed across the front pages of newspapers around the world in the following week; the same image features in one of the collages adorning the covers of the five-volume TRC Report, and has been shown repeatedly in documentaries about the TRC's work. A careful reading of Benzien's hearing reveals an intense crisis of representation and memory in the Truth Commission's work that hinders its attempts to narrate or map the past. His amnesty process thus exposes an intricate confluence of amnesiac forces that inhibits the work of memorialization or elegy: traumatic memory loss combines with political expediency and nationalist myth-making in ways that make it difficult to distinguish between these phenomena or to render any sort of objective accounting of past events.

Benzien's amnesty proceedings have become a kind of *tabula rasa* on which observers inscribe their own feelings about the TRC's work more generally. Some observers feel that his dramatic and seemingly emotional breakdown during the hearings was evidence of his sincere regret,[1] while others have doubted his sincerity, especially given the selectiveness of his memories and his claims to memory loss under posttraumatic stress. One

Figure 1.1 Zapiro, 17 July 1997, *Mail & Guardian* (courtesy of Jonathan Shapiro).

satirical take is offered in a Zapiro cartoon (figure 1.1): Benzien is pouring a bottle labeled "Benzien: Dissolves Unwanted Memories" directly onto his brain, which the skull has flipped open to expose. The pun between Benzien's name and the industrial solvent benzene implies that his account of the past has been sterilized, with incriminating incidents conveniently washed away or neutralized through omission. Zapiro labels various parts of the brain one through five, with a corresponding key explaining: "1. Chain of command; 2. *Systematic* use of wet-bag technique; 3. Other officers present during torture; 4. Some particularly barbaric details; 5. The true version of Ashley Kriel's death"; these are all things Benzien claimed to have forgotten, and suspiciously, they are all details that might either implicate former colleagues and superiors who did not apply for amnesty, or disqualify his own amnesty application on the grounds that the brutality of his actions exceeded the "proportionate methods" clause of the TRC Act.[2]

In Antjie Krog's words, Benzien's amnesty hearing "seizes the heart of truth and reconciliation—the victim face to face with the perpetrator—and tears it out into the light" (*Country* 73). Certainly the compelling drama of the hearing reveals the extent to which the TRC's process of truth-telling is always a performance, a fact that might explain why so many

South African theater-makers have taken the TRC as subject matter. But far from being a textbook model of reconciliation between perpetrator and victim, the hearing is emblematic of the murkier qualities of the TRC process: victims' accounts of the past are contradicted by the perpetrators, the perpetrators contradict themselves and each other, and memory is inseparably intertwined with forgetting. Mark Sanders observes that in Benzien's hearing, "[i]ncommensurable prerogatives have been thrown together: the 'truth' [the victims] are after is no longer simply forensic...but a truth of their suffering that they want acknowledged by Benzien" (*Ambiguities* 107). In the end, however, it is not at all clear that the victims have received this acknowledgment, and "truth" seems even more elusive than before.

Benzien, still an officer in the police force at the time of the hearings, had been notorious throughout the country as a torture specialist, and he confesses in his amnesty application to having regularly practiced his trademark suffocation technique. Peter Jacobs, one of his former victims, claims that Benzien told him "I will take you to the verge of death as many times as I want to" (Benzien). Benzien applies for amnesty for the killing of Ashley Kriel and the torture of several others. Some of these former victims oppose the amnesty application, and are given the opportunity to cross-examine him at his amnesty hearing in July of 1997.

The scenes that unfold over three days of hearings are high drama. Tony Yengeni insists that Benzien physically demonstrate the wet-bag technique with a pillowcase and a volunteer from the audience: "As [Benzien] explains it to me, I can hear his explanation, but I would want to be given the opportunity by the Commission to see what he did to me, with my own eyes." Later Benzien is cross-examined by another former victim, Ashley Forbes, with whom the policeman remembers developing a "very good rapport." The dialogue reads like a Harold Pinter play, full of absurd *non sequiturs*: Benzien recalls taking Forbes out for Kentucky Fried Chicken and romps in the park, while Forbes responds with further questions about electric shocks administered to his rectum. All of the former victims repeatedly charge Benzien with using additional torture methods such as electric shocks. Benzien either denies these allegations outright, or claims not to remember the events but "concedes yes" when asked about them. On the second day of the hearings, Benzien's counsel presents a statement from his psychiatrist declaring that "because of the trauma experienced by my client, and all the various experiences, there was a psychological block and therefore he cannot remember certain incidents."

From the beginning, Benzien's explanations of his activities display a complicated and seemingly contradictory logic. For example, to the family of Ashley Kriel, an ANC militant whom Benzien shot and killed during an arrest, he says: "Although I deny that I killed him unlawfully and wrongfully, he did however die as a result of an action on my part and for that I apologise." His testimony, most likely calculated to establish a political motive for his activities as required for amnesty by the TRC Act, is a confusing assembly of old right-wing nationalist rhetoric and the new rhetoric of reconciliation and racial harmony. Benzien tells the committee, "As Director Kruse mentioned, 'Jeff, we are all now on the same side.'...It is now reconciliation, forgive and forget at its best." In the amnesty application, on the other hand, he writes that his political motive was "the averting of the onslaught from the ANC/SACP [South African Communist Party] alliance which was aimed at overthrowing the previous government by violent means and destroying the constitutional dispensation." This complicated and inconsistent logic of then-and-now legality leads Benzien to make numerous paradoxical statements, as when Tony Yengeni asks him whether he believes the wet bag and other torture methods were lawful, and he replies: "I was engaged in a lawful activity, using unlawful, unconstitutional methods, yes Sir." Not only does Benzien's testimony contain these apparent contradictions within itself, it is also often at odds with the testimony of his former victims, and several of those victims oppose his amnesty application because they feel he has not disclosed the full truth.[3]

Psychiatrist Ria Kotze testifies that she has diagnosed Benzien as having Post-Traumatic Stress Disorder, with symptoms including auditory hallucinations and memory loss. She tells the TRC that during his time with the Security Branch "he was torn by his belief that he was saving the lives of the public...and the disgust that he felt in the measures he had to take....These thoughts tore him apart and destroyed his self-respect" (SAPA). During the hearing, as he is being questioned by Tony Yengeni, he has a momentary breakdown: describing the torments his family had faced because of his reputation as a policeman, he says, "Yes, Mr. Yengeni, I did terrible things, I did terrible things to members of the ANC, but as God as my witness, believe me, I have also suffered. I may not call myself a victim of Apartheid, but yes Sir, I have also been a victim" (Benzien). Benzien thus appropriates the rhetoric of trauma and victimhood to account for the gaps and contradictions in his own stories.

In some ways, at least at first glance, the Benzien case seems to confirm the claims of the TRC's proponents who see the commission's task as one of restoring the victims to agency through language and narrative.[4] The TRC apparently gives them the opportunity to recover their agency: *they* ask the questions, and the former prisoners become the interrogators. They also become, at least for a moment, the director of a sort of drama, as when Yengeni requests to see the wet-bag torture physically reenacted: "I also want to see it with my own eyes what he did to me." The cross-examination by Benzien's former victims is also intended as a forum for them to present their side of the story, just as the Human Rights Violation hearings were designed to counterbalance the perpetrator-oriented amnesty process; the victims have an opportunity to narrativize their experience and re-externalize the source of trauma. Moreover, because the TRC process exposes the paradoxes and lacunae that render traumatic events unnarratable, and then attempts to narrate them anyway, it generates representational strategies and, more abstractly, psychic echoes that have profoundly influenced post-apartheid literature. Indeed, it is the deep-seated ambiguity and indeterminacy of proceedings such as the Benzien hearing that make them such rich terrain for novels, poems, and plays.

Yet, on closer look, the gaps and inconsistencies in Benzien's accounts and those of his former victims call into question the nature and power of the "truth" constructed through public hearings. The TRC, granted, was less reliant on notions of an empirically verifiable "truth, the whole truth, and nothing but the truth" than Western jurisprudence. Archbishop Tutu's foreword to the TRC Report, for instance, offers an alternative view, referring to the past as a "jigsaw puzzle" of which the TRC is only a piece, and alluding to the TRC's search "for the clues that lead, endlessly, to a truth that will, in the very nature of things, never be fully revealed" (Tutu, "Foreword" 4). In the report itself, the authors describe four notions of truth that they relied on in reaching their conclusions: "Factual or forensic truth," "Personal and narrative truth," "social truth," and "healing and restorative truth" (Truth and Reconciliation Commission I: 110). Villa-Vicencio emphasizes this aspect of the TRC's work, claiming the Commission "saw itself as offering no more than a historical comment from its perspective on a given period of history.... And, even then, the voice or perspective of the Commission was rarely a single, homogenous one" (22).[5]

I would maintain, however, that these polyvocal and heterogeneous aspects of the Report are present largely in spite of, rather than owing to, the Commission's dominant epistemological view of "truth." According to this view, even if the past has been covered up, it can be "excavated" or recovered in its entirety through a careful process of empirical verification, comparable to a legal trial.[6] Yet even in a trial's reconstruction of an individual crime, or a scholar's piecing together of a single historical event, there are always lacunae, doubts, and contradictions, as we can see in the conflicts between Benzien's accounts of his interrogation methods and those of his former victims. With the writing of a truth commission final report, which attempts to weave such individual stories into a larger narrative of national oppression, struggle, and reconciliation, the dangers and controversies inherent in such a reconstruction of the past (especially a traumatic, violent past) are exponentially compounded. And while a simplistic notion of "truth recovery" can be initially comforting to a nation in transition, it runs the danger of leading to disenchantment and bitterness when the actual process of piecing together the past proves to be fraught with difficulties and paradoxes, as it inevitably will.

If the dominant mode of the TRC Report relies too heavily on these false hopes and oversimplified epistemologies, however, the larger TRC process still contains within it possibilities for imaginative, productive engagements with the past. If not forensically verifiable, these strategies of remembrance nevertheless make possible the type of large-scale reconciliation and nation-building envisioned in the Commission's genesis. As André Brink says, "the kind of whole the [TRC] exercise is aimed at can never be complete and... ultimately, like all narratives, this one must eventually be constructed around its own blind spots and silences.... Hence my argument in favour of an imagined rewriting of history or, more precisely, of the role of the imagination in the dialectic between past and present, individual and society" (37).

Even as they are public articulations of imagined counter-narratives and counter-memorials, such testimonies are also deeply political acts that resist state power by documenting and publicizing its abuses. Under the white minority regime, the stories of Africans suffering under apartheid policies and police abuse were excluded from the public sphere, and relegated to the private spaces of home and church. The TRC hearings, and the handful of criminal trials that have taken place, have generated testimony that turns this public-private spatial divide on its head and brings private traumas into the public eye.

In this light, the effectiveness of victim testimony is often judged by the speaker's fidelity to a documented and well-measured reality, and here the paradoxes and impossibilities of traumatic telling become acutely problematic. For the survivor of gross human rights violations, much of the difficulty in narrating the past results from three conflicting functions of traumatic testimony. Testimonial literature serves, first of all, as evidence (historical and cultural, if not legal) of the crime committed against the victim—the TRC Report's "factual or forensic truth." According to this function, testimony should be accurate and objectively faithful to the events as they happened. Second, such writing should convey some sense of the horror and psychic damage the victim has suffered, and should overcome the phenomenon of "psychic numbing" (Phelps 124). This second function, which overlaps with the TRC Report's categories of "personal and narrative truth" and "social truth," sometimes interferes with the first, for the "psychological truth" frequently cannot be conveyed through an empirically precise account of an event, and at any rate, it is precisely the victim's memories of the past that have been so grievously damaged in the traumatic event.[7] Of course, the notion of psychological truth becomes even more fraught in a case such as Benzien's amnesty hearing, in which the victims report having a vivid memory of the particulars of their trauma, while the perpetrator claims to have been traumatized by his own actions to the point that important details cannot be recalled.

In addition to the tension between factual truth and psychological or personal truth, the imperative to convey the survivor's subjective experience of trauma also contains an internal paradox: to narrate a story requires an agent, but in testimonial literature the narrative describes the destruction of the author's agency. In this sense, the true agent of a torture victim's story is the torturer, a fact that threatens to exile the victim to the margins of his or her own tale. This leads us to the third function of testimonial witnessing and literature, which the TRC Report calls "healing and restorative truth" (I: 114): such testimony should ideally play a therapeutic role, by restoring the victim to subjectivity. This function works against the second one, for as the victim tells his or her story and thereby attains at least a transient agency, the pain and sense of rupture he or she attempts to convey grows less immediate.

All three of these competing functions are operative in any testimony to a traumatic event, and their incompatibilities appear particularly stark in the case of the testimonies given by Yengeni, Gary Kruse, and the others whose stories were contested or called into doubt by Benzien's own testimony. But these challenges are even more acute for "second-order" representations, constructed after the initial act of bearing witness by those who did not personally survive the experience—for instance, the novels, plays, poems, and memoirs that I discuss in part 1. However necessary for keeping memories of the past alive in collective/national memory, such works risk the added insult of consciously or unconsciously appropriating the narratives of other people's personal pain and suffering for their own political agenda, thus robbing the witnesses of the very agency they attempted to recover through the testimonial act.

A final danger, related to those outlined earlier, is that the TRC will monumentalize memories of the past, and thus "facilitate social amnesia" (Bundy 20) by closing off certain narratives and interpretations of the past. We can see this phenomena operating in the Commission's work in the way that certain images and sound bites became icons, representing the apartheid past in public memory: Benzien demonstrating the wet-bag technique and later embracing his former victim; the cry of Nomonde Calata; Lucas Sikwepere declaring that telling his story to the Commission made him feel like he got his sight back. All these and similar images were seized on by the media and by the TRC's proponents as emblematic moments in the project of narrating a national history and achieving reconciliation. In the process, these images focus our narratives of the past on certain "gross" violations, while ignoring other profound material and psychological effects of apartheid and colonial rule. The potential for TRC testimonies to become ossified as "official" accounts of the past also provide incentive for hard-fought contests over how those narratives will be told, mediated, and recorded for posterity; thus, for example, we see Tony Yengeni heatedly challenging Benzien's version of events not only because that version contradicts his own memories of the traumatic event, but also because that version threatens to undermine Yengeni's own legitimacy as a member of Parliament whose position depends on his struggle credentials.

In short, then, the victims' frustration at Benzien's alleged inability to recall the "whole truth," and the fact that many of them continue to oppose the application even after Benzien's dramatic breakdown in his hearing, casts a long shadow over assumptions that this truth will lead to healing and reconciliation in any sort of direct or immediate way. In fact, the tensions and renewed struggles that erupt over appropriation and control of stories about the past contribute to a selective social amnesia, which in turn may serve not only the cause of nation-building and reconciliation, but also the interests of global capital and investment. The Commission's media-savvy public presentation often seemed aimed as much at the international community as at local audiences, and local considerations and the needs of individuals were often sacrificed in the name or in the interests of the national and the global.[8] In this light, the Commission might be seen as trying to navigate between various "scales" of geographic activity: individual, familial, local, national, and global. (This phenomenon parallels the ANC's postliberation economic policies, especially those in the Mbeki era, which are evidently aimed more at pleasing global financiers and the editors of *The Economist* and *The Wall Street Journal* than at addressing structural inequality at the local level.) This simultaneous attempt to "market" the TRC to the international community, achieve national reconciliation, and restore dignity to individual victims explains much of the dissatisfaction at the kind of "truth" it produced.

In appropriating the stories of trauma and loss in the service of a nation-building agenda aimed at reassuring international investors, the TRC threatens to consign those memories to the "archive" of a safely contained history. This, even more than the false expectations created by a conception of truth-telling as simple excavation, is the greatest danger in the TRC as it was conceived in South Africa: ostensibly a mechanism for registering and preserving a record of the past, the Commission might instead serve as a mechanism for obscuring and forgetting it.

* * *

In the ten years since the main body of the TRC concluded its work, a vast interdisciplinary corpus of scholarly literature has arisen to analyze the Commission's history, processes, and moral and ethical implications.[9] I will not attempt any sort of comprehensive survey of that material here; rather, what follows is only the most schematic overview of the TRC's work and some of the debates that have emerged from that work.

The Truth and Reconciliation Commission and the decision to grant amnesty on an individual basis to the perpetrators were born out of impasse and compromise. During the negotiated settlement between the National Party and the resistance movements in the early 1990s, amnesty was a sticking point, with some in the resistance movement calling for full-blown prosecutions against the apartheid security establishment, and that establishment itself demanding blanket indemnity for perpetrators. Rather than granting blanket indemnity to former agents of the state, as happened in many former dictatorships in Latin America, the Promotion of National Unity and Reconciliation Act of 1995 ("TRC Act") gave the Commission the power to grant amnesty to individuals based on a number of criteria, including establishing a political motive for the crime, proving that no "disproportionate" means were used to achieve that political aim, and, crucially, providing "full disclosure" of the truth about past human rights violations.

One concern that came out of the public debates that preceded the TRC's formation was that amnesty hearings would be focused heavily on the perpetrators, leaving victims once again sidelined from their own stories. The result of these negotiations was the creation of two arms of the TRC that would operate independently of the Amnesty Committee (AC): the Human Rights Violations Committee (HRVC) and the Reparations and Rehabilitation Committee (RRC). The HRVC heard testimony from over 22,000 victims, over 2,000 of them in public hearings; ideally it would provide a safe, non-interrogative space in which victims and survivors could tell their own stories and reclaim their human dignity. The RRC, among its other tasks, was to make recommendations for reparations to be paid to those determined to have been victimized by political violence under apartheid. The TRC also held a series of special hearings on the role of institutions such as churches, the news media, and the business sector in perpetuating the system of apartheid, and employed an army of researchers in its Investigative Unit. The first HRVC hearings were held in East London in April 1996. The HRVC and special hearings continued until 1998, when in October the Commission released its massive five-volume TRC Report. The AC began its work several months after the victim hearings had commenced, and continued to hold hearings into 2003, after which the two-volume addendum to the Report was released.

Criticisms of the TRC's work have been myriad and varied, grounded in both epistemological and methodological concerns: the TRC's ambit was too narrow, too constrained by the Commission's political mandate, and it ignored or downplayed whole categories of human rights violations for the good of national stability and reconciliation.[10] Or, the TRC's "particular strategies of inclusion and exclusion" produced a "primarily descriptive rendition of the past, uneven in its discernment of detail and indifferent to the complexities of social causation" (Posel, "TRC" 148). Or, in a related vein, the TRC was too reliant on naive conceptions of Truth as something easily reconstructed through empirical detail.[11] Or, just the opposite, the TRC's standards of evidence were sloppy and unverifiable—the "untested evidence" talking point of the right wing.[12] Or the rhetoric of the TRC created the misleading expectation that telling one's story in public will lead to easy catharsis and healing. And, of course, there are trenchant critiques of the injustice of giving amnesty to confessed murderers and torturers.[13]

Nevertheless, many observers have seen the South African TRC as having accomplished a great deal, especially given its limited budget and short lifespan. The keys to its success arose from several innovations that distinguished the South African TRC from similar bodies in Latin America and elsewhere: the use of conditional amnesty as a "carrot" to coax information out of perpetrators, the balancing of the amnesty proceedings with a process sensitive to the needs of victims, and the very public nature of the truth-finding process[14] have all contributed to the unearthing of more information (of an admittedly narrow and particular kind) about the past than might otherwise have been possible. For example, the information revealed by apartheid perpetrators made amnesia and denial much more difficult for the white beneficiaries of apartheid.[15] Moreover, the TRC's innovations have helped to make the project of constructing a national history a democratic and participatory one, making plausible the argument that the TRC substituted one vision of justice for another, rather than denying justice outright. And it has often been argued that without the amnesty provisions of the interim Constitution and the TRC Act, the country's rival factions would have plunged into total civil war.[16]

Among critics who have studied the TRC in hindsight, a nearly universal consensus has emerged that the rhetoric of "closing the book on the past" and moving on—used by the Commission's early exponents and by the authors of the TRC Report—is premature and misguided, and that in fact the TRC should be regarded only as the first step in forging new social memories of the past.[17] Some have suggested that the real value of the TRC process was not in the Final Report, with its inevitable air of finality and closure, but in the vast archive of testimony and verification compiled by the Commission, which scholars have only begun to explore. Villa-Vicencio and Verwoerd claim that the Report was "intended to constitute a *road map* that would enable others to access the resources on which the TRC's conclusions drew" ("Constructing" 280–81; emphasis added).[18]

Yet even the vast, unexplored TRC archive will be limited in the kinds of information it contains by many of the factors outlined earlier—the almost exclusive focus on political acts and on "gross violations of human rights," for instance. As Brent Harris notes, "The archive itself produces silences. It frames what is consigned in the archive as a unified whole and represses what is left outside the archive, denying its existence and consigning it to oblivion" (165). Recognizing this fact requires us to see the TRC as " 'a site of struggle,' an ideological, conceptual, political, emotional, personal struggle" (Sachs, "His Name" 98). It also requires us to read the TRC findings in terms of what Verne Harris calls the "archival sliver," which helps us to conceive of the TRC not as the final or official last word that will close the book on the past, but rather as the catalyst for an ongoing national project of memorializing that past.

This argument suggests that the task of researchers and scholars is not only to explore the archival sliver made available through the TRC process, but also to counter it with other perspectives to create a "contrapuntal" or multivocal narrative, drawing on different versions.[19] Judging from the comments by Tutu and others, the Truth Commissioners hoped to construct such a multivocal narrative with the TRC Report, even if they ultimately succumbed to the comforting absolutism of statistical analysis. What this contrapuntal dialogue enables, I would add, is a reconceptualization of such fundamental spatio-temporal constructs as the dichotomies between public and private, past and present.[20] In other words, despite its limitations, the TRC has helped make possible a total reimagining of how South African society is organized and of what the country can become. Thus the stories that survivors told at the Commission hearings, the stories put on display at cultural history museums, and the stories told in post-apartheid literature all take part in recalibrating our understanding of South African history and the social spaces it has produced.

My argument in part 1, then, is that fiction, theater, poetry, and memoirs are uniquely suited for the sort of complex social, spatial, and temporal mappings that are required to expand our understanding of the past beyond the iconic "truths" produced by the TRC and the global electronic media. In retrospect, the anxiety in the mid-1990s about what South African writers would write about after the end of apartheid seems unwarranted: whereas the struggle against apartheid tended to subsume ambiguity and complexity into didactic binarism, the collapse of white minority rule seems to have freed South African artists to explore both well-known and forgotten aspects of the past in far more nuanced, sometimes ambivalent ways. Thus we might begin to see the paradoxes and contradictions of Jeffrey Benzien's amnesty hearing, not as a breakdown in the TRC process or an indictment of its failures, but as evidence of how badly the ambiguous truths of literary representation are needed. Ingrid de Kok suggests as much in her poem "What Kind of Man?" which I analyze in section 1.4: In response to Yengeni's question to Benzien, the poet answers, "This kind, we will possibly answer, / (pointing straight, sideways, / upwards, down, inside out), / this kind" (*Terrestrial Things* 27). In place of the "whole truth and nothing but the truth," De Kok suggests that some truths cannot be spoken, but only pointed to ambiguously. The texts I analyze in part 1, and indeed throughout this book, likewise attempt to bear witness to the past without sensationalizing it, fixing or foreclosing its meanings, monumentalizing it, or consigning it to the archive of oblivion.

1.1 The Calcification of Memory: *The Story I Am about to Tell* and *He Left Quietly*

All of the aforementioned risks—especially the danger that narratives of the past will become ossified and/or forgotten—lurk in the Truth Commission's work, where the rhetoric of reconciliation and closure pervaded all proceedings. In literature that incorporates actual TRC testimony into the text, another risk is the possibility of appropriating and reducing the once-empowering process of ritualized public testimony into a collection of empty stock phrases and images that are made to stand in for the past. The first play I will discuss here, a workshop theater piece called *The Story I Am about to Tell* (1997), attempts to circumvent the problem of appropriation by privileging authenticity: three of the six actors are members of the Khulumani Support Group for victims and survivors of state violence who gave testimony at the HRVC hearings, and the stories they tell are their own. Yet as I argue, the play becomes trapped in the forms and rituals established by the Truth Commission, and the stories become calcified in their rehearsed retelling. The piece thus demonstrates a central paradox of the TRC's work, in that it operates simultaneously as a conduit for registering the past and consigning it to oblivion.

Produced in collaboration with human rights activist Bobby Rodwell and poet Lesego Rampolokeng, *The Story I Am about to Tell* has toured across the country and throughout the world. The production I saw in Johannesburg in June of 2000 began with a brief monologue spoken by one of the actors, in which he emphasizes that "we must listen to people's stories to confirm our common responsibility" for the past. The play's cast, he explains, consists of three professional actors and three "real people," by which he means the actual witnesses who gave testimony at the TRC. Other elements of the play are designed to emphasize the "realness" of the people on stage and their stories. The stage setting follows a Brechtian minimalist approach: six folding chairs represent the seats on a minivan taxi. The only other prop is an ax, which, we are told, "has its own story." The lights in the theater are never dimmed, which helps eliminate the sense of distance between the audience and the stage and disrupts the audience's expectations of the genre. After the play has ended, the actors take a brief bow; then, instead of leaving the stage, they arrange the chairs into a semicircle and take questions from the audience, in a discussion that Rodwell says is "a crucial, integral part of each performance, opening debate that hasn't previously been raised" (qtd. in Winer 8).

The core of the play consists of the stories told by the three actual survivors of human rights violations. In some of these, the scenes of original trauma are acted out by the other actors; in others, the rest of the cast leaves the stage and the witness turns to the audience and recreates his or her testimony from the TRC hearing, as if the audience members themselves were Truth Commissioners. Yet, the reenactments are only partly effective at conveying the emotions of the original testimony. One of the survivors is Catherine Mlangeni, whose son Bheki, a human rights lawyer, was killed by a bomb in 1990. Her appearance at the TRC was the first time she had told the story of her son's death in such a public forum. Punctuated by her sobs, the testimony was deeply moving when she gave it in Johannesburg in May 1996, and it has been frequently quoted and excerpted in writings and documentaries on the TRC. By June 2000, when I saw *The Story I Am about to Tell* performed, she had told her story dozens if not hundreds of times. Although still moving, her delivery felt rehearsed, yet halting. Mlangeni's story had perhaps lost some of its force in the calcification of its repeated telling. Ironically, the *literalness* of the play's contrived reenactments detracts from the "realness" of the experiences that the play tries so hard to convey.

The Khulumani group's stories have become standardized in ways that may be necessary for the victims to cope with the trauma. I do not wish to minimize the potential therapeutic value of such public storytelling rituals; for example, Thandi Shezi, a survivor of rape and torture by the security police and one of the victim-actors in *The Story*, claims that "the play has given me the opportunity to confront my demons. There are times when I realise that I am not a victim any more. Through the play, I have been able to give a voice to thousands of women who have been raped but could not 'come out' " (qtd. in Dube 126). Yet, in a cruel irony, Shezi's apparent transcendence of victim status seems to diminish the stories' affective impact on the audience.

In his study *Holocaust Testimonies*, Lawrence Langer makes a distinction that may help us understand this paradox. Langer distinguishes between "common memory," which produces the surface narratives that are related to other people, and "deep memory," which is the trauma victim's unconveyeable truth. Common memory can never adequately represent the "reality" of deep memory, and thus must be continually revised. In some cases, however, Langer suggests that the manifestations of common memory can become calcified in particular, seemingly immutable, forms. In an interview with Langer, for example, one Holocaust survivor interrupts her oral narrative to read aloud from a book she had written about the death camps; Langer expresses the "uncomfortable feeling that the *book's* idiom may be intrusive on and distracting from the more unencumbered flow of the oral testimony" (18).

Perhaps ironically, in *The Story I Am about to Tell*, the idiom that seems to be controlling the oral testimony within the play is not a book but a previous oral testimony, that given at the Truth Commission hearings. Mlangeni and her fellow Khulumani actors seem locked into a mode of telling that prevents the continual return and revision demanded by traumatic narrative. Moreover, as Shezi acknowledges, "I am still pained. I am angry and pained that I am struggling with this, while the perpetrators are walking the streets. I am not free. Their deed will be with me for the rest of my life" (Dube 127). It is precisely this eternal haunting that requires the survivor of trauma to continually revisit and revise the narratives of loss.

In the director's notes to his own work *Ubu and the Truth Commission*, William Kentridge says of the Khulumani play that "what the 'real' people give is not the evidence itself, but performances of the evidence. There is a huge gap between the testimony at the Commission and its reperformance on stage" (Kentridge xiii). Nevertheless, the performed repetitions of the event and its "original" telling transform the victims into minor celebrities through media coverage of the TRC and the play's touring around the world. In the process, the distinctions between the professional actors and the "real people" begin to erode. The play, indeed, is most successful when it breaks out of the carefully rehearsed frame. As Kentridge observes, "The most moving moment for me was when one of the survivors [Duma Kumalo]...had a lapse of memory. How could he forget his own story—but of course he was in that moment a performer at a loss for his place in the script" (xiii–xiv). I have witnessed the lapses Kentridge refers to, both on stage and in person: Kumalo drifts off in mid-sentence, staring into space, as if searching for a word that will never be adequate. As his character in *The Story* says about being on death row, "Is what's happening a dream, or truth? No words can match the pain."

Yet the play seems to assume just the opposite: that the words spoken on stage *can* be adequate to express their pain, because they are "real stories" spoken by "real people." Perhaps the play is too heavily invested in notions of an "excavatable" past, and especially in the authenticity of stories told by survivors of the events described, which raises an important question: what makes the "real people" more real than the actors who help them stage their experiences? The term as it is used in the play has two different, and seemingly contradictory, valences. On the one hand, it refers to the fact that their stories are autobiographical. In other words, the people we see on stage are connected to the events they describe through their memories. On the other hand, whereas the professional actors have not necessarily experienced a life-shattering trauma themselves, the "real people" have experienced such a traumatic ordeal. Trauma, as I use the term, entails a disruption in the survivor's memory and ability to narrate the past, among other symptoms. Thus the viewer of *The Story* is confronted with a paradox: the survivors' "reality" is contingent on their telling the story of an event that resists assimilation into consciousness and thus renders telling impossible. Or to invert the paradox: the Khulumani actors have constructed their characters in the play—and to a large extent their personal identity—around a sort of victimhood in which they were violently robbed of language, but from which they ostensibly recover with each rendering of the story into language.

According to Marlin-Curiel, such a containment of the irreducible pain of trauma is the primary goal of a theatrical rendering of testimony. She claims that both *The Story* and *Ubu and the Truth Commission* (to which I turn in section 1.2) in different ways "reproduce and diverge from TRC conventions in an attempt to manage the instability of the testimonial, violent, and even traumatic aspects of narrating personal stories of suffering in public" (81). Susan VanZanten Gallagher makes a similar point: "Such nightly performed repetitions may be seen as attempts to ascribe boundaries around violence and turn it into a new narrative" (141). Some readers of an earlier version of my argument here,[21] who hold similar assumptions as Marlin-Curiel and Gallagher, have accused me of asking the victims to remain in pain. Yet I question whether freezing traumatic events into "external" or "common" memory truly relieves the pain, or merely provides a numbing, temporary escape from it. Or to put it differently: by circumscribing and containing violence, are the victims not simply trapping it inside their own psyches?

It is a delicate business suggesting that the survivors of torture and violence might sometimes, of necessity, misremember or distort the untellable truth of their experience. To make such an argument is to risk playing into the hands of those who have a vested interest in discrediting the victims and denying their stories. Yet *The Story I Am about to Tell* emphasizes the need for this acknowledgment, by tightly embracing an uncritical privileging of "reality." With each repetition of their tales, *The Story* asserts the survivors' status as subjects capable of narrating their own stories, and simultaneously undermines that assertion by emphasizing their *loss* of subjectivity through trauma and by freezing their narratives into memorized formulae. The play is caught in an endlessly repeated cycle, with apparently no way out; the psychological truth of the events cannot be captured by the conventions of narrative, which reduce traumatic episodes to language and present them in a linear sequence.

The example of Duma Kumalo, a falsely convicted survivor of death row who gave testimony at the TRC and later acted in *The Story*, reveals both the necessity and the inadequacy of codifying trauma into narrative formulae. While *The Story* was still touring the country, Kumalo was interviewed for a documentary film called *Facing Death...Facing Life*, which was about his experiences on death row. Later, with Yael Farber, he cowrote and starred in a piece called *He Left Quietly*, a fringe production at the Grahamstown National Arts Festival in 2002. The very fact that Kumalo continues to search for new vehicles through which to communicate his story suggests a deep psychological compulsion to revisit the scene of trauma and revise the narratives beyond the set scripts and formulae of *The Story*. Indeed, he tells one interviewer that he will never cease demanding "total exoneration from the murder of Councillor Jacob Khuzwayo Dlamini. He wanted a retrial, to establish objectively the innocence he had always vehemently averred" (Matshoba 133). For all the power of the TRC and of theater to give "objective" form to the past, Kumalo has failed to find closure in them, and seeks it instead in the authority of judicial truth. Yet he continues, in *He Left Quietly*, to search for words and theatrical forms through which to convey his experiences.

Moreover, whereas *The Story* relies on an assumed direct correspondence between the narrative and the events it purports to describe, *He Left Quietly* dramatizes the fraught relationship between representation and the unspeakable referent of trauma. The play also emphasizes the necessity for collective participation in rewriting the narratives of the past. *The Story* ends with a question-and-answer session; *He Left* begins with one. Duma[22] takes a few questions from members of the audience, before an actor planted in their midst asks, "What can we do to make sure our stories are told?" After Duma answers the question, the actor joins him on stage, where he sometimes plays the part of prison guards and other third parties, and sometimes plays the role of Duma while Kumalo-the-actor narrates the story.

The play thus establishes a more complex relationship between representation and authentic truth than does its predecessor: Kumalo's coauthorship and presence on the stage obviates the possibility that the play will be mistaken for fiction. Yet the fact that Duma is also played on stage by a second actor allows the play to enact the complicated psychological dynamics of displacement and rupture that characterize testimony to trauma. Farber and Kumalo employ another form of dramatized displacement in the pile of shoes on stage—one pair for each person hanged on death row during the apartheid era. Every time Duma describes the death of a fellow prisoner, the second actor takes a pair of shoes from the pile and throws them across the stage—"Once in an average week on South Africa's death row," he comments. The play thus deploys a metonymic memorialization of the dead very similar to that used by Johannesburg's Apartheid Museum, in which one installation consists of a room full of rope nooses, one for every death row inmate executed for political crimes during apartheid.

I take up displacement as a dramatic strategy in my next section on *Ubu and the Truth Commission*. For now, I also wish to note *He Left Quietly*'s meta-engagement with the very process of writing a play about such horrific experiences. Much of this engagement is carried out by the third, female actor, who plays the role of Farber, and who at one point in the play introduces a suitcase full of letters and diaries that Kumalo kept from his years in prison. She observes that some pages are missing, and she is unsure how to arrange them—chronologically? By subject matter? And she notes despairingly, "You can't arrange the unarrangeable."

Ultimately, the play seems to suggest that such a task exceeds the abilities of a single writer; indeed, it requires the participation of whole communities. This message is conveyed through the play's conclusion, in which Duma invites the audience members in the front rows to join the actors in taking pairs of shoes from the pile and arranging them in a neat row on stage. The play thus emphasizes the need for everyone to take part in reconstructing the past, remembering the dead, and speaking for those no longer able to speak for themselves. Such collective participation in the process of rewriting history might minimize the possibility of the political appropriation of narratives of the past, and the risk of those narratives being frozen into inert "archives" that are all the more easily forgettable for being fixed in historical memory.

1.2 A Theater of Displacement: *Ubu and the Truth Commission*

Where the victims in *The Story* become entangled in the paradoxes of traumatic testimony in their attempts to reconstruct their subjectivity through narrative, *Ubu and the Truth Commission* (first performed in 1997; script published in 1998), another theater piece based on the TRC, might point the way toward a partial resolution of such crises of representation. *Ubu*, like the Khulumani play, includes verbatim testimony from TRC hearings, but rather than reperforming those testimonies literally, the play dramatizes the ruptures and displacements of their telling through the use of puppetry.[23]

Ubu is a complex, multimedia event, modeled in part on French playwright Alfred Jarry's 1896 proto-surrealist play *Ubu Roi*.[24] Staged largely with almost life-sized puppets, *Ubu and the Truth Commission* features only two characters whose parts are performed by actual people: Pa and Ma Ubu. Ubu is an allegorical figure, representing the violence of the apartheid state. He is a composite character who borrows lines from the testimonies of death-squad commanders Eugene de Kock and Dirk Coetzee and other infamous agents of the former regime. Pa Ubu is a living archetype of the security establishment, as when he tells his henchmen, "Remember, we are the tail that wags the dog" (Taylor, *Ubu* 7).

Ma Ubu is an opportunistic Lady Macbeth figure. At the beginning of the play, ignorant of her husband's real job, she believes he stays out all night because he is seeing another woman: "The signs of your lust have given you away. I've seen the red on your collar, and tufts of hair on your sleeve" (3). The reality is that he spends his nights torturing and murdering the "enemies of the state." When Ma learns the truth, she weeps, not from shock but from pride: "The sly old jackal. I had no idea Pa was so important! All along, I thought he was betraying me and here he was, hard at work, protecting me from the Swart Gevaar [Black Peril]" (45). Despite her relief, however, Ma decides to sell the documents to the press, prompting Pa to apply for amnesty—which he had resisted heretofore.

Aside from Ma and Pa Ubu, the other characters are represented by puppets, constructed and operated by the Handspring Puppet Company. Most of these are either victim-puppets or perpetrator-puppets. One of Ubu's assistants is Brutus, a Cerberus-like dog whose three heads represent the foot soldier, the general, and the politician. Connecting these three heads on the puppet is a suitcase belly, which Pa Ubu stuffs late in the play with incriminating documents, thereby turning Brutus into his scapegoat. Another villain-puppet, Niles the crocodile,[25] also has a handbag for a belly. He acts as a sort of *consigliere* to Ubu, advising his master early in the play to confess his deeds to the "Commission to determine Truths, Distortions and Proportions," which can "beyond all ambiguity indicate when a vile act had a political purpose" (17). Ubu rejects this sardonic advice, choosing instead to stuff the incriminating evidence into Niles's mouth, just as the agents of apartheid frantically shredded mountains of paper when the new government came into power.[26] Pa's use of the crocodile to dispose of the evidence, and Ma's discovery and subsequent sale of that evidence to the media, symbolizes one of the central struggles facing attempts to "refigure the archive" in the mid-1990s: the "battle between the paper shredders and the photostat machines" (Kentridge viii), or more broadly the contest between memory and forgetting.

The other puppets in the play represent the victims. These are nearly life-sized human figures, which require two visible handlers on stage, in the trademark *bunraku* style of the Handspring Puppet Company (see figure 1.2). During the testimonies, one of the handlers speaks the lines

Figure 1.2 Basil Jones and Busi Zokufa of the Handspring Puppet Company with a "victim puppet" in *Ubu and the Truth Commission* (photo © Ruphin Coudyzer FPPSA—www.ruphin.com).

in isiZulu, isiXhosa, or seSotho, while an interpreter in a booth translates them into English. Replicating the symbolism of the Truth Commission, the second puppet handler becomes the "comforter" who was always at the side of the victims during the HRVC hearings.

In addition to their presence in the testimony scenes, the victim-puppets often occupy the stage at the same time as Ubu. In the opening act, for instance, a puppet is on stage making soup when Pa Ubu comes along and kicks him. In a later scene, a puppet is setting up a sidewalk "spaza shop" of staple food items and toiletries on a table. At either end of the table, Ma and Pa Ubu are eating dinner. The stage notes say that they are "unaware of the individual presence of the shop-keeper, but become aware of the goods on offer, which they take, gradually and cavalierly, as if all things are available for their own consumption. The shop-keeper throughout is unaware of who steals his belongings, although he is painfully aware of their disappearance" (27). Basil Jones and Adrian Kohler of Handspring explain in the "Puppeteers' Note" that these

> wooden dolls attempting to be people are never seen by Ma and Pa Ubu, though their actions impact fundamentally on their lives. Though they occupy the same space... they appear to be somewhere else. The Ubus eat the goods they loot from the Spaza shop, but cannot see the shopkeeper, who in turn cannot see them. This division between the human clowns and the puppets, mirrors the era of trauma the play describes. (xvii)

Indeed, the use of puppets creates a powerful vehicle for *Ubu and the Truth Commission* to reenact the experience of trauma, characterized as it is by displacement and alienation.

Jones and Kohler further comment on the advantage of using puppets to speak fragments of TRC testimony, which are taken almost verbatim from actual hearings: "Badly handled, such stories could easily become a kind of horror pornography. The puppets assist in mediating this horror. They are not actors playing a role. Rather, they are wooden dolls attempting to be real people.... they cross the barrier of the here and now and become metaphors for humanity" (xvi–xvii). By using puppets to stand in for the bodies of victims and survivors, *Ubu* calls attention to the constructedness of self and the very experience of embodiment. In one scene, the animation on the screen coincides with Pa Ubu's movements on stage, "decoding his own body, using the toilet-brush [Ubu's phallic scepter] as a kind of Geiger counter" (Taylor, *Ubu* 57). The scene thus underscores the connections between memory (represented by the animated images) and the body, like the victims whose stories are displaced across puppet, handler, and translator.

Whereas *The Story I Am about to Tell* attempts to circumvent the danger of producing a "horror pornography" by having the victims play themselves on stage, *Ubu* takes a very different tack, for it is essentially a theater of *displacement*. For instance, conveying emotion through the puppets themselves is very difficult, despite the puppeteers' ingenious use of lighting and expressive gestures. The audience must therefore rely partly on the face of the puppeteer who speaks the testimony. Indeed, at one point in the play the puppeteer who is speaking stops animating the puppet in order to point at his own head as that body part is referred to in the testimony, which shifts the audience's attention from the puppet to the handler (Y. Coetzee 45). In addition, audience members who understand no African language must rely on the translations from the interpreter's booth in order to understand the content of the testimony. Paradoxically, even as it puts a distance between the audience and the victim, this displacement of the testimony brings the audience closer to the victim's experience of trauma. This effect occurs because the spatial representation of the process of remembering and bearing witness—that is, the separation of speaker, speech, and meaning—not only mimics but also draws the audience's attention to the fragmentation of subjectivity experienced by the trauma survivor.[27]

To clarify this point, I should note a very common characteristic of traumatic testimony: the fluidity of pronouns. A former prisoner relating his experiences will suddenly shift from the first person—for example, "I was detained and put into a tiny, dark cell"—to the second- or third person—"when you spend twenty-three hours a day alone in a room, you begin to question your sanity." The "I" who tells the story never entirely equals the "I" to whom terrible things were done, for to tell a story requires *agency*, and the trauma victim is one who has experienced a loss of agency. Thus the person giving testimony must stand outside him- or herself, as it were, and see the events as if they had happened to someone else.[28] *Ubu* dramatizes this paradox, by channeling the story through a teller who stands outside the body of the victim/puppet. In this way, the audience is able to regard the victim as both agent and acted-upon, storyteller and victim, simultaneously. Kentridge notes that in working with puppets, "there's a sense that even though you can see the manipulators working with the puppets, even when the artifice is laid bare, it does not stop you from giving the agency of the action over to these wooden, inanimate puppets" (Cameron 69).

Ubu suggests exciting new ways a society might work through traumatic events via an art of displacement; in the process, the play avoids the calcification of memory that often results from consigning the past to, for instance, a museum exhibit or an archive. Ultimately, however, and despite Kentridge's claim, *Ubu* locates agency and subjectivity not with the victims, but with the perpetrators. In a monologue in Act One, Pa Ubu declares, "Once I was an agent of the state, and had agency and stature" (Taylor, *Ubu* 5). The pun here reveals the ambiguity of the term "agent," which can refer either to a pawn, one who serves others, or to one with the ability to act freely. Ubu declares himself to have been both. Moreover, he speaks in the past tense, for under the new political dispensation, he feels himself to have been robbed of "agency and stature." Like Jeffrey Benzien, Ubu essentially declares that "I, too, have been a victim." And like the white right wing in South Africa more generally, Ubu quickly learns to play the part of the persecuted rather than the oppressor, and to cry out "witch hunt!" against the TRC. As he tells the crocodile, "Oh, Niles, such a vision I had. I saw the Great Truth approaching, a rope in its hand. It demanded I speak of the truth of our land" (17).

There is a world of difference, however, between the "trauma" of Ubu and that of his victims. Whereas the latter are subjected to epistemic violence, their fundamental selfhood unmade by others, Ubu deliberately disavows his *own* agency, following the advice of his shadow: "shift the burden of guilt.... Extract yourself from the plot of your own history" (55). Thus, even as he attempts to adopt the status of victim, he retains his subjectivity—that is, the apparent power to choose his own role in the play. This devious disavowal of responsibility is foregrounded by the structure of the play—again, this is a theater of displacement. Pa Ubu's acts of violence are never depicted on stage, only their aftermath, as when he washes away the "Smell of Blood and Dynamite" (11). Indeed, the only representations of violence are in the images projected on a screen behind the actors. Some of these images are live-action videos, such as footage of police at anti-apartheid demonstrations, or newspaper clippings reporting death squads and torture allegations. For the most part, however, the video screen displays animation by director and artist William Kentridge. Several motifs recur frequently, especially a camera tripod, an "all-seeing eye" (which is interpolated with close-ups of a real eye), the Ubu figure from Jarry's original play, and scenes from a torture chamber.

At times the characters on stage are oblivious to the film, while sometimes they interact with it. Sometimes, too, the animation takes center stage. When Ma Ubu opens Niles's handbag/stomach and discovers the documents and rags, the screen behind her shows a crumpled ball of paper unfolding into an animated image of a sparsely furnished room with a person tied to a chair. The "camera" then pans left and right, up and down between numerous images of people being beaten and tortured (see figure 1.3). Finally, the camera pulls back, revealing that each of these individual images is a window in a giant building that very much resembles the notorious John Vorster Square police station in Johannesburg. Inside each window, a scene of terrible violence unfolds.

Figure 1.3 Kentridge's animated camera tripod as the agent of violence in *Ubu and the Truth Commission* (courtesy of William Kentridge).

Even in the animated sequences, the perpetrator's presence is frequently elided. In one segment, a victim is seated on the chair with his hands tied behind his back; we hear the blows and see the victim reeling from them, but there are no policemen visible. In other scenes, the instigator of violence is the camera tripod—a gun replaces the camera and shoots the victim in the face, or a lion's head jumps out from the camera and lunges toward the victim.[29] The causes of violence are always these mechanized automatons or faceless silhouettes, not the actor on the stage. Yet the audience does not perceive this displacement of the agency behind the tortures, bombings, murders, and disappearances as exonerating Ubu. Rather, the displacement becomes evidence of how insidiously he has covered his tracks, for we see Pa Ubu away from the public eye of the Truth Commission's cameras, we hear his internal deliberations, and we witness his attempts to deny or shift the culpability. "Information," he says, "is the beacon of our enlightenment, but a man is cursed when his information is turned to shine on himself" (35). Thus, he disposes of the evidence into the belly of Niles the crocodile. Later, Ubu stuffs some of the remaining evidence into Brutus's body-trunk, commenting that "we've hopefully muzzled our dogs. Now to cover them in dirt before we send them to the cleaners" (61). In other words, after making them his fall guys, he has them killed when they apply for amnesty.

In part, our "insider" view of Pa Ubu's machinations functions as a satirical commentary on the TRC and on justice in the new South Africa. This is most clear, for instance, when the judge (represented by a giant mouth on the video screen) in the "matter of the state versus Brutus, Brutus, and Brutus" gives three different sentences to the three different heads on the same dog:

> With regard to the first case: a head of political affairs cannot always foresee how his vision will be implemented. We thus exonerate you, and retire you with full pension.
>
> With regard to the head of the military: there is no evidence to link you directly to these barbarous acts. Nonetheless, an example must be made of you, or who knows where we'll end up. You are thus sentenced to thirty years in the leadership of the new state army.
>
> Finally, to the dog who allowed himself to become the agent of these ghastly deeds: you have been identified by the families of victims; you have left traces of your activities everywhere. We thus sentence you to two hundred and twelve years imprisonment. (63)

Two hundred and twelve years, plus two life terms, was Eugene de Kock's sentence. This passage thus satirizes the situation that De Kock himself has decried from his prison cell and in his amnesty hearings: the foot soldiers or "agents" who did all the dirty work have been betrayed and abandoned by the politicians and generals who gave the orders and condoned the crimes. Indirectly, as well, by raising these questions of agency and blame, the play exposes some of the political and personal motives some South Africans have for attempting to propagate a selective amnesia about the past.

The fact that the audience is privy to Ubu's secrets also positions us as coconspirators, accessories to his crimes. It does this by casting Ubu as the protagonist of the play, the subject through whom the audience relates to the action. In her "Writer's Note," Taylor acknowledges that this tactic is deliberate: "Narrative depends upon agency; the stories of those who 'do' are generally more compelling than those who are 'done to' " (v). In an article in the *Rhodes Journalism Review*, she asks a similar question about the South African news media's treatment of the TRC:

> For many journalists, there is the difficulty of distinguishing one story of abuse from another: that one mother's loss is another father's grief is another sister's memory. All victims tell a story with one structure, it seems. What makes the stories of the perpetrators so compelling is, in part, that

> they are agents: they act upon others. All of the psychological structures of desire, power, greed, fear, identification are invoked in these accounts. (Taylor, "Truth" 3)

Taylor's dismissal of victims' stories as all alike is rather disconcerting. It ignores the myriad rhetorical ploys that victims use to rewrite themselves into their own stories. More importantly, her assertion, when put into practice in the play, leads to an erasure of the victims as subjects, thus ironically reenacting the deliberate shattering of their "selves" via the traumatic event to which they have testified. This phenomenon suggests a troubling implication of Jones and Kohler's remark that the victim-puppets "become metaphors for humanity." Granted, the use of puppets makes possible the group's unique theater of displaced testimony, but it also reduces the victims to interchangeable parts. If their stories are all alike, because they lack agency, then the victims themselves appear equally devoid of substance, and any puppet can speak any victim's faceless tale of suffering.

Ubu and the Truth Commission thus undoes one of the key features that distinguishes testimonials from other forms of autobiographical representation. According to Doris Sommer, in traditional autobiography, the author calls on the reader to identify with the "I" who tells the story. Sommer claims that in a testimonial, on the other hand, the survivor is not a "metaphorical" individual with whom the reader is invited to identify, but a "metonymic" figure representing a community of which he or she is part. The reader of a *testimonio*, then, identifies not with the "I" who tells the story, but with the "you" to whom the story is told. In this way, Sommer says, "the testimonial produces complicity" (118).

Ubu also produces complicity, but in a very different way: not by addressing the reader as a juror or witness to the story, but by aligning the audience's gaze with the perspective of the perpetrator. This identification with the torturer is used ironically, and the audience is made to feel uncomfortable, like an accessory to a horrible crime. But in the process, the victims are removed from the center of their stories, and their testimonies are appropriated primarily to emphasize the magnitude of the deeds committed by the protagonist of the story. Whereas *The Story I Am about to Tell* casts the survivors as storytellers even as it privileges their victimhood, *Ubu and the Truth Commission* relegates the victims to the margins of the play, making them both literally and metaphorically puppets in Pa Ubu's tortured fantasy world. In a sense, the play replicates, however unintentionally, the traumatic exile of blacks and political dissidents from apartheid's own fevered vision of a whites-only Africa.

Nevertheless, *Ubu*'s theater of displacement makes it possible to dramatize and represent, if not unspeakable events themselves, at least the ruptures and transferences that render the events unspeakable.[30] In this regard the play resembles director Kentridge's trademark style of draw-and-erase animation, which as he explains in one interview differs from traditional animation in which the object in motion is redrawn many times on separate sheets of cellophane:

> With a [my] technique of animating or drawing, the stages of a movement are drawn on the same sheet of paper, and the previous ones erased, so you have a visible trace of that journey around the table. . . . This is how the effect of erasure and the effect of imperfect erasure puts on to the very surface and into the heart of the drawing or piece of the film itself the fact of time passing, but also makes visible something that is normally invisible. One can perceive the multiplicity of the self passing through time, which would end up as a single self if the moment was frozen in a photograph. (Cameron 67)

This mode of "imperfect erasure," which "can make the temporal visible" (68), suggests a provocative model for any attempt to represent a past characterized by the "erasure" of the black majority from history. Marcia Blumberg says that "this production [of *Ubu*] refuses to allow amnesia and demands engagement" (317).[31] Such a refusal of amnesia is especially important in light of my argument in the introduction that post-apartheid culture is subject to amnesiac impulses from a number of fronts: from perpetrators eager to have their victims "forgive and forget"; from victims unable to confront the horrors of their past; from politicians looking to consolidate power in the new dispensation; but also from the imperatives of late capitalism, which aims to commodify narratives of the past and tends to consign highly selective, depoliticized images to the museum and the archive.

On this last point in particular, *Ubu*'s strategies of displacement and translation offer possibilities for representing postmodern spaces and landscapes and the phenomenon of "time-space compression" that the play itself only begins to explore. This potential is suggested in the opening scene, described earlier, in which the Ubus obliviously steal food from the puppet's spaza shop. As Jones and Kohler note, the Ubus occupy a different "space" from that of the victims, yet those spaces overlap. In the terminology of political geography, Pa Ubu has the mobility to move at will between "scales"—for example, from the local to the regional to the global, or from the private to the public—just as he retains the power to disavow his own agency. The poor spaza shop owner, on the contrary, is confined almost entirely to the township and the street corner.

Similarly, Kentridge's practice of an art of imperfect erasure that can make temporality visible holds great promise for mapping the disjunctive experiences of time in post-apartheid South Africa, as well as for helping to expose the material processes that shape the production of space. He argues:

> One of the ways things are false is when they get locked into being seen as fact, as opposed to moments of a process. To draw an analogy from the studio again, looking out of the window now, I can see the leafy, wooded suburbs of the north part of Johannesburg. It's not to say there aren't lush deciduous trees in the view and outside, but that this current, factual view is oblivious to how that wooded suburb was created. (Cameron 68)

An art of erasure and displacement, used in *Ubu* to dramatize memory and make visible multiple subjectivities through time, has broader potential for representing the new social geographies of post-apartheid South Africa. What Walder describes as the play's "art of multiple viewpoints, multiple perspectives" (160) might make possible a mapping of the very different encounters with space-time experienced by those who continue to benefit or suffer from the spatial, bodily, and psychological traumas of apartheid. *Country of My Skull*, to which I turn in the next section, is engaged in a similar process, attempting to map the author's own privileged history against the traumatic past of the nation at large.

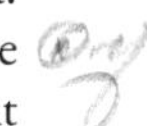

1.3 The Lie Where the Truth Is Closest: Antjie Krog's *Country of My Skull*

Antjie Krog's memoir *Country of My Skull* (1998) takes up some of the same questions raised by *Ubu*: How does one map the intimate networks of memory, identity, body, time, space, and place? And in another vein, why do white South Africans—and international audiences—often seem so much more interested in the stories of killers and torturers than in victims' tales of loss and sorrow? Taylor argues that it is because the perpetrators have agency, while the victims have been robbed of agency. Krog's answer is different, and less comforting; she suggests that, especially where both the perpetrators and audiences are Afrikaners, the fascination with the killers and their motives exists at least in part because a white audience feels a kinship to or an identification with the white perpetrators. Krog, a noted Afrikaans poet who reported on the Truth Commission for SABC Radio, published *Country of My Skull* even before the Commission's Report was released.[32] Krog's book was a bestseller in South Africa, garnering many awards and much international success and critical acclaim for its author. It is undoubtedly one of the most moving and important works on the Truth Commission and on South Africa's violent past. Further, Krog is sensitive to the victims' loss and the ethical dilemmas inherent in reproducing their stories, and she handles their testimonies gingerly without exiling them to the margins of her book.

But *Country of My Skull* is also Krog's coming to terms with her whiteness, with her Afrikaner heritage and her perceived kinship with so many of the amnesty applicants. She dedicates the book "*for every victim who had an Afrikaner surname on her lips.*" She thus puts the black victims of state violence at the center of her project. She also declares a sort of sisterhood with those victims who gave testimony at the TRC, so many of whom were women, even as she acknowledges her complicity in the violence, which was, after all, committed in the name of Afrikaner "freedom" and nationhood. Indeed, the title of the first chapter is "They Never Wept, the Men of My Race," referring both to her immediate family and to the amnesty applicants whose testimony she reported to the nation.

Krog begins by describing the reactions of right-wing Afrikaners to the draft legislation that was to establish the Truth Commission: defiant, combative, unrepentant. She intersperses these scenes with descriptions of a visit to her family at her childhood home in the Free State: "As if back into a womb, I crawl" (*Country* 4). This is the first of many passages in the work that conflate the body (as the site of physical violence and trauma but also as the locus for memory and identity) with the landscape which that body occupies. Sanders points out, moreover, that Krog feels displaced from the home she shares with her husband and children:

> This turning of the authorial self out of its house, at home and away from home, is integral to *Country of My Skull*; it performs, *spatially*, the reversal that makes the country the "country" of Krog's skull. . . . It helps her story to mime, almost in silence, . . . what takes place at the hearings, when witnesses testify to police or soldiers invading their houses, and to being forced from their homes. (*Ambiguities* 158; emphasis added)

Given this widespread sense of dislocation, which Sanders calls a "doubling of spatial displacement" (158), an important aspect of Krog's project in this memoir is to "remap" the relationship of her body to other bodies (those of amnesty applicants and victims, for example) and to the rapidly transforming social geographies of South Africa after the Truth Commission. This process involves rethinking both the history of the country she thought she knew, and socio-spatial relationships in the present.

Such passages as those comparing her childhood farm to a womb, though, also underscore the siege mentality experienced by many rural Afrikaners. While understandable given the recurring outbreaks of violence against white landowners since the late 1980s, this mind-set sours the reaction of many Afrikaners to the Truth Commission and the new dispensation, and therefore makes the renegotiation of space, place, and memory a highly fraught endeavor. Krog's brothers who now run the family farm have to patrol the premises nightly to keep the township residents from stealing their sheep. Their perspective on the country is that "the brutalization of ordinary people that was previously confined to the townships is not disappearing, but instead spilling over the rest of the country" (12). Later, when hearing the testimony of members of the Vlakplaas death squad, Krog comments, "They are as familiar as my brothers, cousins and school friends. Between us all distance is erased.... What I have in common with them is a culture" (96).

The tension exhibited in Krog's dedication, a tension between feeling sympathy for the (predominately female) victims and identifying with the (exclusively male) amnesty applicants, persists throughout her book. At times Krog and the other journalists covering the hearings experience symptoms of "second-order" trauma: Krog felt "powerless—without help, without words" (37). Yet in some places, Krog's and her colleagues' behavior more closely resembles that of the security policemen than of the survivors of their violence. This impression is reinforced by the feelings expressed when the SABC radio team meets in a guest house for a workshop:

> At once we become our own little hit squad. We talk contemptuously and drink destructively. Some people park themselves behind the bar counter for the evening. Others tell stories in front of the fireplace—Truth Commission stories.... Everybody speaks as if they've been in solitary confinement for months. In the end, no one is listening to anyone else, but everyone keeps on talking. (168)

The trauma of the victim, just released from solitary confinement, is conflated here with the forced bravado of the guilty murderers—"our own little hit squad." This rhetorical conflation threatens not only to trivialize the suffering of the victim, but also to legitimize the problematic (if not entirely unjustified) claims of some of those perpetrators to have also been victims.

In addition to her confessed feelings of kinship with the white Afrikaner perpetrators, Krog embraces a conception of truth that threatens to play into the hands of the very right-wing forces who wish to cover up the crimes of the past under a convenient veil of relativism. Krog admits that hers is a subjective notion of truth: "The word 'Truth' makes me uncomfortable. / The word 'truth' still trips the tongue.... I prefer the word 'lie.'... Because it is there... where the truth is closest" (36). Krog is implicitly noting what

Graeme Simpson identifies as a weakness in the TRC's work, an assumption that "there was a 'recoverable' and integrated truth about the roles of these [state] institutions" (224). What Krog makes clear is that sometimes such an empirical notion of truth is not enough, that sometimes it is the lie that comes closest to the truth. In one essay she says that "It is this lacuna in the judiciary, this absence in the legal heart of justice of the meaning of the word *ubuntu*, this lack of any vision beyond respect for law and order, that undermined the usefulness of the TRC process for moral or political processes" ("The Choice" 117).

In *Country of My Skull* she illustrates this lacuna around the word "truth" by presenting several different versions of a Vlakplaas murder, each differing in important details. She says that the amnesty applicants' stories "became part of a whole circuit of narratives: township stories, literature, Truth Commission testimonies, newspaper reports.... every listener decodes the story in terms of truth. Telling is therefore never neutral, and the selection and ordering try to determine the interpretation" (84–85). Kim Wallmach notes the ubiquity of translation and interpretation as both a literal presence and a figurative trope in *Country*: "interpreting and translation do not constitute pure imitation.... there will always be a gap between original and translation; and this gap is not one of language, but of voice, of a speaking subject" (74). It is the truth of this speaking subject that Krog attempts to dramatize or enact through the mediated process of storytelling.

Moreover, the way Krog describes the beginning of the amnesty hearings emphasizes the ways that truth is being rewritten through the TRC's process of storytelling:

> For six months the Truth Commission has listened to the voices of victims. Focused and clear, the first narrative cut into the country....
>
> She is sitting behind a microphone, dressed in beret or *kopdoek* [headscarf] and her Sunday best. Everybody recognizes her. Truth has become Woman. Her voice, distorted behind her rough hand, has undermined Man as the source of truth....
>
> Yet something is amiss. We prick up our ears. Waiting for the Other. The Counter. The Perpetrator. More and more we want the second narrative.... There can be no story without the balance of the antagonist. (*Country* 56)

The malleability of truth means that the objectified "Others" (women, victims) can mold it through their own stories. Yet their versions can still be contested and unmade through the "second narrative." And like Taylor, Krog suggests that the victim's narrative is incomplete without the agency supplied by the perpetrator's own tale.

Krog's ambivalent relationship to the truth extends to the recounting of her own experiences with the TRC. She writes in the Envoi at the end of the memoir, "I have told many lies in this book about the truth" (281). She also describes a conversation about her manuscript in which a colleague comments, "this is not quite what happened at the workshop [of journalists covering the TRC]." He complains, "you're not busy with the truth!" To which Krog replies,

> I am busy with the truth... *my* truth. Of course, it's quilted together from hundreds of stories that we've experienced or heard about in the past two years. Seen from my perspective, shaped by my state of mind at the time.... And all this together makes up the whole country's truth. So also the lies. And the stories that date from earlier times. (170–71)

In the same spirit, Krog invents a fictional, adulterous love affair between herself and a man involved with the TRC. She invents this episode, she explains, in order to "express the psychological underpinning of the Commission. Surely I can't describe how I eavesdropped and spied on others?" (171). Even if the affair never happened, her use of this invention illustrates the distance she feels from her family, and the fact that, like many trauma survivors, she feels she can talk closely only to those who have shared her experiences.[33] For Krog to convey the subjective truth of her reactions to covering the TRC, it was necessary for her to distill emotions and invent situations dramatizing complex interpersonal dynamics. Anthea Garman notes, moreover, that "[b]y insisting on poetic licence claimed for a book situated within the public... confessional space created by the Commission, in order to reveal the truths that liberate and make history, Krog unsettles the reader's trust in what would be considered to be 'the truth' in the book itself" (338).[34]

In some ways these creative liberties function similarly to the fragmentation of testimony in *Ubu*: They paradoxically render telling possible by enacting the displacements and ruptures of trauma that have heretofore prevented its telling.[35] As Schaffer and Smith put it, "Krog becomes a witness in the second person, staging acts of complicity, guilt, loss, suffering, and apology" (1579). Furthermore, however disturbing the presence of perpetrators' versions of events may be, their stories are necessarily part of the "widest possible compilation" of stories (Krog, *Country* 16). This is not to say that we must consider every version equally valid, or that we should not be suspicious when a confessed torturer's tale contradicts or denies the memories of his victims. Nor does the concept of truth as multiplicity demand that we abandon the search for truth, or fatalistically embrace ambiguity. But Krog implies that we must tolerate some ambiguity and contradiction at the level of individual cases, while looking for the larger patterns of truth revealed in the TRC's findings.

I would argue, then, that Krog's notion of truth is considerably more nuanced than what many of her critics would allow. It might seem that Krog is playing fast and loose with the truth, yet I would argue that in fact she questions the nature and definition of truth systematically and reflectively. Interestingly, in an imaginary conversation with her husband about her imaginary affair, Krog takes a relativist view of truth. But in the retelling, she lets her husband have the last word: "Rubbish. There is always a basic truth: you cheated on me. Why? Where? How? From when to when—all of that is negotiable with the things I already know. So the more I know, the more you will confess. What truth I don't know, you will never tell me" (197). This, of course, is the strategy of a great many amnesty applicants—reveal only the information that is likely to emerge regardless. By including her husband's attack on this strategy (real or imagined), Krog seems to acknowledge that there do exist some irrefutable truths. In South African history, the ultimate manifestation of "basic truth" is the death penalty for political prisoners as well as common-law prisoners. Krog reminds us of this sobering fact immediately after the argument with her husband, through a quotation from a TRC hearing: "The Maximum Security Prison in Pretoria was the head office for hangings—it was a place designed for death" (197).

However sophisticated and self-reflective Antjie Krog's ideas of truth may be, the fundamental tension between the stories of the victims and those of their perpetrators persists. This is not so much a flaw in the book as it is a driving force. Yet this tension does further complicate the central difficulty facing historiography and art during the post-apartheid era: how to represent the past, and particularly the victims of that past? This is a multifaceted problem that Krog first faced as a journalist reporting on the TRC. Radio is the most democratic news medium in South Africa, accessible to those who cannot read or afford a television. Moreover, short news bulletins are heard even by those (especially whites) who consciously avoid news about the TRC. Thus, she writes, "[W]e will have to use the full spectrum of hard news techniques and where necessary develop and reform them according to our needs" (31). The danger is that the stories of victims will be compressed into sound bites, as meaningless and toothless as the acronym "TRC" would be. Part of the team's strategy to minimize this risk is to let the victims speak for themselves, and to follow the same ethic that the TRC itself proclaims: "trust the victim, believe the poorest of the poor, treat the simple and illiterate with the tenderest of respect.... Through the Commission we have come to accept that poor people seldom have reason to lie, whereas the well-dressed rich often have every reason you can think of" (232). Krog's mission, both in her broadcast reporting and in her memoir, is the formation of what Mark Sanders calls "an ethics of advocacy, the task of giving the domain of words over to the other" ("Truth" 17). To this I would add that it is in the voices and perspectives of ordinary people—the poor black majority—that Krog is most likely to discover new (or old but forgotten) modes of mapping space, memory, and social relationships.

If reporting on the TRC for the nightly news is like walking a tight wire, writing a memoir about the commission (especially a memoir as overtly fictionalized as *Country of My Skull* sometimes is) raises a whole other set of problems. When her publisher first asked Krog to document her TRC experience, she "initially said no, because when you tackle something as a writer rather than a journalist, you become a vulture. Journalists are also vultures to a certain degree, but there are journalistic ethics" (qtd. in Braude 9). Yet, just as the survivors of a great catastrophe sometimes talk obsessively about the event, Krog feels compelled to tell her story: "No poetry should come forth from this. May my hands fall off if I write this.... If I write this, I exploit and betray. If I don't, I die" (*Country* 49).

The betrayal Krog mentions is double-edged. If she tells the victims' stories, she betrays the understanding out of which those stories were told, by appropriating the narratives for her own project of self-realization. But she also betrays her language and her heritage as an Afrikaner, at least in the eyes of the self-appointed guardians of that heritage. For Carli Coetzee, this second form of betrayal is the crux of the memoir: "It would seem as if the codes of this ancestral language [Afrikaans] speak of another landscape, now rejected by [Krog]—and one that rejects her in turn.... This book, then, is an attempt at a public distancing from the language of the heart, the language of the men of her race" ("They Never" 690).[36]

Krog's declaration that "No poetry should come forth from this" echoes Theodor Adorno's dictum that poetry was impossible after Auschwitz. Her dilemma is to represent the stories of victims without exploiting, trivializing, or aestheticizing them,[37] and to do so in a way that keeps the reader's interest and conveys the psychological impact of the traumatic events. In one article Krog reveals her anxiety, in working with her editor Ivan Vladislavić, to "make the testimonies of the victims and perpetrators readable on paper" ("The Cook" 93):

> Initially I had the name of the victim plus the date and violation upfront and in bold. But people who had been asked to write something for the blurb confessed to "skipping" the testimonies, because they were "too hard to read." I was obsessed with the necessity that people should read the testimonies and asked Ivan why the texts (some taken from the Internet) posed problems.

> "Punctuation," he suggested. We had a long discussion on whether and how one should present on paper an oral delivery's recorded interpretation which has been officially transcribed for the Truth and Reconciliation Commission's Website. I decided to remove everything that would make it visually easy to "skip" the testimony—the bold names, the different font. . . . ("The Cook" 93–94)

When Krog uses this technique, her book sometimes resembles a novel, with the testimonies inside quotation marks mimicking the familiar conventions of fictional dialogue. This practice is highly effective at keeping the reader emotionally involved.

Krog experiments with various other strategies for quoting victims' testimony throughout the book. In Chapter 3, she portrays the first week of the TRC's official work in a list of unattributed quotations from the hearings, each separated by a bit of white space. The effect is ambivalent: reading one horrible story after another does convey some of the overwhelming shock felt by participants and audiences in East London that week. Yet the list is anonymous, and the reader is given no context for the stories, no dates, and not even the names of the victims. As in *Ubu*, the survivors are removed from the center of their own stories and made into interchangeable metaphors. Krog's book thus threatens from the outset to expropriate the stories of victims for her own narrative of being displaced from her country and traumatized by the knowledge of the horrible deeds committed in the name of her people.

Later in the book, Krog begins to include the names of victims in parentheses at the end of each quotation. Yet still she provides little context for their stories, and few explanations of who the speakers are. One reviewer of the book claims that Krog's appropriation of these testimonies approaches "ordinary theft," asking, "Did Krog get permission to use this verbatim text at such length, or to alter its format, and what compensation did she offer the indigent author?" (Ruden 171).[38] Schaffer and Smith anticipate this sort of critique when they claim that in "her empathetic identification with the victims . . . Krog appropriates victim testimony to effect her call for recognition and reconciliation; in so doing, she renarrativizes the asymmetry of subject positions parceled out during apartheid" (1582). I agree that this larger project of making that asymmetry visible outweighs the immediate monetary issues Ruden raises. Moreover, I would argue that Krog is well aware of the dangers she encounters in appropriating the testimonies to create her own narrative of bearing witness.[39] To compensate, she experiments with different presentations of the material. Her use of unattributed quotations early in the memoir, for example, might be explained in terms of what Samuel Durrant calls "works of failed or inconsolable mourning"

(437).[40] Krog's memoir, in other words, refuses an easy closure through artificial mourning.

One of Krog's most remarkable attempts to represent victim testimony is "The Shepherd's Tale" by an elderly shepherd named Lekotse (spelled Likotsi in the TRC transcripts). Krog reproduces Lekotse's testimony in "the exact words in which he spoke it" (*Country* 217)—or at least the exact words into which the TRC interpreter translated them, a distinction Krog curiously fails to make. But rather than presenting the transcript as a block of text that readers might easily skim over, she enjambs the sentences to resemble poetry. For instance, Lekotse's description of the police searching his house, looking for evidence against his children in the resistance movement, appears as follows:

> They said every door of the house should be opened.
> They pulled clothes from the wardrobes.
> I said, "When a jackal gets into the sheep
> it does not do this—
> please unpack neatly and pack them back neatly."
>
> They did not provide an answer.
> They pushed us outside.
> I fell on my shoulder: *kaboem!* (211–12)

At the end of the testimony, Ilan Lax, the chairperson of the hearing, asks whether Lekotse had reported the incident to the police. He replies:

> We never took any initiative to report this matter to the police, because
> how can you report policemen to policemen?
> They were going to attack us.
> That is why I said to them,
> "Kill us all
> so that there is no trouble thereafter.
> It is much better to die—
> all of us."
> . . .
> If one of these policemen is around here,
> I'll be happy if one of them comes to the stage
> and kills me immediately. . . . (215–16)

Reluctant to bring forth poetry out of pain, Krog nevertheless uses the familiar conventions of poetry to underscore the dignity of the old man's narrative. Presenting the testimony as poetry adds suspense and emphasis to the shepherd's already very moving words; the enjambment and end-stopping lends force, for instance, to Lekotse's claim that death would have been preferable to his traumatized existence after the raid.

Krog's use of poetic enjambment—which is, incidentally, a kind of spatial rendering of the painful hesitation that characterizes Lekotse's tale—also acknowledges that this poor, uneducated old man has a gift of eloquence worthy of being called poetry.[41] Furthermore, she follows "The Shepherd's Tale" with a four-page exposition, implying that his story contains a depth and richness that requires a systematic literary analysis to fully appreciate: "They were worse than jackals, says Lekotse. And since the jackal is the shepherd's greatest enemy, a threat to the flock night and day, he means that the security police exceeded his worst expectations of evil. As a shepherd he often had to measure up against the sly jackal—but against this opponent he was at a loss" (218). Krog thus manages to represent the paradox of traumatic telling: Lekotse has been shattered and desymbolized by his experience—"his ability to understand the world around him is taken away," Krog says (218). Yet he is, in his own way, a master storyteller, using metaphor and narrative tension skillfully, and he thus stakes out his own subject-position as narrator even as he describes the destruction of subjectivity.

Moreover, the broken, uneven lines of "The Shepherd's Tale" replicate the effects of Lekotse's trauma: the story comes erratically, in fits and starts, rather than in one sustained, linear narration. The nonlinearity of Krog's presentation of Lekotse's story, which I see as deliberate and strategic on Krog's part, is one of Sarah Ruden's complaints about the memoir. She claims that "Lekotse's story would be more 'real' if the scenes were rearranged into the order in which they happened" (Ruden 172). This claim is an extension of Ruden's more general critique of *Country of My Skull*, which she believes lacks "overall structure" and "does not go far enough in [Krog's] synthesis; there is too little that is shaped, too little of a story" (169, 168). To shape the stories in the way Ruden demands, however, would be to impose a structure on them that would suppress or exclude the very elements that render the events traumatic. Ruden says that to "imagine the testimony with no intervention at all is to realize how naïve it is to think that the oppressed can speak for themselves if the rest of us just stand back" (172–73). Far more naive, I would suggest, is Ruden's faith in the ability of language and narrative to fully and accurately represent the traumatic past. While the success of her efforts is open to debate, what Krog has set out to do is create a form in which victims can be allowed not only to "speak for themselves," but to do so in a way that animates the disjunctures and displacements of trauma. In the case of Lekotse's tale, the production of a chronologically and empirically accurate accounting of external events is less important than registering the very impossibility of creating such narratives.

Nevertheless, many commentators have noted the compulsion to narrativize and externalize the past in *Country of My Skull*.[42] Such readings typically focus on language as constitutive of selfhood, identity, and community. They generally do not, however, note *Country of My Skull*'s attempts to remap social space and the experience of embodiment within which identity and community are forged. One exception is Susan Spearey, who argues that "testimony becomes less a singular act of archaeological retrieval . . . than a dynamic and open-ended process of *narrative mapping*, of exploring and testing the limits and boundaries of the multiple and shifting landscapes being traversed together by witness and audience" (73; emphasis added). This notion of narrative mapping, which will recur repeatedly throughout my study of post-apartheid literature, is crucial to understanding Krog's ultimate project in *Country of My Skull*: to create a new space—and a new understanding of space—for living in the "New South Africa" as a white Afrikaner. Krog acknowledges as much herself—and, significantly, does so in geographical/nationalist terms: "When the Truth Commission started last year, I realized instinctively: if you cut yourself off from the process, you will wake up in a foreign country—a country that you don't know and that you will never understand" (*Country* 131).

The memoir's mapping of Krog's imagined "country of her skull" begins with her trip into the "womb" of her parents' home in the Free State. It continues as she follows the TRC hearings around the country, beginning in the Eastern Cape and Port Elizabeth. As the narrative turns to each locale, Krog includes a brief history of the place, often borrowing on Noel Mostert's popular history *Frontiers*. She describes Queenstown (134), Oudtshoorn (196), Pietersburg (205), and Ladysmith, which is "my landscape. The marrow of my bones. . . . This I love. This is what I'm made of" (210). Through these descriptions, she notes the ways in which the past is inscribed on or interred in the physical landscape: "Queenstown. On the surface a normal platteland town among the soft, grass-covered mountains of the Eastern Cape. But Queenstown holds buried the most gruesome of histories" (134). Other passages emphasize the way that places and buildings are haunted by the past: "Every respectable historical building has its own live-in ghost. The South African Parliament in Cape Town has several" (122).

If *Country* charts the ways that the traumatic past has been encoded and memorialized on or through the landscape, it also charts many hopeful transformations to geography and memory. One example can be seen in the sculpture garden in Pietersburg, which contains statues of Piet Joubert, Magnus Malan, Pik Botha, and other heroes of Afrikaner nationalism. But Krog also notes that, "Just lately, the King of Kwela, Lemmy Special Mabaso, has been honoured with a bronze statue in the Garden of Pietersburg. The famous pennywhistler is the first black man to be honoured in this way by the town. His statue stands beside the *boere-orkes*, as if they just might invite him to join in on the next number" (206–07). With so much nationalist rhetoric relying on symbolic spatializations of the past, such subtle gestures as the Mabaso statue mark a small but significant transformation in how South Africans publicly conceive of history and symbolic social space. Krog shows us a similar reconfiguration of symbolic memory in the removal of the paintings inside the Parliament building, three of which "provide an insight into three distinct eras of our past" (107): one of the legislature at the time of Union in 1910; one of Hendrik Verwoerd explaining his Bantustan policy to his Cabinet; and one of P.W. Botha's Cabinet from 1984. The removal of these paintings from South Africa's official legislative chambers marks the end of the narrative of whites-only power and Afrikaner nationalism as sketched by these paintings.

In two recent works, Susan VanZanten Gallagher and Teresa Godwin Phelps both argue that narrative and storytelling are crucial to resolving the conflicts of the past and moving into the future. Krog's memoir confirms this claim, as for instance when she quotes her friend Professor Kondlo, who suggests that "to get that memory, to fix it in words, to capture it with the precise image, is to be present at the birth of language itself" (*Country* 42). Yet Kondlo's analysis and *Country of My Skull* as a whole suggest the need for something more than oral and written narratives of the past. They both call for *spatial* renderings of memory—images, statues, monuments, memorials of various sorts.

Krog further recognizes that in changing the way that the past is encoded and inscribed on the landscape, the Truth Commission is changing the contours of the landscape itself, and people's understanding of social space. Thus the comic book that Kondlo proposes about Nomonde Calata's HRVC hearing into the murder of her husband and the three other members of the "Cradock Four" by security forces is entitled "*The Contestation of Spaces*" (37). The opening frames depict the "Male Storyteller (Historian)" (37) and a female storyteller, "Socializer of Children" (37), whose spaces have literally been invaded by the stamped words "MIGRATION, URBANIZATION, FORCED REMOVALS"; "And then starts the actual story of Nomonde Calata as a woman, sitting in the male space of the British Colonial city hall of East London, and relating a story as part of the official history of this country" (38). For Kondlo, Calata's testimony is about reclaiming the space formerly delimited as a whites-only area by British colonial and apartheid rule: "By choosing the city hall in the centre of town and not a community centre in the township, the Truth Commission wants to portray a symbolic break with the institutional frameworks of the past. This city hall is no longer the official domain of whites and perpetrators: it now belongs to all of us" (38–39). It is this project, of reclaiming space and recovering certain forgotten aspects of precolonial conceptualizations of space, that Krog seems to posit as a prerequisite for reconciliation and healing in South Africa.

Krog's project, then, is one of mapping loss on multiple levels simultaneously: the loss of self that results from the assault on the body, such as that experienced by N.E. Zingxondo, who testified that she kept a cloth covered in pus from her battered breast and tufts of her hair ripped out by the police, and has the rag to this day (*Country* 114); the loss of loved ones and community, such as Sheila Masote's, who gives "a summary of what I was stripped of.... I had a family that was home and togetherness. That was destroyed" (187); the loss of knowledge about those lost, as with Cynthia Ngewu, who laments about the police who killed her son: "Why did they just kill everyone, absolutely everyone? Not leaving even one to give witness. Now nobody knows the real-real story" (192); and the loss of determination over one's own private spaces, as embodied in the plight of Lekotse, who has been unable "to redefine his own space" (220). Such a redefinition of space is central to Krog's project, and it is clear that her use of the term "space" is more than metaphorical. This is also the case when she praises Winnie Madikizela-Mandela for her non-apology: "A space was created for the first time for both her and her followers to admit in an honourable way that things went wrong" (260). At the beginning of the hearing, Krog had been worried because "[t]his hearing is about my country.... And whether there is space for all of us. And the conditions for this space" (258).

The final chapters of *Country of My Skull* see an intensified condensation of the tropes of nation, community, landscape, body, language, memory, and the past. The suggestion is that the TRC has at least laid the groundwork for a transformation of space and memory that can allow perpetrators, beneficiaries, victims, and survivors to coexist in post-apartheid South Africa. We get an intimation of this hopeful prospect in Krog's apostrophic reaction to Madikizela-Mandela's hearing: "Ah, the Commission! The deepest heart of my heart. Heart that can only come from this soil—brave—with its teeth firmly in the jugular of the only truth that matters. And that heart is black. I belong to that blinding black African heart.... for one brief, shimmering moment this country, this country is also truly mine" (259).

The transformative, perhaps even redemptive, potential of the Truth Commission is ultimately emphasized in the poem that concludes the memoir:

> because of you
> this country no longer lies
> between us but within
> ...
> in the cradle of my skull
> it sings, it ignites

my tongue, my inner ear, the cavity of heart
shudders toward the outline
        new in soft intimate clicks and gutturals

of my soul the retina learns to expand
daily because by a thousand stories
I was scorched

a new skin.

I am changed for ever. I want to say:
        forgive me
        forgive me
        forgive me

You whom I have wronged, please
take me

with you (278–79)

Carli Coetzee reads these lines in terms of a "rebirth": "It is as if her body wants to negate the identification with the men of her race, to grow a new skin—scorched, dark perhaps. This new skin will be the mark of having been born into a new language and a new lineage; it will qualify her to be taken 'with you' " ("They Never" 693). But body, skin, and language have been conflated with landscape so thoroughly by this point—the body contains cavities and countries, the heart is born of the soil, truth has a jugular, language holds spaces—that the birth of the new skin must also be seen as a new configuration of the land, a reclaiming of space.

1.4 Words That Look Like Acts: Ingrid de Kok's *Transfer* and *Terrestrial Things*

In my first two sections of part 1, I suggested that theater, with its capacity for nearly infinite variation and improvisation, might be a particularly effective medium for conveying the psychological dynamics of a traumatic history. I argued furthermore that the most effective drama in this regard is that which, rather than trying to reproduce a linear, empirically precise accounting of the traumatic event, attempts to make visible the obstacles and paradoxes that make such an accounting problematic. Yet even in a play such as *The Story I Am about to Tell*, there is a real danger of psychic numbing, in which the event is rendered inert through the sheer repetition of a particular dramatic idiom. This danger is all the greater in a written prose narrative, in which the representation of the traumatic event is fixed in one immutable form.

Yet as we saw in section 1.3, Antjie Krog demonstrates the possibilities of formal experimentation for circumventing psychic numbing, again by making explicit the impossibility of telling. One technique that she employs is to present TRC testimony as poetry through a strategic use of enjambment; I hinted that this technique constitutes a *spatialization* of narrative—it draws the reader's attention to the speaker's occupation of space and place, not merely the temporal duration represented in the words.

In this section, I develop that argument at greater length by studying the poetry of Ingrid de Kok, whose work explores the intersections of space, place, and memory through both content and form.[43] Like *Country of My Skull*, the poems in two of De Kok's collections—*Transfer* (1997) and *Terrestrial Things* (2002)—address the impossible necessity of narrating stories about traumatic loss. And like Krog, De Kok suggests that the key to unraveling this paradox lies in remapping the intimate, complex connections and displacements between memory, landscape, and the body. Anthony O'Brien notes this characteristic in his reading of "Two Places, Two Dreams," a poem in De Kok's first collection *Familiar Ground*: "This poem uses landscape to suggest the phenomenology of how place memory persists" (O'Brien 142). O'Brien argues further that in the "found poems" in the final section of *Familiar Ground*, "the reconnection or healing toward which the poems strive can come only through a reconstituting of both child's and woman's place" (162). One could characterize the lessons of De Kok's two more recent collections in similar terms: they reveal a need for a feminist remapping, with the aim of reconstituting South Africans' relationship to and encounters with space and place.

De Kok dramatizes the persistence of place memory immediately in "Transfer" (*Transfer* 13–14; *Seasonal Fires* [*SF*] 57–58). It depicts the narrator's family homestead, now abandoned by its white residents and occupied by "dark tenants" (36)—"Seven strangers" (6) who have let the property fall into disrepair, rust, and "rankness" (20). The opening lines establish images of displacement, disarrangement, and wildness: "All the family dogs are dead. / A borrowed one, its displaced hip / at an angle to its purebred head, / bays at a siren's emergency climb / whining from the motorway" (1–5) The dogs, symbol of domestic protection, are no longer around, and a pervasive sense of menace and insecurity fill their absence.

The third and fourth stanzas further develop this image of a siege giving way to a ransacking:

> Forty years ago the house was built
> to hold private unhappiness intact,
> safe against mobile molecular growths
> of city, developers and blacks.
> Now rhubarb spurs grow wild and sour;
> . . .
>
> Townhouses circle the inheritance.
> The fire station and franchised inn
> keep neighbourhood watch over its fate.
> The municipality leers over the gate,
> Complains of dispossession and neglect,
> dark tenants and the broken fence. (21–36)

Having established this scene of ruin, the closing lines turn in an unexpectedly optimistic direction: "But all the highveld birds are here, / weighing their metronomic blossoms / upon the branches in the winter air. / And the exiles are returning" (37–40). The image of a bird bringing songs of unanticipated hope will recur throughout both volumes of poetry, as I discuss at further length in the following pages. For now let me remain with the trope of the house, which Patrick Cullinan reads as "a metaphor for the 'old' South Africa, and since the blossoms (metronomic or not) are appearing on the wintry branches, they can be seen (or heard) to prefigure the spring of the 'new' South Africa" (153).

Clearly the house is the source of some ambivalence for the narrator: it was a refuge from the "city, developers and blacks," but also a container for "private unhappiness." And the very fact that the architecture of the house is designed to exclude blacks is a source of discomfort for the narrator, who oscillates between the scandalized perspective of the "municipality" (and, perhaps, of her family who formerly occupied the house) and her own more detached, ironic perspective. It is this ambivalence and slippage in narrative point of view that Fiona Zerbst overlooks in her review of *Transfer* when she complains about De Kok's "muddled narration": "The last line, 'And the exiles are returning,' is a triumphant declaration—but by whom? Surely not the narrator who says 'All the family dogs are dead'?" (63). Yet surely the narrator is capable of lamenting the death of her childhood pets while still celebrating the demise of the exclusionary system that the dogs had unwittingly played a part in reinforcing. From the first poem in the collection, then, De Kok reveals the unhealthiness and misery that both reproduce and are produced by the spatial regimes of apartheid, implicitly making the case for the reworking of those configurations of space, place, and history.

If "Transfer" begins to probe formations of "place memory," the poem "What Everyone Should Know about Grief" (*Transfer* 21–22; *SF* 63–64) deepens the picture through a metaphorical conflation of mourning, landscape, and the body. The poem's title is taken from a headline in a women's magazine in which "grief finds its marketable stage" (5) The narrator first mocks the article, which "advises talking as the healing cure, / commends long walks, and therapies, / assures the grieving that they will endure, / and then it gently cautions: let go, move on" (12–15). But the last three stanzas take a more sober turn, conjuring a corporeal landscape of grief and suffering that seems to prefigure Krog's language in *Country of My Skull*:

> But everyone knows sorrow is incurable:
> a bruised and jagged scar
> in the rift valley of the body;
> shrapnel seeded in the skin;
> undoused burning pyres of war.
>
> And grief is one thing nearly personal,
> a hairline fracture in an individual skull;
> homemade elegy which sounds its keening
> in the scarred heart's well;
> where it is too deep to reach
>
> the ladder of light
> sent down from land above,
> where hands write words
> to work the winch
> to plumb the shaft below. (16–30)

Like Krog, De Kok draws connections between mourning, traumatic memory, the injured body, and the ravaged landscape with an insistence that suggests that these connections transcend the merely metaphorical; the implication seems to be that the healing of one must involve the healing of all at once.

"What Everyone Should Know about Grief" also introduces a theme that recurs throughout *Transfer* and *Terrestrial Things*: the untellable nature of grief and loss, which nevertheless demands to be told. The shortening of the lines in the last stanza, the use of short, staccato monosyllables, and the breaking of the final sentence across two stanzas, all reinforce the sense of descent or underwater excavation—of plumbing the depths of a well in which grief lies "too deep to reach." Most importantly, this exploration is presented explicitly as a metaphor for writing—"where hands write words / to work the winch"—and perhaps for storytelling more generally. The implication of this metaphor is that the truth can only be reconstituted inductively, by paying attention to the absences, gaps, seams, and traces.

Similar images and tropes appear throughout the two volumes: "The Talking Cure" (*Transfer* 44–45) repeats "Grief"'s ridicule of the facile "talking cure" for trauma and mourning:

> Sometimes a man walks away from a window
> just as light splinters the screen.
> Sometimes a diver hired to resurrect beauty
> secretly buries the brightest pearl.
> Sometimes the story keeps winding back to the same place.
> And who would believe the gristle and lung
> in our short conversations?
>
> Mouthing under water
> Wetly jewelled words,
> we are acrobatic aquanauts
> in a chest of swords. (1–11)
>
> . . .
>
> Here too: riddle, spiral, ruse,
> a ridge of words that look like acts.
> On a suspension bridge,
> we tightrope into talk:
> silver, dancing alphabets
> strung with loops and hoops,
> arabesques of words on a swaying net. (24–34)

In the opening stanza, De Kok highlights the elusiveness of truth and insight into the past, and the need to query what the "story" is avoiding, obscuring, or distracting itself from by continually "winding back to the same place." The successive lines can be read as an implicit critique of the Truth Commission, which shared certain assumptions with the proponents of the talking cure. The poem satirizes the TRC's processes of bearing witness as a kind of circus sideshow, as aquatic/diving metaphors (a variation on the motif of plumbing the depths of a well, perhaps) give way to images of acrobatics and tight-rope walking. De Kok again seems to question the substance of "words that look like acts."

De Kok devotes an entire section of *Terrestrial Things*, titled "A Room Full of Questions," to poems about the TRC, and here too she thematizes the impossibility of telling stories about trauma. The first poem of the section is entitled "Parts of Speech"; the final poem in the section is called "Body Parts," and the pairing of the two titles suggests another deep-seated connection between stories and the body. In "Parts of Speech" (21; *SF* 96) the narrator describes the TRC, no longer as an acrobatics display but as a shambling song-and-dance routine:

> Some stories don't want to be told.
> They walk away, carrying their suitcases
> held together with grey string.
> . . .
>
> Some stories refuse to be danced or mimed,
> drop their scuffed canes
> and clattering tap-shoes,
> erase their traces in nursery rhymes
> or ancient games like blindman's buff. (1–10)

The TRC here becomes a parody of a Vaudeville show, an institution poorly equipped to track the erasures and displacements of trauma into encoded cultural symptoms. Moreover, when it does turn to the task of discovering the truth, the TRC is depicted as proceeding in a clinical, institutional way: "And at this stained place words / are scraped from resinous tongues, / wrung like washing, hung on the lines / of courtroom and confessional, / transposed into the dialect of record" (11–15). The narrator seems to see the TRC's self-appointed task as one of sanitizing the past rather than elegizing it, leading her to despair in the final stanzas at the ability of stories to transcend pain:

> Why still believe stories can rise
> with wings, on currents, as silver flares,
> levitate unweighted by stones,
> begin in pain and move towards grace,
> aerating history with recovered breath?
>
> Why still imagine whole words, whole worlds:
> the flame splutter of consonants,
> deep sea anemone vowels,
> birth-cable syntax, rhymes that start in the heart,
> and verbs, verbs that move mountains? (16–25)

Gallagher argues that "confession in post-apartheid South Africa participates in creating a new identity through narrative" (113); the narrator of "Parts of Speech" is decidedly less convinced. The "stones" that weigh down stories are multivalent: they symbolize at once the landscape on which memory is encoded and described, and also the material conditions of those who tell the stories—many of them still poor, still suffering from irreplaceable loss. The narrator here almost mocks the idea that stories—mere words, which as we have seen can only "look like acts"—are enough to "move mountains" or effect changes to material space.

De Kok continues to explore the untellability of traumatic episodes in "How to Mourn in a Room Full of Questions" (*Terrestrial* 23; *SF* 99), the title of which is both an apt description of a TRC hearing and a spatial metaphor for the process of reconstructing the past through narrative:

> The witness tells it steady:
> the breathing of a boy deep asleep
> the way the young, even the watchful young, sleep;
> the window splintering,
> shaking shack walls,
> raked breathing of the shot, same, boy.
> The mother and her spreading blanket.
>
> Old sorrow holds down anger like a plug.
> And juridical questions
> swab swab the brains and blood off the floor. (1–10)

As with "Parts of Speech," the TRC is depicted here as engaged in an institutional sanitization, swabbing away memory like blood from the scene of a crime. The "room full of questions" in the title likewise suggests an analytical, legalistic, almost antagonistic aspect to the proceedings: the questions ironically hinder mourning rather than enabling it. The notions of "common" or "external" memory that I discussed in relation to *The Story I Am about to Tell* in section 1.1 prove useful in understanding the second stanza: "Old sorrow" might be read as the congealed or codified narratives that the victim has long used to distance herself from the pain of her son's murder enough to "tell it steady." In the line "raked breathing of the shot, same, boy," the one-word interjection "same" literally means "the one referred to in line two above," but it also evokes a weariness—he is the "same" boy whose death she has been reliving privately for years.

Again and again, the poems in *Terrestrial Things* question the capacity of storytelling to produce truth, as the title of "Tongue-Tied" (24; *SF* 100) suggests. The poem begins with the oath, "Do you promise to tell the truth, / the whole truth and nothing but the truth?" (1–2), but the rest of the poem soon shows the assumptions underlying the oath to be somewhat simplistic, even naive, as the image of speaking underwater (repeated from "The Talking Cure") suggests: "Someone's been hurt. / But she can't speak. / They say she's 'tongue-tied'. / . . . / Now she's speaking underwater, / to herself, to drowning, / to her son, her lost daughter" (3–9). The image of drowning here is a distant echo of the image of the diver inadvertently burying the "brightest pearl" in "Talking Cure." Unlike a land burial, which can be exhumed and autopsied, something lost under water is often irretrievable, like the depths of a well "too deep to reach." The victim's tongue-tied testimony soon reveals the absurdity of claiming to tell "the whole truth" about such a loss:

> "They came for the children, took, then me,
> and then, then afterwards
> the bucket bled. My ears went still.
> I'm older than my mother when . . ."
>
> The gull drags its wing to the lighthouse steps.
> "That's the truth. So help. Whole. To tell." (15–20)

If telling the "whole truth" requires being able to tell a coherent, unfractured story, then this victim's honest answer to the oath's question must be no, she cannot swear to do so. And just as the narrator of "Parts of Speech" doubts the ability of stories to burst into unencumbered flight, here De Kok compares the victim's story to a gull with a broken wing.

If the poems already mentioned highlight the inadequacy of language for representing the victims' pain and loss, "What Kind of Man?" (*Terrestrial* 25–27; *SF* 101–04) makes clear its further inadequacy for understanding the motives and makeup of the perpetrators. The title is taken from Tony Yengeni's questions to Jeffrey Benzien at the latter's amnesty hearing, which De Kok quotes in the epigraph, but the poem goes on to question several other instances of inhuman brutality revealed by the TRC hearings. Such behavior is so inexplicable, the narrator suggests, that it can perhaps only be understood through pseudo-science and superstition: "What type? We ask and he asks too / like Victorians at a seminar. / Is it in the script, the shape of the head, / the family gene? / Graphology, phrenology, or the devil?" (21–25).

The tone of the rest of the poem, though, gradually becomes more somber and serious, as the narrator searches for explanations in the perpetrators' faces, hands, mannerisms: "Nothing left but to screen his body. / We have no other measure / but body as lie detector, / truth serum, weathervane" (26–29). J.U. Jacobs notes that in *Country of My Skull*, Krog is "scrupulous about recording the signs of psychological damage that punctuate the perpetrators' versions of their deeds to the Commission" ("Reconciling" 44): the twitch in Brian Mitchell's jaw, Dirk Coetzee's gulping Adam's apple, et cetera. De Kok's narrator pays similar attention to the bodies and tics of the perpetrators: to one's "misshapen cheek" (30), another's "elastic pantomime" mouth (33), a "sagging chin, glottal Adam's apple" (34). The poem acts like Pa Ubu's Geiger counter/toilet brush, "decoding" the body of the perpetrator. Yet, like a weathervane, the opaque bodies of the killers and torturers point only toward distant horizons, not fixed truths:

> VI
> Though of the heart we cannot speak
> encased in its grille of gristle
>
> the body almost but doesn't explain
> "What kind of man are you?"
>
> VII
> This kind, we will possibly answer,
> (pointing straight, sideways,
> upwards, down, inside out),
> this kind. (48–55)

The conclusion clearly reveals language to be inadequate to answer the question in the poem's title, a question that so urgently demands an answer. What is needed is some set of coordinates, a location; but decoding the body can only yield directions that lead outward (or inward) to further questions.

After several such poems devoted to the TRC hearings and the victims and perpetrators at their center, De Kok dedicates two poems to those in less visible positions behind the scenes—"The Transcriber Speaks" and "The Sound Engineer"—which serve to thematize the extent to which the TRC is a mediated public spectacle. "The Transcriber Speaks" (*Terrestrial* 32; *SF* 109) is spoken by a first-person narrator, "the commission's own captive, / Its anonymous after-hours scribe, / Professional blank slate" (1–3). A scribe is charged with his society's history, and is expected to be neutral and objective. Yet the transcriber reveals his or her job to be a precarious assembling of words: "Like bricks for a kiln or tiles for a roof / Or the sweeping of leaves into piles for burning: / I don't know which: / Word upon word upon word" (7–10). Like Krog and many other post-apartheid writers, De Kok depicts the process of transcribing and recording history as one of re/assembling fragments. But there is much ambiguity in the narrator's attitude toward that process: bricks placed in a fire become tough and hard, but useful as building blocks, while leaves set on fire are reduced to barren ash. The anguished "I don't know which" reveals the speaker's deep ambivalence about the TRC's monumental project of archiving aspects of the past: she does not know whether these stories, "Word upon word upon word," are contributing toward a new, greater narrative, or simply immolating the past in the singular crucible of the TRC.

"The Transcriber Speaks" is perhaps, of the poems in this volume, the one in which De Kok's lyrical elegy is most poignant and effective. In a stanza that evokes the closing image of "What Kind of Man?" the narrator describes a witness pointing in a direction that refuses iterability through its very indeterminacy:

> But how to transcribe silence from tape?
> Is weeping a pause or a word?
> What written sign for a strangled throat?
> And a witness pointing? That I described,
> When official identified direction and name.
> But what if she stared?
> And if the silence seemed to stretch
> Past the police guard, into the street,
> Away to a door or a grave or a child,
> Was it my job to conclude:
> "The witness was silent. There was nothing left to say?" (13–23)

The victim's finger and her gaze point toward meanings, pasts, and futures that the transcriber's and the poet's language alike are unable to decode: present absences of dead loved ones and lost children. This indecipherability is reinforced by the fact that six of the last seven sentences in the poem end in question marks. "Transcriber" thus reveals the ostensibly transparent and objective task of transcribing TRC hearings to be a fraught, hopelessly insufficient archiving of the truths to emerge from the testimony.

"The Sound Engineer" (*Terrestrial* 33; *SF* 110–11) likewise demystifies the heavily mediated process whereby "sound bites" from the TRC hearings make it to the nation's television screens and radios:

> From the speaker's mouth
> through the engineer's ear,
> sound waves of drought and flood
> are edited for us to hear:
> dunes filtering burnt desert sand,
> corrupted wells, and shocks, shouts,
> no longer muffled in the cochlea shell.
>
> Listen, cut; comma, cut;
> stammer, cut;
> edit, pain; connect, pain; broadcast, pain;
> listen, cut; comma, cut.

Bind grammar to horror,
blood heating the earphones,
beating the airwaves' wings. (1–14)

The engineer's job is both to "edit" and to "broadcast" pain. In one interview, De Kok describes this seeming paradox as equally central to the functioning of poetic form: "Especially, perhaps, when material is painful, formal systems...do two things—they both contain and they intensify. Both effects must be present, or the poem could end up being either sentimental or patronizing; or exploitative" (Kelly 35). In the case of the second stanza just quoted, we can see this dual operation of containment and intensification at work through the use of commas and semicolons, as well as through the repetition of the words "comma" and "cut." The caesurae created by heavy punctuation certainly serves to *contain* the pain, horror, and blood being described, to the point of rendering it almost cold and clinical. This surely reflects the experience of the sound engineer, whose work requires her to regard the testimony as neutral bites of sound information. Yet, by making it visible to the reader how thoroughly inadequate the tools of the sound engineer are to capturing that pain and horror (like the tools of the transcriber and the poet), De Kok's conflation of poetic conventions of punctuation with the mechanical processes of sound production also *intensifies* the reader's understanding of a particular sliver of the past—or at least, it intensifies our understanding of how profoundly unspeakable that past may be.

The same tension is evident in the sound engineer's work in the next stanza: "For truth's sound bite / tape the teeth, mouth, jaw, / put hesitation in, take it out: / maybe the breath too. / Take away the lips. / Even the tongue. / Leave just sound's throat" (15–21). Here the term "tape" is ambiguous: it could mean to record to a tape, and thus to document the story; or it could mean to cover with tape—that is, to gag the storyteller. To edit and broadcast, contain and intensify. The engineer's job involves both senses of taping, for if you take away tongue and lips and leave "just sound's throat," you are left with a primal growl, with no ability to articulate words.

The second stanza quoted earlier ends with the image of blood "beating the airwaves' wings." The fourth stanza returns to this image of the testimony, developing into a winged creature attempting flight to avoid drowning, flying over "history's topography" and recording the suffering there:

Keep your ear to the ground,
to pain's surfacing,
its gulps for air, its low ragged flight
over history's topography.
The instrumental ear

records the lesions of eroded land
while blood drums the vellum of the brain. (22–28)

This stanza gives us still more linkages between testimony, body, and earth, here with the "ear" as the recording equipment able to pick up the whole country's pain. But the closing stanza makes clear that such pain can damage that equipment in turn: "The sound engineer hears / his own tympanic membrane tear" (36–37).

Throughout *Terrestrial Things*, De Kok both invokes and calls into question the image of the testimony as a bird in flight, and the bird song as symbol of hope. The volume's title is taken from Thomas Hardy's poem "The Darkling Thrush," the significance of which Jane Commin explains: "the speaker [of Hardy's poem] evokes a desolate landscape in which a bird carols hope and beauty though the speaker perceives none. The 'terrestrial things' of the landscape barely contain the seeds of life or love, but the speaker imagines an outside force, present in the air that may germinate these things" (64). De Kok confirms this reading when she tells Erica Kelly that the "blessed hope" represented by the bird in Hardy's poem is important because:

> Hardy's "I" imagines it as a possibility but is "unaware": both in the sense of not noticing it and not being shown it exists. He reads a different meaning and lesson from the landscape. The environment the poem describes—of deep winter and despair at the turn of the century—militates against "Hope": however the bird's song projects a potentially optimistic reading/ perspective; and the poem is capable of containing the latter within its sceptical framework. . . . (34)

Simon Lewis sheds further light on the significance of Hardy's poem: "without such stubborn hope [as Hardy's poem invokes] the terrible beauty of tragic events is lost and we are left with meaningless, inexplicable calamity. The process of singing as well as the poet's struggle with words, meaning and rhythm *is* the hope."

At first glance Lewis's interpretation seems to contradict the lesson of the poems cited earlier, in which trauma and loss are seen as defying the capacity of "words, meaning and rhythm" to bear witness to them. Yet this paradox is crucial to understanding De Kok's poetry, as she herself tells Kelly: "I feel no despair that language fails or has limited expressive range or access. That tension and paradox is at the root of the activity of writing poetry itself. It is its very material. . . . On the one hand, verbs can, and on the other they cannot, 'move mountains' " (35). She also claims:

> Reconstruction is a political act but also a symbolic one. Writers also deal with shards. . . . I [do not] believe that art "remembers and acknowledges"

> stories in any simple way—I am less interested in its anthropological or historical purpose than its transformative one. The brief extracts I use from...the TRC are not reproduced but recomposed, transformed into meaning by poetic languaging. (Kelly 37)

In another interview, De Kok says about Derek Walcott's image of African history as a broken vase that must be lovingly glued back together that the metaphor is "about *keeping the scars present, but in a reconstituted form*" (Rich 115; emphasis added). In other words, she urges us to keep the traumatic past alive in social memory, in ways that can be "transformative." And as we saw in the early poems in *Transfer*, written before the TRC hearings began, De Kok clearly sees a transformative potential in poetic form to help us "reconstitute" the fundamentally masculine, colonialist configurations of space and land that represent one legacy of white minority rule.

Again and again, De Kok's poetry cautions us against romanticizing the capacity of narrative to bring about closure and healing, and questions the tangibility of "words that look like acts." She acknowledges to Kelly that "[e]legiac poetry (or any art) cannot heal the burden of the past. It can only symbolically reconfigure the past, own its burdens and losses" (37). And repeatedly, her poetry brings us back to the "gristle and lung" of embodiment (*Transfer* 44) and to the "lesions of eroded land" (*Terrestrial* 33)—in other words, to the terrestrial things where the scars of the past are recorded. The poem "At the Commission" (*Transfer* 28; *SF* 70) questions the TRC's emphasis on documenting forensic truth through language and confession:

> Would it matter to know
> the detail called truth
> since, fast forwarded,
> the ending is the same,
> over and over?
>
> The questions, however intended,
> all lead away from him
> alone there, running for his life. (7–14)

Along with "What Everyone Should Know about Grief" and several other poems, "At the Commission" suggests that for De Kok the grief of victims and survivors should be the singular "truth" that we must not lose sight of—the scar that we must keep "present, but in a reconstituted form." Likewise, "Bandaged" (*Transfer* 29) implores us through apostrophe to pay attention to the material and bodily spaces in which victims live and testify:

> O listen, let us not turn away
> from seeing and hearing
> the witness speak with bowed neck.
>
> Prayer, apostrophe, curse.
>
> A bandaged story about
> the broken world, stumps
> on which to hang our shame
> as useless hands, forever. (10–17)

Here again, De Kok draws on a poetic convention to invoke the transformative potential of poetry: the apostrophe serves as a moral appeal to the reader, implicating us as fellow witnesses to the "bandaged stories" told, however inadequately, to the TRC. This is the first instance of many we will see of the second-person direct address being used to confront readers or audiences with a past they might sooner leave forgotten; in the work to which I turn my attention in the next section, Sindiwe Magona creates a similar effect through the use of a second-person epistolary form.

The lesson I draw from both of De Kok's collections is that, if we need words to give flight to stories, we need a connection to terrestrial things to maintain bearings and balance in an era prone to amnesia and loss of direction. This reading is confirmed by the last poem in the "Room Full of Questions" section of *Terrestrial Things*, called "Body Parts" (37; *SF* 113):

> may the wrist turn in the wind like a wing
> the severed foot tread home ground
>
> the punctured ear hear the thrum of sunbirds
> the molten eye see stars in the dark
>
> the faltering lungs quicken windmills
> the maimed hand scatter seeds and grain
>
> the heart flood underground springs
> pound maize, recognize named cattle
>
> and may the unfixable broken bone
> loosened from its hinges

now lying like a wishbone in the veld
pitted by pointillist ants

give us new bearings. (1–13)

The opening image immediately evokes the recurring linkage of bodies and stories, symbolized throughout the collection by winged creatures, and the linkage of bodies to "home ground." The "punctured ear" evokes the sound engineer's torn "tympanic membrane," but now it hears the "thrum of sunbirds," perhaps carrying the same unimaginable hope as Hardy's darkling thrush. Indeed, the entire poem speaks of rebirth and new life being breathed or flooding into the landscape. Even the broken, dessicated, "unfixable" bone becomes a wishbone, implying some hope for a better future—something worth wishing for. Only through remapping and transforming the interconnections between language, self, body, and space, De Kok's poetry implies, can the decaying ruins of the past "give us new bearings."

1.5 Irredeemable Blood, Irretrievable Loss: Sindiwe Magona's *Mother to Mother*

The plays, poems, and memoir I have discussed up to this point have all grappled with the Truth Commission fairly directly as source material, or as dramatic spectacle. They have also engaged with the TRC as a new "road map" for exploring and narrating the past, or at least as a repertoire of social-cartographic tools for carrying out the authors' own projects of reconfiguring space and memory. In her first novel *Mother to Mother* (1998), Sindiwe Magona[44] also takes her inspiration from a real event that eventually came before the TRC, and not just any incident: the murder of white American Fulbright student Amy Biehl by youth in Guguletu in August 1993 was one of the most internationally notorious events of the transitional era between Mandela's release from prison in 1990 and the first democratic elections in 1994. This event also gave the TRC some of its most iconic moments, as Biehl's parents dramatically forgave one of the perpetrators during his amnesty hearing and subsequently founded the Amy Biehl Foundation to carry out the kind of work in the townships about which their daughter had been passionate.

Magona takes some liberties with the actual event—for example, attributing the murder primarily to one character, Mxolisi. But ultimately the novel is not about Amy Biehl or Mxolisi, but rather about the latter's mother, Mandisa, a domestic worker with two other children. The novel is her first-person letter to Biehl's mother; it is also Magona's attempt to diagnose the social and psychological disorders that engender such unspeakable, unexplainable acts of violence, rendered through a complex temporal, spatial, and social mapping of the multiple traumas visited on Mandisa, her children, and her community.

Mother to Mother is clearly a work of fiction, but insofar as it confronts the very real crisis of bearing witness to the past through individual, fictionalized scenarios and characters, it nevertheless stands in a synecdochical relationship to larger communities represented by the characters, much as Doris Sommer argues that the subjects of autobiographical *testimonios* in Latin America stand in for the traumatized, politically silenced communities from and for which they speak. As Meg Samuelson notes, "Magona's mother-as-witness allows the act of witnessing to extend beyond the lives of Mandisa and her son into the story of 'entire communities,' while simultaneously enabling the empathy between individuals that the TRC attempted to foster" ("Mother" 131). In other words, Mandisa and several generations of her family play out in microcosm the private dramas and traumas of millions of black Africans under apartheid: forced removal and dispossession, manual labor in white homes, and being subjected to a spatial infrastructure designed to confine and control black bodies. Through this diagnosis, Magona implicitly offers a prescription for reknitting the fabric of a ruptured society, a prescription she makes explicit in an interview with Renée Schatteman: "South Africans need to participate in the governing of their country.... Political transformation does not guarantee social transformation. Social transformation can only be achieved in South Africa if we join hands and we work boldly and in a concerted effort to change lives so that people remain hopeful about their futures" (163). In diagnosing the causes and effects of these regimes of socio-spatial control, Magona keeps alive memories of the past that are needed, if only as cautionary tales, but she also provides provisional coordinates for future remappings of what might yet become a truly democratic South Africa.

* * *

The first chapter of the novel, titled "Mandisa's Lament," is in the form of a letter written directly from Mandisa to Biehl's mother, which begins with the sentence "*My son killed your daughter*" (1). Excerpts of this letter are interspersed throughout the rest of the novel in italics. The effect of this second-person confessional mode is jarring, and immediately implicates the reader in the process of constructing what Susan Brison has called "speech acts of memory" that potentially have the performative power of "transforming traumatic memory into narrative memory or...recovering or remaking the self" (72). It is through the power of speech acts of memory that Mandisa hopes that describing her son, his world, and her own grief "might ease the other mother's pain...if a little" (vi). In trying to understand "these monsters our children have become" (2), Mandisa is obliged to explore the history of the country and her family, and marvels at the irony of Mxolisi's situation: "Why now, when he's an outcast, does my son have a better roof over his head than ever before in his life?...living a better life, if chained?" (3).

Subsequent chapters alternate between the week of 25 August 1993, the date of Biehl's murder, and flashbacks to earlier eras and episodes in Mandisa's and Mxolisi's lives. Some of the former scenes attempt to piece together both Mxolisi's and Biehl's movements throughout the day. The two trajectories intersect in the last chapter of the novel when the narrative finally describes Biehl and the carload of friends she was taking to their homes on the Cape Flats crossing paths with Mxolisi and friends just leaving a highly charged political meeting. These chapters commence with headers announcing the place and time of the events described, which is part of Magona's spatio-temporal mapping of this unspeakable event.

But that mapping extends much further than the events of one day, through the flashbacks that depict a series of traumatic events and displacements, some of which are obviously instigated by the oppressive apartheid state. The central trauma of Mandisa's life was the forced removal from the semi-urban village of Blouvlei in the name of "Slum Clearance" (29). Though Blouvlei as she describes it is far from a romantic utopia, she emphasizes the sense of community that was destroyed by the forced removals: She complains, "[W]here before we had been members of solid, well-knit communities, now we were amongst strangers" (29), and notes that "we lived in Blouvlei because we wanted to live there. Those were shacks we had built ourselves, with our own hands...built them where we wanted them, with each put together according to the wishes, whims and means of its owner" (33). For the young Mandisa Blouvlei was "the only place I had ever known...had ever called home" (60). One of the elders in the location emphasizes the close connection between the place and the communal identity of the residents: "The afterbirths of our children are deep in this ground. So are the foreskins of our boys and the bleached bones of our long dead.... Blouvlei was going nowhere" (55). As in Krog's and De Kok's descriptions of South African landscape, Magona draws a tight symbolic connection between land and body, asserting a deep-seated attachment to the soil. The key distinction between Magona's characters and the white writers, of course, is that Mandisa, her family, and the other residents of Blouvlei were uprooted violently from that land decades before, while whites have anxiously retained most of the land even throughout the political transition.

The shack settlement in Blouvlei is remembered even more fondly as a result of the contrast with their new location in Guguletu, which quickly became a worse slum than Blouvlei but one in which community and family ties were severely strained. Through Mandisa's narrative, Magona reveals to us the devastating impact of the Group Areas Act and attendant legislation as seen through the eyes of one poor, working-class woman. On hearing from her employer's suburban Cape Town home that there is trouble in Guguletu, she reflects:

> Trouble is, there is always trouble in Guguletu . . . of one kind or another . . . since the government uprooted us from all over the show: all around Cape Town's locations, suburbs, and other of its environs, and dumped us on the arid, wind-swept, sandy Flats. My first impressions of the place are still vivid in my mind, etched inside my eyelids, fresh today as they were all those many years ago when I was still but a child, not even ten. . . . (26)

Notably, the memory of this painful episode appears to her mind's eye like a picture, an embodiment of a particular intersection of space/place and time. And the picture that emerges of Mandisa's family's arrival in Guguletu in 1968 is one of "pandemonium": "People choking the morning streets. . . . Children roaming the streets aimlessly even in that early hour. And then the forest of houses. A grey, unending mass of squatting structures. Ugly. Impersonal" (27).

The dominant metaphors that recur in Mandisa's descriptions of Guguletu are of hauntings and of cataclysmic natural events: The wind on the Flats howls "like the despairing voices of lost souls. In fact, some said what we heard of nights were the voices of Malay slaves lost in a ship wrecked hereabouts, when the area was still all sea" (30). This gesture toward the early history of colonialism in the Cape implicitly extends Magona's analysis of the traumatic roots of violence centuries before even the events of 1968 that she describes firsthand. And like a ship wrecked in a tempest, the forced removals are compared to violent meteorological phenomena: "As for myself, I came to Guguletu borne by a whirlwind . . . perched on a precarious leaf balking a tornado . . . a violent scattering of black people, a dispersal of the government's making" (48).

But if the metaphors of tempests and tornados imply a blind, impersonal destructiveness, other descriptions of Guguletu make it clear that the devastating social impact of their new homes is an intrinsic and deliberate quality of the very architecture of apartheid townships: "The very houses—an unrelieved monotony of drabness; harsh and uncaring in the manner of allocation, administration and maintenance—could not but kill the soul of those who inhabited them.... the small, inadequate, ugly concrete houses seemed to loosen ties among those who dwelled in them" (34). Magona thus implies that understanding the corrosive effects of the physical structures of apartheid on social and familial bonds among the poor majority, and understanding the trauma inflicted by the removals, are prerequisite to understanding the spiraling violence that led to Biehl's murder. More generally, understanding such things is necessary to understanding the uneasy impasse that poses as reconciliation in the era of the TRC and its aftermath.

The removals themselves are described as the actions of "[a]n army of invasion: a fleet of police" (65); after the homes are destroyed, "[l]ike *imfecane* fleeing Shaka more than a century ago, our parents trekked" (66). Here again Magona/Mandisa suggests that historical traumas in South Africa have much deeper roots than the inception of formal apartheid in 1948, and that the condition of displacement and uprootedness is an old one with many causes. Some of those catalysts, such as the *imfecane*—the great scattering of tribes in the early nineteenth century—are not at all attributable to British or apartheid rule. Mandisa's use of the word "trek," moreover, inevitably evokes the Afrikaner *Voortrekkers* venturing into the untamed interior to escape the constraints of British rule. Magona thus points out that the African majority, too, has "great treks" in its history, and simultaneously appropriates the iconography of the *Voortrekkers* in the service of a new victim-myth.

The result of these centuries of trauma and displacement, according to Mandisa, is a generation of children that have degenerated into savagery, as the "Young Lions" of the resistance movement burn the houses and bodies of suspected *impimpis* or informers: "Our children fast descended into barbarism. With impunity, they broke with old tradition and crossed the boundary between that which separates human beings from beasts. Humaneness, *ubuntu*, took flight. It had been sorely violated. It went and buried itself where none of us would easily find it again" (76). The word *ubuntu* now inevitably evokes the TRC and Tutu's theology of restorative justice, but Mandisa's cynicism here implies that the quality of human compassion underlying this philosophy has been destroyed.

The prevalence of spatial metaphors in the short passage just quoted is also striking: tradition provides a *boundary* of human behavior that the children have crossed; as a result, human compassion has *taken flight* and *buried itself*—the contradictory metaphors suggesting the difficulty one would have excavating this elusive lost quality of *ubuntu*. The spatial tropes also imply that tradition and the identity for which it provides a potential basis is rooted in specific *places*, a fact that makes dispossession under apartheid law an especially bitter pill to swallow and explains the Blouvlei elders' refusal to be removed from the land.[45] The dissolution of family ties is further exacerbated by the system of labor in place for black women, which typically takes them out of their own homes and puts them to work in the homes of white families, thus imposing yet another kind of spatial dislocation.[46]

Another key traumatic event that Mandisa narrates occurs when Mxolisi is a young child just learning to talk. Two of his older friends attend a political rally and, pursued by the police, hide themselves in a wardrobe in Mandisa's house. The family have almost convinced the police that the boys escaped over a back fence when Mxolisi, thinking all of this excitement a game of hide-and-go-seek, shouts out the boys' location. After the boys try to flee and are shot dead by the police, the traumatized Mxolisi "kept silent for nearly two years. And when he did speak again, it was to ask me a question to which I had no answer" (159)—that is, the whereabouts of his father who abandoned them years before. Thus Mxolisi seems to recover from the loss of language only to attempt to find the words to express other kinds of loss in his life.

Years later, in a sort of historic echo, Mandisa's home is again invaded by police, this time searching for her son in connection with Biehl's murder. In the process, they destroy her sons' *hokkie* or backyard shack: "Outside in the backyard, they simply dismantled the boys' *hokkie*. They tore the planks off, breaking each and every one of them. Breaking them so that we would never be able to put them together again" (86). This narrative of irretrievable loss contains certain parallels to the shepherd Lekotse's story of the police permanently breaking the door to his shack when they raided it in search of one of his children, discussed in Krog's *Country of My Skull* (1.3). In this scene from *Mother to Mother* quoted earlier, likewise, the police leave a permanent "scar" or reminder of the violation they have perpetrated on the home. Indeed, Mandisa notes that "[w]e could never go back to who we were before they had come. We could never go back to that time or place. Nothing would ever be the same for us. We had been hurtled headlong into the eye of a raging storm" (87). Yet again, the actions of the apartheid government are depicted as a destructive force of nature. And this description of the life-changing effects of the police invasion could apply with equal accuracy to the visit of the police to Blouvlei for the forced evictions, or to the police search of the Guguletu home; all three are instances of "[i]rredeemable blood. Irretrievable loss" brought about by the agents of apartheid (210).

Other traumatic memories in Mandisa's life are more difficult to ascribe directly to the white minority government's policies. The most important of these is a fluke of biology—her falling pregnant despite practicing only non-penetrative sex with her boyfriend China; in the words of the village elder who inspects her and confirms her virginity, "*Utakelwe!* She has been jumped into!" (112). As a result of this "violation" by the seed that becomes Mxolisi, she is forced to abandon her very promising academic career and marry China. She then finds herself trapped in her in-laws' home, and prohibited by patriarchal strictures from continuing her studies. Her father at first gives his consent for her to attend school, but then retracts it because her future in-laws object and his clan intercedes: "Custom dictated that he listened to the counsel of the clan.... decisions affecting my life were not his to make" (131).

In light of this total regimentation of her own body through the mechanisms of both apartheid and patriarchy, the only form of agency that Mandisa can exercise is through narrative; her letters to Amy's mother, then, can be seen as symbolic reclamations of space and identity. Yet the narrative in some ways seems to swallow itself, structured as it is around a "present absence." Margaret Daymond uses similar terminology to describe the absence of African oral tradition in Magona's story sequence "Women at Work," which "evokes, as a partial absence or a remembered presence, the narrative practices of an oral community that uses tale-telling as a means of purveying its wisdom and rules of conduct" ("Complementary" 333). Yet the clan's decision to override Mandisa's father's permission to return to school demonstrates that the "rules of conduct" of this community can impose oppressive spatial strictures of their own, especially on women. This fact is perhaps connected to the long history of "indirect rule" and Bantustan regimes that used "tribal" authorities to implement colonial and apartheid policy, as well as patriarchal regimentation of domestic space.[47]

In all of the examples quoted earlier, Magona is attempting to map, spatially and temporally, the losses and traumas that accumulate in the historical trajectory leading to her son's murder of the young white woman. The extent of this loss and the depths to which the people still feel it is expressed in several passages in the novel. For example, in the taxi from Gungululu to Cape Town after Mxolisi's birth, the taxi driver points out that they have been driving for more than one hour through one man's farm, and complains that the whites stole the land and the livestock from the Africans (116). The refrain "White people stole our land" (e.g., 173) echoes throughout the book. And when Mandisa's grandfather hears the colonial/apartheid version of the story that Mandisa learns in school of Nongqawuse, the prophetess who called for the Xhosa cattle killing of 1856, he gives her an alternative, corrective version. Whereas Mandisa's teacher claimed that the cattle were killed out of primitive superstition, her Tatumkhulu (grandfather) attributes the act to the amaXhosa's desperation to be rid of the white settlers; he "explained what had seemed stupid decisions, and acts that had seemed indefensible [in school lessons] became not only understandable but highly honourable" (183). To phrase this notion in the language of subaltern studies, Tatumkhulu is providing what has been systematically excluded and effaced from the official narrative—the agency and resistance of subaltern people.[48]

The stories Tatumkhulu tells Mandisa about Nongqawuse and also about Jan van Riebeeck's landing at the Cape can perhaps be read as fragments of an older oral tradition that was ruthlessly excised from the official school curriculum precisely because it offers alternative visions for relating to space and land beyond those imposed by apartheid. Daymond's comments on Magona's two-volume autobiography and her semiautobiographical short stories are relevant here as well: "In drawing on the oral tale-teller's repertoire, Magona's story-telling is not a harking back to ancestral voices but a demonstration that ancient modes and motifs can, in certain circumstances and within certain constraints, be used to represent the modern world" ("Complementary" 346). The recurring figure of Nongqawuse serves just such a function in *Mother to Mother*: in the last chapter, describing the "irrevocable moment" (Magona 209) at which Mxolisi stabs Amy Biehl, the narrative takes a short, abrupt detour:

> Nongqawuse saw it in that long, long-ago dream: A great raging whirlwind would come. It would drive *abelungu* [white people] to the sea. Nongqawuse had but voiced the unconscious collective wish of the nation: rid ourselves of the scourge.
>
> She was not robbed. She was not raped. There was no quarrel. Only the eruption of a slow, simmering, seething rage. Bitterness burst and spilled her tender blood on the green autumn grass of a far-away land. Irredeemable blood. Irretrievable loss. (210)

Here again, the explosions of violence typified by the attack on Biehl are characterized as natural phenomena—whirlwinds and volcanoes. This passage also makes clear that the rage which produces such cataclysmic explosions has been simmering for decades; as Hermann Wittenberg puts it, "Amy Biehl's death is claimed as part of the long history of the Xhosa's resistance to white rule" (320), and thus part of the reclaiming of space and land, the "irretrievable loss" that is at the root of the collective trauma Magona diagnoses.

Reading Wittenberg's review, however, one might think that the novel therefore celebrates Biehl's murder, when in fact Magona depicts it as a senseless act of barbarism, perhaps doomed to the same dark fate as the followers of Nongqawuse. Mandisa does indeed provide a rationale for Mxolisi's violence, just as Tatumkhulu provided a rationale for the cattle killing; but in both cases the rationale is one borne of desperation and social dissolution. Mandisa moreover implicates herself in the disintegration of her own family, as when she describes taking young Mxolisi to a *sangoma* (traditional healer) to cure his speechlessness, and the sangoma tells her, "You must free this your son.... resentment can be worse than hate" (Magona 154). Perhaps this more than anything is what Mandisa is "confessing" to Biehl's mother: she feels responsible for Mxolisi's crime because she had always secretly resented him for "taking her virginity."

But in the end Mandisa recognizes that the real trouble lies far beyond her own rearing of her son, and is perhaps ultimately incomprehensible: "I do not pretend to know why your daughter died... died in the manner in which she did. Died when the time and place and hands were all in perfect congruence; cruel confluence of time, place and agent" (210). Her efforts to track the trajectories that culminate in this congruence are partial and inadequate, as any such mapping must be. But, by emphasizing that the causes of a traumatic political incident are always rooted in earlier traumas and extend far beyond the lives of the individuals involved, Magona deepens the TRC's cultural project of remembrance in valuable and provocative ways.

Conclusion

All the works discussed in part 1 have engaged deeply with the issues of history and memory, truth and justice that have confronted South Africa in the era of the TRC. In the case of the Khulumani Support Group and the theater made by its members, we saw the importance of flexible, tentative modes of telling, lest the sheer repetition of a particular version of a particular narrative result in a sort of psychic numbing to its horror. Thus, I argued, Duma Kumalo remained unsatisfied with having told his story first to the TRC, and then again and again to audiences of *The Story I Am about to Tell*; and so he later collaborated with Yael Farber on *He Left Quietly*, crafting another vehicle for giving theatrical embodiment to his memories of prison. I also pointed out the constantly changing presentation of victim testimony in *Country of My Skull*, arguing that Krog was trying to avoid the anesthetizing effect of being presented with one horrifying tale after another.

By the same token, I believe that the need to perpetually revisit and revise these stories in constantly changing form explains the diverse proliferation of generic forms that I have assembled,[49] all of which deal with similar themes and ideas. Thus Krog and De Kok no doubt attended some of the same hearings, but Krog elects to deal with the experience through a heavily lyrical memoir form, while De Kok chooses elegiac verse as her vehicle. We see even within the corpus of individual authors a curious generic restlessness: in addition to *Country of My Skull*, for example, Krog has revisited the TRC in her Afrikaans poetry, in the play *Waarom is Dié wat Vóór Toyi-Toyi Altyd So Vet?* ("Why Are the Women Who Dance the Toyi-Toyi Always So Fat?"), and in *The Unfolding of Sky*, a documentary that Krog produced in collaboration with Ronelle Loots. And Jane Taylor, who authored the script for *Ubu*, recently published a novel called *Of Wild Dogs*.

The great outpouring of literary and dramatic expression in South Africa in the last decade, in such a plethora of genres, suggests that contemporary artists are hungry for models and forms that can help make sense of the bewildering geographies of the present and the recent past. What is more, if any given mode of telling will always be inadequate to conveying the "Truth about the Past," then a serious understanding of history demands all the more urgently that we hear stories about the past from as many perspectives and through as diverse a range of forms as possible.

It is curious, then, that the eight texts I have chosen to study in parts 2 and 3 are all novels. The reason, I believe, has something to do with the unique capacities of the novel for what I term "narrative mapping." Theater offers the representation of memories or psychological states through the use of symbolic visual space, lighting, and staging. Poetry's intense concentration on language—its sounds, its visual qualities, its play with semantics and symbolism and condensation of meanings—helps the reader more readily understand the impossibility of telling. The memoir form intrinsically raises questions of truth and authenticity. But prose fiction employs unique strategies for mapping the multiple imbrications of personal and social memory, with all its conscious and unconscious associations, and particular places in the urban or rural landscape.

The novels in part 2 describe social and built landscapes in the urban metropolises of Johannesburg, Cape Town, and Durban, which the books navigate for us in particular detail. Though the cities seem all the more perplexing and protean the more carefully they are archived, that is in fact the central quality of the post-apartheid cityscape, which the novel conveys more convincingly than any other form. Likewise in the narratives of rural landscapes in part 3, the complex narrative structures of the postmodern novel—full of misremembered fragments and half-forgotten flashbacks—lend themselves to exploring multiple time frames in the history of particular landscapes. Each novel thus becomes through its own internal structure a metaphorical stand-in for urban palimpsests and the palimpsests of landscapes. In the next two parts, then, I cease this restless cycling through genres, and focus my attention on several examples of the post-TRC novel.

Part 2

Post-Apartheid Urban Spaces

Introduction

For three days in October 1996, the Truth and Reconciliation Commission (TRC) held Human Rights Violation (HRV) hearings in Alexandra, an impoverished township on the northern outskirts of Johannesburg that borders the affluent suburb of Sandton. Many of the witnesses gave testimony about the events of the so-called Six-Day War in April of 1986. This uprising turned the township into a "no-go zone" for police and outsiders for six months afterward; it included consumer boycotts, youth-led anticrime patrols, and people's courts, even in the midst of occupation by the South African Defense Force; eventually the alleged leaders of the rebellion would be charged with treason.

Though the uprising was sparked by the shooting death of a thirteen-year-old boy by a security officer in February of that year, African National Congress (ANC) councilor Obed Bapela in his TRC testimony ascribed it to much larger systemic causes, as diagnosed by the State Security Council's own Joint Management Committee:

> They analysed all the demands of the community of Alexandra such as poor dilapidated housing and sewerage, no untarred streets and at the time only Selbourne Street was tarred. The electrification of the township, only phase 1 and phase 2 were electrified at that time. Poor recreational facilities and an end to the bucket system night soil and a better life for all and an end to overcrowding. At that time there were about 40 people in one yard. (Bapela 3)

Bapela as a community leader had publicly denounced these conditions, and was charged with "treason, subversion and sedition" (3).

Belinda Bozzoli gives a thorough and detailed analysis of the Alexandra revolt in her book *Theatres of Struggle and the End of Apartheid*. In her telling, the Six-Day War was not simply a challenge to the authority of the apartheid government, nor was it merely following the ANC's prescription for making the townships "ungovernable," as many ANC advocates have argued. For Bozzoli, the rebellion challenged the fundamental spatial policies and relationships that both underlay and made possible the apartheid government's mechanisms of control:

> [It] was to some extent the geographical space of the township itself that produced a stratum of people with a revolutionary spirit.... The world of the residents was "turned upside down." Ordinary people in Alexandra Township not only came to visualise an alternative world, a Utopia: for a while they actually brought it into being. Their Utopia was not a particularly beautiful one—the kind of idyllic new world dreamed of by middle-class intellectuals.... Instead it was harsh, even cruel, closer to the Cultural Revolution than the communes of California. (2)

The physical layout of the township, which had been designed to confine its residents and limit resistance, was ironically inverted by the rebel youth[1]: "Private spaces became places to hide, regroup. Public spaces were refigured and reimagined" (Bozzoli 15). Streets, schools, and landmarks were renamed; public spaces were reclaimed and transformed; "people's parks" were created out of waste dumps; the borders of the township no longer served to keep the residents in, but to keep others out; self-appointed youth patrols would keep the peace and enforce their views of "moral behavior." As Bozzoli writes, the young rebels "began to write a new script. They reinvented 'good' and 'bad' spaces" (66).

In short, the Alexandra rebellion illustrates both the possibilities and the perils enabled by the collapse of apartheid in the late 1980s; social spaces were suddenly open to reform and renegotiation, for better and sometimes for worse. The novels I analyze in part 2 both represent and take advantage of the collapse of apartheid's regimentation of urban space. A text such as Aziz Hassim's *The Lotus People*, for example, illuminates the interstices within which resistance was always being fomented, even in the darkest days of National Party rule. Moreover, as Bapela describes it, the people of Alexandra "wanted really to also begin a process of establishing those structures of the street committees, the block committees and the yard committees within their own areas, within their own townships" (12). By implication, the struggle within the township was in large part a struggle for autonomy and control over the social spaces inhabited by its residents. As novels such as Vladislavić's *The Exploded View* and Duiker's *The Quiet Violence of Dreams* make clear, this struggle was not resolved by the first democratic elections in 1994, nor by the TRC hearings a few years later, but in fact continues into the twenty-first century, as people continue to negotiate and reshape the cityscapes around them.

The struggle over urban space is also partly a contest over how the struggle itself will be remembered and represented. Indeed, the Alexandra revolt was relatively short-lived, and before it even ended it was being contested in public memory. As Bozzoli describes it, much of the inversion of spatial regimentation was being carried out by loosely organized youth, with little oversight by the adult ANC or United Democratic Front (UDF) leadership. But Bozzoli raises "the question of how this event was constructed by the ideologues of the transition . . . and how it was more 'officially' remembered in the subsequent ten years" (253) through the media coverage of the Six-Day War, the trials that happened in the late 1980s, and especially the Truth Commission hearings. Those hearings deferred to the adult community leaders, especially those such as Bapela who had ANC connections: their version "precluded the telling of another story—that in which intrepid youths manned the barricades, reconstructed social and cultural relations, and tried to create alternatives to the governance of the township" (Bozzoli 269). By contrast, the stories of ordinary residents of Alexandra who gave their testimony to the Commission "did not cast their memories in terms of larger images of community, nation or social movement, but rather on a more intimate, but no less socially constructed, scale. The body, the soul and the personal space provided the main markers of this universe" (265). In some cases these witnesses called for modest but significant transformations of public space that seem continuous with the young rebels' own wholesale inversion of spatial dynamics during the revolt itself; for instance, M. Mkhuanazi, one of the women who testified at the TRC's hearings in Alexandra, says: "We were so badly injured and we would also be happy if those who died can be honoured by erecting tombstones on their graves" (5).

The kind of seizure and transformation of social space that characterized the Alexandra rebellion is dramatized (albeit in less militant and obvious forms) in many of the novels to which I turn in part 2, in which people reshape the cities around them simply by interacting with cityspace. Many of these texts, furthermore, depict how such contests over the formations of social space, and spatial registrations of collective memory, continue well into the post-apartheid era. The political and psychological obstacles to memorialization that I catalogued in part 1 continue to figure heavily in these texts, but they are further compounded by the rapidly shifting postmodern cityscapes of the twenty-first-century South African metropolis.

In this context, the notion of "urban palimpsests," which often register past spatial configurations only through the marks of erasure and change, will be especially useful.[2] As Carrol Clarkson notes about several recent urban South African novels,

> What is past...is buried, but the past surfaces in ways that disturb complacent assumptions about the supposed stability of the present. The sedimentary patternings of the characters' own cultural identities have found expression some place else, in a different time, so that the *present*, in both a spatial and a temporal sense, is a site of transitory dislocation. ("Visible" 85).[3]

In response to this dislocation, the novels by Dangor, Vladislavić, Mpe, Duiker, and Hassim practice modes of narrative mapping that record not only built environments and physical spaces, but also the movement of city inhabitants through those spaces over time. Such mapping, the texts suggest, is a necessary first step in reconfiguring spatial relationships so that truly autonomous zones of self-determination can be developed. At the same time, it is in these novelistic representations of contemporary urban space that another key challenge to the operation of mourning and remembrance emerges, in the form of Jameson's "weakening of historicity" in the postmodern cultural artifact. It is in South Africa's huge metropolises that "late capitalism" and consumer culture have most deeply penetrated people's consciousness, and their unconscious.

* * *

If we are to understand South African cities as urban palimpsests, imperfectly and ephemerally marked by multiple histories, then one of the most important "scars of history" that we need to consider is apartheid city planning, which was driven by contradictory impulses within segregationist thinking in the mid-twentieth century: on the one hand, the desire from certain sectors for "total segregation" leading to a "whites only" urban paradise, with blacks relegated to distant reservations; and on the other hand, the need for a pool of cheap labor close at hand to serve as miners, factory workers, farmhands, and domestic workers.[4] The result has been a schizophrenic sort of racialized geography, in which largely white, affluent towns and cities are encircled by satellite black townships containing stark poverty.

To achieve this partially deliberate state of affairs, the apartheid state practiced a particularly brutal form of spatial engineering in which black, coloured, and Indian residents of the cities were forcibly removed—most famously from District Six in Cape Town and Sophiatown in Johannesburg, but also from Fordsburg, Pageview, Cato Manor, and many other working-class, inner-city areas—to distant townships. The very street plans of black townships make clear that space was deliberately engineered to effect social control over the black urban population.[5] The effect of forced removals and distant township ghettos, according to Achmat Dangor, was "the slow destruction of Johannesburg as a city of communities" ("Apartheid" 360).

In the 1980s, as political unrest continued to spread throughout urban and rural areas of the country alike, the racialized spatial schemas of apartheid began to break down. Inner-city neighborhoods slowly became "grey areas," places in which landlords rented first to Indian and coloured tenants, then to blacks, while the authorities looked the other way or were unable to contain the phenomenon. In 1986, an estimated 20,000 black people lived in Hillbrow (the densely populated and once trendy suburb bordering Johannesburg's Central Business District) out of a total population of 120,000. The "darkening" of the demographics of inner-city Johannesburg accelerated in the transitional period of the early 1990s: by 1993, 85 percent of residents of inner-city Johannesburg were black, and by 1996 only 5 percent were white (Tomlinson et al. 13). The inner city, and especially Hillbrow, has also became a way station for African immigrants from beyond South Africa's borders: in 1995 an estimated 23,000 Congolese nationals resided in Johannesburg, and in 1999 an estimated 3,000 Nigerians lived in the inner city alone (ibid. 14). These changes have also, unfortunately, been accompanied by sharp rises in crime.

One common response among black South Africans to this influx of African immigrants has been a virulent sort of xenophobia, and many blame the crime epidemic on the immigrants whom they derogatorily refer to as *Makwerekwere*. Meanwhile, the almost universal response of white South Africans to the reclaiming of the inner city by blacks (both local and foreign) has been "white flight" to the northern and far eastern suburbs. The wholesale abandonment of the inner city by capital and white residents has been so profound that Sandton in the distant north suburbs is now the de facto business capital of South Africa, and a large number of national and multinational corporations have established their headquarters in Midrand, along the highway connecting Johannesburg to Pretoria. Middle- and upper-class residents have likewise responded to spiraling crime rates by erecting concrete walls with electric fences or razor wire around their houses. Recent years have seen a concerted effort by government and business interests to reclaim the inner city, with some promising results,[6] but the corporate headquarters that have remained in or returned to the business district have become tightly controlled citadels.[7] Part of this fortification of urban space can be attributed to the fear of crime, but crime is only one force affecting the growth and development of post-apartheid cities, which in many ways resemble the American model of sprawling urban agglomeration.[8]

The juxtaposition between barricaded affluence and devastating poverty and crime—readily apparent, for example, in the proximity of wealthy Sandton to impoverished Alexandra Township, and in the view of the shanty towns surrounding the retired nuclear power plant on the Cape Flats from the opulent campus of the University of Cape Town—is blatant evidence of *uneven development* in South African cities and townships.[9] One corollary of this unfortunate state of affairs (which is by no means exclusive to South Africa) is that people who occupy one scale of development—the world of the middle class, say—experience space and time differently than those, even in the same city, who live at another scale altogether. For instance: a custodian who lives in Soweto and cleans offices in Sandton might spend more time every day on trains, minibus taxis, and walking to work than a businessman who lives in the East Rand might spend flying to Cape Town for a business meeting. The point is that different kinds of "maps" may be needed to register different ways of interacting with the city, and the most useful way to think about urban space is not as fixed or static environments but as a palimpsest through which the reader may decode the multiple lost histories accessible only through marks and phantoms.[10]

The concept of the urban palimpsest or the footprint from the past has suggestive implications for the encoding of memory on the cityscape, especially in contemporary Johannesburg. For example, the mostly black but also coloured and Indian residents of Sophiatown were removed to the Meadowlands and other remote townships southwest of the city. The new whites-only area was officially renamed Triomf ("Triumph"), only to become a mixed-race suburb once again in the 1990s, and then renamed Sophiatown in 2006. Similarly, the designers of Constitution Hill seemed to be conscious of the palimpsestic qualities of the old prison site on the edge of Hillbrow, and worked not only to preserve elements of the site's previous functions but to make those elements explicit and call the viewers' attention to them.

This "reregistering" or making visible of memory is the crux of the challenge facing those who would rewrite the spatial codes of post-apartheid urban space, whether they be architects and city planners or authors of urban fiction. The postmodern phenomena of technological change, hypermobility, planned obsolescence, consumerism, commodification, and time-space compression all act to thwart this inscription of memory onto urban spaces. In this context, the impulse to *archive* and preserve the past must be seen not as contradicting the amnesiac tendencies of late capitalism, but rather as *responding* to them by searching for cultural stability and identity through fixed spatial configurations.[11]

This "amnesiac archiving" impulse is characteristic of global culture in the late twentieth- and early twenty-first centuries in general, but is especially evident in the South African novels I analyze in part 2. For some of the characters, especially Budlender of Vladislavić's *The Exploded View* (2.2) and Silas Ali in Dangor's *Bitter Fruit* (2.1), traditional modes of archiving and documenting are not so much means of preserving the past as of obscuring it in an unmanageable flood of information. Yet archiving, like mapping, takes many forms in these novels, as it does in the real world. The narrator of *Bitter Fruit*, for example, describes one township home as consisting of an "archive of smells" documenting the inhabitants' lives together. By far the most common trope in these books is of *walking* as a form of archiving. Through descriptions of such peripatetic activity, the narrators map the fixed spatial forms of the city—streets, parks, businesses, homes—thus documenting both the reality of those built environments and the subjectivity of the persons moving more-or-less freely through them. What I draw from my study of urban fiction by Duiker, Dangor, Vladislavić, Mpe, and Hassim, then, as well as from recent studies of African urban spaces,[12] is a model of the city in which forces of globalized consumer capitalism play a certainly decisive but not totalizing role in the production, consumption, occupation, and representation of space.[13] The forces of late capitalism, besides falling prey to their own internal contradictions, are perpetually contested by the everyday use and transformation of space by the inhabitants of the city.[14]

One obvious instance of what Alison Brown terms "contested space" is the enormous "grey market" that exists in Johannesburg and other metropolitan areas of the country. We can make sense of this phenomenon by seeing it as the importation of cultural practices and attitudes from the townships and other African cities into the formerly whites-only city and suburbs.[15] Johannesburg drivers encounter beggars and street hawkers aggressively selling newspapers, sunglasses, soft drinks, rubbish bags, condoms, cell phone accessories, and everything else imaginable at almost every red traffic light or "robot." Just as the rebel youth in Alexandra in 1986 inverted apartheid's mechanisms of spatial control, so the traffic light marketplace subverts bourgeois schemas such as zoning, sales tax, and the very notion of a public/private divide.[16]

Many of the characters in post-apartheid urban fiction inhabit the in-between zones in which the spatial regimentation of the state and private property is limited. But other characters explore means of reclaiming and transforming the spaces around them; this can be as simple as, in *Bitter Fruit*, the grass verge near Silas's apartment in inner-city Berea to which he retreats with a six-pack of beer and which "provided some relief from the hot criss-cross of streets" (Dangor 9); or it can be as elaborate as the Cape Flats community established by local Rastafarians in Sello Duiker's *The Quiet Violence of Dreams* (2.4). Most of all, though, the characters in these novels lay claim to the city by walking. In their walking, these nomadic characters not only subject themselves to the disorienting currents of globalization, they also reshape those currents in subtle, not always visible, ways.

This appropriation and transformation of public space has the same psychological effect that the Alexandra rebellion had for many of its participants: "In spite of the Truth Commission's sequestration of memory, the rebellion left a legacy of pride. A sense of assertiveness and power, of ownership of the space had for a brief moment been born, and this was indeed a matter for self-respect for residents" (Bozzoli 277). Just as importantly, in the process of cataloguing their characters' perambulations through the city, the authors develop powerful modes of "mapping" the intricate networks that make up the city. The various tactics of narrative mapping employed in these novels can help make visible the networks of social memory that alternately inscribe traces of the past onto, and erase them from, the physical environment.

2.1 Peace through Amnesia: Achmat Dangor's *Bitter Fruit*

A central conceit in the rhetoric of the TRC is that truth, obtained through an archiving of the memories of victims and the confessions of perpetrators, will lead to reconciliation. Achmat Dangor's *Bitter Fruit*[17] (2001) is a cautionary tale that depicts a very different trajectory for the processes of remembering and confessing, one in which memory is damaged, confession is always hampered and embittered, and reconciliation is undercut by revenge.[18] This arguably failed trajectory is laid out in the respective titles of the three sections of the novel: "Memory"; "Confession"; "Retribution." In this regard, *Bitter Fruit* constitutes an extended critical evaluation of the TRC process through its microcosmic dramatization of the conflicts and confrontations that drove the TRC's work. Furthermore, the novel presents a critique of uneven development in the post-apartheid city. It maps the conflicts arising from the past onto the spaces of Johannesburg, in ways that emphasize the continuing perpetuation of the ills of apartheid, segregation, and patriarchy through the structuring of space and the containment of mobility. The novel furthermore points to numerous forms of archiving, traditional and otherwise, but warns that such archives can become not a link to a stable past but rather a disorienting labyrinth—amounting to another form of confinement. The challenge that the novel poses is how to preserve and give voice to the past without being trapped in it or possessed by it.

The novel tells the story of Silas Ali, an attorney working for the minister of justice in Mandela's administration as liaison to the TRC; his wife Lydia, a part-time nurse; and his son Michael, a first-year student at Wits University. The story begins with Silas encountering François du Boise, a retired police lieutenant, who, nineteen years earlier, had raped Lydia while Silas raged helplessly inside a police vehicle nearby. The chance encounter two decades later sets off multiple chains of events: it evokes agonizing memories that Silas and Lydia had struggled for years to suppress; it compels Du Boise to apply to the TRC for amnesty for assaulting Lydia and others; and it leads Michael to discover that he is a "child of rape" (114) and sets him on a quest throughout the city as if to reestablish his ties to the past. Ultimately, this chain of events prompts Lydia to leave her husband, and leads Michael to assassinate Du Boise outside the very shopping mall where Silas first encountered him.

Like *Mother to Mother* (see section 1.5), *Bitter Fruit* plays out the aftermath of apartheid violence in a fictional vehicle; it thematizes the paradoxes of traumatic memory and of telling impossible stories about being robbed of language and self. Silas remembers that Lydia "had never been the same since the night she was raped. Somewhere inside of her that *other* Lydia was hiding, shielding herself from the memory of being raped and from his response to it" (57). He knows that even before he encountered Du Boise, "Lydia really wanted to explore some hidden pain, perhaps not of her rape, but to journey through the darkness of the silent years that had ensued between them" (59). Nevertheless, she rejects the TRC's mode of public confessional, concluding that "[n]othing in her life would have changed... because of a public confession of pain suffered" (140–41).

Lydia's method of coping with the trauma collapses, however, when Silas tells her about his encounter with Du Boise: she gets drunk, breaks down, and deliberately cuts her feet badly on broken glass. Silas tries to convince himself that her "wounds were not self-inflicted, not provoked by his obsession with remembering the past" (21). But the narrator tells us that "this physical pain was Lydia's way of displacing a much deeper, unfathomable agony" (22–23). The novel itself performs this same act of displacement in the larger symbolic register, by exploring how a single event continues to have ramifications in the present for a large group of characters at various removes from the original encounter between Du Boise, Lydia, and Silas.

The only outlet Lydia seems to have for her pain and trauma is the diary that she started shortly after the rape. It is in this diary that Michael first learns that he is a "child of rape." She describes her decision to keep the baby, which she made only when Silas responded to the news of her pregnancy with fear and silence: "At that moment, in Smith Street, Noordgesig,

I crossed over into a zone of silence" (117). Thus her memory of this painful repression of memory is inscribed (at least in her own mind) onto a particular locale in the urban landscape through the archive of the personal diary. Her last diary entry dates from 16 May 1994, shortly after the first democratic elections. After the Du Boise encounter, though, she takes up the diary again, and "Now it is a true journal, a record of daily events" (149). History has apparently restarted, and the anesthetized amnesia of the Mandela era is giving way to the conflicts of the twenty-first century.

As for Silas, his response to the rape might be characterized as a retreat from memory into the archive. Depending on one's perspective on the TRC, this makes him either an ironic or an appropriate choice to help oversee the commission's work. Michael notes the irony to himself: "My father the stoic, can't tell you a thing when you look him in the eyes. And yet, there he is, dealing with the country's problems, trying to reconcile the irreconcilable" (30). And Lydia notes caustically that Silas's forgetfulness was not "an unconscious, pain-induced suppression of things too agonizing to remember, but a deliberate strategy, something thought out behind a desk.... That's why he was so good at his job, helping the country to forget and therefore to forgive, a convenient kind of amnesia" (110).

It should be noted that this uncharitable assessment of Silas's behavior is narrated through Lydia's embittered, depressed consciousness; Silas's fainting attack in Lydia's hospital room when he is forced to remember a painful aspect of the rape suggests that his amnesia may indeed be a "pain-induced suppression." Nevertheless, her observation contains real insight into Silas's compulsive archiving of his and the country's past as a strategy for forgetting. Prying through Silas's study one day, Lydia thinks: "This was her husband's world, filled with recorded knowledge, a desperate orderliness of catalogued books and research papers. A history of the world, a *containment* of history, of civilisations won and lost through the rule of law" (140). This phrase perfectly encapsulates Silas's ulterior but probably unconscious motives for archiving the past: not to keep it alive, but to keep it contained.

Michael knows his father well enough to realize that his obsessive documenting of the past is a way of avoiding coming to terms with it: "Does Silas grapple with his memories when he's alone? No, he blunts their impact by declaiming them loudly, and usually when he is drunk" (117–18). Silas's own thoughts seem to confirm this, when he recognizes that to accompany Lydia on her journey through the past "would require an immersion in words he was not familiar with, words that did not seek to blur memory, to lessen the pain, but to sharpen all of these things. He was trained to find consensus, even if it meant not acknowledging the 'truth' in all its unflattering nakedness" (59). Such a journey away from consensual truth is especially daunting to him in light of the expectation of objectivity in his role in the government and with the TRC.

Indeed, insofar as Silas's own strategies for avoiding the past through archiving parallel the methodologies of the TRC, the novel can be read as a critique of those methods and the "consensual truth" they produce. Dangor notes in one interview that if *Bitter Fruit* has "any ideological starting point at all, it is probably my feeling that in wanting to forgive and forget so quickly, we swept a lot of things under the carpet—we didn't deal with a lot of issues and they've festered there" (Young, "Interview" 57). Elsewhere he echoes these remarks: "Everyone was in such haste to forget the past and to forgive.... It might just come back to haunt us" (De Beer).

The metaphor of haunting is an important one, and recurs throughout *Bitter Fruit*. Insofar as it shows us that the past will come back to torment us if it is not dealt with adequately, the novel in fact seems to criticize the "forgive-and-forget" rhetoric of the TRC era. The critique is offered through irony, for example, in its depiction of Silas's brother-in-law and childhood friend Alec, who comments that "a happy nation has no memory. That's the problem with this country, we want to forgive but we don't want to forget. You can't have it both ways" (79). Yet much of the TRC's rhetoric resorted to metaphors such as "closing the book on the past" to describe its ultimate aims; the implication is that the nation must remember and record the past before it can forget it, but also *in order to* forget it. Derrida notes that with the death drive, Freud introduces, "*a priori*, forgetfulness and the archiviolithic into the heart of the monument.... [The death drive] even threatens every principality, every archontic primacy, every archival desire. It is what we will call, later on, *le mal d'archive*, 'archive fever'" (12). Silas himself notes the ephemerality of public monuments: looking down on Pretoria from his office, he observes "the usual array of triumphalist squares and shat-upon statues spawned by all pretentious political minds.... God, hope that fate never befalls Mandela. Bronze likenesses burning in the African sun, stench of bird droppings, pigeon shit the worst" (91).[19]

Yet, if Silas sees the futility of these attempts to enshrine political memory in public consciousness, he is only partly conscious of the ways in which his own archival compulsions enact a similar process of forgetting-through-inscription. His methods of archiving attempt to fix, contain, and foreclose memory, rather than opening it up. Verne Harris argues that the "archival endeavour as a whole, should be about the releasing of meanings, the tending of mystery and the disclosing of the archive's openness" ("Shaft" 71). For Silas, the archive serves no such purpose. The fact that his archival compulsion includes collecting keys that could potentially open unknown or long-forgotten locks (Dangor, *Bitter Fruit* 31) suggests that the possibility for "disclosing the archive's openness" does indeed exist, but Silas prefers to keep the past locked down and compartmentalized. This practice allows him to retain a fantasy of the past, "increasingly summoning up happier times, epochs of greater clarity, times without this ambiguity he sees everywhere. In his home, in his office, in the country . . . there is a growing area of grey, shadowy morality" (148). This romanticized notion of the past serves as a kind of oasis for Silas, not unlike the grass verge near his house in Berea to which he likes to retreat with a six-pack of beer: the verge, as the narrator tells us, forms a "border between the past and the future" (133). Ideally, Lydia thinks, the climate in the Ali household upon her release from the hospital would be a "forgiving truce. Peace through amnesia" (138).

That the youth of a coloured man under apartheid could be described as "happier times" speaks to the power of Silas's selective forgetting. And his archival practices are akin to his habit of "blunting" memory by speaking it aloud. Contemplating confronting Alec with his suspicion that his brother-in-law was involved in his own arrest and Lydia's rape, Silas remembers that "[s]peaking the unspeakable out loud had saved his sanity in the past, confused his interrogators, and, above all, allowed him to retain his sense of *space* (solitary confinement disoriented you, made you think you were among friends . . .)" (93; emphasis added). This need for a sense of space and place is especially compelling in light of both the rapid pace of change in the city of his youth, and the distortions and fickleness of memory; visiting his childhood neighborhood in Newclare, he marvels at "[h]ow time seduces the memory, makes the past seem grander than it could ever have been. This was where he had grown up, where he had been shaped, where his world-view had been formed. How miserable it seemed now" (195). If Silas is experiencing something that anyone who has visited a childhood home after years away can relate to, the experience is nevertheless all the more intense for the many changes Newclare has been through: first a mixed-race suburb, then an all-white area, and finally now a majority-African neighborhood that is still in rapid transition.

If Silas craves the stability of a fixed past and an identification with a particular place, for other characters in the novel—especially the female characters—the inscriptions of the past on the places around them become a trap from which they are desperate to escape. In one passage, for example, Lydia's sister Gracie lies sleepless in bed, cursing her stuffy township house that preserves the smells of her and Alec's lives together there: "The history of their sojourn here, preserved within these walls. An archive you browsed with your nose" (75). Gracie's thoughts point to a different kind of archiving from the physical paper trail that Silas favors, an archiving that is unconscious and not always voluntary or welcome—again, it presents as a sort of haunting that cannot be contained so easily among Silas's library of books and papers.

As Gracie's complaints about her township house make clear, these traces or fragments of sensory memory are often inscribed on the home. And whereas Silas finds a numbing sort of comfort from his documents and collections, the women characters in the novel find the constant, involuntary reminders of the past to be oppressive. The description of Silas's house in Berea, seen through the eyes of his friend and comrade Kate, emphasizes its palimpsestic qualities: The house was "a survivor of Berea's grander days. . . . High ceilings made of pressed steel that a succession of less ostentatious, or simply much poorer, inhabitants had painted over in plain white until elaborate floral patterns faded, becoming gloomy reminders of lives left behind" (70).

Such is the evocative power of these inscribed memory-traces that they arouse in Kate "a swirl of recollections about her own childhood and the house she had grown up in" (71). Yet the physical space itself shapes the relationships between its inhabitants, as it did in the first house Silas and Lydia lived in after their marriage: "the newly-weds' household was hot and quiet, its smallness making it impossible for them to escape each other physically. They had to create interior spaces of their own, private rooms of the mind in which to hide their emotions" (97). What is more, Dangor's characterization of Silas and Lydia's alienation from each other as creating "interior spaces" and "private rooms of the mind" emphasizes the Foucauldian ways in which people internalize and reproduce the strictures of material space and built environments in their behaviors, expectations, and unquestioned assumptions.

Lydia's confinement in the home is more than metaphorical, as Silas owns the only car in the family. After they have an argument, he drives off quietly: "He is the only one able to escape in this way. Lydia takes buses, or walks down to Louis Botha Avenue to catch a kombi-taxi when she needs to go and see Mam Agnes and Jackson [her parents] in Soweto" (146). Her reliance on walking and public transportation contrasts to the lifestyle of Silas, who works in Pretoria and spends much of his day in the car. One day in traffic, he thinks about how things had changed from even ten years ago, when he would have been practically the only dark face driving a private car: "Now the lanes were clogged with people like him, black and white, travelling in contradictory directions, just like a normal city anywhere in the world" (88). In contrast with Silas's world of middle-class hypermobility, as Michael notes, the taxis and taxi ranks are part of a "forgotten world, one that he suspects Silas rarely sees these days" (164), but one inhabited by the great majority of the Johannesburg area's carless residents.

Despite Silas's observation about the number of black faces now driving private cars, the divisions of late capitalism still fall along mostly racial lines in South Africa. As Lydia's and Gracie's responses to the confinement of domestic space make clear, the production of urban space also has a gendered dimension, and the fact that Lydia relies on Silas for transportation points to a kind of uneven development even within the scale of the family. Significantly, her relationship to Silas and their home changes when she buys her own car, thus becoming, as Silas notes, "free to do things independently. Strange how a mechanical object like a car could hasten the estrangement between people. She no longer needed him" (228). In the end, when Lydia finally leaves him, he reflects that the "car had become the real instrument of her freedom. Gave her the ability to cover great distances without his help" (242). And indeed, the last time we see Lydia she is driving across the karoo, fleeing the confinement of gendered spaces that are inscribed with memories of her rape, freed at last from the "Burden of the mother" (251). Before she leaves, however, Lydia takes the opportunity of Silas's birthday party to symbolically break free of him, of his history, and especially of his archives. She gives him the diary of his father, Ali Ali, which his mother had given to her, and which presumably tells the story of Ali's flight from the British authorities in India, his travels around the world, and his arrival in South Africa. She contrives to hand "Silas his heritage... then walk away, free of him and his burdensome past" (225); with this gesture, she frees herself from the prison of Silas's archives.

My analysis so far has focused on how Silas and Lydia cope respectively with memories of the past, and on how their different experiences of time-space and of posttraumatic stress affect the registering or expression of those memories. But perhaps the most interesting character is their son Michael, who did not live through that past and yet is a product of it. As Ronit Frenkel puts it, "Lydia, Silas, and Mikey each represent a different course of action for dealing with the past.... For both Lydia and Mikey, the past must be dealt with outside of the TRC" (163). But whereas Lydia has been haunted by the past since her rape, Mikey fails to register the impact of that past on his own life until he learns the bitter secret of his own parentage. As a child, Kate notes that Michael, unlike most children raised in the township, did not fear dogs: he was "[t]horoughly freed of his past" (139). Then one night his father comes home whispering the name Du Boise, and his mother breaks down and hospitalizes herself. Bracing himself to read Lydia's diary, he contemplates the name Du Boise:

> A ghost from the past, a mythical phantom embedded in the "historical memory" of those who were active in the struggle. Historical memory.... It

> explains everything, the violence periodically sweeping the country, the crime rate, even the strange "upsurge" of brutality against women. It is as if history has a remembering process of its own, one that gives life to its imaginary monsters. Now his mother and father have received a visitation from that dark past, some terrible memory brought to life. (32)

After reading the diary and learning that he is a "child of rape," Michael's rootedness in the past, which he had always taken for granted to the extent of disavowing it, is thrown into crisis: "He can no longer think of the future without confronting his past" (119), and that past is suddenly shrouded in mystery but begins to churn up stories and images beyond his control. He ponders his paternity, at first assuming that Du Boise was white, then realizing that it could have been a "traitorous black man" (118). Michael finds the very core of his identity, the paternity assumed in the surname "Ali," to be shrouded in doubt. This is one of many examples we will see of murky ancestries, a theme that emerges with special clarity in Mda's *Heart of Redness* (3.3) and Wicomb's *David's Story* (3.2), and one that is also prominent in Dangor's earlier collection of stories *Kafka's Curse.* Indeed, the contested or gap-ridden nature of genealogies in post-apartheid literature seems to reflect in microcosm the new nation's own fraught relationship to its past.

Michael has always scorned his father's philosophy of "peace through amnesia," and by extension the Truth Commission's methods, which he sees as rooted in the Christian doctrine of confession and forgiveness: The Church teaches you to confess your sin, "but confess it only once. There true salvation is to be found. In saying the unsayable, and then holding your peace for ever after" (115). And he has similarly scorned his father's compulsive attempts to document the past through its tangible traces. But after learning the dark secret of his conception, Michael decides in the grip of a peripatetic restlessness to retrace his family's "township sojourns. It is an impulse, sentimental, bizarre. It is the kind of thing Silas would do.... Michael hates dwelling on the past, looking back is such a fruitless exercise.... Yet he feels it is something he must do, perhaps to get away from the claustrophobic fervour of the 'new South Africa' " (163).

Thus *Bitter Fruit* offers the first instance of what will emerge as a crucial motif throughout the novels to follow in part 2, in which the characters walk compulsively through the city streets. "Mikey walks, endlessly, strides away, long, loping steps" (147); he "walks through the deserted streets, seemingly unafraid of their dangers, or he is oblivious to them" (175); he walks through the inner city, through Newclare, through Noordgesig; he walks through the north suburbs, and in one surreal scene encounters

Nelson Mandela in a limousine outside his mansion in Houghton. One night at home after one of these ramblings, Michael

> contemplates the purpose of this quest. He is like a tourist doing the apartheid heritage route. What is the point of going from one ramshackle point of reference to the next? Perhaps it is true: our memories are chained to poverty, we cannot live without our apartheid roots.... He dismisses this thought. Must every pursuit have a utilitarian purpose? Is it not enough to want to discover your roots simply for the sake of it? Yes, he can write his history and the history of a whole country, simply by tracing his family's nomadic movements from one ruined neighbourhood to the next, searching through photographs, deeds of sale, engineering reports. (167)

Yet if Michael begins to adopt his father's habits of archiving, there is a key difference in his methods, in that they are less prone to freezing the past into static, inert data that can be neatly filed away. Rather, Michael sees the city as containing multiplicitous, shifting, phantasmal networks through which social relationships and thus social memory are formed. Marveling at how smoothly the taxi ranks operate without any central control system, for example, Michael thinks: "It is as if unseen hands direct everything, some intelligence out there" (164). His observation offers an astute insight into the "flexible, mobile, and provisional intersections of residents" that Simone labels "people as infrastructure" ("People" 407). For a rather macabre example, after obtaining the handgun that he will later use to kill Du Boise, Michael "ponders the exotic journeys that guns make. Where does this one come from, Palestine, Kosovo, Kashmir, another home in Johannesburg's northern suburbs?" (Dangor, *Bitter Fruit* 216). Michael obtained the gun through a network of Islamic radicals, one of the many vectors that feed into the globalizing metropolis of Johannesburg, and it is through this same network that he disappears after the murder.

The example of the gun's journey into Michael's hands reveals the dark underbelly of the global networks of which Michael becomes aware. Arguably, his mode of archiving the city does open the ruins of the past up to the future and renders the loss they represent "oddly fecund, paradoxically productive" (Butler 468). Yet what Michael has lost are his roots, his connection to any community except the mosque in Newclare where his grandfather—or, at any rate, Silas's father—formerly presided as spiritual leader (and those connections he forged for himself). Moreover, the future that his excavations of the past open up is a bleak one. The trajectory traced by the section titles, beginning with memory and confession, does not culminate in peace and reconciliation but in retribution—against Du Boise, but also against "an entire system of injustice" that his actions represent (176). Moulana Ismail confirms for Michael that "[t]here are certain things people do not forget, or forgive. Rape is one of them" (182). If the ruins of the past are "creative" or "fecund," they yield a bitter fruit indeed in Dangor's novel.

Indeed, Michael's past leads him to nihilism, as symbolized by his changes of name. Early in the novel he had insisted that his friends and family call him "Michael" rather than "Mikey," which Vinu declares passionately is a "brave" move: "A child's given name is an instrument of self-identity, of freedom" (185). In the end, though, he goes into hiding, and thinks: "He, too, is going to a death of sorts. Michael is to die, Noor will be incarnated in his place. / May Michael's truth live on after him" (247). Having discovered that the identity assumed in a name is a fragile sort of mirage, Michael becomes free to "kill" personas and invent new ones, partly by forging the identity documents that help create the illusion of officialdom and permanence associated with a person's name and identity. Thus, again, where Silas sees the archive as bestowing fixity on the past it purports to document, Michael sees archives and documentation as tools that can be infinitely manipulated to suit his changing needs and circumstances.

There are hints that ultimately even Silas comes to accept Michael's more cynical (but arguably more effective) view of the archives. Silas gives up his dreams of reconciling the conflicts of his country's past and of his own through the compilation of records and artifacts: "Perhaps it was time to go, to leave this place, this house, this country and its contorted history?" (200). Yet Dangor, perhaps thinking of the trilogy he plans to write about Michael's story, describes the novel as ending "on a strangely optimistic note, the themes of rape, incest and murder notwithstanding" ("Being Short-Listed"). Perhaps the basis for this optimism lies in what one reviewer describes as Michael's "insistence on 'nowness,' a determination to keep his own identity open to change" (Gbadamosi). This psychological flexibility is increasingly needed to live in the rapidly changing social landscape of urban post-apartheid South Africa, as we shall see in all the novels in this second part of my survey. But Dangor's novel serves us with a sobering warning about the opposite extreme: new, more open-ended maps or cognitive archives of South Africa could just as easily lead to a path of vigilantism and violent retribution as to a democratic rainbow nation.

2.2 The City Dissected: Ivan Vladislavić's *The Exploded View*

As I have been suggesting, the postmodern African city, with its multiplicity of social and commodity flows interacting in complex ways with the built environment, resists representation either of its own spaces or of the memories encoded in those very spaces. The challenge for the new urban literature in South Africa, then, is to pioneer modes of representation that can either circumvent these resistances, or at least make them visible. In his third novel, *The Exploded View* (2004), Ivan Vladislavić does so through the metaphor embedded in the title itself.[20] An exploded view, as the character Gordon Duffy explains, is an illustration of a building project in which each piece of wood, nail, screw, et cetera is detached and floating as if in mid-air to demonstrate where the builder should place each piece. Duffy used to pore over the exploded views of projects in his father's DIY magazines, and in one scene "[h]e closed his eyes and began to detach the components of the house one by one as if easing apart a delicate puzzle.... The universe was expanding, we were causing it to expand, by analyzing it" (189–90).

The interconnections between memory, representation, and public space remain curiously undernoted in existing criticism of Vladislavić's work, despite the author's long-standing interest in architecture and urban space—revealed, for instance, in his coediting the volume *blank___: Architecture, Apartheid and After* with Hilton Judin. Christopher Warnes suggests that in "Propaganda by Monuments," which focuses "on the apparent terminations of the narratives of communism and apartheid, the reminder is that closure itself may be provisional and artificial" ("Making" 80). Though quite true, this reading seems to posit closure as a primarily *temporal* characteristic of narrative. Mike Marais, conversely, does use spatial metaphors in his discussion of closure in *The Restless Supermarket*, but in a way that never fully transcends the metaphorical ("Visions").[21] His reading of closure centers primarily on questions of language and discourse—as do the arguments of many other critics.[22] Similarly, Stefan Helgesson argues, "Rather than document change in a realistic mode, Vladislavić thematises language itself as the very material of understanding and being" ("Minor Disorders" 777). Echoing this idea, Vladislavić himself compares the process of writing to the building of mechanical objects: "[O]ften when I talk about writing, the language I use is appropriate to building or engineering, the construction of the text, as if it was an object. The text feels like a construct" (in Miller 117).

All the aforementioned critics offer compelling interpretations of Vladislavić's works; yet, with the exception of Helgesson, all fail to note Vladislavić's depictions of the processes whereby language and discourse shape and are in turn shaped by the physical and social spaces of the city. The novelist tells Warnes,

> As people write about the making and re-making of South African cities, the question of what's changed and what hasn't becomes urgent. What

> the project [of editing the anthology *Blank*___] confirmed for me is that the actual physical structures of apartheid are going to be difficult, if not impossible, to erase, and that we're going to be living within those structures for a very long time. (Warnes, "Interview" 278–79)

In this same interview, Vladislavić demurs at the idea that he has a particular political project in view as he writes; Felicity Wood warns, moreover, that through their use of the ludic and the carnivalesque, his works elude "our attempts to bring any single, definitive critical response to bear on them" (22). Nevertheless, a recurring theme in all of Vladislavić's writing is that the disorientation and historical amnesia that characterize post-apartheid life and culture result at least in part from the contestation on several fronts of spatial configurations that reinforce older social formations.

One of these contesting forces is the tendency of computer-age technology to make invisible the material processes and infrastructure that undergirds daily urban life. Duffy, pondering his "surgical ability to see how things fitted together," goes on to wonder how useful that ability has become in a world dominated by microcircuitry: "this skill seemed to him increasingly outmoded in the world he lived in. It was no longer clear even to the most insightful observer how things were made or how they worked. The simplest devices were full of components no one could see, processes no one could fathom" (190). Nevertheless, Vladislavić takes up the metaphor of the exploded view as a representational strategy through which he exposes the multifaceted social and physical infrastructures of contemporary Johannesburg. This strategy extends to the very narrative structure of the text itself, which is not a unified novel in the traditional sense so much as four vignettes featuring four sets of characters whose paths interconnect in subtle ways. The four protagonists' careers are diverse and seemingly unconnected: Budlender in "Villa Toscana" is a statistician for the census; Egan in "Afritude Sauce" is a sanitary engineer; Simeon Majara in "Curiouser" is an artist famous for his representations of genocide in Rwanda and elsewhere; and in "Crocodile Lodge," Gordon Duffy's company erects signs and billboards, specializing in signs announcing the future use of construction sites. Yet each character's perspective allows us to see different facets of the complex cultural and material processes that make everyday life in the city possible.

* * *

Budlender likes to make lists and catalogs; he also has a "passion for statistics" (5), which he uses as a means of archiving the changes happening all around him. The extent of his faith in technologies of archiving is revealed in his notion that the most trivial facts must be "lodged somewhere in the circuitry of his memory" (22), though he is frustrated at his inability to recall those facts at will. Budlender also has a keen awareness of the effect of architecture and other built spaces, as we see when he approaches a new housing development, Villa Toscana, on the northern outskirts of the city to interview a woman about her census form:

> The boundaries of Johannesburg are drifting away, sliding over pristine ridges and valleys, lodging in tenuous places, slipping again. At its edges, where the city fades momentarily into the veld, unimaginable new atmospheres evolve. A strange sensation had come over [Budlender] when he first drew up at the gates of Villa Toscana, a dreamlike blend of familiarity and displacement.... [H]e was like a man in a film who has lost his memory and returns by chance to a well-loved place. (6)

If the changes that have taken place in the city center reflect the grimy underside of uneven capitalist development, the new developments and "edge cities" that have sprung up in the far-flung outskirts of the city reflect in turn the glittering aspirational lures of postmodern/global consumer culture; as Helgesson notes, the "destabilization of boundaries is a prerequisite for the identification of this metropolis with an African modernity" ("Johannesburg" 29). The aforementioned passage in particular makes clear the disorienting amnesiac effect of edge-city architecture, which creates the uncanny effect of *déja vu* through its simulations of older forms of European buildings.

The faux Tuscan architecture of Villa Toscana exemplifies what Achille Mbembe calls "an architecture of *hysteria*": its evocations of an imagined European past are like the "reminiscences" of hysterics, "repressed memories that fail to be integrated into the psyche" ("Aesthetics" 402).[23] For Budlender the new faux European subdivisions pose a bewildering experience, one that he finds strangely intoxicating. Returning from one of his many visits to Iris du Plooy, the woman at Villa Toscana with whom he grows increasingly obsessed, Budlender gets lost: "At first, he was irritated. Not just with himself for his carelessness, but with the whole ridiculous lifestyle that surrounded him, with its repetitions, its mass-produced effects, its formulaic individuality. But then this very shallowness began to exert a pacifying effect on him" (30–31). The postmodern spaces of the edge city seem to resist the ordering compulsion that Budlender craves; as Titlestad and Kissack note about *The Exploded View*, "Cartographic plans...are constituted in the gaze of the planner, and link more directly to a desire for an ordered and predictable future than to the actual rivalries, expectations, conflicts, histories and vested interests that comprise the ways in which individuals inhabit cities" ("Secular" 14). Like Egan in a later scene in the book, Budlender finds that there is "no elevated position from which he can control the shifts and disruptions of metropolitan life" (Helgesson, "Johannesburg" 34).

If Budlender finds his lived experience of the city disorienting because of his inability to gain the ordered perspective of the cartographic overview, he encounters a similarly hypnotic disorientation from watching television, which he rarely does until he meets Du Plooy, a continuity announcer for SABC1. The music videos in particular, with their dizzying strobe of jump cuts and close-ups, cause him to despair for his culture: "Why did everything have to happen so quickly? So incompletely? It was nothing but bits and pieces of things" (24). He complains about the images flashing across his television, an "endless jumble of body parts amid ruins, a gyrating hip, an enigmatic navel... sign language from a secret alphabet, fragments of city streets, images flaring and fading, dissolving, detaching, floating in airtime, dwindling away into nothing" (24).

Given Budlender's ambivalent relationship to the newly emergent consumer culture, it is interesting that he develops an infatuation with Du Plooy, whose job seems the very embodiment of postmodern surface and simulation. Watching her on television, Budlender notices the "odd interiors" in which she and her fellow announcers were filmed: "generically decorative spaces with crimped and puckered surfaces, draped and folded satin sheens... in which they moved stiffly like overdressed mannequins, animated goods" (23). Budlender recognizes that within this space of pure artifice, identity is a fluid, malleable thing, and wonders whether Du Plooy had been honest on her census questionnaire about whether there was a man in her life: "She might have made up a new persona for herself. She could be anyone she chose" (40). Though Budlender does not make the connection, the notion that people might use the census form as a means of inventing their identity has destabilizing implications for his project of archiving and documenting the world through ordered facts and statistics.

As if acknowledging this shortcoming in the kinds of archiving practiced by Budlender, in the vignette entitled "Afritude Sauce" Vladislavić turns to the perspective of Egan the sanitary engineer. He recognizes ruefully that "[s]ooner or later, everyone figured it out: you were in the shit business" (55). Though it provides fodder for his self-deprecating sense of humor, waste management is of course absolutely integral to the functioning of the modern city, and Egan's perspective gives the reader a glimpse into the mostly invisible material infrastructure and processes that undergird the city's visible facades. Because he is involved in new housing developments from the earliest stages, he sees such developments as the product of layers of "permanence"—pipes and cables underneath the surface, houses that rest "lightly on their bases," electrical poles, paving and brick, et cetera. "Permanance grew like a crust. Each layer added depth" (58). Furthermore, in a metaphor rich in possibility for my ongoing discussion of the relationship between bodies and social spaces, Egan compares the infrastructure of the city to the human body undergoing surgery: "Workers clustered around a manhole, surrounded by striped barriers under a makeshift awning of green canvas, would remind him of nothing so much as surgeons in the operating theatre" (58).

In the novel's present, Egan is employed on a project for the government, building permanent houses for shack dwellers, and he is proud of the contribution he is making to the country's transformation. Or at least, he wants to be proud of it, but he is forced to recognize the faults in that contribution by the complaints of the new residents who have already moved into the barely completed homes. Many of the problems have nothing to do with Egan's job, but he is required to listen to these complaints by his employer in the name of "doing your bit for reconciliation" (62). One woman, Mrs. Ntlaka, complains that the doorways are too narrow, there is no ceiling separating the room from the roof, one wall is cracked, the toilet is positioned too high for her feet to reach the floor when seated on it, and everything is too small and generally "fucked," the word she repeats with emphasis. Egan privately dismisses Mrs. Ntlaka's complaints as the rantings of a "drama queen" (71), but those complaints nevertheless effectively draw the reader's attention to the shortcomings of the post-apartheid government's efforts to transform systemic spatial inequities. Egan's lack of empathy for the plight of the people who must live in the houses he helps build is symptomatic of a mind-set that regards the country's housing shortage as an abstract policy problem to be addressed by bureaucratic social engineering, with scarcely more regard for the needs of residents than was shown by the apartheid policies that created the housing crisis in the first place.

Furthermore, though Egan's view of the city as comprised of "layers of permanence" provides a valuable insight into the material processes that constitute and produce those urban layers, it proves little help to him in navigating the new *social* geographies of post-apartheid South Africa. This is driven home when he is invited to a business dinner at Bra Zama's African Eatery attended by five town officials and members of the Residents' Association. At first the conversation is conducted mostly in English, and "Egan began to feel like one of the boys" (85), part of this complex new network of power. But then:

> Slowly, peristaltically, Egan felt himself moving to the edge of the conversation. They were talking mainly in Sotho now, switching back into English

> occasionally to include him.... [H]e began to suspect that *nothing* important was being discussed with him. That the real purpose of their exchange, in which he appeared to be an equal partner, was in the sidelong chatter, the small talk he didn't understand. It was possible, wasn't it? That everything that mattered lay between the lines? (86–87)

Egan tellingly uses spatial metaphors to describe his alienation—"the edge of the conversation," "between the lines." Meanwhile the adverb "peristaltically" implies a bodily metaphor, with the body here standing in not for the city more generally but specifically for the networks of power that govern the production of space, at least on the small scale of this peri-urban town.

Several bottles of wine later, when one of his hosts spoons some of the restaurant's trademark "Afritude Sauce" over Egan's steak without asking, Egan wonders, "What did it mean? Was it a sign of sharing, of hospitality?... Or was he being ridiculed? Why did he even think this was a possibility? He could no longer tell the difference between kindness and cruelty" (90). His inability to decode the simplest of cultural signifiers points to another source of disorientation for many white South Africans, beyond the socioeconomic forces underlying postmodern time-space compression. Egan struggles with only partial success to find his way in a new social landscape in which the backroom deals that shape the physical landscape are conducted in languages he does not understand.

Simeon Majara, the protagonist of "Curiouser," faces a similar identity crisis and disorientation in the face of the complex social geographies of the post-apartheid era. A successful black artist, Majara struggles not with the linguistic multiplicity of the country, but rather with his own position of privilege in the midst of a continent full of poverty. He established his reputation with a series of works on the theme of genocide—first the Holocaust, then in Bosnia, and finally in Rwanda. While visiting the site of a massacre in Nyanza, Majara meets a "cross-cultural adventurer" from Europe who has toured genocide sites around the world. When asked what he does, Simeon refuses to admit that he was an artist: "The idea made him queasy. It suggested an intolerable common purpose with his fellow traveller" (105). His disavowal of his true profession suggests an unconscious discomfort with what could be seen as an exploitative or parasitical relationship to the subjects of his art. And given that his art purports to commemorate the dead, his discomfort reads as a cautionary tale about memorialization projects more generally—perhaps including, by implication, the TRC.

Unexpectedly, Majara runs into equally uncomfortable questions of authority and authenticity and the ethics of art with his follow-up project entitled *Curiouser.* The title, besides containing a sly allusion to *Alice's*

Adventures in Wonderland, is a punning reference to the African masks, statues, and other curios that he cuts into slices and arranges on wall-size surfaces. The project was born when the owner of Bra Zama's African Eatery asked Majara to design the new restaurant's interior décor. He managed to buy several crates containing thousands of the masks and curios, some of which he turns into lamps to hang spookily on the walls of Bra Zama's; the narrator notes that "he had chanced upon a talent for frightening people, for giving them goosebumps by doing violence to their ordinary clutter" (120). This effect, incidentally, goes some way to explaining Egan's discomfort during the dinner scene in the earlier vignette, surrounded by Majara's masks; the two passages together reveal Vladislavić's awareness of the ability of architecture and design to affect social interaction in subtle ways.

After finishing the Bra Zama's project, Majara finds himself with thousands of curios left over, and thus he begins the *Curiouser* (or "Curio-user") project. He slices wooden statuettes of animals into pieces, in a kind of "mechanical compulsion, a tirelessly repeated dismemberment" (137). He soon finds that he "could graft the parts of different animals into new species, the head of a lion, the horns of a buffalo, the legs of a hippopotamus, exquisite corpses, many-headed monsters for a contemporary bestiary" (137). At the closing party, Majara's friend John comments that he thinks *Curiouser* is about "*re*construction.... It's about putting things together in new ways" (125). In this sense, then, Majara's artistic process resembles the work of the detective or the historian, putting fragments of past narratives together in ways that make sense of them for the present world.

Then, however, the conversation takes an uncomfortable turn, reminding us that these fragments have a material reality and that to appropriate them as part of a current narrative has material consequences. Another party attendee accuses Majara of dealing in stolen property with the masks he bought on the street at a suspiciously large discount. Later in a private conversation, even Majara's friend Amy raises a similar concern, pointing out that "You carve up a cheap curio and put it in a gallery, and suddenly it's worth a packet" (145). He attempts to dismiss her point with abstract arguments about popular craft versus high art, but Amy boils the matter down to simpler terms: "I can't help being aware of the balance of power, the imbalance, one should say. The way you live here [in affluent Greenside], the way the people who made these masks must live" (146). This conversation evokes the reluctant memory in Majara of a conversation he had at university with a fellow student who forced him to think about the means of production that go into the making of such simple items as a can of soda: the farmworkers who grow the raw materials, the miners who extract the aluminum from the earth, the factory workers who make the paint for the can, et cetera. "These things had been put here by thousands of people, tens of thousands of people, bound together in a massively complex web of work, whose most surprising characteristic was that nearly all of it was invisible and unacknowledged" (148).

Majara's reluctance to acknowledge these complex webs of work that underlie even the simple carved wooden animals he deconstructs in his art suggests a kind of postmodern existential despair, one resulting from the consuming subject's extreme alienation from both his or her own labor and from the objects of consumption. Within this free-floating web of social and material vectors as described by Vladislavić, an artist's power of narrative mapping is most intensely challenged, but also most urgently needed. We can further see both the challenges and the urgency in the figure of Gordon Duffy, protagonist of the final section of the novel, "Crocodile Lodge." I discussed earlier his lament for the irrelevance of his intuitive mechanical skills in a world where "the simplest devices were full of components no one could see, processes no one could fathom." He goes on to wonder, after some hypothetical massive catastrophe, "What could be saved of our high-tech world? How many people knew what went into the manufacture of a fibre-optic cable, a compact disk, a silicon chip, a printing press, a sheet of paper? How was information coded digitally?" (191). Such specialized technologies and pools of knowledge are another factor contributing to the difficulty of memorialization in the age of information: how can you ensure the survival of your memories of the past if the technology you choose for recording your narratives might not be readable in twenty years' time?

Despite the mind-boggling impossibility of comprehensively mapping all of the social, material, and economic elements that constitute the post-apartheid city, Vladislavić persists in constructing his "exploded view" of contemporary Johannesburg.[24] He does this, for instance, through Duffy's uncomfortable awareness of the material derivation of commodity goods, as his thoughts reveal when stopped at a traffic light where street vendors sell their goods between cars. One of them is selling a miniature balsa-wood schooner that "came sailing through the Highveld air. From a distance there was an illusion of intricacy and craft; from close up it was shoddily made, stuck together with staples and glue. A slave ship, mass-produced, he supposed, by children in a sweatshop somewhere in Hong Kong or Karachi or Doornfontein" (162). These few lines contain an entire allegorical critique of consumer capitalism: that which glitters and appears to float unencumbered in the air is in reality rooted in a system of human sweat and desperate poverty. And by including Doornfontein, a manufacturing area in central Johannesburg (very near to Vladislavić's home, incidentally), at the end of a list of cities infamous for their sweatshops, the author implies moreover that South Africa is equally caught up in the massive web of transnational capitalism.

Vladislavić applies the same demystifying process—laying bare the layers of work and infrastructure that underlie the apparently superficial—to one of the most characteristic features of the postmodern landscape, the billboard. Duffy puts them up for a living, specializing in billboards outside construction sites for new developments. In an essay on youth culture in contemporary Johannesburg, Sarah Nuttall discusses billboards as one of many "urban visual forms, which embody concepts of the urban, of race, and of culture that have much to tell us about Johannesburg as it participates in global cultures of circulation" ("Stylizing" 432). Vladislavić's treatment of billboards does indeed invite discussion in terms of surface images and simulacra. For example, Duffy wonders why the convention of labeling the illustrations of future housing developments as "Artist's Impression" has lapsed, and speculates: "Now that the fanciful images were practically indistinguishable from the photographically real, were more vividly convincing in fact than the ordinary world, disclaimers were no longer required" (*Exploded View* 187).

Here again, however, the novel also reinforces the material reality behind the production of those images; for instance, the Crocodile Lodge billboard had "taken a week to put up. It was on rocky ground, on a sloping stand beside the N3, and sinking the posts had been a performance. Josiah and his team were breaking rock with a jackhammer for a solid day while the agency breathed down his neck" (174). The billboard may be the very embodiment of the postmodern simulacra, but Vladislavić reveals that even that symbol of consumerist ephemera contains a history of human labor, a palimpsestic history that, after the fact, can be detected only through inference.

The grim conclusion to *The Exploded View* likewise suggests a certain skepticism toward romantic ideas about the liberating potential of information technologies. Whereas Egan views the city as composed of layers of permanence, Duffy views it as an intricate network of mechanisms and flows that he is able to "jack into" and navigate skillfully with the help of technology such as the radio traffic report:

> Usually it was reassuring, this invocation of rises and dips and the states associated with them, *a map of sensations keyed to his own body*.... It would soothe him to hear that each of the named intersections had become the hub of a failed mechanism, the end point of an incomplete trajectory, and that he was implicated in none of it, he was still on course. (159; emphasis added)

The radio thus seems to function as an extension of his senses, linking his body not just to his immediate surroundings but to the larger network of the city, which he explicitly thinks of in terms of a *map*.

Yet his faith in the system is shaken at the beginning of the vignette, when, leaving the construction site for the day, he hears the radio announcer report a traffic jam he is already stuck in. This inauspicious beginning to his evening foreshadows darker events, which begin when he realizes he has misplaced his cell phone—another piece of technology literally connecting him to larger networks. Turning his car around to look for it, he finds himself disoriented by its absence: "Twice in the space of a kilometre he thought he should call [his wife] to say he'd be late, and twice he had to remind himself that the phone was gone. A broken record player, he said to himself" (164–65). Significantly, he has become another "failed mechanism" like that resulting in traffic accidents; even his short-term memory seems to falter without the technological crutch of the phone (which for many people doubles as an address book and appointment planner). Fumbling in the dark for his phone at the construction site of the future Crocodile Lodge, Duffy is attacked by the occupants of a taxi-van that Budlender had earlier remarked as suspicious, but the license number of which Budlender was unable to recall from the "circuitry of his memory"—yet another failed mechanism.

Read together, the stories in *The Exploded View* paint a portrait of contemporary Johannesburg as containing almost unfathomably complex interactions between fixed spaces (houses, office buildings, shopping malls, streets), movements (of people, commodities, money, information), and the mechanisms that both facilitate and regulate those movements (traffic lights, fiber optic cables, cell phone towers).[25] Compounding the complexity of Vladislavić's cityscape is the fact that the fixed spaces are not so permanent as they might seem, but are in fact subject to rapid transformations that render problematic attempts by the inhabitants of those spaces to navigate through them, as well as attempts to inscribe social memory on them. Indeed, the novel points out the utter inadequacy of any single existing mode of archiving and documenting the city's past or present. Budlender's obsession with statistics is emblematic: killing time in a restaurant straddling the freeway, he counts cars: "He counted women drivers, did the conversion. Cars for men, cars for women. Rivers of drivers.... Entire lifestyles, dissolved in the flow like some troubling additive, like statistical fluoride, became perceptible to his trained eye" (15–16).

Yet Budlender's compiling of statistics equips him poorly for everyday life in the dizzying, shifting geographies of Johannesburg, where memories tend to follow the route of his attempts to recall the license number of that taxi: "There had been a motto too, in the back window, and a name printed by hand on the panel below. But all of it was gone" (22–23). Despite these challenges, though, Vladislavić's characters carry on trying to map and archive and make sense of the world around them, as do the characters in the work to which I next turn my attention—Mpe's *Welcome to Our Hillbrow*.

2.3 Linguistic Trips: Phaswane Mpe's *Welcome to Our Hillbrow*

So far we have seen Johannesburg depicted from the perspective of relatively privileged characters. Silas Ali in *Bitter Fruit* is of mixed-race and Muslim heritage, but holds a prestigious position with Mandela's government. And *The Exploded View* shows us the city from the points of view of three middle-class white men and a successful black artist. The next few novels I survey show us a different side of the post-apartheid city, one closer to Appadurai's vision of "globalization from below." For instance, Phaswane Mpe's *Welcome to Our Hillbrow* (2001) depicts the city from the perspective of a young student just arrived in Hillbrow from his rural village.[26]

The second-person narration of *Welcome* engages in a kind of narrative mapping or archiving in the process of describing the protagonists' movements through Hillbrow and its surrounds. Significantly, the first chapter of the novel is entitled "Hillbrow: The Map," and the narrative does indeed sketch out the map of the area. Mpe maps not just fixed structures but also the social and economic networks and flows within the city and those that connect Hillbrow to rural spaces and to other cities in South Africa and beyond. His innovative narrative technique, rather than circumscribing and regimenting the spaces it describes, opens them up in a multiplicity of directions as spaces of loss but also of fecundity and transformation. This is, I believe, what Neville Hoad means when he claims that Mpe's novel is an "elegy for African cosmopolitanism" (113). By "cosmopolitan," Hoad means "not an individual or even an attribute of an individual. Instead it is something like a structure of feeling, a web of relations between the living and the dead, the rural and the urban, the healthy and the sick, the kinsman and the stranger, Africans and the world" (116).

One of the mechanisms through which Mpe establishes or makes visible this "structure of feeling" is the second-person mode of narration, which is immediately and consistently jarring, and in which the "you" continually shifts and expands to include an ever-larger web of relations. The narrator seems to be the collective voice of the people of Hillbrow, or alternately Hillbrow itself, or the village of Tiragalong; at other times still it seems to be narrated by the ancestors from "Heaven" or the afterlife. The narrative is addressed directly to Refentše after his suicide, and in the last chapter directly to Refilwe, Refentše's childhood sweetheart who follows him from Tiragalong to Hillbrow just before his death; Refilwe then goes to Oxford, returns to Africa, and dies of AIDS. Thus the first paragraph begins:

> If you were still alive, Refentše, child of Tiragalong, you would be glad that Bafana Bafana [the South African national side] lost to France in the 1998 Soccer World Cup fiasco. Of course you supported the squad. But at least now, you would experience no hardships walking to your flat through the streets of Hillbrow—that locality of just over one square kilometre, according to official records; and according to its inhabitants, at least twice as big and teeming with countless people. You would remember the last occasion in 1995, when Bafana Bafana won against Ivory Coast and, in their jubilation, people in Hillbrow hurled bottles of all sorts from their flat balconies. (1)

The narrator describes the city from the perspective of what Refentše would see and feel were he still alive to do so. The narrative is thus structured around a perpetually present absence, preserving the memories of the lost one by recalling the traces of his movements in life, and reinforced by the perpetual use of subjunctive and conditional tenses in the novel.[27] The notion of a present absence from the past echoing in the present is developed further later in the novel, when Refilwe in a pub in Oxford sees a "stranger-whose-face-was-Refentše's" (110). The narrator says that "If Refentše were still alive, he might have written a poem for her, called *For Refilwe Who is No More*" (112). Thus mourning and loss are compounded in layer upon palimpsestic layer, with Refentše mourning for Refilwe and being mourned by her and the narrator in turn.

The traces of the characters' movements constitute a map of the inner city, as when the narrator describes in that distinctive blend of conditional voice and present tense Refentše's first arrival at his cousin's flat in Hillbrow:

> If you are coming from the city centre, the best way to get to Cousin's place is by driving or walking through Twist Street, a one-way street that takes you to the north of the city. You cross Wolmarans and three rather obscure streets, Kapteijn, Ockerse and Pieterse, before you drive or walk past Esselen, Kotze and Pretoria Streets.... On your left-hand side is Christ Church, the Bible Centred Church of Christ, as the big red letters announce to you. On your right-hand side is a block of flats called Vickers Place. You turn to your right, because the entrance to Vickers is in Caroline Street, directly opposite another block, Da Gama Court. (6)

Gugu Hlongwane notes that in Mpe's novel, the "simple act of walking the city... becomes extremely significant even though the prevalence of

English and Afrikaans street names which virtually mark the whole of South Africa suggest not a new post-colonial South Africa but a neo-colonial one" (73). I would argue that this careful catalog of street names is more than a form of protest against living conditions in "a country where the poor live in desperate poverty," as Hlongwane suggests (73). It also serves to unearth the layers of historical sediment that have contributed to the making of South Africa's cities, from the Portuguese (Da Gama) to the Dutch and English, and even to black American missionaries who brought evangelical Christianity.

Moreover, if this narrative map focuses in special detail on Hillbrow and its vicinity, it also includes a much larger area, as the repeatedly invoked refrain "Welcome to Our ..." is expanded throughout the course of the novel beyond Hillbrow to include the rest of Johannesburg, Tiragalong, Oxford, all of England, and, finally, "Heaven" and "the World of Our Humanity." The effect is similar to a satellite image zooming out from central Johannesburg to show a much larger picture. By doing so, Mpe maps not only the built environments—the physical spaces—of the city, but also the layers of history as well as the sociocultural networks that bind together the people who occupy, use, move through, and (re)produce those spaces. Michael Green notes that the novel's "failures, along with its successes, are a product of a range of voices struggling to speak to each other in awkward translation" (14).[28] For instance, Mpe's Hillbrow is linked to the rural village of Tiragalong through Refilwe and Refentše; to other parts of Africa through the many foreign immigrants; and to Europe through the characters' travels. *Welcome to Our Hillbrow* thus portrays contemporary Johannesburg as fed by and constituted out of infinitely complex local, regional, and global networks.[29]

The narrator engages in similar mapping when Refilwe goes to Oxford: "If you drove there from the corner of Gipsy Lane and Headington Road you would take the route to the city centre, drive past the main entrance to the Headington Hill Campus, and turn right into Marston Road" (104). Memory is further inscribed in spatial terms in the description of a pub in Oxford that reminds Refilwe of her favorite pub in Braamfontein, and "in which resided so many of *the memory landscapes of home*" (111; emphasis added). In part 3, I use the term "memory of landscapes" fluidly both to describe people's memories of particular places, and to characterize the memories that sometimes seem to be contained in the land itself and can be aroused involuntarily in the presence of the land. Mpe's expression "the memory landscapes of home" is similarly suggestive, pointing to the power of places to transport people back in time.

The narrator thus takes the reader on a "linguistic trip" through the places the characters have visited, mapping time as well as space, just as Refilwe takes Lerato through such a trip in Heaven (68). The narrative mapping is most intense in the first chapter, "Hillbrow: The Map." Mpe then sets his characters in motion through those fixed spaces in the remaining chapters, whose titles reflect this peripatetic restlessness: "The Journey through Alexandra"; "Refilwe on the Move"; "The Returnee." Green argues that the "insistent mapping of Hillbrow that dominates the first section of *Welcome to our Hillbrow* is an almost compulsive attempt on the part of the narrator to site his protagonist in the city" (7). Mpe uses this technique again in the long, unpunctuated catalog paragraphs that end several of the novel's chapters, such as this excerpt from the end of the first chapter:

> And when you finally come to this part of your journey that ends in the blank wall of suicide...with the spinning of cars the prostitution drug use and misuse the grime and crime the numerous bottles diving from flat balconies giving off sparks of red and yellow from mid-air reflections of street and flat neon lights only to crush on unfortunate souls' skulls the neon welcoming lights the peace of mind you could see in many Hillbrowans the liveliness of the place and places collapsing while others got renovated.... Chelsea Hotel closing down robbery moving flowing from Hillbrow into its neighbours especially Berea and Braamfontein as the media had it *Mail & Guardian* and David Philip Publishers and others changing offices moving out of this increasingly dilapidated and menacing Braamfontein while others found it to be quite an investment and so coming in to build and occupy their lush offices...*Makwerekwere* [derogatory term for foreign Africans] drifting into and out of Hillbrow and Berea having spilt into Berea from Hillbrow according to many xenophobic South Africans...coming to take our jobs in the new democratic rainbowism of African Renaissance that threatened the future of the locals Bafana Bafana fans momentarily forgetting xenophobia and investing their hopes in the national team...also investing in the Moroccan team the Nigerian Super Eagles and singing at least they are African unlike the French the English the Danes. (25–27)

I have quoted this passage at such length because it illustrates so richly the strategies of narrative social mapping that Mpe employs throughout the novel. The absence of punctuation creates in the reader a disorientation not dissimilar to that experienced by the residents of a city that is transforming so quickly before their eyes.

Yet by identifying various loci of social interaction such as churches, residential hotels, and football stadiums, Mpe points to possible foundations for identity that rely neither on nationalism nor on highly localized places such as a village or city block. Such an identity comprises instead a multiplicity of social roles and relationships.[30] Nuttall notes that "Mpe offers a revised inventory of the city, comprising a path along its streets, both tracking and breaching historical constructions of space. Built sites along the streets symbolise specific practices, demarcate racial identities in particular ways and in turn determine *how* one walks" ("City Forms" 743). I would emphasize here the importance of determining how different social classes walk, or drive, or otherwise experience the city. What makes Mpe's novel so important is precisely its efforts to map a "grassroots globalization"—that is, to register the ways that ordinary people navigate the complexity of the contemporary urban landscape.

Yet the long passage quoted earlier also illustrates the role that people themselves play in determining the production and distribution of space.[31] In Mpe's depiction, capital lacks the power to unilaterally shape spaces, but rather shifts its resources in response to changes beyond its control, as with the *Mail & Guardian* staff and David Philip Publishers fleeing Braamfontein's crime wave. And like other passages in the novel, this one suggests that ordinary people have an intuitive awareness of the national and transnational flows that feed into the city. Some of these flows do indeed emanate from the western metropole and are transmitted via electronic information technology, such as the televised Hollywood images that help shape children's perceptions even in remote Tiragalong: "Crime was glamorised on the screens and robbers were portrayed as if they were movie stars.... the little boys of Tiragalong emulated their TV heroes, driving their cars made of wire with wheels of tennis balls" (5). But information flows along multiple axes, each of which is subject to its own forms of framing and distortion. For example, the fact that many of the South African characters in the novel blame the AIDS epidemic on *Makwerekwere*—who, they believe, have brought the virus with them from north of the border—suggests a partial and imperfect, but nevertheless significant, understanding of the phenomena of border crossings and global flows.

One of the primary vehicles for perpetuating these (mis)perceptions is village gossip, which thanks to technology and the migrant labor system extends to Johannesburg and beyond. The narrator tells Refentše how word of his suicide spread through the country: "It was minibus taxis and migrants' cars that transported the news. It was Telkom's telephone lines that performed a similar function. It was Vodacom and MTN, South Africa's giant cellphone service providers. And credit must be given, too, to the villagers' abilities to imagine well beyond the known and the possible, in order to embellish the story of your suicide" (30–31). Later the narrator describes another round of gossip, this time about the mother of Refentše's girlfriend Lerato, who was struck by a strange illness: "So the word went around the fields of Tiragalong—much faster than any radio news could have spread it—until all the fields were left empty" (72–73). Initially these flows of gossip and information attribute Refentše's suicide to his mother's witchcraft, but then "Refilwe rewrote large chunks of the story that Tiragalong had constructed about you.... In this version of things, you had been bewitched indeed—but not by your mother; by a loose-thighed Hillbrowan called Lerato" (42–44).

Refilwe's ability to reshape the stories about Refentše, and the village's eagerness to believe her stories about the loose women of Johannesburg, underscores the fact that knowledge of the past is always constructed out of socially shared interpretations and assumptions. Mpe suggests moreover that, in the dizzying chaos of post-apartheid Johannesburg, such memories will be even more fragmented and ephemeral. Indeed, a fixed, final, totalizing memory of the past might not be possible until one reaches Heaven, and even then Mpe implies that memory is an artifact of the human archive: "Heaven is the world of our continuing existence, located in the memory and consciousness of those who live with us and after us. It is the *archive* that those we left behind keep visiting and revisiting.... *Continually reconfiguring the stories of our lives*, as if they alone hold the real and true version" (124; emphasis added). Even in Heaven, then, the past is never fixed, but can be refigured just as the TRC refigured official apartheid history and as the TRC's narrative will need to be recalibrated in turn.

If both personal and social memories are constructed from residual fragments of the past, it follows that both individual and group identities (founded as they inevitably are in particular versions of the past) are similarly manufactured out of shared social relationships and practices. This notion of identity or selfhood not as a unified whole but as an assemblage of memories, places, and connections to social networks is dramatized through the displacement of the author's/narrator's/protagonists' subjectivity in the novel. Green points out some of the autobiographical resonances to many aspects of Mpe's characters: like Refentše, Mpe studied literature at Wits University, and like Refilwe, he went on to study at an English university; like Refentše, Mpe has written a collection of poems called *Love Songs, Blues and Interludes*, and a novel that grew out of a short story; and just as Refentše's story was written "in order to steady [himself] against grief and prejudice, against the painful and complex realities of humanness" (*Welcome* 59), so Mpe has admitted that *Welcome to Our Hillbrow* was written, in Green's words, as "an alternative to suicide" (9).

What is nevertheless noteworthy about Mpe's attempt to "objectify the subjective so that it may be mapped accurately against post-apartheid's inflection of the postmodern" (Green 12) is the way in which that subjectivity is incarnated and displaced across multiple sites of selfhood. This displacement takes on the effect of two mirrors facing each other when Refentše writes a story about a woman who has written a novel about

Hillbrow and Tiragalong—all this, of course, appearing in a novel about Hillbrow and Tiragalong. Mpe is thus able to explore the vexed questions of identity, subjectivity, and representation throughout several degrees of remove. He accomplishes this through the fictional technique of embedding stories within stories within stories, and through multiply displaced bodies/sites—similar to what *Ubu and the Truth Commission* (1.2) accomplishes through puppets, handlers, and interpreters.

Together, these works emphasize the value of being able to shift among multiple avatars or sites of subjectivity in negotiating the labyrinthine postmodern social geographies of post-apartheid South Africa. Emma Hunt suggests that the "metafictional nature of Mpe's novel is a means of writing the city through storytelling and establishing the city's links to multiple places" (116). Dangor has his character Michael Ali perform a similar trick in *Bitter Fruit* (2.1). And we can see this shifting of performed identities in the novel to which I turn next as well: Tshepo in *The Quiet Violence of Dreams* is able to forge new identities for himself in order to navigate within and between the still-segregated social worlds of post-apartheid Cape Town.

2.4 Peripatetic Mapping: K. Sello Duiker's *The Quiet Violence of Dreams*

In a recent article on youth culture in contemporary Johannesburg, Sarah Nuttall pays "close attention to modes of stylizing the self increasingly common among young people in the city. By *stylization of the self*, I am referring to how people seek to transform themselves into singular beings" ("Stylizing the Self" 432). She is careful to emphasize that her "focus on self-styling avoids easy equations between the young, post-apartheid generation in Johannesburg and a global youth culture. Generation Y cannot be reduced to mere surface(s), nor is it simply a subcultural critique of 'official culture'" (432).

It quickly becomes apparent from Nuttall's analysis, however, that this styling the self is essentially a process of consumption, as evidenced in the "[b]ooks, CDs, comic strips, advertisements, food, urban design, and techware" reviewed in the pages of the youth-oriented *Y* and *SL* magazines (446). The unexplored implication is that the ability to shape one's own identity in the post-apartheid, postmodern city is contingent on a certain level of financial and educational privilege, and, as Michael Watts notes, the "question of what the Y generation represents politically, of what a 'stylistics of the future'...means, remains enigmatic and elusive"

(185). Nuttall does acknowledge the aspirational qualities of this youth culture—it reflects where teenagers would like to be, not necessarily where they come from—and she does recognize that the poor are not welcome at a favorite hangout of middle-class youth, the Zone at Rosebank (434). But she never addresses the question of how "stylizing the self" might play out for the desperately poor, for whom the world of middle-class consumerism seems alien and unattainable.

K. Sello Duiker's[32] second novel, *The Quiet Violence of Dreams* (2001), might be read as a critique of the limited kinds of subjectivity seemingly made possible through stylizing the self in the age of the globalization of consumer capitalism. If he portrays the potential for South Africans in the new century to forge new identities, that potential lies not in the patterns of consumption Nuttall describes but in the ability of city residents in the post-apartheid era to carve out spaces of their own. Such autonomous cultural spaces include, for example, the "brotherhood" that Tshepo finds among his fellow male prostitutes at Steamy Windows; Peter Tosh Hall and Marcus Garvey Square, the rasta club and haven on the Cape Flats; and the gay clubs in Green Point. But if these places hold out the promise of a somewhat secure basis for self-styled identities, the spaces are perpetually contested and under threat—from the harassment of police, and from the homogenizing impulses of global consumer culture, among other forces. Moreover, the danger of these self-determined spaces is that they will become exclusionary citadels, as happens with the club for gay white men from which Tshepo is rudely ejected late in the novel. The novel thus poses, and only partly resolves, a great challenge for post-apartheid reconstruction: how to create such safe autonomous zones of self-determination, where true renegotiations of selfhood can take place, without creating a society of disconnected, balkanized communities resembling the spatial stratifications of apartheid.

* * *

One of the most frequently recurring tropes of the novel is schizophrenia and mental illness; early on we follow Tshepo on one of his many confinements in the Valkenberg Mental Hospital. The novel's depiction of mental disintegration is reflected in and reinforced by the complicated narrative structure, with each section narrated in the first person by a different character. Until late in the novel, Tshepo's worst breakdowns are narrated not through his consciousness and point of view but by other characters who observe his behavior in bafflement. In such scenes we do not hear Tshepo's internal ruminations, only his friends' muted perception of what he is thinking and feeling. Later in the book, however, as Tshepo finds a sense of belonging with the fraternity of male prostitutes and begins to feel secure in his sexual identity, his narrated sections become longer and more coherent, and we see less of him through other people's eyes and more through his own. When Tshepo does reflect on his own mental state, it is significant that he thinks of it through metaphors of space, time, and motion: In Valkenberg, he thinks, "There is the possibility of never being found or of never finding yourself, forever lost in dementia, a tight space smaller than the distance between two letters" (62).

Like so many characters in post-apartheid urban fiction, Tshepo experiences an almost involuntary compulsion to walk—perhaps because of the sensation of being "forever lost in dementia." As Certeau suggests, such peripatetic impulses seem born out of the structures of the city itself: "To walk is to lack a place. It is the indefinite process of being absent in search of a proper.... the city itself [is] an immense social experience of lacking a place" (103). Sometimes Tshepo's compulsion seems to be a sort of self-medicating therapy, a search for some stability in his world of fragmentation and disconnection: "I must decode the logic of my own madness.... I must walk till there is nothing left till I have no energy left to expand on ideas of a father" (*Quiet Violence* 91–92). The need to search out his roots—the "ideas of a father"—partly explains the compulsion Tshepo feels to walk, even if only through the hospital grounds.

It is this aspect of his condition that most resembles the "schizophrenia" that Fredric Jameson proposes as an "aesthetic model" (26) for discussing the cultural effects of a postmodern culture of surface and simulacrum, in which the experience of schizophrenia is potentially intoxicating as well as disorienting.[33] Indeed, in the midst of his peripatetic restlessness Tshepo sometimes finds a strange connection to the people around him, as if tapping into the larger social and cultural networks of the city: He says that he experiences synchronicity "with frightening intensity. There was a period during one of the days when I was just walking around Cape Town when everything made sense and everyone seemed to be communicating with me" (*Quiet Violence* 38).

Sometimes, the compulsion to walk seems to be a symptom of his schizophrenic-like condition: he walks "around the city aimlessly like unclaimed baggage drifting on an airport conveyer belt" (90). Late in the novel, after earlier seeming to have found his mental equilibrium, he finds himself again walking aimlessly: "I don't know where I am going. The road is itching for my feet, aching to be walked on, lusting to be explored" (425). He ends up in the desperately poor black township of Nyanga; he thinks to himself that the word "nyanga" is isiXhosa for "to heal," but "I don't feel healed by the walking.... I walk further into confusion, my mind wrapped around finding home. The township is a maze" (429).

The "home" Tshepo is searching for is not literal—he grew up in Soweto, hundreds of kilometers from Nyanga—but figurative: a sense of connection both to his past and to some larger community. Ultimately, though, he finds little basis for either in Cape Town, which he thinks of as more European than Europe: "In some places in Cape Town you don't feel like you're in Africa. And this is what they call progress, obliterate any traces of the native cultures" (420). Tshepo's feelings of uprootedness and alienation result in an identity crisis, emblemized by the changes to his name. When he begins working as an escort at Steamy Windows, he adopts the pseudonym "Angelo"; soon that becomes the name by which he is primarily known, to the extent that the chapters narrated by him are headed "Angelo." Later, though, the chapters are titled "Angelo-Tshepo" (see 378, for example), and in the final chapter, when he has returned to Johannesburg, he becomes just "Tshepo" once again. As Shaun Viljoen puts it, Tshepo "insists on seeing himself not as a psychotic man or a black man or a gay man but rather as a rich amalgam of shifting, intermingling identities" (51). If his constantly shifting identity is a source of anxiety for him and his friends, it is also perhaps the only form of identity that can successfully navigate the social geographies of the post-apartheid city, which shift and transform just as rapidly.

Quiet Violence suggests a complicated aggregation of causes underlying Tshepo's mental illness. On a personal level, his traumatic childhood surely plays a role: his mother was raped by a gang of men when he was young, while he and his father were locked in a nearby bathroom; when they finished with her, they hauled Tshepo out of the toilet and administered the same treatment to him (76–77).[34] Tshepo, moreover, is extremely sensitive not only to his personal traumas but to those of the country as a whole: He tells one of the many flatmates he has over the course of the novel, a Congolese immigrant, that the past is "still fresh to me. Can't you understand that? It was like yesterday. . . . And the vicious lies that come with horrible deaths, I can't forget them. I won't forget them" (97). Like Michael Ali in *Bitter Fruit* (2.1), Tshepo recognizes the power of a kind of "historical memory" to echo in and affect the present, as with black Americans for whom slavery has "branded their memory" (317). As the conversation with the roommates reveals, Tshepo's own memory is "branded" by the memories of apartheid violence, and by personal violence. The paradox of his situation is that even as the marks of history are erased from the city spaces around him, they continue to haunt him—demanding to be continually revisited and "remapped."

The psychological disturbances that lead to Tshepo's disorientation, in fact, often present as a sort of haunting. One scene in particular suggests that involuntary memories are inscribed on or haunt particular places, and that such places have the power to communicate the past even to those far removed from it. He visits the family home of his Afrikaans friend West in Somerset West; asleep in West's bedroom, he dreams about British soldiers tormenting Afrikaner women and children in a concentration camp during the Anglo-Boer War. When he wakes up, Tshepo notes that "I feel strange, disoriented. I feel as if the room swallowed me and infected me with its stories and histories.... The image of emaciated women and children with dirty clothes and broken faces sticks to my mind" (368). It seems significant that this vision comes to Tshepo while he is in a small town in the Cape, where the palimpsest of history is less densely layered than in the city and the scars of traumatic events are more readily visible.

If Tshepo's mental alienation is partly rooted in these memories of personal and collective trauma that dwell only partially in his own mind, it is also related, as Jameson's analysis suggests, to newly emerging economic formations. Tshepo notes that race has been supplanted by class and consumer status symbols as the principal mode of social differentiation: The people at the trendy clubs in Cape Town "want to see you wearing Diesel jeans with a retro shirt and Nike tackies [sneakers].... They want to live out their Trainspotting odyssey of excess in a culture rapidly blurring the borders between the township and the northern suburbs" (34). Cape Town, he often reflects, "wants to be New York, London or Paris" (35); people there want to see others and to be seen consuming both branded goods and foreign cultures.

On a number of occasions Tshepo directly links his schizophrenic-like condition to the postindustrial capitalist landscape and to what he sees as the rampant corruption of the post-apartheid dispensation. During one of his breakdowns, he visits a nature reserve and sees visions in a lake there—which he narrates as if to his mother: "[I]n the lake I see terrible things, Mama; poverty and children with kwashiorkor [malnutrition] playing with guns.... I see industrialists drinking the blood of rivers and defecating on our fears. I see old men tired of protest leading us further into darkness laughing and joking" (94). Tshepo continues, "I walk because of them and all the ugliness they have left us. But the ugliness from which we are trying to run is us" (95). Tshepo thus directly attributes his perambulatory compulsion to an attempt to escape a landscape scarred by industrialization, war, and crime. But this passage further suggests that he walks in response to a profound loss, the "deep raw gashes" in memory, and the "ugliness" the past has left inside him. The second-person apostrophe to his dead mother, a rhetorical device that recurs throughout the novel, has a similar effect to that evoked by Mpe's *Welcome to Our Hillbrow* (2.3), centering the narrative around a continually present absence.

Such centering and reorientation is both especially necessary because of, and especially complicated by, the enormous complexity of urban space. Duiker depicts Cape Town as a highly variegated assemblage of places and pathways, with people moving through the city variously on foot, in taxi vans, by train, or in private car. In the process people produce very different kinds of interactions with the socio-spatial networks around them, and thus require different modes of mapping those spaces and encounters. The novel likewise emphasizes the severity of uneven development in Cape Town, especially evident in the stark poverty of the Cape Flats. Chris, one of Tshepo's roommates (who turns out to be a psychopathic rasta gangster), describes the Flats as "like a complicated underground sewage system.... You stop being a person if you spend your whole life in the Cape Flats, if you don't go out for a while, even for a day" (154–55). Tshepo sees this for himself in his last walk through the shanty towns: "There are no parks to go to, no video arcades to explore, just dirty streets and longdrops festering with disease.... There are no public toilets, no bushes or trees, only shacks and people" (430–31). The maze of unpaved streets and ramshackle hovels constitutes a kind of network of its own, one that Tshepo attempts to decipher through walking: "Everywhere I go I look. I feel like I'm decoding the madness, wrapping my brain around it, facing it.... Maybe it is called capitalism, making money for the sake of making money, not building communities" (431–32).

I have already suggested that Tshepo seems to succeed in finding at least a transient source of stability and identity over the course of the novel. Part of this stability derives from his "decoding" and coming to terms with his sexuality. For instance, he describes one of his clients as "an expert, a tourist guide traveling through a foreign country" (392), a line that confirms my sense that, through his interior explorations of his sexuality and his body, Tshepo is developing "maps" that can guide him through the disorienting metropolis. Related to this evolving sexual identity is the sense of community he finds among the workers at Steamy Windows. After Tshepo's first successful session with a client, West welcomes him aboard and tells him, "[Y]ou're one of us now. We're like brothers here. You will see things that not many people get to see in one life.... We are all brothers. We all look after each other. We know each other well" (244–45). To some extent, this sense of community also extends to the gay bars in Green Point and Sea Point.

Quiet Violence, in fact, is frequently concerned with the ways that groups lay claim to and develop spaces of their own. Tshepo's flatmate Chris explains that he goes as often as he can to Peter Tosh Hall and Marcus Garvey Square "where rastas have their own place and they can do their own things without the interference of the white man's law" (161), though they are still harassed by police outside the square for possession of cannabis. Inside the club, nevertheless, the rastas create their own "vibe," which Tshepo experiences as a "deep feeling that resonates throughout my body as I dance" (161). Later, after being arrested for possession of cannabis, Tshepo finds himself in a jail cell full of rastas, and discovers that they create their own space wherever a group of them meets: "I suddenly become aware that I'm in their space, that even though we're all in the same situation I'm still a guest" (185).

Such self-defined spaces offer great potential for groups seeking to establish and control their post-apartheid identities. They also, unfortunately, create the possibility of a society of exclusionary, insulated enclaves, as Tshepo discovers the hard way in a gay hothouse: "I look around me and feel my aloneness as one of the few black faces in the room. I am sick of that. With all their moaning, crying and campaigning for equal rights gay men are also just as bigoted.... [G]ay friendly places are still a white male preserve" (417). Later, after walking all night and desperately needing a refuge, he is turned away from a bar he frequents in his better dressed guise in the company of his white friends. The doorman's refusal to admit him further emphasizes the exclusionary nature of many such partially autonomous places for identity formation.

Perhaps ironically, one possible solution to this unfortunate tendency is suggested in the Afrikaner's pioneer history. Visiting West, his family, and his friends in Somerset West, Tshepo realizes for the first time that Afrikaners can be human and sensitive: "How little I knew. How small my world was.... I didn't realise that [West] was opening up his world to me" (355). At a party, one of West's friends jokes about moving to an island in the South Pacific and starting his own rugby team and brewery, and Tshepo thinks to himself, "he probably would. They are like that, pioneers. Perhaps they are here to show us that anyone can live anywhere. Perhaps their lesson is to learn how to live with other people without interfering with their culture" (364). If Tshepo's is perhaps a selective, even romanticized interpretation of pioneer history in the Cape, this scene nevertheless anticipates an important theme that will emerge more forcefully in part 3: amid all the oppression and struggle, the past also contains possibilities obscured until now by apartheid. There are lost traditions and beliefs and rituals, as well as alternative ways of understanding and interacting with others and with social spaces. If these lost practices can never be excavated and recuperated wholesale, their fragments can nevertheless be recovered and assimilated into new narratives of the present and future.

Despite the optimism implied by Tshepo's newfound insights into Afrikaans cultural history, the ending of the novel is somewhat ambiguous. After his father dies, Tshepo experiences another mental breakdown, and finally moves back to Johannesburg and gets a job working with orphans in Hillbrow. The novel ends on a note of hopeful reconciliation: "I know where my greatest treasures lie. They are within me" (457). It is difficult, though, to read the novel hopefully in light of its significant autobiographical component and the knowledge of Duiker's suicide in January 2005, reportedly because his psychiatric medications interfered with his creative work (McGregor).

Yet, if it is hard to read the novel as an optimistic tale of redemption, it is equally difficult to see the conclusion as utterly bleak—as Tshepo finds even within his madness an indication of future potential growth. He thinks to himself that he cannot "follow" whites, Indians, coloureds, or the greedy and corrupt blacks in the new dispensation: "So I follow the Africans, the enlightened ones, the elusive ones.... I follow the ones I read about, I sense in the air, the ones time always remembers and never forgets. They are part of the changing African landscape" (*Quiet Violence* 438). These men are keepers of ancient traditions, but have also adapted to the multilayered networks of (post)modern life, part of "the changing African landscape."

Back in Johannesburg Tshepo also meets such "special men" who give him "blueprints for survival, for building a new civilisation, a new way of life.... There are better ways, they keep telling me, capitalism is not the only way. We haven't nearly exhausted all the possibilities, they say. We know that the future depends on everyone working together" (455). This strikes me as a summary of Duiker's own project in this novel: to construct blueprints for survival and new modes of social and spatial organization, based partly on forgotten remnants of the past and partly on resourcefulness and flexibility. John Hawley remarks that "the role that Duiker's character envisions has really very little to do with capitalism—though paradoxically, much to do with globalization" (76). Indeed, if Duiker sees any promise in the new South Africa, it lies not in the political transition and the embrace of neoliberal capitalism—the book repeatedly rails against the corruption and opportunism of the new government—but in the shifting and opening up of spaces so that people can reclaim a space for their own communities and work together to forge new provisional, nonexclusionary identities.

2.5 Excavating the City: Aziz Hassim's *The Lotus People*

Aziz Hassim's *The Lotus People* (2003)[35] provides a natural bridge between the urban novels I have been analyzing in the second part of this book and the works in part 3, which depict the post-apartheid impulse to excavate and document forgotten histories of places. The plot of Hassim's debut novel culminates in Durban during the state of emergency in the late 1980s, and the agonized dilemma facing four middle-aged businessmen who must decide whether or not to join the ANC and take an active part in the resistance. But these chapters are interspersed throughout the novel with chapters that explore over a century of Durban's past, especially the Indian commercial district in the city center known as "the Casbah." This history is presented from the perspective of "two great dynasties" of business families, started when Yahya Suleiman and Pravin Naran enter into a business pact in 1882. Part of their history includes the 1949 riots, in which Yahya is killed and both families lose many of their investments; it also includes the devastating effects of the so-called Ghetto Act, which forced the removal of Indians from the suburbs close to the city. The novel maps these losses onto the landscape of the city, and in the process illuminates the crucial role of Durban's Indian community in the history of resistance to white minority rule as well as the central role of Indian women in that struggle.[36]

Whereas characters such as Michael Ali in *Bitter Fruit* (2.1) and Tshepo in *The Quiet Violence of Dreams* (2.4) feel utterly severed from their own pasts, Hassim's novel reveals a bedrock faith in the citability and traceability of history. He spells out his moral explicitly and repeatedly; as Yayha tells his son Dara, who in turn tells his children Jake, Sam, and Ayesha: "You must remember your past before you can build a future" (144; see also 471). Accordingly, in the very first paragraph we learn that the Suleimans are descended from Pathan warriors who successfully repelled Alexander the Great's assault in 325 BC. The novel itself tells the story of four generations of the Suleimans, the Narans, and their friends, providing exactly the kind of genealogical rootedness of which Michael Ali, for example, feels the lack so acutely. This fictional history is given a certain verisimilitude by the appearance of various real historical figures in the novel, including Mohandas Gandhi, Fatima Meer, and Allen Boesak.

Despite the foundation provided by this history, *The Lotus People*, like virtually the whole of post-apartheid South African literature, is a tale of loss: loss of family members to the machinations of the state, loss of dignity under such humiliating policies as the pass laws, and loss of land to repressive legislation such as the Ghetto Act. Indeed, the novel narrates over a century of repressive white minority rule, with its increasingly harsh methods of disenfranchising, dispossessing, and controlling the movements of the Indian population. Early in the novel, a young revolutionary named Jammu complains about the treatment of Indians in the Natal colony, who are invited by the government to settle in South Africa—only to be treated as slaves on sugar plantations, subjected to passbook controls, et cetera (62–63).

Next, in the aftermath of World War II, we see the community's response to the "Asiatic Land Tenure and Indian Representation Bill" (1946) or "Ghetto Act," which one leader describes as the government "formulating even more unjust laws to give a so-called legitimacy to their usurpation of our wealth" (89). In response to the burgeoning resistance movement, Jan Smuts's regime accelerates this process: "At a stroke of the pen, overnight and with breathtaking audacity, it declared the affluent sections of the city as exclusive areas for White occupation," and expropriated Indian homes (100). Hassim's novel thus makes clear that for the Indian community as well as for black Africans, the spatial partitioning that dominated their lives began well before the formal introduction of apartheid in 1948.

The novel devotes a particularly strong focus to the effects of the Ghetto Act. One didactic passage emphasizes the ways in which the spatial schemas of apartheid and segregation functioned as instruments of social control and repression:

> [I]n an environment where the energies of the inhabitants were devoted solely towards keeping the body and its meagre possessions intact, the inclination to protest against moral issues was bound to be diluted. All that was required was to police the edges of the ghettoes, to ensure the violence within did not spill over into the exclusively white areas and impinge on the safety and the sensibilities of the master race. . . . In addition, the demarcation of exclusive settlement zones, restricted to the sole occupation of a specific race group, acted as a neat hindrance to racially unified political resistance and fostered a degree of friction amongst the African, coloured and Indian citizens. (168)

These divide-and-rule policies of social confinement and control are reinforced with tight controls over the flow of information, so that by "January 1947, the [Indian] family owned weekly, *The Leader*, stood out as the only paper anywhere in the country that dared to openly defy the government" (111).

While the novel makes clear that these mechanisms never succeed in totally eliminating political opposition, the protest that does exist is driven by a deep sense of loss, as manifest, for example, in the strike of June 1946, when "Indians throughout the country downed tools and declared it a national day of mourning" (98). The losses of the past create a present absence, a rupture in the temporal fabric that echoes in the present—through memories, but also through repetitions of history: when blacks begin looting and pillaging Indian homes and businesses in 1986, apparently at the instigation of the white authorities, Dara Suleiman remarks that "[f]or us, it is like 1949 all over again" (23), referring to the period of riots that destroyed the fortunes of many Natal Indians. These riots disrupt the community's sense of history and connection to its past—quite literally in the case of the Gandhi settlement in Inanda, which in the 1986 riots "has been totally destroyed, all the historic archives and documents lost in the fire" (30).

In the face of this monumental loss, *memory* plays a crucial role in connecting the community to the places of their past; this is as true of the old Indian districts such as Cato Manor in Durban as it is of District Six in Cape Town or Sophiatown in Johannesburg. Yet at the same time, Hassim reveals that memory is intimately intertwined with the places themselves and can take on a reality of its own, often involuntarily, in a phenomenon I describe in part 3 as "the memory of landscapes." Nithin (Nits) Vania, one of Jake and Sam Suleiman's good friends, makes this clear in a flashback he experiences standing near his old school: "When Nithin looked at the playground he could actually see the events as they had unfolded, it was like looking at a movie screen" (319). Sam also experiences a similar flashback to his childhood, when he used to listen to an old man in the Casbah tell stories about his own boyhood. Thus memories are embedded within memories in a flashback that is again described in cinematic terms: "The picture faded, as if the reel had come to an end, and Sam was back in the present.... The magic of that day was gone forever" (459).

Sam encounters these memories while walking through his old neighborhood, from which all the Indian inhabitants had been removed years before but which was never developed for white occupation:

> Sam had the eerie sensation that he was the sole survivor of some monumental upheaval that had wiped out every other living being.... He took a few hesitant steps back in the direction he had driven up from, and was attracted towards what seemed to be a black spot considerably darker than its surroundings. As he drew closer a vague shape rose before him and he suddenly stopped, rooted to the spot. He couldn't believe his eyes. There, before him, looking incongruous in the dark, was the Pather home, intact, solid and well-maintained in spite of its age. Sam was certain he was hallucinating, looking at a mirage from the past, created entirely by his imagination and his disorientated brain. He approached the structure with trepidation, expecting that at any moment his eyes would clear and all that would remain would be an empty hole before him. (461)

The present absence of the past is manifest here in almost tangible form, to the extent that Sam is unable to distinguish what he is really seeing from what his imagination and memory have constructed. The built cityscape has been bulldozed, the inscriptions of history erased, but memory resides in the place and seems to have an independent existence of its own.

These evocations are no less strong in Verbena Road, where Sam lived as a child, and which had now "simply disappeared, as surely as death obliterates life, leaving only the memories that live on in the minds of those that still remember" (462), except for a few palimpsestic traces such as the children's names etched in the concrete sidewalk. As Sam runs his fingers over the etchings, "His memories went into free-fall. In vivid detail he could see the girls in knee length blue poplin dresses and white bobbie sox" playing hopscotch: "His body responded to the thrill of recollection, involuntarily trembling as long forgotten images surged through him. . . . This was not his memory reliving the past, he was physically there with them, in form and substance" (463). This tangibly present absence, perhaps inevitably, is likened to the haunting of ghosts: Sam thinks to himself, "Too many ghosts. . . . They're still here, all my old friends. And I'm somewhere there too, caught in a time warp, forever a part of this environment" (464).

Sam goes back to Verbena Road one last time, after his brother Jake's death at the hands of the Special Branch when he is deciding the best way to respond to the state's accelerating repression and violence. He has been having nightmares, and continues to hear voices from the past. Looking perhaps for peace, perhaps for a sign, he goes back and searches for 15 Verbena Road, which he blames himself for having failed to protect from looters during the riots years earlier: "He seemed to be measuring distances with his eyes, his memory serving as a yardstick, directing him one way, then another"; while there, he "heard the voices as clear and distinct as the day on which he had first heard them" (474). When he later tells his friends about this quest, and they wonder why the whites seized the land only to let it fall into ruin, Sam answers, "the spirits wouldn't allow them to settle there" (500).

Even amid this climate of dispossession, mourning, and haunting, however, the Casbah district remains in the hands of Indian shopkeepers, and provides a stable basis for identity formation and resistance. The area is described several times over the course of its history; in the early twentieth century, for example, "The Casbah on a Saturday morning was like no city anywhere on earth" (108). The narrator sketches a map of the city spaces and the social functions they contain: "Each street served a specific function. The eastern end of Victoria Street was theatre-land, the western half reserved mainly for the markets and grocery stores. Grey Street, from the racecourse to the West End Hotel in Pine Street, was the clothes-horses' paradise" (109). Despite the drastic changes that happen over the ensuing decades, the Casbah retains its distinctive identity: "In the late forties Grey Street, and the roads bisecting it, were a miniature replica of a major city in India" (168), and the Casbah "was inhabited almost exclusively by Indians, with a fair sprinkling of coloureds" (169). Though the streets of the Casbah become plagued by crime and ruled by gangs, it remains a kind of haven for those who belong to it. When Sam decides to walk away from his brother's gang, Jake's friend Sandy approves but warns him, "When you belong to it the street is your best friend. It's a cocoon that's safer than a mother's womb. Walk away and it's your greatest enemy" (223).

The Casbah can thus be read as one of the interstitial zones within which Nuttall claims that creolized identities are forged, and within which a politics of resistance is galvanized ("City Forms" 734). When Fatima Meer and Dr. Goonum begin making speeches and organizing a Passive Resistance Campaign in the district, Grey Street and the neighboring roads "became the focal point of the resistance movement" (95). Life in the Casbah, the narrator tells us, "was about politics too. Children were weaned on it. . . . There was no other area of under a square mile that could equal it for the intensity of its emotions and its pursuit of justice" (109). Though infiltrated regularly by spies for the state, the Casbah exists partly outside that state's mechanisms of surveillance and control: Jake tells his brother,

> The Casbah is another world, Sam. Another country. When you know your way around an army of cops wouldn't find you. You could disappear for weeks, move around freely. And don't ever think this is the only such place. You can lose yourself just as easily in the Dutchene or May Street or in any of a dozen other mini Casbahs. (193)

Later Jake abandons passive resistance and becomes the pimpernel freedom fighter known as *Aza Kwela*, "the man who dances in and out of the Security Branch's clutches with impunity" (163). As with so many post-apartheid urban characters, Jake is possessed by a peripatetic restlessness: He "never stopped in one place for long. He seemed to be restless, on the move all the time, constantly alert" (184). For him, the in-between spaces in the heart of the city become the base for his resistance campaign; for instance, he prepares for a bombing in the post office by disguising himself as a beggar and retreating to an abandoned railway station nearby. Indistinguishable from the down-and-outers who inhabit this space, Jake is virtually invisible to the hordes of policemen guarding the post office—a fact he uses to his advantage. This invisibility is a recurring theme in the novel, as a number of Indian and coloured waiters, servants, and clerks in white establishments act as moles, feeding information to the resistance movement. Nits thinks to himself that for whites, Indians hardly exist, so the Indians make no effort to hide their machinations from their employers and other whites: "And because they don't see us they fail to realise how much we observe and how perspicacious we are" (357). Thus the families are able to find chinks even in the armor of the Security Branch (SB), whose members Nits claims are "unapproachable. They move in a closed circle" (280). Yet the families are able to communicate with Jake's wife Hannah even in SB custody through a coloured prison cook, named Mousey, who declares "We all darkies here.... United we stand, *ou pa*. Divided we still don't fall" (284).

Indeed, the primary mode of resistance operative in the novel takes advantage of the porosity of the boundaries constructed by the state and engages in transgressive border-crossings. Jammu, whose activities in the early twentieth century prefigure Jake's guerilla campaign, had escaped from one of the sugar plantations, but "I have slipped in and out of there often since then" (65) stirring up insurrection. Similarly, Fatima Meer tells a group of Indian women that it is time to leave the talking to their men: "Now we take our bodies to where our mouths haven't reached.... Into the white enclaves" such as public parks (97). In a system in which space is constructed so as to control the movements of bodies, those bodies become the instruments of resistance simply by moving outside the designated zones. The role of Indian women in the multiplicity of resistance movements is the sort of history whose fragments the novel is devoted to excavating. At one gathering of women in the Casbah, Zainub Asvat tells them "in the final reckoning you, each of you, is the real decision maker in your homes" (90), and indeed Sam is continually amazed at how much the women in his and Karan Naran's family accomplish by working subtly behind the scenes.

Finally, grudgingly, along with many of his characters, Hassim's novel concludes that passive resistance was no longer adequate by the mid-1980s to counter the multitude of injustices inflicted by the apartheid state. Karan tells Sam that "this new State of Emergency [in 1985–86] is different from anything we've been through before.... They can lock anyone up, without access to legal representation.... Even the newspapers aren't allowed to publish any such detentions" (32). Even as a young man Jake rejects the philosophy of nonviolence, insisting that while "[y]ou cannot fight evil with evil" you can "fight it with justice" (84). *The Lotus People* ends ambiguously, with all four friends undecided about joining the ANC and taking up armed resistance. But the trajectory of the novel suggests an inevitability to their plight: even if they choose to remain passive, their much more militant children have already committed themselves to the struggle, and the parents find it impossible to condemn their children's militancy.

Moreover, of course, the novel was written in the post-apartheid era, when the outcome of their struggle was already known. In that light, the novel should be read as an assertion of the Indian community's belonging to the new dispensation; as Sam tells his friend, "we know no other country, Karan. Like the Afrikaner and the Coloured, we are here to stay" (42). Hassim suggests that it is in the Casbah, which resisted all the state's efforts to fragment and break the will of the Indian community, that the traces of the past are inscribed for that community—and it is out of the ruins of that past that the future can grow.

Conclusion

One goal that some artists have in common with many city planners and architects is a desire to transform the way social and urban spaces are used and perceived, while preserving and making visible the palimpsestic traces of history. This goal is perhaps easier in the Casbah district of Durban than in many other places, as the area's long status as a bastion of the Indian community survived the siege of apartheid relatively unscathed and continues to be a thriving commercial and residential district. But even the Casbah's distinctive "Afrindian" identity[37] will face pressure in the coming years under the homogenizing forces of globalization and Americanization (as well as African nationalism that sometimes appears to be maneuvering to cut Indians and coloureds out of power just as Afrikaner nationalism had done before it).

In other parts of Durban, and in Johannesburg, Cape Town, Pretoria/Tshwane, and Port Elizabeth, the amnesiac forces of globalization and rapid change threaten to altogether overwhelm any effort at commemorating or elegizing the ancient or even immediate past. Older methods of archiving and mapping no longer serve, so these post-apartheid novelists have formulated their own tropes and models for reading the palimpsests of urban space: Vladislavić's exploded view; the narrative archiving and mapping of Dangor, Mpe, and Duiker; the excavation of layers of history in Hassim. This later trope links *The Lotus People* to the novels I discuss in part 3, in which digging holes and unearthing the past are central motifs. And while these texts reveal the impossibility of a fixed and totalizing map, and thus the inadequacy of any given representational method, taken as a whole the texts show us a breathtakingly complex portrait of the contemporary South African metropolis and a provisional set of coordinates for mapping its histories.

Part 3

Excavations and the Memory of Landscapes

Introduction

In March of 1997, six formers members of the security police applied for amnesty for the murder of, among others, Phila Portia Ndwandwe—who became "the most senior woman commander ever of Umkhonto we Sizwe" (Du Preez 203). She had been kidnapped in October 1988 from Swaziland with the help of two former comrades-turned-*askaris* (police collaborators); the security police had hoped to turn Ndwandwe herself into an *askari*, but in the words of one of her captors, "She was brave this one, hell she was brave.... She simply would not talk" (Krog, *Country* 128). She was killed and buried on Elandskop dairy farm near Pietermaritzburg in KwaZulu-Natal, where nine years later the amnesty applicants would lead investigators to her remains. The TRC Report quotes Commissioner Richard Lyster's description of her death and exhumation:

> She was held in a small concrete chamber on the edge of the small forest in which she was buried. According to information from those that killed her, she was held naked and interrogated in this chamber, for some time before her death. When we exhumed her, she was on her back in a foetal position, because the grave had not been dug long enough, and had a single bullet wound to the top of her head, indicating that she had been kneeling or squatting when she was killed. Her pelvis was clothed in a plastic packet, fashioned into a pair of panties indicating an attempt to protect her modesty. (Truth and Reconciliation Commission II: 543)

Ndwandwe's was the first of at least fifty bodies to be exhumed by the Commission during its operations; two other bodies would later be found at the same farm. Thus began a series of exhumations that the architects of the TRC never foresaw, but which would become emblematic of the entire Truth Commission enterprise.

Reading the Final Report's findings on the dozens of exhumations carried out by the Commission gives the sense of a rural landscape full of mysteries waiting to be excavated. Gail Reagon captures this in her report on Ndwandwe's funeral on SABC-TV's *Special Report*: "The rich soil is turned endlessly. But the furious digging and scooping, digging and scooping, is not to prepare the land for harvest; it is to unearth some of the secrets of the past: bodies—skeletal remains—of ANC activists thought to have disappeared, now known to have been killed and buried on South Africa's death farms" (Episode 45). The ways in which Ndwandwe's death and exhumation have been memorialized also suggest that the trauma of her murder lingers on the landscape like the half-erased inscriptions on a palimpsest. Most notably, a triptych commemorating Ndwandwe's sacrifice hangs in the Constitutional Court building in Johannesburg; it is entitled *The Man Who Sang and the Woman Who Kept Silent* by artist Judith Mason. The centerpiece is sculpture in the form of a dress made of plastic bags (figure 3.1), which recalls the plastic bag out of which Ndwandwe fashioned her makeshift panties. On either side are paintings of the same blue dress (figure 3.2). An accompanying placard reads: "Memorials to your courage are everywhere. They blow about in the streets and drift on the tide and cling to thornbushes. This dress is made of some of them."

The sense of a rural landscape haunted by the past that lies interred in its earth pervades many of the works of South African literature written since the Truth Commission, and especially the novels by Anne Landsman, Zoë Wicomb, and Zakes Mda that I consider in part 3. My title for this part contains a deliberate and productive ambiguity: I use the phrase "memory of landscapes" throughout my discussion of these novels to refer to the memories that people have of particular places, but also to the memories that seem to inhabit a particular landscape itself. Several themes and implications emerge from studying this phenomenon of the memory of landscapes. Excavations, holes, caves, and wounds become multilayered tropes for the ways in which loss and traumatic memory are registered in social consciousness: obliquely, partially, and through absence and silence as much as utterance and sign.

Yet the "excavations" (literal and figurative) carried out in these texts are often ambiguous and indeterminate. This is equally true of the TRC's exhumation project: in Ndwandwe's case, her family was able to learn of her fate after a decade of agonizing uncertainty about

Figure 3.1 Judith Mason, *The Man Who Sang and the Woman Who Kept Silent* (sculpture from triptych—central panel), 1998; mixed media; collection: Constitutional Court (photo credit: Bob Cnoops).

Figure 3.2 Judith Mason, *The Man Who Sang and the Woman Who Kept Silent* (painting from triptych—left panel), 1998; oil on board; collection: Constitutional Court (photo credit: Bob Cnoops).

her whereabouts; but for every mystery that the Commission solved, it raised new ones and left many others clouded in doubt.[1] Similarly, the excavations we see in the novels by Landsman, Mda, and Wicomb seldom result in unequivocal answers, even as the authors diagnose and map out the complexly intertwined operations of remembering and forgetting that characterize the post-apartheid social landscape. The narrator of Wicomb's *David's Story*, for example, describes a hole as a "thing of absence" which, once refilled, can only be detected by the "presence" of its walls (55). As all three novels make clear, the memory of landscapes and of loss is precisely such a thing of absence, knowable only through its effects and traces.

If the trope of digging and excavation is firmly established in the post-apartheid era by the TRC's project of exhumation, it is especially significant that the first body uncovered by the Commission was that of a woman freedom fighter. In many ways, Phila Ndwandwe could have been a model for the character Dulcie Oliphant in Wicomb's *David's Story*. She became the commander of Umkhonto we Sizwe's Natal Operations, the highest appointment ever achieved by a woman in the ANC. Her former senior officer during her guerrilla training in Angola, who later became the father of her son, says that Ndwandwe, like Dulcie, "never acted like a woman, she did everything the men did.... She was seen as a tomboy" (Du Preez 203). But the fact that her captors kept her naked must have made the pretense of masculinity impossible to maintain, a fact that gives the pathetic power of the plastic-bag panties such force. Indeed, it is Ndwandwe's femaleness that post-TRC representations of her murder tend to emphasize—Max du Preez, for example, titles his chapter about Ndwandwe "The Breastfeeding Warrior."

To the extent that Ndwandwe became a symbol of the TRC's larger project of "excavating" the past, then, her case shows the gendered dimensions of that project. More specifically, her case reveals the ways in which the past is often "mapped," and conceptions of the nation are often constructed, around women's bodies, as Meg Samuelson has convincingly argued (*Remembering*). Blunt and Rose point out that "[r]epresentations of women and landscapes as sites of colonization were often codified through mapping.... Theoretical parallels can be drawn between the disciplinary power and surveillance imposed on landscapes by mapping and imposed on the body by, for example, discourses of medicine and sexuality" (10). In the novels by Landsman, Wicomb, and Mda, the land and landscape take on a rich, multifaceted, almost mythical status: the land is the site in which social memory and cultural identity are invested, and also the site of struggle over fundamental questions of nationalism, equality, dignity, and justice. This struggle both resembles and occasionally intersects with the continual battle fought over the "terrain" of women's bodies. As Sarah Nuttall says of two other South African novels from the transitional period, such texts "address the political and gendered myth-making to which the land has been subjected, showing it to be caught in a set of contemporary white, and largely male, fantasies" ("Flatness" 219).

These novels not only lay bare the processes by which the land has historically been subjected to colonizing technologies such as surveying, mapping, and translation; they go further, to engage in what Catherine Nash has called "remapping," seeking out alternative modes of living with the landscape and the histories that have been inscribed thereon.[2] Mda's *The Heart of Redness* grapples with this issue most specifically through one of the most fraught problems facing South Africa in the twenty-first century: the "Land Question." Decades of apartheid and segregationist policies, including forced removals and the creation of the Bantustans, led to devastating poverty and lack of development in the rural areas, and a housing shortage in the urban and peri-urban areas that continues to grow more severe with each passing year.[3] Apartheid policy also created an extreme, racialized inequity in landownership, with almost 90 percent of the land owned by white individuals and enterprises ("Land Ownership").[4] Given the strong attachment many Africans feel toward the land, and the connection it provides to the ancestors, such a massive loss of landownership must surely be accompanied by a collectively shared sense of mourning. Yet, as David Johnson has argued, the struggle for land restitution "discloses a hierarchy of loss in which mourning the loss of loved ones (managed in South Africa by the Truth and Reconciliation Commission) takes precedence over the loss of land (managed by the Land Commission)" (278). This hierarchy has persisted despite evidence that, at least for the Griqua, "the major concern is material loss," not personal loss (293).

If Johnson is right that the loss of land leads to a form of mourning in relation to which "Marx's ideas on land . . . appear more suggestive than Freud's on personal loss" (293), then clearly the symbolic reparations and expressions of condolence that Mark Sanders applauds as a success of the TRC must be accompanied by material compensation and land redistribution.[5] Yet the baleful legacy of dispossession and of domination through control of the land also requires more than the complicated land redistribution and agricultural reform that has slowly taken shape in the post-apartheid years; what is called for is a fundamental rethinking of the relationships of people to land and space.[6] In other words, part of the process of "remapping" the landscape entails a subversion of the gendered codes that make possible these spatial regimes of social control in the first place. Post-apartheid literature has already made its own modest and often indirect contributions to this process; in *The Devil's Chimney*, for example, Beatrice Chapman's attempts to free herself of her husband's domination coincide and overlap with her efforts to become that unheard-of thing, a successful woman ostrich farmer.[7] Moreover, like Wicomb in *David's Story*, Landsman puts active women characters at the center of the history of the land, thus countering the nationalist mythologies that paint men as conquering and ruling over a passive, feminized landscape.

The process of remapping the land and reclaiming lost narratives of the past, these writers teach us, opens up opportunities to create a system in which people have a degree of control over their own social space. Marinda

Weideman's complaint about land reform in South Africa is that "the poorest and most marginalized sectors of South African society were not part of the policy development process" (219).[8] In other words, the demand for autonomy on the part of South Africa's poor has been addressed in only the most nominal and superficial way by the architects of land reform. Weideman's diagnosis correlates quite comfortably with Mda's implicit prescription for a rural development policy in South Africa that would prioritize the autonomy of the poor.

Another theme related to the loss of land that arises in studying these works is that the land is deeply and intimately connected to the human body, and that the memory of landscapes can behave much like bodily traumatic memory: the trauma is paradoxically both inscribed on and perceived as external to the body/land, and the memories generated by the inscription are involuntary, arising in the survivor almost like a demonic possession. A corollary of this observation is that these novelists more or less overtly reject the amnesiac impulses characterizing the post-apartheid era, because a willful amnesia cannot bring about the desired numbness to painful memories if those memories stubbornly insist on haunting and possessing the survivor. Given this inevitable and involuntary recurrence of memory, these writers suggest, it is better to work through memory in a conscious, productive manner—even if, as Wicomb's work implies, putting the pieces of the past together can sometimes get you killed.

The question that *David's Story* leaves unanswered is "killed by whom?" Was the character Dulcie Olifant assassinated by agents of the former apartheid government, or by her own comrades? This emphasis on the anti-apartheid resistance movements' own crimes during the struggle, and on the growing venality and nepotism of some factions of the new ruling party, marks a distinct shift from South African literature of the 1970s and 1980s, which was typically strident in its condemnation of white minority rule and open in its admiration of the resistance movements. Notwithstanding the fact that the ANC was more transparent than any other political body in South Africa in investigating human rights violations in its own ranks and in presenting its findings to the TRC, it is easy to understand why the party's leaders would wish to repress from the nation's collective consciousness the memories, for example, of torture in the Quatro Camp run by Umkhonto we Sizwe (MK—the armed wing of the ANC) in Angola—where many cadres such as Phila Ndwandwe received their guerrilla training. Yet Wicomb, and less directly Mda, refuse this convenient public amnesia and shine a light instead on the struggle's own occasionally ugly history.

Another reason these writers reject the amnesiac option, I believe, is that they recognize on some level that to forget the past runs counter to the crucial project of reclaiming and redistributing land, and to the still more fundamental project of rethinking socio-spatial relationships. Even the least explicitly political book of the trio, *The Devil's Chimney*, points out the need for a kind of "remapping" of the land and its social history. In those forgotten histories of the pre-apartheid and even precolonial past lie immense possibilities for rethinking relationships between races and genders, between public and private, and between present and past—possibilities heretofore obscured and buried by apartheid's spatial engineering and historical revisionism. All three writers look for these forgotten possibilities in the stories and lives of women: Wicomb's characters hunt for evidence of inclusive, nonethnic nationalist thought in the writings and speeches of historical figure Andrew le Fleur; and Mda and Landsman both suggest that traditional African beliefs can help provide new spatial coordinates and modes of mapping post-apartheid social geographies.

3.1 A Map of Echoes: Anne Landsman's *The Devil's Chimney*

"Ever since Pauline Cupido's disappearance during the Christmas holidays in 1955, I have been trying to remember things" (Landsman 1). This opening sentence of Anne Landsman's[9] *The Devil's Chimney* instantly raises many of the motifs that recur so insistently in South African literature after the TRC—memory and forgetting, loss, hauntings, and present absences. Pauline, we learn, got lost on a tour of the Cango Caves in the Great Karoo, and was never found again. Thus the Caves, where many of the novel's key events take place, come to represent the repressed traces of trauma and loss, lying just beneath the surface of the landscape and yet apparently non-recuperable.

The Devil's Chimney, however, is not about Pauline Cupidos, but rather about two other women who occupy the farm above the Caves at two different times, decades apart. In the novel's narrative present of the mid-1990s, at the beginning of the TRC proceedings, we meet the narrator: Connie, an aging white alcoholic still mourning the death of her infant child years before. Connie is trapped in an emotionally abusive but codependent relationship with her husband Jack; she lives in a state of perpetual neurotic meltdown, drinking gin, methylated spirits, or even mouthwash to distract her from her many phobias. More deeply, the novel itself might best be described as an exercise in displacement and denial of the memory of her son's death from heart problems, no doubt brought on by her heavy drinking during pregnancy.

The second woman is Beatrice Chapman, an invented-historical figure who is the subject of Connie's story-within-the-story, and onto whom Connie maps (figuratively speaking, through her narrative) her own repressed fears and desires. Miss Beatrice, as Connie always refers to her, was an English woman who immigrated to the Cape with her husband Henry and bought the farm above the Cango Caves in 1910. This is a significant date, as it marks the formation of the Union of South Africa as a self-governing entity after eight years of restive occupation by the British armed forces following the Anglo-Boer War's conclusion. Those first two decades of the twentieth century were a period of transition and reconciliation between bitter enemies; they contain great resonance for the closing decade of the century as well—another period of rapid and unpredictable social transformation.[10]

Connie, though, is only dimly aware of political happenings, either in her own time or in the Union of Beatrice's day. Consequently, any conclusions drawn about the significance of the two parallel historical periods must be based on inference and speculation. Connie's preoccupations, instead, are with the personal: the efforts of Miss Beatrice to succeed in the ostrich farming business despite her husband's increasingly debilitating mental illness (and, for several months, his disappearance); Beatrice's passionate affairs with her neighbor, the "Ostrich King" Mr. Jacobs, and with her coloured servants Nomsa and September; and with Beatrice's pregnancy, after which she loses her baby in the Cango Caves. In recounting the story of Miss Beatrice (sometimes to her deaf sister Gerda), and in visiting the Oudtshoorn Museum, where many of Beatrice's possessions now lie, Connie attempts to map her own relationship with the present through a past that has been both inscribed upon and erased from the landscape. I intend the term "mapping" here to refer to Connie's negotiations both of the literal, physical Karoo landscape and of the figurative landscape of shared or social memory.

Indeed, land and the landscape are crucial motifs throughout the book. Connie tells us that Miss Beatrice's farm "was so big you could get lost on it" (53), and Beatrice herself becomes a cipher for loss/being lost and forgetting/being forgotten: Connie believes "people just don't want to know about [Beatrice] which is why there's that big sandstone wall around her house" at Highland (46). For Connie, the figure of Miss Beatrice offers the chance to project onto someone else her own anxieties about feeling trapped and confined, and to play out her own wish-fulfillment fantasies about escaping and taking flight. Thus, in one interlude, the wall around Beatrice's old house reminds Connie of when her own mother took her, aged seven, and Gerda, aged nine, to a prison "where bad people were" (48) to frighten her as punishment for having run away.

Significantly, this memory, which might go some way toward explaining Connie's claustrophobia and other neurotic behaviors, is immediately followed by a section break, then by an observation about ostriches, the famously neurotic birds that often run themselves to death after a fright: "The first thing you have to learn with ostriches is patience. You can't force them to do anything because they will run away or hurt themselves" (48). Juxtapositions such as this one thus establish symbolic parallels between the female protagonists and the ostriches, parallels that run deeper than just the imagery of confinement and flight. The comparison is spelled out blatantly in Chapter Two:

> [Beatrice] can see the ostriches in the *kraal*, the black and white plumes of the males, the brown-grey feathers of the females. She knows that she is the female ostrich, dressed in the colours of the earth, set here, on this piece of land, to belong. In a split-second, everything is different. She cannot live here with Henry. She no longer wants to lick that envelope like a good girl. She will not go back to England. This land is hers. She is the Queen Bee. (32)

Perhaps what makes the ostrich curiously appropriate as a figure of loss, as well as a symbolic parallel to Connie and Beatrice, is its status as a flightless bird. This point comes into focus through the Khoi folktale told to Beatrice by her farmhand September of why the ostrich does not fly: The Mantis tricked Ostrich into flying to the upper reaches of a tree and dropping the fire he kept safe under his wings: "The Mantis grabbed his fire and ran away. Now the Ostrich always keeps his wings close to him in case the fire falls out again. He doesn't flap his wings and fly" (66).[11] The Mantis is the trickster-god of the Khoi peoples, but the Ostrich seems to stand in for the people themselves, wary and suspicious after a long history of being deceived and exploited. The ostrich's nervousness makes it an appropriate figure for Connie's narrative consciousness, as well; so does the ostrich's reputation for burying its head in the sand, which symbolizes Connie's state of denial about her lost baby.

If ostriches become central figures of loss and helplessness in the novel, the Cango Caves operate as an even more transparent symbol of psychological loss and absence. The land under which the Caves lie is already curiously, stubbornly resistant to registering the history that passes over it. Perhaps because of the vastness of the place and the difficulty of mapping it, the descendents of the *Voortrekkers* and subsequent immigrants have long attempted to survey, fence, and police the land, but largely in vain. Connie describes her region, the enormous semidesert of the Great Karoo, as "bigger and emptier and harder than most places.... It's where the Voortrekkers fought with the Natives, where they drew up their *laagers* and loaded their shotguns" (28). Yet, already by the time Henry and Beatrice arrive in the Cape, "the Voortrekkers were gone. They had been gone since the Great Trek and that was a long time ago" (27).

Beneath the surface of this landscape, one finds, not depth or signification, but rather a vast blankness. Mr. Jacobs complains, "[S]ome of his land didn't count because it was just air and big holes and animals could fall in it" (45). Yet the empty space of a cave seems to invite imaginative investments of loss and desire. After Pauline Cupidos's disappearance, the coloured tour guides refuse to go anywhere near the cave called the "Devil's Chimney" (1). Regarding the money from a race organized by Henry Chapman that went missing, Connie speculates that "[m]aybe somebody *skopped* it into a hole by mistake and the hole was part of the Cango Caves and now that money is sitting somewhere turning into a stalagmite" (24).

Frequently, too, the Caves are the sites of literal loss: of life, or of loved ones. Most crucially—a fact that the narrative circles around reluctantly until nearly the end—Miss Beatrice wanders into the Caves with her newborn daughter Precious, and mislays the baby inside, where she is found and rescued/kidnapped by Beatrice's former servant Nomsa. The same section of the Cave is the site of one of Beatrice and Mr. Jacobs's first sexual encounters, and is also the site of a mudfall that killed eight people in 1870: "They got in but they couldn't get out. The saddest part was a tiny picture on the bottom of the rock of two women with babies in their stomachs" (137). This image resonates powerfully with Connie, whose own baby is buried in the backyard, but who does not know the infant's sex, because "sometimes the less you know the better" (13).

The comparison of the Cango Caves to a woman's womb is inevitable, and Connie's narrative indeed draws the parallels between the land and human bodies extensively throughout the novel.[12] One implication of the two material artifacts—land and body—being symbolically linked in such an explicit way is that the memory of landscapes operates very much like bodily memory[13]: involuntary and fragmentary, and composed largely of blind spots, ruptures, and present absences. In this regard, the memory of landscapes is a kind of traumatic memory—a memory made up of *wounds* and holes, and a trauma born sometimes as much out of love as out of violence. For instance, Connie says that Miss Beatrice's reaction to Mr. Jacobs leaving her was like when "[y]our body loses a wing or a shoulder. There's a big piece missing where that other person used to be" (74).[14] Connie uses similar language in the novel's final chapter to describe Beatrice—her daughter missing, September murdered and the other servants having abandoned her, the ostriches mostly dead due to Henry's greedy overplucking, and Henry himself killed by one of the remaining ostriches: "When something dies there is a hole, like a shadow, that stays behind. That's what Miss Beatrice was crying for as she rode. All the gaps and holes where people or *goggas* [insects] or ostriches used to be. You can't fill them in. They're just gone forever and ever, no matter what the ministers say" (264).

The Cango Caves, then, are vivid embodiments of the kind of loss or absence best described as a *hole* or *wound*, and those are indeed common tropes throughout the novel more generally. One of the more puzzling examples involves a hole that Beatrice had dug in the middle of the house during Henry's long, unexplained absence, intending it to be a fountain. Unfortunately, though, ostriches and other animals kept falling into the hole and drowning: "It was like a floating cemetery for the animals and birds that strolled in and out of the house.... So she filled up the hole with cement and that was the end of that" (76). But that is not the end—the hole in the center of the house is mentioned again and again, as are various other kinds of graves and cemeteries. For example, after Henry kills September, Beatrice dreams that "she watched September dig a deep hole in the ground.... Then he put her in the hole with him and the earth all around them was damp" (198–99). The womb-like earth, then, is neither warm nor comforting in Landsman's novel, but is rather a source of claustrophobia and panic—somewhat like a common symptom of post-traumatic stress.

Figurative holes recur throughout the novel as well; indeed, perhaps the best way to think about the novel's representation of memory is to think of ghosts and hauntings as holes in particular times and places. Drunk with Jack on methylated spirits on Christmas Eve, Connie writes: "The baby's ghost lies between [Jack and me] like the ghost of baby Jesus except Jesus is alive after so many years and our baby is dead" (199). Similarly, even the grotesquely self-absorbed Henry is able to feel a tangibly present absence on the farm after he murders September. With Nomsa and the other servants missing the next morning, "The kitchen was empty, and felt like a ruin or an old cave" (200); Henry is reluctant to enter the sorting shed where he broke September's neck, because "[e]ven if the body was gone, it would always be there" (201). Inside the shed itself, "it felt as if something had been stolen. As if there was a hole in the air where something used to be" (202).

Holes and caves are only the most poignant set of tropes for loss and amnesia in the novel; indeed, it would be no exaggeration to claim that *Devil's Chimney* is a book *about* forgetting. As Connie tells us, Beatrice realizes she is pregnant, then forgets again; Connie asks herself, "How much can one person forget? Ma told me she forgot when I was born. Was it night or day, I wanted to know. I forget, she said. It could have been either" (98). Sometimes amnesia is a state that Connie actively endorses and seeks: when Gerda, inspired by an article in the paper about the Truth Commission, prods her to tell the truth about her baby's death,[15] Connie rejects the idea: "I want to tell the truth, [Gerda] says, and it sounds like the worst thing I have ever heard. *Ag* no, man, I say, let bygones be bygones. *Moenie ou koeie uit die sloot grawe.* Don't dig old cows out of the grave" (248). Being linked so explicitly to the TRC, this translation of the graphic Afrikaans expression suggests that any attempt to "excavate" the past will be a disturbing and messy process, one best not ventured in the first place.

Yet the messy, violent, wounded past has a way of coming to the surface of its own accord, and even Connie's binge drinking gives her only the most unsatisfying sort of oblivion: "How do you forget when something terrible happens like my baby with a leaking heart? I drink and it goes away but the next morning it's all back, and I have to start all over again. And each forgetting with the bottle is different" (252). Forgetting, as Connie relates it, can be as painful as remembering, and never lasts long. So in addition to drinking away the memory of her loss, she also *displaces* her own grief through the narrative of Beatrice, who becomes a paradoxical figure of both remembrance and amnesia. On the one hand, there is the wall of forgetting around her home, which "sprang up in front of the house at Highlands after the New Year [of 1915]. Who put it up nobody knew" (267). But on the other hand, artifacts of Beatrice's life are preserved and put on display in the Oudtshoorn Museum: a green dress, a railway ticket, ostrich feathers—most of which make it into Connie's imagined reconstruction of Beatrice's life story.

Of course (as we have seen in several post-apartheid texts), museums, monuments, and archives are often spaces of consignment to oblivion rather than a means of keeping aspects of the past alive in present consciousness. Certainly that is true in the dusty old Oudtshoorn Museum, which is frequently closed and usually empty. Moreover, once Connie has exited the museum, it immediately seems dreamlike and unreal in her memory: "The old man is locking the door behind us and I'm wondering if we were in the *blerrie* Museum at all" (84). Similarly, Connie wonders whether an "old green frock" (110) on display really belonged to Beatrice. Her description of the exhibits also emphasizes their sterility: "The program [for a Sarah Bernhardt show the Jacobs had seen in America] is also at the Museum, laying in the glass case, right next to the umbrella" (112). Significantly, it is the belongings of the Chapmans and the Jacobs that end up in the Museum: the English couple and the Jewish family, tolerated but mistrusted outsiders in the Afrikaans-dominated Great Karoo. In this regard, the Museum might function much like the wall erected around Beatrice's house—both structures allow the community as a whole to set aside and forget a part of the town's history. Note that both methods of consigning the past to a neutralized "history" involve a spatial containment through the built structures of the wall and the Museum building.

This strategy of containing or repressing painful or incongruous narratives from the larger social or communal memory have grave consequences, not only for one's understanding of history but also for finding one's way through the contemporary world. Recall that Jameson considers the "weakening of historicity" to be a cultural expression of the depthlessness and disorientation characterizing late capitalism. Such disorientation is readily apparent in Connie's narrative, and can be accounted for only partly by her drinking, as when she says "I am sorry I was born too late. I wish I could have seen what it was like [in Beatrice's time]. The world is so far away now. You can only see it in magazines" (81).

The absolute disconnect from both past and present also makes possible the common refrain among white South Africans that they had no idea the old Nationalist government was committing such terrible crimes. For instance, at the end of the novel, Connie tell us: "I saw all those Bantu people on the TV standing in long lines to vote and then I saw a film on the TV about Robben Island, where they tortured people and of course we didn't know anything" (275). The disclaimer at the end feels rote and empty, like a phrase often repeated but rarely interrogated. For Connie, the "great miracle" of South Africa's political transformation is a distant spectacle seen on the television screen, not too different from the objects placed under glass at the Museum. Yet her use of the antiquated and somewhat offensive term "Bantu" for black Africans makes it seem like *she* is the museum piece, a forgotten relic of the bygone age.

Ironically, though, what saves Beatrice—what reanimates her from the limbo of musealization—is Connie's own narrative imagination. As Connie declares from the outset, "Miss Beatrice. This is her story and I have to do all the parts myself" (15). What her story does, in effect, is to lift Beatrice out of the mausoleum-like confines of the Oudsthoorn Museum, and to align her, on the one hand, with the rhizomic labyrinths of the Cango Caves, and, on the other hand, with the skittish, fleet-footed, and difficult-to-corral ostrich. In the process, Connie is grasping for alternative modes of mapping and traversing space, and is ironically (given her amnesiac tendencies noted earlier) using the past for her compass. As Wendy Woodward notes, "[S]ome potential for transformation exists in Connie's narrative which contradicts linear time and locatable space, is episodic and slips between the different eras of Connie's present, in the 1990s, as well as into her past, in the 1950s, and Miss Beatrice's past in 1910. What gradually develops through the narratives is Connie's strong connections with narratives of other women" ("Beyond Fixed Geographies" 27).

Unfortunately, though, these attempts at mapping the present through landscapes past and present largely fail so long as Beatrice remains the center of the novel's imaginary cartographies. In fact, it is only very late in the book, when the 1914 story's narrative consciousness shifts from Beatrice to Nomsa (Beatrice's servant and September's spouse), that Landsman begins to hint at how a society devastated by loss might begin to recover its bearings. It is difficult to know what to make of Landsman's representation of Nomsa; for much of the story she is part handmaid, part midwife, and part *sangoma* or traditional healer. Through Beatrice's eyes and Connie's imagination, she is thus an exotic figure of power and mystery. But Nomsa is also shown to have an almost instinctive capacity for finding her way through the baffling terrain of Karoo and caverns. This is especially true when Miss Beatrice loses Precious in the Cango Caves: "The cry came back right next to [Beatrice]. She grabbed into the air and all she got in her arms was a big empty echo" (241). By contrast with Beatrice's helpless paralysis, Nomsa is compared to "the bat. She was clicking her way to the child, *following the map of her echoes*" (241; emphasis added).

To attribute animal features to an African woman is of course to flirt with a most base form of racist stereotype. This risk is compounded by Connie's initial depiction of Nomsa as almost a dark witch who steals Beatrice's child—though by then we know that Precious is also September's child, and in a strange sense Nomsa's as well. At the end, however, a curious shift occurs, and we see the same scene replayed from Nomsa's perspective. Suddenly she seems like the protective, maternal figure shielding Precious from the biological mother's sickness: "Nomsa wasn't sure if Miss Beatrice was dead or a ghost or the sister of a *tokolosh* [a goblin or mischievous demon]. All she knew was that she must get this child away from her, from those clutching hands and that chicken head" (269). Connie even seems eager to buy into a rumor "that what really happened to Pauline [Cupidos] was that she wasn't really Pauline, she was Precious, the child raised by [Nomsa's grandmother] *Ouma* on the farm outside Meiringspoort" (274).

Connie might simply be engaging in a wish-fulfillment fantasy, projecting a happy ending as a means of taking control over her own grieving; indeed, she sounds a bit desperate when she insists that "Precious did live, not like my poor baby" (274).[16] Certainly Landsman's last paragraph, in which Connie decides she wants to move to the coast and learn to swim despite her phobia of the sea, is too trite to be considered a serious engagement with the deep crisis of memory and forgetting that the novel renders so powerfully. But where the novel offers real hope and insight is in its narrative shift that begins to acknowledge Nomsa's and September's central roles in this tale. It is a shift beyond the perspective of the white immigrant landowner to an understanding that when Nomsa fights for Precious, "the anger inside her wasn't just Precious. It was all her children who she had left and lost, and all the white noses and bums she had wiped, long lines of them" (242). If Beatrice is in some sense an icon for white women who have lost children, farms, or lovers, then Nomsa comes to represent the loss of an entire country's dignity and self-determination, but she is also the embodiment of "an old order from before" (243).

Landsman, by shifting to Nomsa's perspective at the end, is showing us her ideal of the post-apartheid white South African. Such a figure would embrace both the new order of integrated democracy, and certain aspects of the "old order" from before the days of apartheid and colonial domination. If Beatrice does not quite live up to this ideal, in choosing to ally herself with Africa she at least provides a sharp contrast to Henry, who longs for England and hates the African soil: "It was hard getting him into the Karoo ground... because people said he didn't want to be buried there and his soul was making the spades buckle and the *volkies* who were digging the grave fall down" (265). *The Devil's Chimney* is full of solipsistic characters very much mired in their own internal, isolated worlds; Henry is the worst in this regard, in that he stubbornly remains fixated on his own fantasy of returning to England even after death. The first step toward remapping socio-spatial relations in South Africa, Landsman suggests, is to eradicate this attitude that fetishizes a myth of Europe at the expense of a connection to the African soil.

Indeed, the characters who are able to chart a more successful course through the landscapes of memory and loss are the ones who eventually learn to see beyond their own solipsistic perspective. If white privilege breeds blindness, the antidotes are empathy and imagination, or so Landsman implies. Beatrice, for example, is described in the end as mourning more than just the loss of her baby and the death of her husband:

> That day coming back on the mare Miss Beatrice cried for everything. She cried for September who would never see Precious.... She cried for her mother who was sad when she married Mr. Henry.... She cried for the ostrich that died trying to eat a quince and she cried for the ones that danced too much and broke their legs. Then she cried for the Russian dogs and everything else she had known that had died. (263–64)

Until this point Beatrice had lacked such empathy, which is not unlike that attributed to Nomsa (242), and it is possibly this ability to project herself into other subject positions that allows Nomsa to construct her own "map of echoes" to the baby Precious. This empathy and cognizance of the external world might also explain a cryptic line in a dreamlike passage in the novel: Beatrice "found Nomsa outside, squatting on the ground. Nomsa beckoned and Miss Beatrice squatted down next to her, half falling, half laughing, her bum in the air. You must learn, Nomsa said, you must dig your own hole" (176–77). She must learn to sit like the Africans, Nomsa tells her; more broadly, she must open herself to African ways of thinking about space and time, belonging and loss; only then, the novel suggests, can Beatrice and other perceived "outsiders" in South Africa dig their own holes, make their own places, and tell their own narratives of the past.

3.2 Buried Footprints: Zoë Wicomb's *David's Story*

Like *The Devil's Chimney*, Zoë Wicomb's[17] ambitious novel *David's Story* (2000) uses a complex system of spatial-corporal-narrative mapping to lay bare the ways in which the past continues to flow into and haunt the present. And Wicomb's novel similarly follows multiple plot lines across distinct but parallel historical periods. The narrative present of the novel is 1991, in the uncertain midst of transition and negotiation; David Dirkse, an MK guerilla, is attempting to narrate to an unnamed woman amanuensis the story of the last decade of his life, a story he is loath to admit revolves around his unacknowledged, unconsummated relationship with his mysterious comrade Dulcie Olifant.

As the vague outlines of the story begin to emerge from the half- and mis-remembered fragments David can convey, we learn that Dulcie, a high-ranking officer of "coloured" descent, has most likely been forced to serve as concubine for the male troops in the field; that she was tortured in the ANC-run prison camps in Angola; that her name appeared on a hit list; and that she may in fact have been killed, though whether by right-wing forces or as a result of power plays within her own organization remains murky. These passages in the novel resonate deeply for readers of apartheid-era South African fiction, who are accustomed to accounts of police assaulting and raping detainees. In Wicomb's telling, though, we see how even within the resistance movements, power struggles play out on human bodies, and especially (as throughout history) on the bodies of coloured or Khoi-San women.

David, however, finds this traumatic history difficult to recount. He says of Dulcie that "I think of her more as a kind of... a scream somehow echoing through my story" (134). Yet paradoxically, Wicomb describes Dulcie in an interview as "the necessary silence in the text; she can't be fleshed out precisely because of her shameful treatment which those committed to the Movement would rather not talk about" (Meyer and Oliver

190–91). As the narrator notes wryly, "Dulcie has, after all, always hovered somewhere between fact and fiction" (*David's Story* 198); and David, having tried and failed to bring his story around to describing Dulcie's role in it, engages instead in what the narrator peevishly terms an "exercise in avoidance" (33). He "chose to displace her [Dulcie] by working on the historical figure of Saartje Baartman instead" (134); as Gillian Gane remarks, these are "layerings of displacement among which it is virtually impossible to find a 'real,' 'true' Dulcie" (Gane 106). David wants his narrator to begin the story with Krotoä, the Khoi woman renamed Eva by the Dutch settlers for whom she became an interpreter. The narrator refuses to incorporate this material, but she does include some of his notes on the later historical figure of Sara or Saartje Baartman, hauled around Europe on display as the "Hottentot Venus" in the early nineteenth century. Both women's stories become urtexts for the women in David's life—in other words, they are historical phantoms whose later incarnations include Dulcie, the narrator, and David's wife Sally (called "Saartje" or "Little Sara" as a child).

Later in this section I have more to say about Eva-Krotoä and Sara Baartman, as well as about the most important parallel narrative in the novel—which concerns the actions and words of Andrew Abraham Stockenstrom le Fleur, David's ancestor by an indirect route, who led the Griqua people on a series of treks in the 1910s and 1920s. The inclusion of all of these real historical figures, I argue, is one means by which Wicomb reveals how the past continues to echo in and haunt the present. But at the level of David's individual psychology, his detours into the Griqua past are indeed an "exercise in avoidance"—a way of putting off the question of what happened to Dulcie.

Before I analyze the novel's many metatextual layers, then, let me first grapple with its difficult and elliptical structure, which is itself a symptom of the untellability of David's story. David insists early and often, and the narrator tries to keep up the pretense, that her role in the telling of his story is one of neutral amanuensis, capturing the key events and putting them in a sensible order (see, e.g., the narrator's comments on pages 141, 142, 147, and 151). In fact, one of the central concerns of *David's Story* is the impossibility of telling stories about apartheid's bloody past, and the superficiality of linear telling as a mode of conveying psychological damage.

In one interview, Wicomb speculates that the nonlinearity of the narrative is characteristic of all her fiction, but that in the case of this novel in particular it is a necessary conceit given her intrinsically disruptive subject: "I do now wonder if I'm capable of writing a linear, chronological novel and perhaps it's because I'm not capable of doing it.... Because the story is by nature an incomplete story, it can't be told" (in Willemse 144). Any such narrative will have to forego an easy sense of beginning, middle, and end; the narrator pleads, "[L]et us not claim a beginning for this mixed-up tale. Beginnings are too redolent of origins, of the sweaty and negligible act of physical union which will not be tolerated on these pages" (*David's Story* 8–9). This story's endings are no more straightforward; again the narrator remarks, "Dulcie and the events surrounding her cannot be cast as story.... There is no progression in time, no beginning and no end. Only a middle that is infinitely repeated, that remains in an eternal, inescapable present" (150).

For David, then, Dulcie is a sort of ever-present haunting, and his rambling narrative tangents serve precisely to distract him from the subject of her end. David's difficulty in talking about Dulcie is best encapsulated in the "mess of scribbles" he gives his scribe at the end of the manuscript on Sara Baartman, on which Dulcie's name has been written and struck out several times, and on which he has begun the story in various places and angles on the page, "as if by not starting at the top or not following the shape of the page he could fool himself that it is not a beginning" (135). The resistance to beginnings is perhaps born out of fear of the ending; yet the ending is already foreshadowed in the specter of Dulcie's name written down and then struck out, just as it was on the hit list left mysteriously in David's hotel room in Kokstad.

David's incapacity to come to terms with Dulcie's fate likewise presents as a rupture in his ability to use language. The narrator continues her description of the scribbled mess: "Truth, I gather, is the word that cannot be written. He has changed it into the palindrome of Cape Flats speech.... TRURT... TRURT... TRURT... TRURT... the trurt in black and white... colouring the truth to say that... which cannot be said the thing of no name" (136; ellipses in the original except for the first set). David's apparent inability to write the word "truth" evokes Antjie Krog's words in *Country of My Skull* (see section 1.3): "The word 'Truth' makes me uncomfortable. The word 'Truth' still trips the tongue.... Even when I type it, it ends up as either *turth* or *trth*" (Krog, *Country* 36). The novel's oblique evocation of the TRC (never mentioned by name) suggests that Wicomb's skepticism about the supposedly panacean virtues of realist representational modes extends beyond fiction and historiography to the work of the Truth Commission and its own narratives of past trauma. Dulcie's story, in contradistinction to the TRC's conceit that "revealing is healing" (Adam and Adam 33), is "a story that cannot be told, that cannot be translated into words, into language we use for everyday matters" (*David's Story* 151).

Dulcie, in short, is an overdetermined cipher—on the one hand, the incarnation of unrepresentable trauma; on the other hand, as Wicomb puts it, "a figure who is pure body, a body that is tortured" (in Meyer and Oliver 191). Driver helps to resolve the seeming contradiction: "the notion of the unrepresentable, so fashionable a concept in postmodern and postcolonial debate, is deconstructed in Wicomb's text: it is given a historical context and a political force" (232).[18] Indeed, Dulcie is a linguistic construct or lacuna only from the point of view of the narrator, who does not remember meeting Dulcie and sees her as "surrounded by a mystique that I am determined to crush with facts:...necessary details from which to patch together a character who can be inserted at suitable points into the story" (78). David refuses to address questions about such details; the narrator therefore feels "I must put things together as best I can, invent, and hope that David's response will reveal something" (80). She even suspects that "Dulcie is a decoy. She does not exist in the real world; David has invented her in order to cover up aspects of his own story" (124).

For David, on the contrary, it is Dulcie's very realness—the materiality of her body, and the devastating violations perpetrated on it—that makes her story so essentially untellable. It is Dulcie's role as "pure body" that makes her such a powerful illustration of the spatial-material dimensions of trauma. In one passage, for instance, the narrator imagines Dulcie being visited and raped in the night by men in black balaclavas, who then proceed to treat her like a prisoner in an interrogation session. Indeed, her passivity in these scenes—for example, when the men bring a doctor to examine her—suggests that perhaps the visits are historical echoes of Dulcie's earlier trauma experienced in the ANC's Quatro Camp in Angola. The power of these scenes is in their ability to help the reader understand how profoundly Dulcie's sense of herself as an autonomous body moving freely in space has been ruptured and disoriented.

In short, then, Dulcie represents a mapping of the past—or at least the phantom traces of the past residing in what Eyerman calls "cultural trauma"—through the material body of the coloured woman, and through the echoes of the past that affect the present in very real and immediate ways. As Eyerman cautions, "Viewing memory as symbolic discourse...tends to downplay or ignore the impact of material culture on memory and identity-formation" (8). In *David's Story* Wicomb makes no such mistake; in fact, her project could fairly be described as one of generating a system of corporal mappings. In other words, it is a project of symbolically and metonymically linking physical bodies and material places with memories of the past, through the medium of the landscape on which that past has been inscribed and erased. Two such mechanisms of corporal mapping feature prominently in Wicomb's novel: scars and steatopygia.

* * *

The narrator's description of Dulcie early in the novel is noteworthy for the emphasis it gives to Dulcie's physical body, and especially the scars on her back. The image of the "criss-cross cuts on each of her naturally bolstered buttocks" (*David's Story* 19) anticipates the motif of steatopygia, and links Dulcie's body to other Khoi women with "bolstered buttocks." The scars on her back also offer a potent metaphor for understanding how struggles for power have been literally and figuratively inscribed on Dulcie's body:

> This square [of her back] is marked with four cent-sized circles forming the corners of a smaller inner square, meticulously staked out with blue ballpoint pen before the insertion of a red-hot poker between the bones. The smell of that singed flesh and bone still, on occasion, invades, and then she cannot summon it away.... One day a nice man of her own age will idly circle the dark cents with his own thumb and sigh.... Perhaps a man called David, who will say nothing and who will frown when she speaks of a woman in *Beloved* whose back is scarred and who nevertheless is able to turn it into a tree. (19)

The description of the scar as "staked out" evokes an image of land surveying, reinforcing the link between land and body. And this passage highlights the paradox of the traumatic "memory of landscapes," which is unavoidable but unconveyable: for Dulcie, the scar arouses such painful memories that she cannot "summon it away"; but for David, the scar is an inexplicable mystery, and not one that he is terribly interested in exploring.[19]

The scars, then, become an ambivalent figure for the ways that trauma is transmitted from one generation to the next. They become symbols, that is, of what E. Ann Kaplan calls "transgenerational trauma." Her discussion of Native American and African American trauma seems equally applicable to dispossessed populations in South Africa such as the Griqua people: "subjects are haunted by the trauma of their parents even as their lives may take on less catastrophic forms" (Kaplan 106); in contrast to the actual survivors of catastrophe, whose memories are often blocked, "in transgenerational trauma subjects are haunted by tragedies affecting their parents, grandparents or ancestors from far back without conscious knowledge" (106). The notion of being haunted by the tragedies visited on one's ancestors explains much about the recurring echoes of Baartman, Adam Kok, Le Fleur, and other historical figures in *David's Story*.

If the scar, as a physical reminder linking the past to the present, symbolizes this transgenerational trauma, other motifs, such as steatopygia, connect the women of the novel's narrative present to the country's past in even more explicit ways. Steatopygia is a term for the deposits of fat typically found in the buttocks of Khoi women, including the Griquas. "Steatopygous Sally," as the narrator calls her, is unaware of the link her figure provides to the "queens of steatopygia"—Rachel le Fleur and Sara

Baartman (16)—but the narrator does make the connection explicit for the reader. Furthermore, when Rachel hides the records of her husband's anticolonial activities in the hollow of her back created by her steatopygia, she creates a symbolic link between her husband's advocacy of a Griqua national identity, Griqua women's bodies, and the land in which the documents had previously been buried.

Through such symbolic motifs as the scar and the steatopygous rear end, then, Wicomb establishes links connecting David, Dulcie, and Sally (in the present) to Andrew and Rachel le Fleur and to Baartman (in the past). In doing so, she emphasizes the extent to which the historical traumas embodied in those figures from South Africa's past continue to echo in the late twentieth century, haunting the lives of the entire Cape coloured population, and especially those who identify as Griqua. Moreover, through these links, Wicomb develops a system of spatio-temporal mapping that draws our attention to the material manifestations of that trauma. What gives these corporal mappings such power, in fact, is how seamlessly they interact with other representational strategies in the novel; working together, these various spatial and corporal mechanisms show us new understandings of history, memory, and cultural trauma. Wicomb's key spatial tropes and themes include the image of the haunted landscape; fractured and gap-ridden genealogies; troubled definitions of the nation; diggings and excavations; and, overlapping all of the above, various types of palimpsest.

* * *

In *David's Story*, as in so many works we have seen in this study, landscapes are haunted, in a sense, by the histories to which they have born witness. This theme is more than merely symbolic; the linking of land to traumatic episodes in history effectively draws our attention to the ongoing material ramifications of colonial and apartheid policies that led to today's inequitable distribution of land. Indeed, the corporal mapping that I described earlier should be seen as part of Wicomb's larger project of making visible how the past has been inscribed onto particular places and landscapes in a complicated interplay with physical bodies, social relations, and group identities. Yet she also shows us that the inscription of memory on space is more complicated than what storytelling or confession can convey alone. Huyssen identifies and suggests a causal link between two key forces that oppose memorialization: postmodernism, with its intense compression of space and time, and historical amnesia: "After the waning of modernist fantasies about *creatio ex nihilo* and of the desire for the purity of new beginnings, we have come to read cities and buildings as palimpsests of space, monuments as transformable and transitory, and sculpture as subject to the vicissitudes of time" (Huyssen 7).

Perhaps nowhere can the disorientation and dehistoricization that accompanies the encroachment of globalization be seen so clearly as in South Africa, where the rewriting of the past under political transformation has coincided with the country's newly intensified immersion in the global system of consumer capitalism. If the traces of the past continue to haunt a site thus transformed, such a site nevertheless resists the kind of inscription that can make those traces readily visible. This paradox is buried deeply within the Kokstad that David finds on his quest to recover the history of Le Fleur's Griqua tribe: "Kokstad carries no traces of Andrew Abraham Stockenstrom le Fleur. There are no street names, no monuments, and it would seem no memories" (*David's Story* 137); indeed, even the townspeople David meets avoid talking about the Griqua chief. Yet even as Le Fleur has been erased from public memory in Kokstad, his ghost seems to haunt the landscape there. And the "present absence" of Le Fleur in the collectively remembered history of British Settler country is mirrored by the fractured genealogy in the family tree that prefaces the novel. Between the European ancestor Eduard la Fleur (a fictional creation of Wicomb's) and Andrew le Fleur's father Abraham lies nothing but two Xs, representing who knows how many generations of interbreeding between European and Khoi-San ancestors. As Easton remarks, "[I]f Wicomb's novel makes gestures to the lives of Krotoä-Eva and Saartje Baartman, it also creates gaps, false links, difficult genealogies" (238).

This knowledge has the effect of undermining Andrew le Fleur's ethnic nationalism based on notions of a "pure" Griqua people.[20] In one interview Wicomb calls this notion of racial purity "crazy," and says "That's why I invented his French ancestry, as well. This he then had to completely wipe out of the picture" (in Willemse 146). Elsewhere she elaborates on the novel's false genealogies: "[The] representation of genealogy has always been bound up with identity construction, with producing a literary identity for a region or a group and with founding myths" (in Meyer and Oliver 192). The novel thus uses genealogies to establish historical analogues between present and past, while troubling reductive assumptions about cause-effect and the capacity of genealogy to render a spatial/visual model of linear progress through time.[21] As I have already hinted, moreover, *David's Story* challenges the precepts of post-apartheid nationalism, which is after all a spatial conceptualization of collective group identity. Nationalism also depends on the two assumptions which, as I have just shown, are undermined by Wicomb's novel: a stable connection to the land, and a linear genealogy that can determine who "belongs" to the nation and who is excluded from that citizenship. Indeed, one thing Wicomb makes clear in this text is that in a country such as South Africa, where national or tribal identities have long been conceived in relation to the landscape, displaced symptoms of trauma often shift from violated bodies to damaged landscapes and back again in a movement that conceptually binds the body tightly to the land.

Given that nationalism inevitably defines inclusion and exclusion in spatial terms, and given the damage that spatial engineering has perpetrated in South Africa, it should not be surprising that Wicomb is suspicious of nationalism in the postliberation era. In particular, as she depicts it in *David's Story*, ethnic nationalism is intrinsically predisposed to the absolutism and intolerance that characterized the apartheid dispensation. Wicomb confirms this in interviews conducted around the time of the novel's publication, in which she discusses nationalism as a formerly useful strategy that has now outlived its utility: "Let's just forget about the bloody nation now, because it has run its course. It's done its job. We know what it led to in Europe. I know what it means in Scotland" (in Willemse 151–52).[22] Read in this light, *David's Story* might become a cautionary Fanonesque tale about the pitfalls of nationalism in the postliberation era. Indeed, the novel seems to oppose a growing tendency for both ruling and opposition parties to invoke racial or ethnic nationalism in their political rhetoric.

Beyond using the motifs of haunted landscapes and fractured genealogies to critique ethnic nationalism and its inclination toward spatial domination, Wicomb employs at least two other spatial/visual tropes to help the reader discern the phantom traces of a history of loss. One such trope is the theme of holes and digging. This is most explicitly dramatized when Rachel le Fleur helps her husband uncover some incriminating records of his anticolonial politics, and then, when the hole is refilled, has the idea of redigging it and reburying the empty pouch:

> Again they dug into the earth, making for a second time a hole where a hole had already twice been. Taking the spade out of his hand she carefully lifted out the earth, sensing from the density the site of the original walls of the hole, for a hole being a thing of absence, she focused on the presence of its walls. (55)

The trope of digging helps Wicomb to reveal the processes by which certain narrative truths and the perspectives of certain groups and places have been effaced or obscured from history. Further, in performing this function, digging a hole acts as a metaphor for the novel itself. If we read the aforementioned scene as an allegory for reconstructing or "excavating" the past, then we begin to see that narrating a past such as David's and Dulcie's is like excavating an archaeological site: a negative and inductive enterprise involving the reconstruction or reinvention of the absent. The "present absence" of the hole in the earth contains a further absence, in the form of the documents missing from the reburied pouch.

Indeed, with the hole that Andrew and Rachel le Fleur dig, what is most telling is not what the hole contains (or conspicuously does not contain), but the simple *process* of digging and redigging this "thing of absence," in a symbolic embodiment of Freudian compulsive repetition. The narrator's attempts to "excavate" the truth about Dulcie confront precisely such a present absence, as the horror of her fate precludes registration in David's consciousness and in his story; the narrator, too, must attempt to reconstruct the contents of the empty pouch—the Truth about Dulcie—within a hole that is a "thing of absence." This understanding helps explain the novel's complex meta-narrative structure—*David's Story* is more about the process of telling the story (or digging the hole) than it is about the story itself (or the absent documents).

The final representational strategy that Wicomb employs to lay bare the spatial operations of collective historical trauma has been already much hinted at: the palimpsest, which Wicomb uses on several levels as a trope for the ways in which historical injustice is conveniently erased from social memory, yet continually reveals itself by making visible the gaps and erasures inherent in the selection and emphasis of the narrative elements.[23] The story of Rachel redigging a hole to bury an empty pouch is one such palimpsestic metaphor, but perhaps the novel's most striking example is the portrait of John Glassford and his family ca. 1767, which David recalls having seen hanging in the People's Palace in Glasgow. As he stared at the painting, he saw the ghostly image of a black man's face staring out of an empty space in the painting; only afterward did he read the plaque to learn that the painting had originally included a black slave in that space, which was subsequently painted over. David tells his narrator that he "did not expect to find the effacement of slavery to be betrayed in representation, as an actual absence, the painting out of a man" (193). The symbolic portent of this vision of erased presence is compounded when David realizes that a waiter who gave him *déjà vu* in the hotel in Kokstad is the same man whose face he saw in the painting in Glasgow many years before. This realization leads David to arrive at what might be the novel's central premise: "Surely memory is not to be trusted" (195). The novel presents the "memory truth" that emerges from this painting as something protean and elliptical, spurring him to worry: "if I once believed the first version to be true, who knows whether this one is not another invention?" (142).

This notion is extremely troubling to David, who has a strong belief in common sense and discipline. But as Daymond notes, "*David's Story* ranges the need for political certainty and control against the question of liberty and compels the reader to experience ways in which language itself, especially in its written form, can be made to serve both or... neither" ("Bodies of Writing" 30). When David realizes that memory is more like a spectral haunting, ephemeral and mischievous, than it is like a mechanical, objective playback machine, he is forced to question the political absolutism and moral certitude that had always underpinned his soldier's identity. And it is the palimpsest of the Glassford portrait, with the phantom slave's face that has been subjected to imperfect erasure, that precipitates this crisis of faith and identity for David. Michael Rothberg notes, "While the traumatic combination of the extreme and the everyday blocks traditional claims to synthetic knowledge, attentiveness to its structure can also lead to new forms of knowledge beyond the realist and antirealist positions and outside of traditional disciplines" (6–7). This is precisely the function served by Wicomb's palimpsestic narrative, which, according to M. Neelika Jayawardane, "calls deliberate attention to its elaborate and multilayered structures—an architecture that mirrors the multiplicities of the narrative histories contained within" (62). In other words, Wicomb's novel draws the reader's attention to its own structure and thus leads to "new forms of knowledge" that David, with his reliance on black-and-white certainty, finds deeply threatening.

* * *

To recap, then: to give her readers a glimpse of both the fundamental unspeakability and the materiality of South Africa's history, Wicomb deploys a complex combination of corporal mappings—scars and steatopygia foremost among them—that work together with various spatial and visual tropes—haunted landscapes, fractured genealogies, troubled nations, digging a "thing of absence," and palimpsestic traces of that which has been imperfectly erased—to animate the ruptures and blind spots of cultural trauma. Finally, then, let me illustrate how these various motifs and narrative strategies operate in two of the novel's seeming diversions from the story of the last days of apartheid. Both of these tangents concern the history of the Khoi peoples of southern Africa, and especially of the Griqua (who would have been categorized as "coloured" under apartheid law).

In fact, these are not irrelevant tangents at all, but instances of the larger cultural trauma Wicomb attempts to map for us in the novel. Few groups on earth can claim to have suffered a more calamitous trauma than the so-called Hottentots, who as a collective were severed and alienated from the land they had always wandered and who therefore experienced disruptions to their rituals and customs of recording and transmitting historical knowledge, and to their more fundamental notions of land, space, time, and identity.[24] This resistance to temporal inscription or memorialization is intensified in the era after Mandela's release from prison. Ouma Sarie, for instance, finds many of the transformations happening around her discomforting: the world, she thinks, is changing "rather unevenly, too fast in some ways and not fast enough in others" (*David's Story* 173). Indeed, it is in unwitting response to a sense of rapid, unchecked transformation that David feels compelled to excavate and document an origin or some sense of being rooted in the past.

The narrator foregrounds David's compulsion immediately in the opening pages, through his obsession with Krotoä/Eva and Sara Baartman, which the narrator mentions in the first page of the novel's preface. David's story, she tells us, started with Eva/Krotoä—which section she left out, but he insisted on including a piece on Saartje Baartman: "One cannot write nowadays, he said, without a little monograph on Baartman; it would be like excluding history itself" (1). David, it seems, feels compelled to resist the sense of uprootedness and the fragmentation of genealogies that characterize his era. His trip to Kokstad is partly an attempt to find traces of "the Old Ones, the Grigriqua ancestors who once roamed these plains and whose spirit the Chief [Le Fleur] said they would capture here as a new nation. The Old Ones had left the world as they had found it, their waste drawn back into the earth, *their footprints buried*" (97; emphasis added). The trip furthermore constitutes an attempt to map a future through the past, by excavating the traces of these buried footprints and rediscovering forgotten paths and alternative modes of existence, in opposition to the homogenizing and flattening impulses of the postmodern, post-apartheid landscape. In other words, our protagonist attempts to decode the partially erased traces of the past on the palimpsest that is the Griqualand countryside. And if, as the narrator believes, David "was using the Griqua material to displace that of which he could not speak" (145), I would insist that the unspeakable here includes not just Dulcie and her fate, but also centuries and generations of dispossession, violence, and forced migrations among Dulcie's and David's ancestors, resulting in a "transgenerational" or "cultural" trauma similar to that described by Kaplan and Eyerman. The irony, then, is that by displacing his traumatic memories of Dulcie onto the figures of Baartman and Le Fleur, David in fact finds himself tangled in a much larger web of collective and historical trauma.

As I suggested earlier, one of the key mechanisms Wicomb employs to help us see the historical continuities between past traumas and present symptoms is the steatopygia that symbolically links Dulcie and Sally to Baartman and other Khoi women throughout history. Indeed, the most tragic elements of Baartman's story stem from her European captors' fascination with her nether regions. She was brought to London in 1810, supposedly of her own volition, though the conditions under which her consent was given are murky and disputed. She was displayed around Europe as part of a freak show, with the emphasis on her supposedly grotesque anatomy, especially her steatopygia and (more whispered about than spoken aloud) her enlarged labia. As Hobson drolly proclaims, "Perhaps no other figure epitomizes the connections between grotesquerie, sexual deviance, and posteriors than the 'Hottentot Venus'" (89). Louise Bethlehem likewise calls Baartman "a powerful synecdoche for the intertwining of imperialist and patriarchal violence" (56). Moreover, both Krotoä and Baartman are apt sites for displacing David's anxiety about Dulcie, precisely because all three women's stories are so shrouded in uncertainty. Yvette Abrahams makes the case for "speculative history" as a necessary methodology for attempting to reconstruct Krotoä as a figure with any kind of historical agency, because the "memory of her enemies is all I have to go on" (Abrahams 4).[25] Speculative history, in this sense, is analogous to digging and redigging a hole that is a "thing of absence."

One danger of such a speculative historical method, however, is how easily it lends itself to attempts to appropriate and claim authority over the stories of Krotoä and Baartman. Indeed, in Wicomb's novel these two figures serve as cautionary tales regarding their status as almost mythological but hotly contested icons[26]—that is, for Wicomb they represent the ways in which women's bodies become overdetermined signifiers, representing very different things to different groups of people over a long period of time, and she casts a skeptical light over contemporary efforts to recuperate such historical figures in the service of new political agenda.[27]

Wicomb seems equally ambivalent about the struggles being waged at the time she was writing this novel between advocates for the Khoi and San communities and the French government over the control not just over the image or remembrance of Sara Baartman but over her physical remains, which Cuvier had dissected, preserved, and continued to display after her death. The impassioned character of these debates over burial rites gives a peculiar urgency to Wicomb's use of digging and excavations as tropes in the novel; yet, if the author is sympathetic to the need to repatriate Baartman's remains, she is, as we have already seen, also deeply suspicious of the ethnic nationalism and identity politics that so often drive such campaigns in the post-apartheid era. Yet Baartman likewise represents a trauma that refuses burial (notwithstanding the fact that her remains were returned to South Africa for burial shortly after *David's Story* was published). The knowledge of her humiliation, of having her genitals on display for strangers even after death, is part of the abiding cultural trauma of colonialism in southern Africa.

This collective trauma of the Khoi and San peoples plays out again and takes on deeper layers of significance in another time period much explored in Wicomb's novel: the early twentieth century, when Andrew le Fleur led the Griqua people on multiple treks in the search for a promised homeland for nationalist Griqua separatism. David's research into Le Fleur and Griqua history is rooted in more than mere romantic nostalgia. Shaun Irlam notes that by "staging a figure of retrieval as well as critical reflection on that project, [Wicomb] offers an astute critical and satirical variant on the typically rather earnest pursuits of lost identities and traditions" (712). Part of the "critical reflection" enabled by the novel involves a deep skepticism toward a naive belief in *archiving* as a mode of objectively documenting empirical reality. In one telling passage, for example, Le Fleur's wife Rachel Kok silently questions the work of archiving newspaper accounts about her husband, and she begins to misfile and reorder the archive in unpredictable ways (86). Rachel's selective retention and arrangement of the print record of her husband's activities underscores the intrinsic subjectivity and fallibility of the archiving process.

And yet, however fallible, the archive—the physical residue of history—is all that these characters have to help them piece together the partially erased fragments of the past. Just as David's search for roots leads him to Kokstad in search of information on Le Fleur, Le Fleur himself begins with a search for the "bones" of his ancestors—a figurative sort of archaeological archive. His messianic vision began in 1885 in Kokstad, where, standing on the crest of Mount Currie "like Moses of old," he was visited by a burning bush, which told him: "These are your people who have lost their land, who have become tenants on their own Griqua farms. It is you who must restore to them their dignity" (41). This vision led Le Fleur to the resolution, "Griqualand for the Griquas and the Natives. This is our land. We will wipe out the stain of colouredness and gather together under the Griqua flag those who have been given a dishonourable name" (42). In another, later vision, the voice of God tells him to "Gather the scattered bones of Adam Kok and lead your people out of the wilderness," and young Andrew sees that what appeared to be pebbles strewn in the valley were in fact "acres of bones, bleached bones picked clean by sun and rain" (44). Wicomb here establishes an alternative archive—an intricate web of connections between people, bones and bodies, places and haunted landscapes. David tries to use the figure of Le Fleur as a sort of lodestone in his attempt to map this network.

Despite (or because of) the conservative nature of the Griqua community, which under Le Fleur's leadership began calling for ethnic nationalism and separatism long before the NP came to power,[28] David apparently hopes to recuperate the figure of Le Fleur for the postrevolutionary era. He seizes, for instance, on Le Fleur's slogan "Griqualand for the Griquas and the Natives. This is our land" (42), which David takes as evidence of an inclusive, nonracial vision that is opposed to white domination and declares solidarity with the "Natives" or black Africans. Driver remarks that David needs a "recuperated, nonethnic" Le Fleur, "uncorrupted by racism . . . as a model to live by, and as a model for present-day Griqua and others" (225). More generally, David perhaps is hoping to recuperate earlier, more open-ended ways of thinking about identity, land, space, and nation, of the kind held by Le Fleur before *realpolitik* induced him to make fatal concessions to an incipient Afrikaner nationalism and white domination.

If David's attitude toward Le Fleur is deeply conflicted, Le Fleur plays a still more complex and ambivalent role for Wicomb herself, often serving as a cautionary figure against nationalist zeal. For instance, one link between the novel's narrative present and Le Fleur's campaign for Griqua nationalism in the early twentieth century is that both eras saw the emergence of competing nationalisms struggling to capture power and influence the rebuilding of the country after a long, destructive period of conflict (the Anglo-Boer War at the beginning of the century, the struggle against apartheid at the end). Stéphane Robolin nicely sums up the contradictory impulses that arise from this transitional moment when he compares the Griqua settlement in Wicomb's novel to the town of Ruby in Toni Morrison's *Paradise*: "The black American and Griqua communities work to imaginatively remap their own worlds . . . in part by evolving their own collective memory. However, it becomes evident that both communities insufficiently reconfigure their subject-territories, as both too readily redeploy the discourses of purity" (300).

Presumably because of the Griqua leader's failure to "reconfigure [his] subject-territories," David looks scornfully on the "apartheid" that Le Fleur offered to Botha; indeed, Le Fleur's solution for "God's stepchildren" is shown to be a spatial segregation that anticipates National Party policy by almost three decades, when he calls for "absolute separation. From white and from black" (161). Yet the implications of Wicomb's critique of Le Fleur are most profound in the immediate aftermath of apartheid, another time of intensive social and political transformation, in which we are seeing emerge "new notions of 'colouredness' and essentialism" (Wicomb, qtd. in Willemse 145–46). Ultimately, though, even if the novel highlights the many parallels between the two historical periods, there is no simple key that will allow the reader to decode the narrative of Le Fleur as an allegory for David's story. Wicomb can only tell the story of trauma negatively—that is, not through a linear accounting of facts, but by dramatizing and making visible the marks of the erasure or rupture or displacement that render telling impossible.

At any rate, if Wicomb sees any lessons of redemption in David's recuperations of history, they do not lie with Le Fleur's patriarchal, messianic, and separatist vision of ethnic nationalism. Rather, we should look for those lessons in the previously unwritten stories of women: Le Fleur's wife, Rachel Susanna Kok; Krotoä; Sara Baartman; Antjie Cloete (David's great-grandmother, whom the novel implies was "inspired" with a child from Andrew le Fleur); and David's grandmother Ragel, who told him stories of the Le Fleurs and her mother Antjie. Just as Le Fleur's search for a Griqua homeland echoes and collapses into the earlier *Voortrekker* mythology, so the figures of Khoi women across time overlap and merge in complicated ways. Dulcie, Sally, and the narrator become overdetermined figures of "coloured" women whose social space has historically and repeatedly been inscribed through their bodies. As David complains to his scribe, she has filled the story with so many women that it is no longer "a proper history at all" (199). In fact, it becomes a kind of counterhistory, seen through the eyes of generations of African women. And the representational strategies that make that counterhistory possible are precisely the various tropes of spatial and corporal mapping I have described.

* * *

I conclude this section with a final example of how Wicomb turns her own novel into a palimpsest, thus allowing us to discern the spatial, material, and collective or transgenerational dimensions of the traumas she depicts. The narrator proposes using the "middle voice" for Dulcie's story (197), and in fact does use it with increasing frequency in the novel's closing chapters. The proposed middle voice elicits a strong negative reaction from David, so, to convince him, the scribe demonstrates an approximation of the middle voice with a parable about "Bronwyn the Brown Witch" who uses her magic to help her friends, "until one day her friends, the sticks in the forest, come clattering together, lay themselves down on top of each other until they are a mighty woodpile. There is no way out. Bronwyn the Witch must die on the stake" (203). The absence of agency and rationality—of anyone responsible for Bronwyn's lynching—perfectly encapsulates the story David has recounted about Dulcie: terrible, nameless things have happened to her, but no one seems to be to blame.

Wicomb's use of the middle voice even in this seemingly frivolous example lends credence to Hayden White's argument that it may be necessary, in the wake of the mass traumas of the twentieth century, to recuperate the middle voice and intransitive mode, which he conflates together and associates with the "modernist style, that was developed in order to represent the kind of experiences which social modernism made possible" (White 52). LaCapra, questioning White's argument, wonders "in what sense it is possible to make truth claims in the middle voice and to what extent that question is suspended by its use" (26). In the case of *David's Story*, though, LaCapra's objection seems to be beside the point: Wicomb's goal is not to create the perception of a less frangible and elusive truth, but to make it explicit to us why such a remembered truth *is* so elusive and partial. What Rothberg says of Art Spiegelman's representation of the Holocaust in *Maus* is true of Wicomb's novel as well: "there emerges the possibility of *indirect* reference through the self-conscious staging of the conundrum of representing historical extremity" (103). The middle voice is, if you will, the syntactic equivalent of the palimpsest, drawing attention to that which has been erased and excluded, and to the conundrums of telling.

Later examples of the middle voice as a sort of linguistic palimpsest perform this work more pointedly. On the penultimate page of the novel, after David's suicide and funeral, the narrator returns home to her computer to find several days' work on the book gone, replaced by a phrase in a sort of middle voice, "*this text deletes itself*" (*David's Story* 212; emphasis added). Wicomb's novel ends with a "last warning" bullet striking the narrator's computer, and her disavowal of the story: "My screen is in shards. / The words escape me. / I do not acknowledge this scrambled thing as mine. / I will have nothing more to do with it. / I wash my hands of this story" (213). Yet the narrator (or someone else?) must have turned her hand to it again for the reader to be holding the book in the first place. Thus, as with the conspicuous middle voice, the novel's conclusion makes explicit the crisis of agency and representation inherent in a tale as damaging and damaged as David's story. "What we are left with," Easton summarizes, "is a co-authored text which negotiates versions of the truth, and the icons of Krotoä and Saartje reside as palimpsests, while the haunting figure of Dulcie 'echoes like a scream' throughout the pages, refusing to fully emerge or disappear" (245).

What these palimpsestic tracings make possible, as Kentridge observes about his draw-and-erase animation process (see section 1.2), is a kind of mapping of experience across and through space, time, and embodied states. Wicomb's use of the palimpsest as both motif and narrative strategy reveals traces of the erased past, even as it makes clear that the erased texts are never fully recoverable. The palimpsest also reveals the material and spatial dimensions of collective traumatic memory. In exposing these truths, Wicomb reminds us of what is ultimately at stake in the representation of a traumatic past. If we elide the ways in which time defines and is interpenetrated by space, and the ways in which language depends on a material referent, we create a curiously depoliticized conception of "bearing witness" as an individual process of working through the traumatic aftermath of an event, rather than a collective contest over public configurations of space, place, and memory.

Wicomb's novel has the effect of throwing cold water over post-apartheid triumphalism and nationalist bromides; it becomes harder to celebrate the successes of the Truth Commission as an exercise in confession and historical reconstruction when confronted with the deep ruptures in South Africa's sense of space and time, language and body dramatized so searingly in *David's Story*. On reading Wicomb's masterpiece, one begins to see that South Africa's road to radical democracy has only just begun, and the process of rendering the past must be ongoing.

3.3 Burdened by the Scars of History: Zakes Mda's *The Heart of Redness*

Zakes Mda's third novel *The Heart of Redness* (2000), like *David's Story* and *The Devil's Chimney*, attempts to map the social geographies of contemporary, rural South Africa through a parallel narrative of an earlier historical era.[29] In the narrative present of the late 1990s, the progatonist Camagu leaves Johannesburg for the tiny and remote Eastern Cape coastal village of Qolorha-by-Sea. There, in what Wendy Woodward notes is an inversion of the classic "Jim goes to Jo'burg" plot line so common in South African literature and film (Woodward, "Jim"), Camagu finds a true community that makes room for the wandering stranger; in the process, he also finds a sort of antidote to his sense of alienation and malaise and begins to "build a new life" for himself in this far-flung locale (131).

Yet the community Camagu finds in Qolorha is one deeply divided between two feuding clans: on the one hand, the Believers who follow Zim, embrace the "redness" of traditional Xhosa culture,[30] and oppose modernization and capitalist development; and, on the other hand, the Unbelievers, who follow Bhonco, disdain what they see as the superstitions of the Believers, and passionately want to instigate development in the area by bringing in a casino and luxury resort. The feud between Believers and Unbelievers dates back to the 1850s—the parallel narrative time frame of the novel—when Zim's ancestor Twin chose to follow Nongqawuse and the other prophets of the cattle-killing movement, while his twin brother (Bhonco's ancestor) Twin-Twin rejected the prophecies.

Camagu eventually discovers that it is impossible either to erase or to ignore this deeply engrained history. Yet his vision for the village's future refuses to take sides: he rejects the impersonal and amnesiac postmodern landscape of casinos, golf courses, and luxury homes, but also rejects the reactionary nostalgia of the Believers. Instead, Camagu argues for preserving the history and tradition of the place while using resources and land in a way that benefits and preserves the autonomy of the village as a collective. In this regard, Mda's novel is decidedly the most didactic and programmatic work I have studied in this book. But my interest in the novel concerns not the political efficacy or practicality of Mda's prescription for post-apartheid South Africa, but rather his attempts to graph a narrative map of trauma, loss, and dispossession over a 150-year history of colonization and its aftermath in the Eastern Cape.

The dual temporal structure in *Heart of Redness* is even more complicated than in Landsman's and Wicomb's novels. The narrative continually shifts between the 1850s and the 1990s, a bifurcation immediately hinted at in the genealogy that appears as the epigraph to the novel: both Twin and Bhonco are descended from the same "Headless Ancestor," Xikixa, so nicknamed because he was beheaded by British soldiers with the help of trader and explorer John Dalton. The family tree shows Xikixa's sons Twin and Twin-Twin, Twin and his wife Qukezwa's son Heitsi, and Twin-Twin's "many wives" and "many children," before descending into the vagueness of "THE MIDDLE GENERATIONS." The phrase "Middle Generations" most literally refers to those born into colonial rule and, later, apartheid; that is, to those born into dispossession and white domination. But this large gap in the novel's own genealogy is significant on multiple levels. Most importantly, as with the similar blank spaces in the genealogy that precedes Wicomb's *David's Story* (3.2), the gap is Mda's means of casting doubt on the notion of a past that is easily retrievable, or at least wholly reconstitutable.

The family tree only resumes with Zim and Bhonco and their wives and children in the present, with many repetitions of earlier names on the Believer side: Zim has a son named Twin and a daughter named Qukezwa, who in turn has a son named Heitsi. Mda has great fun moving between the two time frames, often shifting in mid-chapter to draw the reader's attention to some ironic parallel between Zim and Twin or Bhonco and Twin-Twin. For most of the novel, it is possible to sort through any confusion about which time period is being narrated by paying attention to the verb tenses: the 1990s are told in continual present tense, while the events of the 1850s are related in the past tense. This structure breaks down in the final chapter, which visits the original Qukezwa and Twin-Twin once again, but this time in present tense. This has the effect of bringing the past into the present, or rather of showing the Eastern Cape of 1998 to be a palimpsest, constantly revealing traces of the past.[31] As Mda himself notes in one interview, "I am not using a flashback technique. It is the kind of novel that has no respect for time and space. The characters of the present time interact with characters in the year 1856 on different levels" (in Naidoo 260).

Another symbol of the past's tendency to haunt the present is exhibited in the "scars of history" (26) that Bhonco and Twin-Twin alike wear on their backs. Twin-Twin received them when he defended his wife from the Believers' accusations of witchcraft and was flogged for it: "After many months the wounds healed and became scars. But occasionally they itched and reminded him of his flagellation" (17). Such is the power of these corporal reminders of Twin-Twin's humiliation that they extend beyond his own generation: "Every first boy-child in subsequent generations of Twin-Twin's tree is born with the scars. Even those of the Middle Generations, their first males carried the scars" (12). Bhonco's scars from a wound he never received are both a symbol and a physical manifestation of "trans-generational" or "cultural" trauma, in which, as Eyerman explains, "direct experience of an event is not a necessary condition for its inclusion in the trauma process" (12).

Eyerman goes on to argue that *representation* plays a key role in the collective remembering of a traumatic event. This assertion implies that collective memories of trauma are malleable and subject to reshaping, rather than fixed and monolithic. Bhonco's decision to revive the Cult of the Unbelievers confirms this: it does not matter to him "that people have long forgotten the conflicts of generations ago. He holds to them dearly, for they have shaped his present, and the present of the nation. His role in life is to teach people not to believe. He tells them that even the Middle Generations wouldn't have suffered if it had not been for the scourge of belief" (*Heart* 4). One manifestation of this odd, intransitive refusal to believe is the Unbelievers' insistence on never laughing; another is an extreme ambivalence about the past.

Paradoxically, however, if the Unbelievers define themselves according to the "conflicts of the past," they are more likely than their rival clan to buy into the post-apartheid "insistence" on amnesia:

> The sufferings of the Middle Generations are only whispered. It is because of the insistence: *Forget the past. Don't only forgive it. Forget it as well. The past did not happen. You only dreamt it. It is a figment of your rich collective imagination. It did not happen. Banish your memory. It is a sin to have a memory. There is virtue in amnesia. The past. It did not happen. It did not happen. It did not happen.* (157; italics in original)

This insistence on amnesia is especially pronounced in Bhonco's daughter Xoliswa Ximiya, the principal of Qolorha's secondary school. Despite having one of the village's most prestigious jobs, she regards the area as backward and embarrassing, and she longs to have "big stars like Eddie Murphy and Dolly Parton" (74) vacation in Qolorha: "Cape Town is now becoming a celebrity paradise. Qolorha can be one too if these conservative villagers stop standing in the way of progress" (75).

This equation of American-style consumer capitalism and celebrity worship with "progress" is fundamental to the modern Unbelievers' conception of themselves and their relationship to the past and present. Just as his ancestor Twin-Twin was forced through his feud with the anticolonial brother Twin into an uncomfortable collusion with the forces of British colonialism, so Bhonco embraces the economic and cultural imperialism of American-branded global capital. In one public meeting, Bhonco declares, "We want to get rid of this bush which is a sign of our uncivilised state. We want the developers to come and build the gambling city that will bring money to this community. That will bring modernity to our lives, and will rid us of our redness" (105). An attitude of willful amnesia is necessary to maintain the Unbelievers' rigidly pragmatic view of the landscape and the organization of social space; a strong attachment to the land and the past it embodies would interfere with the capitalist project of privatizing, bulldozing, and rebuilding the landscape into a profitable configuration.

In short, then, Bhonco and his followers have crafted a collective identity for themselves based on a complex combination of remembering and forgetting the colonial and precolonial past. But if the Unbelievers are free to rework the representations of the past that make this identity formation possible, others are equally free to recast those representations—to contest or reject those narratives offered by the Unbelievers. Zim, for instance, advocates a relationship to the land and to the ancestors that runs directly counter to the Unbelievers' embrace of amnesia and capitalist development. He responds to Bhonco's argument by denouncing his desire "to destroy the bush that has been here since the days of our forefathers. What kind of progress is that?" (105). The Believers' relationship to the past is perhaps best symbolized in the wild fig tree that grows in Zim's compound, and under which he regularly goes to doze, to communicate with the birds, and to find solace, because it is linked to "all of Twin's progeny who planted it more than a hundred years ago. Now the trunk is as big as his main hut. As soon as it leaves the ground its branches twist and turn in all directions, spreading wide like an umbrella over his whole homestead" (40–41). Complex and intricate, the fig tree metaphor suggests a past deeply rooted in the land but arching over and burrowing under every aspect of daily life for the Believers. The tree becomes a figure for the memory of landscapes, which ineluctably both permeates the present and hangs over it as an external, involuntary reminder of the past.

In many ways Mda seems more sympathetic to Zim's side in this contest over the clan's relationship to the past. Yet even the Unbelievers, despite their insistence on amnesia, feel a deep need to establish connections to the world of the ancestors. This need is readily evident in the Unbelievers' dance, borrowed from the abaThwa or San peoples, which connects them to the ancestors; the narrator calls it "a memory ritual" (83) and explains that "the elders seem to induce death through their dance. When they are dead they visit the world of the ancestors" (82). Bhonco's wife NoPetticoat tells Camagu that the dance was invented by the Unbelievers only recently: "When the sad times passed and the trials of the Middle Generations were over, it became necessary to create something that would make them appreciate this new happiness of the new age" (82). What is significant in NoPetticoat's explanation of the ritual is the explicit connection she draws between the past and the present; according to her, the Unbelievers are commemorating the past so as to live better in the present.

Clearly, then, the Unbelievers' relationship to the past is much more complex than a simple desire for amnesia, and is also related in complex ways to the Believers' own views on the past; the two groups' memorial practices are in fact like two sides of the same coin. For instance, the narrator explains: "While the Unbelievers lament the sufferings of the Middle Generations, Zim celebrates the end of those sufferings" (40). And like Bhonco and the Unbelievers, Zim feels a deep connection to the past and to the landscape of his upbringing, speaking "passionately about this valley. When he began to walk, he walked in this valley. He looked after cattle in this valley. He was circumcised here.... His whole life is centred in this valley" (50–51). This passage is yet another example of memories and narratives of the past and cultural identities becoming inextricably enfolded with particular places.

To Zim's horror, given his attachment to the valley, his daughter Qukezwa talks of leaving for Johannesburg's better economic opportunities (51); it is also telling that, whereas many of the Believer women wear the traditional red robes called *isikhakha*, when Camagu first meets Qukezwa she is wearing "a black woollen cap which is emblazoned with the P symbol of Pierre Cardin in green and yellow" (62).[32] Qukezwa thus initially appears to embody the incursion of amnesiac consumer culture and modernity even into remote Qolorha, and even into the insular clan of the Believers. As Rita Barnard notes, Mda presents Qolorha as "a contact zone, a place where 'natives' and colonizers, dwellers and travelers encounter each other—and where the distinctions between such groups can at times be quite blurry" (162). This blurriness extends to the memories of landscapes that Zim feels are so indelible, and indeed, Qukezwa's willingness to leave the valley likewise calls into question her father's assumptions about the permanence of the memory of the landscape. She demonstrates moreover that the Believers are just as anxious and divided among themselves in their relationship to that history as are the Unbelievers.

Yet it is Qukezwa who, along with Camagu, helps Mda articulate his own views on development and modernization versus tradition most directly in the novel.[33] For instance, when the village elders charge her with vandalism for chopping down alien vegetation, she defends herself by saying, "The trees that I destroyed are . . . the lantana and wattle trees. They come from other countries . . . from Central America, from Australia . . . to suffocate our trees" (*Heart* 248). Thus, after her initial appearance as a rebellious city-bound youth, Qukezwa later reveals herself to be "the guardian of a dying tradition," as Camagu thinks when he first hears her split-tone singing (175). And as with Zim's fig tree, the indigenous trees which Qukezwa fights to protect come to embody that tradition and the past from which it grows.

What Qukezwa has in common with the Believers, the Unbelievers, and those Qolorhans who try to stay neutral is a reverence for tradition, the ancestors, and the memories of landscapes (however differently those things may be conceived by the different factions), tempered by an eagerness to find new ways of incorporating those traditions and memories into the modern world, in which the "landscape has changed already" because of holiday cottages being built all along the coast (76). The reverence for the past and connection to the land is what Camagu seems to find regenerative about life in the seaside village. Whereas Johannesburg had made him bitter, and he "sinks into utter depression" at the thought of moving back to the United States (111), in Qolorha Camagu comes close to finding what apartheid had destroyed for his own family: "Camagu is filled with a searing longing for an imagined blissfulness of his youth. He has vague memories of his home village, up in the mountains. . . . Then the government came and moved the people down to the flatlands, giving them only small plots and no compensation" (65). The "present absence" implicitly evoked by this nostalgia—a fondly remembered childhood of blissful, almost transcendental connection with the land and the community—is ruptured by the rude infringement of apartheid.

Qolorha-by-Sea seems to offer an antidote to this trauma, and a hope of recuperating some of the prelapsarian idyll of his remembered childhood. Koyana puts it well: "[I]n combining place as symbol with place as landscape, Mda is suggesting that for him the spirit of Qholorha represents the ideal spirit of the new South Africa, the true spirit of the 'African Renaissance.' People in Qholorha are able to debate, organise, plan, and implement their own ideas while taking into account what is happening around them" ("Qholora" 59). Woodward also notes that, despite the interconnections between place and identity in the novel, "identities are fluid" ("Jim" 174). It is the fluidity of these identities, I would argue, that prevents particular configurations of space from becoming totalizing, in that people are free to continually redefine their own identities and relations with the landscape, rather than having them imposed from outside.

If living in Qolorha proves therapeutic for Camagu, *The Heart of Redness* suggests that the traditions and practices still partially preserved in such places offer regenerative and practical value to the nation as a whole as it embarks on its collective project of memorializing and reconciling itself with the past. Mda's depiction of amaXhosa oral tradition emphasizes its capacity, proven over many centuries, to serve as a technology for transmitting historical memory from one generation to the next. Naming traditions, for example, have a tremendous power to keep alive certain memories of the past, such as with the popular name NomaRussia—which originates with the Russian victory over British forces led by the detested Sir George Cathcart in the Crimean War in 1854 (70). As violent as Cathcart's command over the amaXhosa people may have been, the fact that he is remembered by the residents of the Cape a century and a half later suggests that they have formed their identity partly in remembered opposition to him, to the extent that they still name their children after his enemies.

Folk songs and dance have a similar power to inscribe certain narratives of the past into social memory. For example, Camagu, who grew up in another part of the Eastern Cape altogether, nonetheless learned about Nongqawuse in school, and sang songs about her as a child (67). These insights are commonplace enough, but have deep and manifold implications for a national project of registering individual memories of the past in collective memory. As I argued in part 1, the TRC was generally at its most effective when it allowed participants to bring their own modes and traditions of storytelling to the hearings, rather than tightly structuring the testimony and subjecting it to rigid standards of forensic verification. In such cases the TRC began to realize the potential of oral and performance traditions to transmit historical memory in ways that clearly engross the dramatist in Mda.

Insofar as these stories keep alive the memory of anticolonial resistance going back 150 years or more, they offer a counternarrative to apartheid's official accounts of pioneers laying claim to an empty landscape, and to British imperial narratives of civilization's conquest over savagery. Furthermore, in the instance of the "memory ritual," the narrative structure of the novel enacts the very function of the dance: after telling us that through ritual the Unbelievers "fleet back through the Middle Generations, and linger in the years when their forebears were hungry" (83), the narrative itself immediately shifts to the time of the cattle killing.

The Heart of Redness shows us still another value conveyed by amaXhosa oral and performance tradition in the post-apartheid era: it gives people a degree of autonomy and control over their own stories and histories, rather than making them passive consumers of the inert, officially determined history of school textbooks and state-funded museums. In this sense, oral tradition is both a paradigmatic example of, and an ideal vehicle for, Mda's larger vision of a truly democratic development in rural South Africa. As he lays out this program through the alter-ego of Camagu,[34] its most crucial feature is its inclusive, participatory nature that gives people the power to make their own decisions: Camagu tells John Dalton, for instance, that Dalton's mistake in building the village water project was in imposing it on people as his own personal charitable project: "[The villagers] should be part of the whole process.... Then it becomes their project. Then they will look after it" (207). In its radical departures from the neoliberal economic policies of the ANC government in the transitional period, in which centralized private monopolies or parastatals deliver essential services such as water only to those who can afford to pay monthly bills or feed meters, Mda's model offers a powerful alternative. He offers a system in which people take control of servicing their own basic needs, and thereby renegotiate the fundamental notions of public and private space and resources through what Titlestad and Kissack call a "zig-zag epistemology" ("The Foot" 266).[35]

Mda's emphasis on nurturing forms of development that give autonomy and opportunity to the people extends to public registrations of the past—though in the case of Qolorha, the traumatic past in question is not the immediate apartheid-era history of violence and struggle, but a much older struggle—the Believers' war against the Unbelievers and the colonizers—and the cataclysm of the cattle killing. In the modern narrative, this conflict continues to play out in new permutations, in which the "colonial masters" (127) with whom the Unbelievers have now allied themselves are rich developers eager to bring casinos and luxury homes to the valley. Mda clearly rejects this project, but neither does he buy wholesale into the Believers' obsessive preoccupation with Nongqawuse and Mlanjeni and the other prophets. Rather, his ambition in this novel is in keeping with his notion of a theater (and, by extension, a fiction) of reconciliation that "will address the past solely for the purpose of understanding the present, of understanding why it is absolutely necessary for us to have reconciliation" ("Theater" 44).

Camagu's own vision for Qolorha's development is to foster environmental and cultural tourism; he shrewdly acknowledges the need for localized differentiation to attract global tourism, but in ways that will protect the environment, the local economy, and the autonomy and traditions of the villagers. Accordingly, he begins a cooperative society with several women in the village: initially they harvest oysters and other shellfish and sell them to hotel restaurants in Grahamstown, and then they branch out into sewing traditional amaXhosa clothing and making beadworks to sell in Johannesburg. Moreover, Camagu argues at one village meeting that many tourists would come to experience the unspoilt beauty of the landscape and the "hospitality of the amaGcaleka clan" (*Heart* 275). The notion of using local culture as a tourist draw is of course nothing new; what makes Camagu's proposal significant is his insistence that these amaXhosa traditions be shown as living, evolving practices rather than as a carefully preserved cultural essence, fixed and unchanging. But he is also not averse to using the history of the place as an added selling point. Indeed, given the village's long-standing feud over the cattle-killing prophecies, the most controversial part of Camagu's plan is his idea to promote the area as the birthplace of the prophets, as some tourists will come to see "a place of miracles! This is where Nongqawuse made her prophecies!" (277). In sharp contrast to the total amnesia and abandonment of tradition desired by Xoliswa Ximiya, Camagu wants to use the area's traditions and history strategically, to help the village adapt to the new, fast-changing world.

The Unbelievers are predictably outraged by Camagu's ideas. John Dalton takes inspiration from them, but in many ways he serves as the whipping boy for Mda's critique of cultural tourism in South Africa. Dalton goes beyond Camagu's idea for a backpackers' hostel: They should "construct a cultural village owned and operated by the villagers" (284), in which tourists watch dancing, stick fighting, and (usually private) initiation rituals. When Dalton explains that the initiates will in fact be actors in costume, Camagu rejects the plan outright, because "[i]t's too contrived.... It is just a museum that pretends that is how people live" (285).

Dalton's ideas are typical of a certain school of cultural tourism, which tends to treat indigenous traditions as quaint museum installations, to be trotted out for tourists on demand. What Camagu argues for instead is a tourism that recognizes both the ancient traditions and the modern lives of South Africa's people; or as Attwell puts it, "Camagu, and therefore the novel, offer a modernised Africanism as the inevitable path into the future" (199). Significantly, Camagu phrases his critique of Dalton's cultural village as a wrongheaded attempt to *excavate* tradition: "When you excavate a buried precolonial identity of these people...a precolonial authenticity that is lost...are you suggesting that they currently have no culture?" (286). Camagu's argument here echoes Mda's own hopes for an "African Renaissance" that aims to "rediscover" forgotten cultural elements rather than "revive" a "pre-colonial authenticity that is lost" (in Nuttall and Michael, "African Renaissance" 117). Two of the central ideas I have noted in South African literature after the Truth Commission intersect in these two very similar critiques of post-apartheid rhetoric and social policy: the notion that the past can be excavated wholesale, and that it can be tamed by consigning it to the archive.

Camagu rejects both modes of coming to terms with the past (or of refusing to do so), and emphasizes instead the need to harness the power of historical narrative and living tradition to enable the local people to achieve self-reliance.[36] He tells Dalton:

> I am interested in the culture of the amaXhosa as they live it today, not yesterday. The amaXhosa people are not a museum piece. Like all cultures their culture is dynamic.... I am talking of self-reliance where people do things for themselves.... This project will be fully owned by the villagers themselves and will be run by a committee elected by them in the true manner of co-operative societies. (*Heart* 286)

Such is Mda's prescription for development in post-apartheid South Africa, and it is a vision much at odds with the new government's actual policies of privatization and Black Economic Empowerment that enrich only an elite handful. Mda's vision thus serves to counter the ahistorical and amnesiac impulses of late capitalism by memorializing the past in ways that help to map the South Africa of the present, and to conceptualize alternative maps for the future. Barnard questions how permanent this victory will be: "The reader is left to wonder if Dalton's ethnic village does not represent a postmodern version of pacification: a domestication and commercialization of otherness, and a collapse of both time and space" (169). Certainly, though, Mda sees Camagu's renegotiation of the village's future as preferable to the purely neoliberal alternative. And the real lesson is that such renegotiation—of social spaces and of the memories they contain—must be ongoing, flexible, and open to continual revision.

Conclusion

Mda's work has always tended toward the prescriptive and didactic. *The Heart of Redness* is no exception, and is certainly the most overt of the three novels I have examined in part 3 in terms of laying out an agenda for political transition in the twenty-first century. But the more elliptical approaches taken by Landsman and Wicomb do nevertheless reveal their own visions of how social space is and can be constituted, organized, and used.

All three novels share a preoccupation with the land, seeing it as containing or embodying the histories of the people who have occupied it. All three are skeptical of attempts to excavate or recuperate those histories, even as the texts themselves engage in precisely such a reclamation project. But for these three writers, representing the past is never a simple process of unearthing its fragments and piecing them back together. For them, the holes one digs will always be empty, genealogies will always have gaps, and coordinates will always be in flux. Rather than denying these ineluctable barriers to truth-telling, filling in the holes, and claiming the results to be absolute truth, South African literature after the Truth Commission teaches us to make the gaps and seams visible, to learn from them, and to make that very indeterminacy a common ground for mapping the post-apartheid future.

Conclusion

In May of 2008, as I was preparing the final version of this book for publication, waves of what the press called "xenophobic violence" broke out around South Africa. The attacks on African immigrants from Zimbabwe, Mozambique, the Congo, Nigeria, and elsewhere began with three murders on May 11–12 in Alexandra Township, site of the "Six-Day War" of 1986, which I discuss in part 2. By May 15 the violence had spread to Diepsloot, a township northwest of Johannesburg that in recent years has frequently been rocked by protests (sometimes violent) against failures in housing and service delivery. A week later, violence had spread throughout Gauteng, KwaZulu-Natal, and the Western Cape. By the end of the month, military vehicles sent to suppress the violence had rolled through South African townships for the first time since 1994; 62 people had been killed; and over 30,000 foreign nationals had become refugees in special camps set up for their protection. As of this writing, over 13,000 people remain in those camps, unable to return to their previous homes because of threats and fear of further attacks (S. Khumalo). With chilling *déjà vu,* ghosts from South Africa's past once again flashed across the world's television screens and newspaper pages: armored vehicles doing battle with crowds armed with rocks and traditional weapons; reports of a right-wing "Third Force" stirring up unrest in the mining hostels; and, most chillingly, in Ramaphosa Village in the East Rand, a Mozambiquan man named Ernesto Nhamuave was assaulted and set afire in a "necklacing" attack like those used against suspected police informers in the 1980s and early 1990s.

As it happens, while these tragic events were transpiring, I was reading the book *Narrating Our Healing* by Chris van der Merwe and Pumla Gobodo-Madikizela. In one chapter the authors describe a group of young girls that Gobodo-Madikizela once saw playing in a township in the Eastern Cape. The girls were too young to have witnessed the most recent necklacing that happened in their township years before, yet they nevertheless played a game in which they acted out the process of placing an imaginary tire around a victim's neck, filling it with petrol, and striking the match, while the victim begged for mercy and, finally, mimed a macabre death dance. The authors comment that "the unspoken events of the past...had become imprinted on [the children's] minds....Re-enacting the death dance of a necklace victim may well have been a way of transforming its memory into something more accessible, and less fearful for the girls" (33). In short, they suggest that the "game" is the children's way of narrating and making sense of a psychic rupture that affects their generation even though they did not directly experience or witness the traumatic events themselves.

The xenophobic violence in May of 2008 is a more extreme symptom of the collective, transgenerational trauma that continues to haunt South Africa's present. But in this most recent case, the repetition of the traumatic act of necklacing is no assertion of control through harmless narrativizing, as Van der Merwe and Gobodo-Madikizela claim of the child's game. Rather, the repetition is literal, and therefore a further source of death, pain, and psychic rupture, perpetuating the downward-spiraling cycle of violence that South Africa was once believed to have escaped. It may also portend, tragically, that the window of opportunity has already begun to close for the kind of radical transformation of spatial relationships that I have called for in these pages.

If these horrifying outbreaks of assault, murder, rape, and looting more than ever prove the urgency of materially refiguring South African social spaces, they also demonstrate the perils of such post-apartheid nation-building. In part 2 I expressed the concern that post-apartheid South Africa is being broken into self-selective, exclusionary citadels that might ironically replicate the spatial segregation of apartheid city planning, and which could also lead to a (re-)traumatizing struggle between ethnic and interest groups over the organization and use of social space. During the episodes of xenophobic violence, such struggles broke out at every scale—from the squatter camp to the nation. Even South African nationals who spoke one of the smaller minority languages such as Shangaan, Venda, or even Pedi were attacked and told to "go back to Limpopo" ("Gauteng").[1] Perhaps most importantly, the recent violence teaches us a lesson: the rhetoric of postliberation reconciliation and nation-building must be joined with a sustained program of material, economic, and spatial compensation and physical rebuilding. After more than a decade of the ANC's neoliberal program of privatization, which the government has implemented at the expense of precisely such an ambitious program of social justice, it is fairly predictable that one or more criminal and/or political elements would be able to exploit the frustrations and resentments of the poor in South African society, channeling their wrath onto the even more poor and vulnerable economic migrants from elsewhere in Africa. Such is the power of ethnic nationalism and other spatial regimes of social control.

* * *

The xenophobic violence, the continuing ravages of HIV/AIDS, crime, rape, and other social problems all promise a foreseeable future of continuing struggle, conflict, and hardship in South Africa. Yet the literature of the last fifteen years, some of which I have studied herein, does contain a sense of flexible, open-ended possibility and indeterminacy that South African society as a whole needs more sorely than ever. What is more, these works foster this productive indeterminacy not only toward the future but also toward the past, making space (literal and figurative) for myriad narratives and accounts, even conflicting ones, to coexist.

This is not to claim that all of the authors offer an optimistic or enthusiastic account of the "Rainbow Nation." The conclusions to some of the texts, in fact, are decidedly bleak: Duffy in *The Exploded View* is attacked by a van full of thugs, for example, and the computer on which the narrator of *David's Story* composes her tale is shot by unseen assailants after David's mysterious death. Yet even in these darker representations of contemporary South Africa there is generally a sense that we can learn from the past without becoming mired in it, and that in the process of mapping that past we can reinvent modes of existence and social interaction that can sketch the trajectory for a different future. Wicomb, for instance, rejects Andrew le Fleur's vision of ethnic nationalism, yet identifies in his slogan "Griqualand for the Griquas and the Natives" an alternative model for reclaiming the land for all who have inhabited it.

In their different ways, the collection of works I have examined teaches us that to memorialize the past is necessarily to remap the land and to reconfigure the spatial structures left behind by centuries of white minority rule. At first glance cartography might seem to offer an ironic range of metaphors for the process of mental decolonization I have described, given the close historical relationship between mapmaking, imperial conquest, and social control. But the "remapping" that I see taking place in so many works of post-apartheid literature more closely resembles Deleuze and Guattari's understanding of the map as rhizome: "The map is open and connectable in all of its dimensions; it is detachable, reversible, susceptible to constant modification. It can be torn, reversed, adapted to any kind of mounting, reworked by an individual, group, or social formation" (12).[2] If traumatic memory disorders demand a certain flexibility to continually revisit and revise one's stories about the past, as I argue in part 1, then the rhizomic map would appear to be ideally suited to navigating one's way through the political and psychological minefields of traumatic narrative.

Indeterminacy and flexibility are prerequisite qualities of Deleuze and Guattari's "anti-cartography" (Titlestad 13), furthermore, because the "lines of flight" recorded on a map are perpetually shifting, growing, disappearing, and reappearing. A map of loss must be a palimpsest, then, showing not just fixed locations in space, but also trajectories through time-space. Deleuze and Guattari themselves hint at such a necessity: although they oppose the map to the "tracing," whose goal is to "describe a de facto state... or to explore an unconscious that is already there from the start" (12), they also maintain that "*the tracing should always be put back on the map*" (13; their emphasis). In the case of post-apartheid urban space, where the ephemeral and shifting Deleuzian rhizome can be seen at its most dramatic, such tracing—for instance, of a character's peripatetic wanderings through the city—is especially important, even though (or precisely because) a second trajectory through the same street or the same building might later yield a very different tracing.

But if Deleuze and Guattari's anti-mapping provides a useful metaphor for understanding the "remapping" performed by so much literature after the TRC, these convenient parallels only take us so far. The refiguring of space and memory in post-apartheid South African literature and culture has involved a more or less overt rejection of mapping as an instrument of male power and colonization, yes, but it has also entailed a feminist renegotiation of spatial relations, and it frequently turns to African tradition for alternative models of understanding and occupying social space. Emblematic of this thread of thought in post-apartheid fiction is Tshepo's resolution to "follow the Africans, the enlightened ones" who are "part of the changing African landscape" (Duiker, *Quiet Violence* 438). Duiker and the other writers I have discussed in these pages occupy a (figurative) space that is at once part of the larger national project of witnessing and documenting the past, and yet distanced from and even critical of that project. Writers such as Vladislavić and Dangor take the country's archives and museum industry as tropes, subjects, and settings in their writings; indeed, twenty-first-century artists in general, in South Africa and internationally, have much to learn from such sites as the District Six Museum and Constitution Hill, which I discussed in my introduction. The architects of those sites have innovated novel strategies for the fixed spatial rendering of the memories of ordinary people who lived through and suffered under apartheid—in the Constitutional Court's painted shingles illustrating the stories of children from Hillbrow, for example, or the annotated map of District Six on the floor of that Museum.

Such representational devices give ordinary people, who suffered under and struggled against apartheid without notice or glory, a stake in the nation's shared narratives of the past. Indeed, many works of post-TRC South African literature have developed intriguing narrative and representational strategies that point from the fragments and recollections of the uncertain past into unforeseeable futures. Through these radical acts of memory and imagination, which bring many and diverse narratives of the past into present consciousness, South African artists and authors are doing their own modest part to remap the strictures built into their social spaces.

These models and strategies for making explicit what is untellable about traumatic violence, and for mapping the endless layers of loss, are much needed today, in South Africa and in the world. Within the country, many people have experienced what might be called "TRC fatigue," and are simply tired of talking about the country's violent past. The novels, plays, poems, and memoirs I have discussed here give us two reasons to resist this amnesia born of truth fatigue: first, a traumatic past that has been repressed rather than mourned will come back to haunt the survivors (and even their children) regardless; and second, the process of community mourning is one that must be continually reperformed, both to keep the loss contained and, perhaps paradoxically, to keep the absent one alive in social memory. With a whole generation now coming of age whose members were born after Mandela was released from prison, and for whom apartheid seems to be ancient history, the power of elegiac art to keep remembered narratives of the past alive will become increasingly urgent.

What I would hope, then, is that South Africans and outside observers will regard the TRC process not as a closing the book on a past so as to put it behind them for good, but rather as a document of provisional coordinates that provides a beginning point for the constant process of remapping the lines between past, present, and future. This remapping is happening at the local, the national, and (with the influx of African immigrants in recent years, and with the staging of the TRC as global spectacle of nation-building) the international level. It is finding expression in many forms: literature and theater, clearly, and also art, film, public memorials and museums, architecture, music, and dance. These imaginative cartographic projects are open to all—and indeed, many of the authors I have discussed emphasize the need for inclusiveness, participation, and autonomy—but those who wish to take part must lay themselves open to the "Africanization" of space, which involves not just redistribution but radically different conceptions about ownership and use of land and resources.

International readers also have much to learn from South Africa's literature of memory, truth-telling, and reconciliation. It has become commonplace to note the ubiquity of memory questions in the twentieth century,[3] but the past decade has presented its own distressingly large share of political violence and trauma: On the African continent alone, political chaos in Zimbabwe and war and genocide in the Congo, Sudan, Uganda, and other countries have displaced millions of shell-shocked refugees (many of whom are ending up on the unwelcoming streets of South Africa's cities). And in my own American context, there are of course the terrorist attacks on New York and Washington DC on September 11, 2001; the destruction of New Orleans due to Hurricane Katrina and official malign neglect; the invasions of Afghanistan and Iraq; and such national disgraces as the Abu Ghraib prison scandal and similar scandals at the U.S.-run Guantanamo Bay detention facility.

In the case of the last-mentioned example, it seems significant that the earliest theatrical work to attempt to deal with the experiences of British-born detainees released from Guantanamo Bay was *Guantanamo: Honor Bound to Defend Freedom*, codevised by South African writer Gillian Slovo. In her fiction, especially in *Red Dust*, Slovo has dealt extensively with the dilemmas of agency and memory inherent in the TRC process. In *Guantanamo*, Slovo and coauthor Victoria Brittain bring to bear on the detentions without trial in Gitmo the collaborative strategies of such TRC-inspired drama as *The Story I Am about to Tell*, *He Left Quietly*, and *Ubu and the Truth Commission*. If operations such as Vlakplaas were, until Eugene de Kock's trial and the TRC amnesty hearings, a great lacuna in South Africa's understanding of even its recent past, then Guantanamo Bay is a vast blind spot in the U.S. public's perception of itself and of America's place in the world. Brittain's and Slovo's play uses detainee narratives to take us inside one of the dark, sequestered spots on earth, and "maps" for us in dramatic form that which has been lost in those prison cells.

In all the far-flung situations in which narratives of the past play crucial roles in political struggle and group identity—which is to say, in every country of the world—various forces compel a sort of political amnesia, or at least a highly selective remembering. South Africa makes a particularly illuminating test case, as the predictable elements of nation-building expediency, perpetrator denial, and victim anguish have combined with a veritable "flash flood" of globalized consumer capitalism to create a sort of laboratory for studying the processes of remembrance and forgetting.

Notes

Introduction: Mapping Loss

1. The spelling of Kumalo's surname seems to be contested: it is spelled "Khumalo" in the TRC transcripts and in the program notes for the 2000 production of *The Story I Am about to Tell*. But it is spelled "Kumalo" in the program for the 2002 Grahamstown Festival at which *He Left Quietly* debuted (except for one instance of "Khumalo"!) and in his obituary that appeared in *The Guardian* on 20 March 2006. I have chosen to spell it Kumalo except where doing so would change a citation or quotation.
2. The category "coloured" was used in apartheid law to describe the mixed descendents of the indigenous Khoi-San peoples of the Western Cape, Asian slaves brought to the early Cape Colony, black Africans, and white settlers. I use the term "coloured" guardedly, aware of its painful apartheid baggage, yet unaware of a satisfactory alternative term for what, after decades of segregation, has become a de facto community, especially in the Western Cape where coloured people are a majority of the population, united by circumstances and a particular dialect of Afrikaans.
3. Martin Legassick has argued that the British colonial authorities attempted to create a new kind of society in South Africa, a central aspect of which was "native policy"—i.e., they saw the need to "proletarianize" the natives (46). Harold Wolpe similarly argues that the decline of agricultural production in the reserves created "a substantial economic prop of cheap labour power" (76). Of course, such socio-spatial engineering was not unique to South Africa, but was in fact characteristic of European policies in settler colonies everywhere.
4. Lefebvre further notes that if "space is a product, our knowledge of it must be expected to reproduce and expound the process of production" (36). Neil Smith poses the same idea succinctly as "the *political* question: how does the geographical configuration of the landscape contribute to the survival of capitalism?" (xiii).
5. I am updating Harvey's list somewhat: the commercial Internet and cellular phone networks did not exist in 1990 when Harvey published *The Condition of Postmodernity*. But the development of such technologies has only heightened and intensified the phenomenon of time-space compression that Harvey diagnosed two decades ago.

6. For an elaboration, see David Bunn, "Comparative Barbarisms."
7. For a discussion of the implications of Lefebvre's conceptual triad specifically for the study of spatial relationships in South Africa, see Jennifer Robinson. I share Robinson's interest in the power of cultural expression to help us rethink fundamental spatial configuration; she argues that cultural activities "transform city space, as much as—or perhaps even more than—political struggle and institutional reform. The imagination, then, is a crucial part of (re)making city spaces" (165).
8. Many of the theorists discussed earlier have been criticized for overstating the extent to which relations of economic production and reproduction determine the production of space. For feminist critiques of the male theorists of postmodernism—especially Harvey, Jameson, and Edward Soja—see Doreen Massey and Sallie Marston. In the case of South Africa, to ignore apartheid's and colonialism's pathological obsessions with race is as severe an omission as to ignore gender relations. Indeed, to discuss the production of space while treating race as merely an incidental byproduct of specialization in the labor market would be to grossly distort and minimize the socio-spatial legacy of apartheid.
9. Gillian Hart has described the mid-1990s as a "kaleidoscopic moment when everything shifted to form new patterns" (1), and points out "a profound irony of the post-apartheid moment: that political liberation and emancipatory promises coincided with the ascendance of market triumphalism on a global scale, defining the terrain on which the newly elected democratic state came to embrace neoliberalism" (17). Patrick Bond is even more blunt in his criticisms of South Africa's "elite transition," claiming that its inexorable outcome appears to be "[w]orsening class division and social segregation," which makes a mockery of Mbeki's talk about ending "global apartheid" (*Talk Left* 15; see also *Elite Transition*).
10. Brent Harris, e.g., quotes politicians and people involved with the TRC who "presented it as 'shutting the book on the country's past,' as coming to 'terms with our dark past *once and for all*,' and as closing 'a horrendous chapter in the life of our nation'" (162).
11. Thanks to Pallavi Rastogi for pointing out this etymological connection in her reading of the manuscript.
12. Huyssen explains the seeming contradiction by explaining the first phenomenon as a psychological response to the second: "memory and musealization together are called upon to provide a bulwark against obsolescence and disappearance" (23), but "any secure sense of the past itself is being destabilized by our musealizing culture industry and by the media" (24).
13. Derrida notes the plural senses of the term "consignation": "we do not only mean, in the ordinary sense of the word, the act of assigning residence or of entrusting so as to put into reserve (to consign, to deposit)... but here the act of *con*signing through *gathering together signs*" (3). In the context of the South African TRC, the act of consigning evidence into the quasi-official archive is to gather together the "signs" and documents of apartheid violence, and to sequester them from daily consciousness.

14. The Women's Monument and Memorial in Bloemfontein (commemorating the women and children who died in British concentration camps during the Anglo-Boer War of 1899–1902) and Hans Strijdom Square in Pretoria serve similar ideological functions by creating spatial representations of a particular view of history. Bunn argues that "[s]uch monuments are essentially devices for keeping selective memory alive. Past traumas... are contained and recirculated for each new generation of white children" ("Whited Supulchres" 104).
15. Studying the potency of national symbols, Nhlanhla Maake notes that South African history is "an inscription of a series of myths on the landscape of memory" through such vehicles as the flag and the national anthem (147).
16. Steven Robins warns that "the problem of historiographical representation is further compounded by the tendency of both official and popular accounts of collective suffering to serve (ethnic) nationalist agendas" ("Silence" 122).
17. District Six was the densely populated, mixed-race neighborhood in the central city bowl, whose residents were forcibly removed under the Group Areas Act in the 1960s and 1970s. The homes were all destroyed, but ongoing controversies over the space prevented its planned redevelopment as a whites-only area, leaving large swaths of vacant land, with the exception of a large Technikon on the western edge of the district.
18. Hannah le Roux remarks that in the short distance between the dark courtyard of the prison complex and the panoramic ramparts of the fort lies "the territory that, in order to gain a sense of citizenship under the new Constitution, we need to learn to negotiate" (38–39).
19. Patrick Bond's description of the court as "an island of pomp within a sea of decay" (*Cities* 3) seems uncharitable given the relative modesty of the exterior architecture.
20. In reference to plans for an enormous Holocaust Memorial in Berlin, Huyssen notes the irony in the fact that "a country whose culture has been guided for decades now by a deliberate antifascist antimonumentalism should resort to monumental dimensions when it comes to public commemoration of the Holocaust for the reunified nation" (32).
21. Achille Mbembe argues that the impulse to document the past is rooted in Freud's death drive, the compulsion toward oblivion: "Archiving is a kind of interment, laying something in a coffin, if not to rest, then at least to consign elements of that life which could not be destroyed purely and simply" ("Power" 22). Thus, according to Mbembe, the function of the archive is to impose order on the past, enabling a type of forgetfulness crucial to the existence of the nation: "the power of the state rests on its ability to consume time, that is, to abolish the archive and anaesthetise the past" (23). His observations ring especially true in South Africa, where the realities of a negotiated settlement and war crimes committed on both sides of the political divide have rendered a certain kind of historical amnesia necessary to the peaceful transition. Mark Gevisser, content advisor to the team that designed Constitution Hill, explains that one of their goals was to make the site "dynamic" rather than "ossified": "because the South African foundation myth is such a dynamic one—the negotiated

settlement, the nation that talked itself out of war and into democracy—it won't be, it can't be, a project of ossification or memorialization" (518).

22. Recent films that have dealt with the Truth Commission and related issues include *Forgiveness*, the adaptation of Gillian Slovo's novel *Red Dust*, and *uCarmen eKhayelitsha*, an isiZulu adaptation of Bizet's *Carmen* set in the infamous Cape Town township.
23. J.U. Jacobs, e.g., argues that an important aspect of the narrative in Mda's *The Heart of Redness* is "its *palimpsest* structure" ("Zakes Mda's *Heart*" 228); and Kai Easton suggests that the icons of Krotoä-Eva and Saartje Baartman "reside as palimpsests" in Wicomb's *David's Story* (245). The trope of "urban palimpsests" also recurs frequently in the contemporary social sciences, and the novels I study in part 2 of this book reveal the post-apartheid city to consist of just such palimpsestic layers, simultaneously revealing and obscuring glimpses of the past as inscribed on the urban landscape.

Part 1 Spaces of Truth-Telling: The TRC and Post-Apartheid Literatures of Memory

1. Albie Sachs, e.g., recalls "How affecting that was—how contradictory it felt to see this man crying, this horrible person, who was yet somehow feeling ashamed of what he had done" ("His Name" 98). And Frederik van zyl Slabbert singles out Benzien as an exception to the general denials and evasions of the security forces, claiming, "Nobody doubted for a moment that Benzien was telling the truth" (69).
2. In her memoir of the TRC, Antjie Krog likewise offers a dim view of Benzien's performance during his hearing, and poses the thorny question, "How to distinguish between lies and memory loss?" (*Country of My Skull* 78). She also points out that in many ways the experience of facing their former torturer was a retraumatizing ordeal for Benzien's victims: the policeman revealed that Tony Yengeni, an important member of parliament at the time of the hearings, had broken and revealed information after a few minutes of torture with the wet bag. Yazir Henry claims that Benzien "showed very little remorse and in some ways, because of his attitude, continued to torture Yengeni and Forbes and others in his appearance before the Commission" (171).
3. For instance, Gary Kruse grows frustrated at what he calls Benzien's "very selective truth." Benzien claims his memory lapse is so severe that he can remember the names of only seven of his former victims: Of the other names, "I have forgotten them, therefore I also apply [for amnesty] for the cases I cannot remember."
4. This is Sanders's reading: "By reversing roles and asking Benzien questions, are [Yengeni and the others], in effect, not continuing the contest begun ten years before, so that they can wrest control of the situation from Benzien, and retrospectively gain the upper hand?" (*Ambiguities* 101–02). But given how

Benzien turns the tables and uses his testimony to humiliate Yengeni, it is not at all clear how effective the hearing is in restoring control and agency to the former victims.

5. Villa-Vicencio and Verwoerd elsewhere argue that the TRC "sought, however imperfectly, to implement and manage an inclusive, accessible, and transparent process in order to facilitate a pluralistic public account" ("Construction" 289).
6. See Charles Maier for an elaboration of the correspondences between truth commissions and trials.
7. Mark Sanders notes the conflict between these first two imperatives in two of the TRC's four categories of "truth" defined in the *Final Report*, "factual or forensic truth" and "personal or narrative truth" (Truth and Reconciliation Commission I:112). The latter category puts the TRC hearings in the realm of fable and storytelling, but as Sanders points out, "Although [the TRC Report] declares itself hospitable to storytelling, it proves to be more at ease with statements that can be forensically verified or falsified" ("Truth" 20).
8. Posel and Simpson note the ways that the global reception of the TRC shaped the narratives told about it by the local media: "The televised confessional, which is what the public hearings became, created space for the telling of individual stories, but with an overriding sense of their more global, 'human' messages" ("Introduction" 8).
9. The most important volumes devoted (in whole or in part) to the South African Truth and Reconciliation Commission include Asmal, Asmal, and Roberts, *Reconciliation through Truth* (1997); Boraine, Levy, and Scheffer, *Dealing with the Past* (1997); special issue of *African Studies* 57.2 (1998); Bizos, *No One to Blame?* (1998); Nuttall and Coetzee, *Negotiating the Past* (1998); Jeffery, *The Truth about the Truth Commission* (1999); Meiring, *Chronicle of the Truth Commission* (1999); Soyinka, *The Burden of Memory, the Muse of Forgiveness* (1999); Boraine, *A Country Unmasked* (2000); Christie, *The South African Truth Commission* (2000); James and Van de Vijver, *After the TRC* (2000); Orr, *From Biko to Basson* (2000); Rotberg and Thompson, *Truth v. Justice* (2000); Tutu, *No Future without Forgiveness* (2000); Villa-Vicencio and Verwoerd, *Looking Back Reaching Forward* (2000); Graybil, *Truth and Reconciliation in South Africa* (2002); Posel and Simpson, *Commissioning the Past* (2002); Ross, *Bearing Witness* (2003); Villa-Vicencio and Doxtader, *The Provocations of Amnesty* (2003); Gibson, *Overcoming Apartheid* (2004); Villa-Vicencio and Du Toit, *Truth and Reconciliation in South Africa* (2006); Sanders, *Ambiguities of Witnessing* (2007).
10. In this regard, the penetrating insights of Mahmood Mamdani have been influential and often quoted. He suggests that the "real power of the Commission was exercised through the work of its main body. That was the power to define the terms of a social debate and, in so doing, define the parameters of truth seeking" ("Diminished" 58), and asks, "What kind of truth did the TRC produce and will its version of truth hold?" (59). His answer is that the "truth" about the past as exposed by the TRC was too narrow: it "focused on torture, murder and rape, ignoring everything that was

distinctive about apartheid and its machinery of violence" (60). For similar arguments, see Bundy; Rassool et al.; H. van der Merwe; and Robins, "Silence."

11. Frederik van zyl Slabbert argues that the TRC is "based on suppositions and assumptions [about the universal and transferable nature of truth] that, even if they are not demonstrably invalid, are nevertheless misleading and ambiguous" (68). See also Bonner and Nieftagodien; Posel and Simpson, "Introduction"; and Brent Harris.
12. Anthea Jeffery, e.g., asks, "How factual were the victim statements?" and answers that, because testimony was neither given under oath nor subjected to cross-examination, "it would be surprising if even a hundred of its 21,300 victim statements passed muster as 'factual evidence'" (9).
13. The earliest legal battle, e.g., came from the families of Steve Biko, Griffith and Victoria Mxenge, and Fabian and Florence Rebeiro, who unsuccessfully challenged the constitutionality of the TRC's power to give amnesty to their loved one's murderers. Mamdani asks bluntly: "If truth has replaced justice has reconciliation turned into an embrace of evil?" ("Reconciliation" 3). Wole Soyinka is similarly skeptical: "Truth as prelude to reconciliation, that seems logical enough; but Truth as the justification, as the sole exaction or condition for Reconciliation? That is what constitutes a stumbling block in the South African proceedings" (13).
14. Analisa Oboe aptly describes the hearings as "a national ritual, a mixture of religious service, legal interrogation, oral history interview, and healing ceremony that has profiled itself as a performance model of narration" (62). I would suggest that it is the highly public performance of this "national ritual" that made the TRC so relatively effective as a vehicle for working through the national trauma of apartheid.
15. The idea that the TRC should discredit the apartheid dispensation and uphold the heroism of the resistance movements is the central thesis of *Reconciliation through Truth* by Kader Asmal, Louise Asmal, and Ronald Suresh Roberts. Similarly, repeating a well-known line from his *Jail Diary*, Albie Sachs suggests there is a need for acknowledgment that "we got into trouble not for being bad, but for being good," and that "not just you as an individual but your generation, your endeavours, your dreams and your goals were fundamentally right and human" ("Personal Accounts" 23).
16. See, e.g., Lyster for an explicit elaboration of this argument. Even George Bizos, who represented the Biko family in their opposition to the Amnesty Committee, asks, "What justice would there have been in our society if we had not agreed to this amnesty procedure? How many people would have been unjustly killed, maimed or imprisoned in an escalating civil war?" ("Why Prosecutions" 6). Contrarily, Nomfundo Walaza points out that denying individual victims the right to pursue justice against perpetrators in court so as to avert a civil war poses "a conflict between the interests of victims and survivors on the one hand and those of the nation as a whole on the other" (250). She nevertheless acknowledges that without "the process of the TRC, South Africa would not be where it is today" (255).

17. To mention only two examples: Phelps suggests this when she urges us to read the stories of trauma survivors as "tools of disruption. We must allow [Truth Commission] reports to be incomplete, multivalent, heteroglossic" (128). And Gallagher argues, rather charitably, that the TRC's truth is "a narrative truth rather than a propositional one, resisting closure" (135), by which she implies that it is only the first step in a long process.
18. Villa-Vicencio repeats a version of this claim elsewhere: The "academically challenging and morally imperative exercise of reading between the lines, hearing behind the words, looking behind the scenes and honouring the silence behind the words waits to be done" (24). Posel, in many ways critical of the TRC, echoes this sentiment: "Whatever the limits of its report, the TRC has created significant opportunities for an engagement with the past, which have not yet been realised fully. Its large archive promises to be an important resource for academic and popular historians, provided it remains open and accessible" ("TRC Report" 168).
19. This vision of a contrapuntal narrative is close to the one also urged by Ingrid de Kok: "It is in the multiplicity of partial versions and experiences, composed and recomposed within sight of each other, that truth 'as a thing of this world,' in Foucault's phrase, will emerge" ("Cracked Heirlooms" 61).
20. Paul Gready argues that, by holding hearings in locations throughout the country, the Truth Commission "epitomized the newly found capacity to traverse space" (285). More specific to my argument, Erik Doxtader notes the ability of the Truth Commission (in his case, the amnesty provisions) to break down divides between public and private, though he regards it as cause for alarm rather than celebration: "the rationale for amnesty risks the outright collapse of the distinction between public and private, demanding revelation in the name of a unity that obscures precisely the difference which sustains memory's relational potential" ("Easy to Forget" 143).
21. See Graham, "The Truth Commission."
22. Throughout this section, I use the name Duma to refer to the character in the play, and Kumalo to refer to Duma Kumalo the man, actor, and playwright.
23. As Loren Kruger puts it, *Ubu* and *The Story* "take diametrically opposed positions on the ethics of representing the suffering of others": whereas *The Story* "attempts to avoid the charges of inauthenticity or aestheticization by bringing survivors themselves onto the stage to express and to represent their experiences in dialogue with actors and audiences," *Ubu* "uses puppets to represent victims and survivors and thus to highlight the risk of inauthenticity" (553–54).
24. The authorship of *Ubu and the Truth Commission* is equally complex. The script was written by Jane Taylor, a professor of Dramatic Art at the University of the Witwatersrand and author of a novel, *Of Wild Dogs* (2005). But the play was jointly conceived by Taylor; by William Kentridge, a director, animator, and South Africa's most celebrated contemporary visual artist; and by the members of the Handspring Puppet Company, an innovative theater group formed in 1981 whose productions include *Woyzeck on the Highveld* (1992), *Faustus in Africa* (1994), *The Chimp Project* (2000), *Confessions of Zeno* (2002), and *Tall Horse* (2004).

25. The crocodile is associated in South African political discourse with former Prime Minister P.W. Botha, "die ou Krokodil." Botha gained renewed notoriety for his refusal to cooperate with or testify at the TRC. It is somewhat ironic, then, that Niles the Crocodile urges Pa Ubu to confess his crimes at the Commission. Yet, as one anonymous reviewer of my article in *Research in African Literatures* noted, the figure of Botha serves as "a kind of repository for the secrets of a larger, surreal agent."
26. Colin Bundy describes the sections of the TRC Final Report dealing with the destruction of records, noting that there are no surviving records of the Civil Cooperation Bureau (CCB) or the National Security Management System: "At the NIS headquarters, in six to eight months in 1993, the mass destruction of forty-four tons of paper and microfilm records took place" (16).
27. Jill Bennett describes this phenomenon in terms of "the Brechtian 'separation of elements,' by which voice and gesture are distinguished as the products of separate manipulations, [which] works to break down the illusion of character" (120–21).
28. In *Country of My Skull*, Antjie Krog draws attention to the dangerous potential of pronouns when she reports what one of the interpreters for the TRC hearings told her: "It is difficult to interpret victim hearings... because you use the first person all the time. I have no distance when I say 'I'... it runs through me with I." A psychiatrist hired by the TRC tells the interpreter that this is a "disastrous attitude" (129).
29. Jill Bennett observes that the tripod "also functions as an instrument of torture, so that no clear distinction is drawn between devices that record violent events and those that collude, and even intervene, in them" (113).
30. Anticipating one of the central tropes I discuss in part 3, Michael Carklin compares this process to an archaeological dig: *Ubu and the Truth Commission*, he says, offers us

    narratives made up of fragments, clues, intertextual references, and juxtaposed references.... [R]ather than understanding the work of these theatre-makers as being akin to that of the dramatic historian, it is perhaps more useful to understand it as a process of theatrical archeology in which we explore with them layers of imaginative debris, or excavate tangible fragments that could lead us to new insights into the manifold human experiences that constitute our past. (24)

31. In a similar vein, Dennis Walder suggests that the "great strength of *Ubu and the Truth Commission* is that it crosses national, cultural and linguistic frontiers in remembering the past, re-membering or bringing together fragments in the present.... Developing a representation of interiority, of multiple subjectivities, necessarily involves the development of an art of multiple viewpoints, multiple perspectives—hence, too, necessarily, of error" (160).
32. Krog was born in 1952 near Kroonstad in the Free State. She has published eleven volumes of adult poetry in Afrikaans and English, the first appearing in 1970. She won multiple awards for her coverage of the TRC for SABC Radio. Her second book of prose in English, *A Change of Tongue*, was published

in 2003. She was recently appointed Extraordinary Professor in the Arts at the University of the Western Cape.

33. Mark Sanders reads Krog's invented relationship as an "'allegory' for the [TRC] hearings and what is enacted there between questioner and witness" ("Truth" 29); the "affair," Sanders says, "dramatizes... the need for an interlocutor, a 'you'... before whom 'I' can speak" (30).
34. Laura Moss is less forgiving:

    > If *Country of My Skull* is read at least in part as a narrativization of a historical event, such shaping is understandable. If it is read as journalistic documentary, however, it is simply unethical. The problem of extending the "essence of the Commission" into the text is that outside of South Africa *Country of My Skull* has been read as presenting the truth of South African history, rather than the narrator's truth. (87)

    This important critique is given more force by the fact that the American edition omits Krog's admission that the affair was invented.
35. Some of Krog's critics are unconvinced by her logic. Claudia Braude, e.g., calls Krog's insistence on her right to take creative liberties in her representations of events around the TRC "naïve or dishonest" (Braude 9). Braude argues that Krog's definition of the truth echoes the NP's warning in its submission to the TRC of the "elusive nature of truth." Yet Krog is surely no apologist for the former regime, nor, conversely, for the ANC. Neither does her definition of truth devolve into a solipsistic moral relativism. Rather, she believes in a truth that, however real and absolute in itself, cannot be fully and satisfactorily represented, but can only be approximated and reconstructed through language. Krog writes that "[i]f [the TRC] sees truth as the widest possible compilation of people's perceptions, stories, myths and experiences, it will have chosen to restore memory and foster a new humanity, and perhaps that is justice in its deepest sense" (*Country* 16).
36. Louise Viljoen puts it somewhat differently: "The reconstruction of identity... implies dis-placement from an earlier subject position" (43), a process in which Krog engages by dramatizing her own subjectivity.
37. Compounding this difficulty is the sheer number of people who gave testimony during the victim hearings and *in camera* interviews—over 22,000 people. Wendy Orr describes the commissioners' efforts to include a summary in the Final Report of the TRC's findings regarding each victim, beyond a cold list of names: "As it became apparent that we were running out of available space, the summaries had to be rewritten in fewer and fewer words" (341–42). Ultimately, the summaries were not completed in time for inclusion in the initial five-volume Report from 1998, and were not published in full until the release of Volume Seven in 2003.
38. Yazir Henry, an ANC guerilla who under threats and beatings from the police revealed the location of his comrade Anton Fransch, seems to agree with Ruden. Henry has complained about the way in which Krog and others have appropriated his narrative, as when he writes, "I have... had my story located within the context of other stories and had several different histories imposed on me since testifying.... The most hurtful of these 'identities' is one that

places me as the agonised confessor or the betrayer that should be pitied" (Henry 166–67).

39. See Ashleigh Harris for more troubling questions about Krog's practice of "quilting" the truth from various sources in light of accusations of plagiarism in Krog's translations of /Xam poetry.
40. Durrant writes that J.M. Coetzee's decision "not to grant 'proper' names to... his figures of alterity is a sign of his failure—his ethical refusal—to integrate them fully into his narratives. One needs the specificity of the name in order to mourn" (437).
41. In Ursula Barnett's phrase, Krog restores to the shepherd "a poetic dignity by setting out his tale as though spoken in verse" (803).
42. See, e.g., Johan Jacobs, "Reconciling," and Judith Lütge Coullie.
43. Ingrid de Kok was born in 1951, and raised in Stilfontein and Johannesburg. She is associate professor of Extra Mural Studies at the University of Cape Town. *Transfer* and *Terrestrial Things* are her second and third poetry collections, respectively; the first was *Familiar Ground* (1988), and the most recent is *Seasonal Fires: Selected and New Poems* (2006). She is also the editor of *Spring Is Rebellious: Albie Sachs and Respondents on Cultural Freedom* (1990) with Karen Press, and of *City in Words: Poems on Cape Town* (2001) with Gus Ferguson.
44. Sindiwe Magona was born in 1943 in what would become the homeland of Transkei. She was raised in a township near Cape Town. She has published two autobiographies, *To My Children's Children* (1991) and *Forced to Grow* (1992), and two collections of short stories: *Living, Loving and Lying Awake at Night* (1991) and *Push-Push! and Other Stories* (1996). After working for the United Nations in New York for many years, she now lives in Cape Town.
45. Johan Jacobs argues that "[t]he traditional Xhosa forms of politeness that Mandisa recollects belong to the past of the rural village, Gungululu" in the Eastern Cape, where Mandisa is sent to live with her maternal grandmother after she falls pregnant ("Cross-Cultural" 56). Jacobs continues, "The world of the urban African under apartheid is presented in terms of severance from those values" (56).
46. For an incisive discussion of Magona's representation of spatial politics in the life of domestic workers, see Koyana, "Womanism."
47. Koyana notes, "African women have always worked, farming in the fields mostly. It was the dominant patriarchal colonial policies, based on the Euro-Christian and Victorian notions of 'the Good Mother' as the emotional centre of the family, that focused on the domestic world and separated mothers from the world of work and citizenship" ("Why" 47–48). She argues elsewhere that Magona's writing resists this patriarchal partitioning of space into public and domestic, and that it attempts "to challenge society to create a more enabling environment for women in the envisioned new South Africa" (Koyana, "Womanism" 64). In part this happens through the community of women forged despite the antisocial constraints of apartheid; as Magona says in an interview, "all a writer can do is state her truth, her hopes and her fears. Alone she can change nothing. It is in joining others in the community that she can

be an agent of change" (in Koyana and Gray 102). We see a glimpse of this after Mxolisi's arrest, when a group of neighbors visits despite Mandisa's assumption that they were shunning her: her friend Yolisa declares simply, "We have come to be with you in this time," and the narrator tells us, "It is people such as these who give me strength" (*Mother* 201).

48. Zakes Mda undertakes a similar project in *The Heart of Redness* (see section 3.3), in which the cattle killing is again recuperated as a moment of desperate but comprehensible resistance to an invasion of aggressive outsiders.
49. Drama has been a particularly rich generic vehicle through which South African writers have explored the scripts and dynamics of truth and reconciliation. For my take on two such plays (in two articles that began life as sections of this book, but were then cut due to length), see Graham, "I Was Those Thousands," about John Kani's *Nothing But the Truth*; and Graham, "Mapping Memory," about Zakes Mda's *The Bells of Amersfoort*. For my analysis of a collection of short stories that deals with these same questions of memory and memorialization, see my treatment of Ivan Vladislavić's *Propaganda by Monuments and Other Stories* in Graham, "Memory, Memorialization."

Part 2 Post-Apartheid Urban Spaces

1. Rita Barnard points out this same ironic potential: "The fact that the disciplinary space of the township became the crucial locus of resistance in the antiapartheid struggle suggests that we need to be suspicious of totalizing models of power, of descriptions of places that ignore the transformative and creative capacities of human beings" (7).
2. David Harvey develops this notion when he describes an urban environment as "a palimpsest, a series of layers constituted and constructed at different historical moments all superimposed upon each other" ("Contested Cities" 21–22). Andreas Huyssen likewise uses the metaphor of "urban palimpsests" to describe contemporary Berlin; in debates over city planning, a notion is emerging of "Berlin as palimpsest, a disparate city-text that is being rewritten while previous text is preserved, traces are restored, erasures documented" (81). Amin and Thrift use a different variation of the urban palimpsest metaphor, arguing that "the spatial and temporal porosity of the city also opens it to *footprints* from the past and contemporary links elsewhere" (22; emphasis added).
3. Ronit Frenkel similarly notes of Achmat Dangor, "In texts that simultaneously unearth sedimented levels of historical understandings, and establish overlapping and contradictory layers of current cultural histories, he reveals the complex cultural formations that undergird contemporary South Africa" (149).
4. See Deborah Posel, "The Meaning of Apartheid."
5. See Frescura for an analysis of the township as a mechanism of social control.
6. Gentrification efforts are under way in several areas of inner Johannesburg, especially in the Newtown/Market Theatre district, where several clubs,

restaurants, and performance spaces are now located, in the Carleton Centre, where a newly renovated mall has been opened, and in the area around Constitution Hill on the border of Braamfontein and Hillbrow. Such gentrification is also taking place in many areas of Cape Town, Durban, and other urban centers, and government "clean-up" efforts are likely to intensify in the run-up to the 2010 Football World Cup. While mixed-income developments that bring a measure of prosperity and safety back to South Africa's city centers would be desirable indeed, there is considerable cause for concern that gentrification will result—indeed, is resulting, as in other parts of the world—in the poor being forced to relocate to distant areas outside the city. Such an effect would perpetuate the socio-spatial policies of apartheid in grimly ironic ways.

7. Bremner, e.g., describes the office buildings that remain in the Johannesburg Central Business District as fortresses in which everything employees need—"library, restaurant, convenience store, travel agent, bank, crèche—can be found on its secured inner street" (Bremner, *Johannesburg* 57). See also Bremner, "Crime," and Steven Robins, "City Sites" on the fortification of the post-apartheid city.
8. Dear and Flusty "have identified a postmodern urban process in which the urban periphery organizes the centre within the context of a globalizing capitalism" (80). Certainly this observation holds true for Johannesburg, where much commercial and residential development in recent years has taken place in Sandton or the edge cities of the Midrand and East Rand. See André Czeglédy on the "literal *inversion* of the urban structure" (28).
9. Neil Smith argues that uneven development is a strategic and integral part of global capitalist expansion: "Capital, rather than using the underdeveloped world as a source of markets, has instead used the Third World as a source of cheap labour, thus preventing its full integration into the world market" (157). Patrick Bond has argued that "the *uneven development* of South Africa's cities and black townships...was generally *amplified* during the 1990s transition to democracy, which was also a transition to 'neoliberal,' market-oriented ways of organizing urban policy" (*Cities* xiii; his emphasis).
10. The tradition of materialist political geography from which the notion of uneven development derives typically sees the buildings and infrastructure of a city as "*capital*, set in intractable, immovable, and hence confined, space....But in turn, cities are spaces where contradictions in the capitalist mode of production therefore play themselves out most forcefully" (Bond, *Cities* 6). Recently, however, other theorists operating within the Marxist tradition have argued that new technologies and new postmodern forms of socio-spatial organization have decreased capital's reliance on urban spatial fixity: "We now find that capital is no longer concerned about cities. Capital needs fewer workers and much of it can move all over the world, deserting problematic places and populations at will" (Harvey, "Contested Cities" 20).
11. Huyssen asks, "What if the relationship between memory and forgetting were actually being transformed under cultural pressures in which new information technologies, media politics, and fast-paced consumption are beginning

to take their toll?" (17), and suggests that the psychic processes described by Freud of "remembering, repressing, and forgetting in individuals is writ large in contemporary consumer societies as a public phenomenon of unprecedented proportions" (17). My reading of the novels in part 2 suggests that the crisis of memory and forgetting predicted by Huyssen is indeed occurring in contemporary South Africa, and is experienced most intensely in the cities and suburbs.

12. See, e.g., the recent special issue of *Public Culture* called "Johannesburg: The Elusive Metropolis," edited by Achille Mbembe and Sarah Nuttall; Simone, *For the City Yet to Come*; and Dawson and Edwards.
13. In this regard, then, economistic theories that regard the city as primarily a fixed form of capital are inadequate to describe the complexity of the lived experience of the city. Indeed, much recent theory on urban space has worked toward a more comprehensive model that can take into account multiple "contingencies" that shape urban life. Marcuse and Van Kempen argue that globalization "is only one of a number of contingencies in explaining the formation of changes in the spatial order" of contemporary cities ("Conclusion" 266), including natural and built geography, history, race, inequality, and politics. Keil and Ronneberger similarly argue that "globalization should not be fetishized and reified as a steamroller over 'local places.' Rather... it has to be seen as a distinctive set of social practices that are conflictive and contradictory and subject to social and political struggles" (228).
14. Alison Brown sees this as a global phenomenon in the developing world: "Space is controlled by boundaries and social conventions that distinguish between the public and private realm. For the urban poor, private space is restricted and fragmented, and so urban public space becomes an essential resource often ignored in narrow policy focus on housing and shelter" (10).
15. Lindsay Bremner points out a crucial distinction between the "socio-spatial practices" of each location:

    > [In bourgeois socio-spatial schemas, the] private work of the home and the public world of work or leisure are distinct and separate. For the working class, these overlap and merge—inside and outside, public and private, family and community, work and home.... It is this attitude to and use of space which is transforming the roads, streets and pavements of Johannesburg since apartheid loosened its grip on the city, reinstating them, not as thoroughfares, but as common ground for public life. (*Johannesburg* 108)

16. Michel de Certeau's notion of the "pedestrian speech act," in which "the crossing, drifting away, or improvisation of walking privilege, transform or abandon spatial elements" (98), helps to make sense of such activities: as pedestrians who never move from one spot, the hawkers transform the red light—an instrument designed to control mobility—into a makeshift marketplace.
17. Dangor is a Johannesburg-born writer of mixed Indian and coloured descent. He is a poet, playwright, and fiction writer whose prose works include *Waiting for Leila* (1978), *The Z Town Trilogy* (1989), and *Kafka's Curse* (1997). *Bitter Fruit* was shortlisted for the Man Booker Prize upon its publication in the

United Kingdom in 2004. Dangor is currently director of Advocacy & Communications at the Joint United Nations Program on AIDS, and has recently lived in New York and Geneva.

18. As Tim Woods notes, *Bitter Fruit* "suggests that confessing the truth does not lead to freedom, but rather opens fresh wounds that persist in tainting the present" (215).
19. Reading this passage, I immediately think of the enormous and enormously gaudy statue of Mandela in Nelson Mandela Square, an upscale shopping and dining center in Sandton.
20. Ivan Vladislavić first emerged as a fiction writer in 1989 with the publication of a collection of short stories called *Missing Persons*, and he cemented his reputation as an important emerging author with his first novel *The Folly* (1993). In the post-apartheid era he has produced *Propaganda by Monuments and Other Stories* (1996), his sophomore novel *The Restless Supermarket* (2001), and his third novel *The Exploded View* (2004). His piece of short fiction, *The Model Men* (2004), was accompanied by illustrations by Joachim Schönfeldt, and he has likewise established his reputation as a major critic of South African art with his essay *Willem Boshoff* (2005), about one of South Africa's most important sculptors and conceptual artists. His most recent publication is a sort of meditative and novelistic collection of essays about Johannesburg entitled *Portrait with Keys: Jo'burg and What-What* (2006). Moreover, Vladislavić's importance as a writer has been rivaled by his crucial role as an editor at Random House South Africa—he has edited some seminal texts of post-apartheid literature, including Antjie Krog's *Country of My Skull*, Achmat Dangor's *Bitter Fruit*, and *The Free Diary of Albie Sachs*.
21. For example, Marais says that the protagonist Aubrey Tearle "routinely instantiates a colonialist discourse of race in his dealings with others. His obsessive attempts at imposing order on his society are . . . the expression of this discursive formation's territorial desire for closure, its impulse to construct itself as a finite, bounded totality" ("Visions" 104–05).
22. See, e.g.: Gaylard and Titlestad; Saffron Hall; Susan van Zyl; Felicity Wood; and Elaine Young, "Or Is It . . . ."
23. Mbembe explains:

    > The architecture of hysteria in contemporary South Africa is the result of a painful, shocking encounter with a radical alterity set loose by the collapse of the racial city. . . . It bears witness to an irretrievable loss—the loss of the racial city. This is a case of traumatic amnesia and not of forgetting, of the disavowal of time as opposed to memorialization. . . . [T]he mark of the past here is only a trace, not a literal recollection. ("Aesthetics" 403)

    This could be taken as a summary of Vladislavić's depiction of Johannesburg in all his recent work, in which the urban archive serves as a mechanism of forgetting rather than recollection.
24. I would argue that this is an ongoing theme in Vladislavić's writing. For a longer discussion of how Vladislavić uses the palimpsestic structure of his stories and novels to replicate and make visible the partially erased layers of

collective memory, see my article "Memory, Memorialization, and the Transformation of Johannesburg: Ivan Vladislavić's *Propaganda by Monuments* and *The Restless Supermarket*" in *Modern Fiction Studies.*

25. Vladislavić's depiction of the city confirms certain aspects of Saskia Sassen's analysis of "the spatiotemporality of economic globalization itself [which] can already be seen to contain dynamics of both fixity and mobility" (262).
26. Phaswane Mpe was born in 1970 in Polokwane in the northern Limpopo province. In many ways the character Refentše is an autobiographical figure, as he, like Mpe, moved to Johannesburg to attend the University of the Witwatersrand. Mpe published poetry and a small handful of short stories; *Welcome to Our Hillbrow* was his first and only novel. He was training to be a traditional healer when he died in 2004 of an unknown illness, probably AIDS-related.
27. Clarkson offers an extended reading of Mpe's use of the second-person narration, in which she notes a similar effect of this technique: "Mpe's novel is relentlessly written in the second person, and in its explicit address to 'you,' the narrative has the disorientating effect of simultaneously distancing, but engaging the reader in the implied community signalled by the 'our' of the novel's title" ("Locating Identity" 452).
28. Jennifer Robinson makes a similar point about the real-world Hillbrow: "It is not just the flows and connections within cities that reflect and generate their dynamism, and might change their spatiality, but the way they are connected through a wide variety of different linkages to other cities, other places, other times.... Hillbrow is not only connected to townships in Johannesburg and other cities... but the routes of many of its residents stretch the length of Africa" (170).
29. Clarkson reads the novel in terms of a "dissolution of a communal history, of values and obligations that were perhaps once recognised and shared" ("Locating Identity" 453). Certainly we can see signs of this dissolution of identity in the spatial and moral disorientation experienced by Mpe's characters. But I would argue that the novel itself finds its bearings, not in the restoration of older forms of communal history but in an intricate mapping of the global flows that feed into and constitute contemporary Hillbrow and South Africa more generally.
30. Simone declares that "an experience of regularity capable of anchoring the livelihood of residents and their transactions with one another is consolidated precisely because the outcomes of residents' reciprocal efforts are radically open, flexible, and provisional" ("People" 407). Mpe might also be seen as engaging in Walter Benjamin's project of "setting out the sphere of life—bios—graphically on a map," which I discussed in the introduction (*Reflections* 5). Glossing the figure of Benjamin's *flaneur* as "the aesthetic bohemian, drifting through the city like a film director" ("City Forms" 741), Nuttall argues that this figure "invites us to read the city from its street-level intimations, to encounter the city as lived complexity, to seek alternative narratives and maps based on wandering" (741–42). Such bio-mapping, for Benjamin as well as Mpe, involves walking through the city, but it is less interested in yielding a

scientifically accurate scale map—as Mpe's narrator notes, Hillbrow feels at least twice as large as it is to its inhabitants—than it is in noting the social uses of space.

31. Various critics have read Mpe's depiction of post-apartheid Johannesburg in different lights. Manase, e.g., gives an ambivalent view, acknowledging "the new openings arising out of the advent of democracy as well as those openings associated with the country's entrance into current global social and economic linkages" (90) but nevertheless emphasizing the "portrayal of the individual's social dislocation within these cities as well as how this comes about through broader structural forces of apartheid, colonialism and globalization" (89). My own view is closer to that of Emma Hunt, who describes the Johannesburg of *Welcome to Our Hillbrow* as "a cosmopolitan space of connection and opportunity" (114). But this opportunity arises not from anything intrinsic to the city itself, but rather from the ways it is reimagined by its residents and by the author himself.
32. Like Phaswane Mpe, Kabelo Sello Duiker was a promising writer who died at a very early age. He was born in 1974 in Soweto to a family well-off enough to send him to a British-style "public school." His first novel, *Thirteen Cents* (2000), won the Commonwealth Writers Prize for best book by an African writer in 2001. After suffering a nervous breakdown the previous year, he committed suicide early in 2005. His third novel, *The Hidden Star*, was published posthumously in 2006.
33. Jameson borrows Lacan's definition of schizophrenia as a "breakdown in the signifying chain" (26) in which the signifier is divorced not only from the signified but also from the chain of other possible signifiers that give meaning through difference. Jameson claims that "the schizophrenic is reduced to an experience of pure material signifiers, or, in other words, a series of pure and unrelated presents in time" (27). But this can be intoxicating: "This present of the world or material signifier comes before the subject with heightened intensity, bearing a mysterious charge of affect, [often] described in the negative terms of anxiety and loss of reality, but which one could just as well imagine in the positive terms of euphoria, a high, an intoxicatory or hallucinogenic intensity" (28).
34. *The Quiet Violence of Dreams* was published three years after J.M. Coetzee's *Disgrace*, and this scene strongly evokes the scene in Coetzee's novel in which David Lurie is locked in the bathroom while a gang of men rapes his daughter in the next room. Duiker's novel, however, seems to critique the implication in *Disgrace* that rape is some diabolical instrument invented by blacks to inflict revenge on whites: as Duiker makes clear, black women—and black boys and men—have been suffering from an epidemic of rape long before the white population began to have real cause to fear it.
35. Born around 1939, Aziz Hassim wrote *The Lotus People*, his first novel, after retiring from his job as an accountant. It won the 2001 Sanlam Literary Award for an unpublished novel.
36. Pallavi Rastogi notes in post-apartheid writing by Indian South Africans a "turn to the *pre-apartheid* past in order to memorialize the history of Indian

arrival in the African continent" (114). Hassim's novel performs some of this work, but extends it to include the entire history of Indian settlement in Natal.

37. I have borrowed this useful term to describe the identity of South Africans of Indian descent from Pallavi Rastogi.

Part 3 Excavations and the Memory of Landscapes

1. Volume six of the Truth and Reconciliation Commission Report, e.g., reveals that the Commission "received hundreds of requests from families requesting that it trace and exhume the bodies of loved ones. Unfortunately it was not possible to deal with them all: once the Commission's operational period came to an end, it was not permitted by law to continue with this process" (554). Moreover, a task team devoted to making recommendations about future exhumations found "serious corroboration problems" in some 20% of exhumation cases, and "additional corroboration was required" in another 20% (560).
2. Nash argues that art can give us alternative models of mapping closer to Deleuze and Guattari's conception of the map as rhizome rather than a "manifestation of a desire for control" and "an analogue for the acquisition, management, and reinforcement of colonial power" (234). In this view, the "land can symbolize the possibility of fluidity and openness, of multiple and diffuse 'names' and 'maps'" (244–45). This is equally true of, say, Landsman's *The Devil's Chimney*, in which the land beneath Beatrice Chapman's farm is pocked with the labyrinthine, rhizomic Cango Caves, which possess "the possibility of fluidity and openness."
3. To address this historical injustice, the new ANC-led government created the Department of Land Affairs (DLA) in 1994 to oversee land reform, focused on three areas: restitution, redistribution, and tenure. Yet the DLA, following the prescriptions of the World Bank, embraced a so-called Market-Led Agrarian Reform and a policy of "willing buyer/willing seller." These strategies had the desired effect of preventing wholesale capital flight and disinvestment, but were less effective at delivering the promised redistribution of land, which proceeded at a snail's pace. Indeed, by the end of Mandela's term in office in 1999, only 1.65% of total target land had been redistributed (Borras 385), and by 2002, of the over 67,000 land claims filed with the Land Claims Court, only 12,000 had been settled (Commey). As a result of these delivery failures, when Thabo Mbeki's new administration took office in 1999 it created the Land Reform for Agricultural Development bureau, which possessed the power to expropriate land from intransigent farmers where necessary. Even so—and despite the issue's newfound urgency in light of the land invasions and expropriations that began in neighboring Zimbabwe in 2000—by

2005 only about 3% of targeted land had been transferred into black hands, and less than 1% of the government's total budget has been devoted to land reform ("Should Reform...?" 38). Frustrations at the continued sluggishness of land transfer led to what Sihlongonyane calls a "groundswell of grassroots demands for land" (160), represented most visibly by the militant Landless People's Movement and the periodically recurring specter of land occupations and assaults on white farmers. As an illustration of this latter point, between 1994 and 2004, more than 1,500 white South African farmers were violently attacked or killed (Goebel 347).

4. While almost no one disputes the urgency of addressing the inequitable distribution of land and housing, many observers have questioned the DLA's emphasis on *agrarian* reform. In contrasting South Africa with Zimbabwe, e.g., Goebel notes that South Africa's population is much more heavily urbanized, and its economy is far less dependent on agriculture than its neighbors (357–59). Furthermore, Deborah James argues that post-apartheid discourses on land actually continue apartheid's insistence on a firm divide between urban and rural: "Ignoring the interplay of rural and urban sources of income and identity, this set of assumptions is one which envisages the worlds of town and country as separate: it reconstitutes Africans either as rural farmers or as urban wage earners" (93). She calls instead for a policy that both pays attention to the needs of landless city dwellers, and accommodates the desires of rural residents "for country areas to become more like the town" (107), an attitude that would no doubt go some distance toward rectifying uneven development in the countryside.
5. Apartheid, Sanders tells us, "entailed a massive refusal to mourn the dead of the other.... [In] order to make reparation for the violations of the apartheid era, an equally massive joining in mourning would have to take place. Mourning would make good for the violations of the apartheid era. As a system of social separation, apartheid would be undone through condolence" (*Ambiguities* 49).
6. Cherryl Walker argues that "what is needed is a new engagement with the issues—a fresh reading of history, a revised narrative that could support a more robust consensus that could, in turn, underpin a more modestly framed, perhaps, but ultimately more grounded, set of land policies" (823).
7. Granted, in becoming such a farmer, Beatrice Chapman both exploits and perpetuates the situation of colonial dominance, as a white Englishwoman who becomes the "mistress" (in multiple senses) of the servants on the farm, however uncomfortable she is in the role of colonial master.
8. Mather similarly worries that, aside from the historical failure of such initiatives, the Land Reform for Agricultural Development (LRAD) policies constitute "a shift away from what many consider to be the real needs of the rural poor: security of tenure and access to land, resources and employment opportunities" (353).
9. Anne Landsman was born in Worcester in 1959 to a Jewish family in a predominately Afrikaans town. She attended the University of Cape Town, and obtained her MFA from Columbia University in New York. *The Devil's Chimney* was her debut novel; she recently published her second book, *The Rowing Lesson* (2007).

10. The years following Beatrice and Henry's migration to the Cape are also the years in which the foundations of apartheid and its opposition were laid: the formation of what became the African National Congress (ANC) in 1912, and the enactment of the Natives Land Act in 1913, which dispossessed the black majority and exiled many of them to rural reservations. In considering this era from the retrospect of nearly a century later, it is tempting to see in it a cautionary tale about the tendency of new nationalist movements and of reconciliation between two parties to (re)produce injustice against a third party.
11. For the Cape in the 1910s, the ostrich also represented loss for another, more pedestrian reason: for a few brief years, ostrich feathers were an enormous fashion fad in Europe and North America, turning big ostrich farmers such as Mr. Jacobs into very wealthy men. Then suddenly in 1914 the fickle market for ostrich feathers collapsed, devastating the economies of Karoo towns such as Oudtshoorn. Connie (and, by extension, Beatrice) is most likely also preoccupied with the ostriches because the system of fences, *kraals*, and brands involved in farming them leave such a visible impact on the bodies of the birds. Connie notes that even the process of mating leaves a mark on the females: "There by the female's tail, on the left, is a mark. The bigger the mark gets, the more times they've done it. / I wonder if there's a mark inside me" (40).
12. See, e.g., passages on pages 70–71; 82–83; 127; 244; 259. The final passage is particularly explicit in comparing the cave to a vagina.
13. Roberta Culbertson, borrowing from Charlotte Delbo, describes a similar concept. She distinguishes "external" memory, that which we convey to others, from "body memory," the "known and felt truth that unfortunately obeys the logic of dreams rather than of speech and so seems as unreachable, as other, as these [dreams], and as difficult to communicate and interpret" (Culbertson 170).
14. These images of bodies with holes in them take on a poignant if grotesquely literal connotation in the novel in light of Connie's late revelation that her baby was born with a "hole in its heart, and it was leaking" (244)—no doubt the result of Fetal Alcohol Syndrome from Connie's chronic drinking during pregnancy.
15. The terrible truth is that the baby was not stillborn, but lived a few days after Connie's mother took it from her and gave it to Gerda, believing Connie unfit to look after the dying child.
16. It is also possible to project a darker reading onto the notion that Pauline was actually Precious: the baby was lost in the Caves twice, and the whole story is in fact a performative repetition of the loss of Connie's own baby. In other words, this reading would imply, the survivor of loss is doomed to repeat the event over and over, interminably.
17. Zoë Wicomb, a writer of Griqua descent, was born in 1948 in Namaqualand in the Northern Cape. She attended the University of the Western Cape, where she later taught. For many years she has lived in Glasgow, Scotland, where she teaches at the University of Strathclyde, though she returned to the Cape for a while in the mid-1990s. Her first book was *You Can't Get Lost in*

Cape Town (1987), which critics raved about but could not agree whether it was a novel or a collection of interrelated short stories. *David's Story* is her second novel; she recently published her third and fourth books, the novel *Playing in the Light* (2006) and the collection of short stories *The One That Got Away* (2008).

18. Samuelson offers a similar reading: "The body of Dulcie and materiality of the body of the text are presented as fundamentally unstable, disrupting the nationalist desire for re-covery and closure, and allowing us to trace, instead, continuities and disjunctures in the making of nation and the inscription of women's bodies" (Samuelson, *Remembering* 115). Sanders likewise argues that Dulcie's body resists signification of anything beyond itself (*Ambiguities* 85).
19. This disjuncture is further underscored by the contrast to the scene in *Beloved* that the narrator alludes to: in that novel, Sethe acquired her scars under slavery in Kentucky, and in one famous scene she is reunited with a fellow former slave, Paul D, who touches the "chokecherry tree" of scars on her back: "He rubbed his cheek on her back and learned that way her sorrow" (Morrison 17). Whereas Paul D is able to understand some of Sethe's sorrow because he too has suffered similar lessons, David's empathy is more complex and ambivalent, especially since the narrator implies later that he was complicit in her abuse, if not himself directly a perpetrator.
20. Derek Attridge comments on the novel's implicit acknowledgment of "the compulsion to seek for a historical and genealogical grounding for one's sense of identity, even as it offers a telling critique of such enterprises" (159).
21. Michael Marais acknowledges the ways in which Wicomb's novel implicates itself "in the poetics of blood which it so assiduously deconstructs" ("Bastards" 32), but he ultimately arrives at a conclusion similar to my point here when he writes, "Through its sheer hybridity, its 'bastardy,' the novel severs, rather than continues, the genealogical line which it depicts. It does not belong to this line, in that it cannot be contained and determined by the aesthetic of blood that informs it, and which it, in fact, deconstructs" (32–33).
22. See also Meyer and Oliver 92.
23. Ken Harrow also notes the novel's palimpsestic structure on several levels, such as the scars that "are left to be deciphered as the palimpsest of a story that refuses total assimilation into" a narrative (58), and Dulcie herself as "the palimpsest of the Revolution's truth" (65).
24. Pippa Skotnes notes specifically of the /Xam group:

    > For the /Xam the strangers' intrusion into the land was an intrusion into the delicate mappings of spaces and places that provided a web of connectedness to both their cultural heritage and the power the shamans . . . drew from the land. . . . In a symbolic sense the destruction of the fabric of /Xam society was a process of demapping the land, of snapping the threads that tied place to place and people to those places. (307)

25. Julie Wells succinctly sums up what is commonly thought to be true about Eva, born Krotoä: she is "known as a Khoena [Khoisan] girl taken into Dutch commander Jan Van Riebeeck's household from the age of about twelve, who later became a key interpreter for the Dutch, was baptized, married Danish

surgeon, Peter Van Meerhoff, but then died as a drunken prostitute after his death. Yet her persona remains an enigma" (417). Wells frames Eva's story as "that of a woman who exercised an extraordinary level of control and influence over the key men in her life" (418). This aspect of Eva's story parallels Dulcie's situation: she too is a woman able to manipulate the structures of power but unable to control her own body or her sexuality.

26. Like Krotoä, Saartje Baartman has become a figure of subaltern agency, or lack of agency. Bethlehem comments, "We know next to nothing of the interiority of the Khoisan woman, who is neither body, agent nor subject any longer, except that she is neither body, agent, nor subject any longer" (74). For both women, this lack of perceived agency leaves them open to political appropriation; as Kai Easton notes, "The icons of Krotoä and Saartje have travelled through history, shifting and acquiring new definitions" (Easton 238). As icons, I would add, they continue to hold some of the earlier connotations and associations even as their possible significance to the new political landscape is being negotiated and fought over. Carli Coetzee makes a similar point, tracing Krotoä's role as "the biological ancestor of many [that] was long denied in the all-white versions of Afrikaner history" ("Krotoä" 113). Baartman has also become an icon for how history is politicized; in the last twenty years of the twentieth century, in particular, she was an increasingly contentious historical figure, and the fate of her remains became a particularly sore point between South Africa and the French museum authorities. In short, in the years during which Wicomb was writing this novel, Baartman was being intensely debated in South Africa and abroad both as an historical icon and as a desecrated physical body. (Finally, two years after Wicomb published *David's Story* in South Africa, Baartman's remains were returned to South Africa, where they received a state burial in August 2002.)
27. Sadiah Qureshi argues that even in Baartman's own time, her story was taken up by a wide spectrum of political causes. The most recent such appropriation of Baartman as empty cipher, Qureshi notes, is "as a symbol of the colonial treatment of Africans, a role exemplified by her repatriation" (250).
28. D.Y. Saks concludes, based on documents in the National Library, that Griqua separatist and nationalist sentiments predate apartheid-era calls for a "coloured Homeland," and that Le Fleur himself advanced many of these separatist ideals. Saks also discusses one of Le Fleur's "treks," this one leading to a Griqua settlement in Kranshoek, about 15 kilometers outside Plettenberg Bay.
29. Known as a playwright since the mid-1970s, Zakes Mda turned to fiction in the mid-1990s, and has primarily written novels ever since, writing plays only when they are specifically commissioned. He was born in 1948 in the Eastern Cape. His published play collections include *We Shall Sing for the Fatherland* (1980), *The Plays of Zakes Mda* (1990), and *Fools, Bells and the Habit of Eating* (2002); he has also published a collection of poems called *Bits of Debris* (1986). His many novels include *Ways of Dying* (1994), *The Heart of Redness* (2000; discussed in section 3.3), *The Madonna of Excelsior* (2002), and most recently *Cion* (2007). He has also published his scholarly work *When People Play People: Development Communication through Theatre* (1993), written while he

was director of the Theatre for Development Project at the University of Lesotho, in which he lays out his vision of a theater for rural development.

30. "Redness" literally refers to the red dye used in the traditional robes worn by amaXhosa women, but in Mda's novel it becomes a metonym for ancient isiXhosa tradition more generally.

31. Johan Jacobs makes a similar point, arguing that the novel's "split-tone" structure is a "*palimpsest* structure" (228). I would suggest that *The Heart of Redness* is at least equally about reconciling concepts of modernization and tradition and competing attitudes toward space and time—Attwell argues, e.g. that "[i]n Mda's hands, splitting and twinning comprise a warp and woof, a weaving of pattern and tension that gives definition to South African postcolonial modernity" (199)—but I find Jacobs's use of overtone singing as a model for the novel's twinned structure very suggestive and useful.

32. Indeed, except for the rather rigid Xoliswa Ximiya, all of the villagers allow the visible distinctions between Believers and Unbelievers to erode. Bhonco's wife NoPetticoat, e.g., wears the traditional red *isikhakha*, and goes to work in Camagu's co-op making beaded clothing to sell in Johannesburg, despite her husband's and daughter's dismay (186).

33. Samuelson sees Qukezwa's significance as lying primarily in her virgin conception of Camagu's baby: "the representation of female reproductive bodies in *The Heart of Redness*," she argues, "untangles the narrative's temporality, rearranging it into a teleological formation that stretches from colonial loss to postcolonial recovery" (*Remembering* 70). Samuelson concludes that "[w]omen in *The Heart of Redness* are cast as vessels for the messages of men, and they speak loudest through their bodies" (80). This reading, I would argue, completely ignores Qukezwa's crucial role in the novel as the one who *teaches* Camagu his message about the importance of indigenous plants (and by extension, indigenous culture). Mda resolves the losses of the colonial past not only, or even primarily, through Qukezwa's reproductive potential; far more important is the novel's proposed renegotiation of socio-spatial relationships, and it is Qukezwa who shows Camagu the way forward.

34. At the risk of attributing too much significance to the autobiographical parallels between the author and his protagonist, the fact that Camagu, like Mda, has a doctorate from an American university in communications and economic development suggests that Camagu functions as a mouthpiece for the author's own views on development issues.

35. Several critics make the point that *The Heart of Redness* tends to cross the fundamental boundaries of western epistemology. Titlestad and Kissack argue that Camagu "emerges, haphazardly, as an intellectual subjectivity by criss-crossing the seam at which rationality is purportedly divided from irrationality, reason from emotion, civilisation from barbarism, the semiotic from the symbolic, tradition from modernity, faith from knowledge and so on" ("The Foot" 265–66). Koyana discusses a "dialogism of place" that "encompasses the heterogeneity of possibilities of what Qholorha [*sic*] could become in the future—what Qholorha is open to in relation to what it was in the past or is in the present" ("Qholorha" 52). For Woodward what gives Mda's work

transgressive power is its use of satire and a humor that "derives, in part, from the multivocality of the narrative and the echoes of traditional folk tales" ("Laughing" 288). And Wenzel notes of Mda's earlier novel *Ways of Dying* that the protagonist Toloki "illustrates the possibility of transcending time and space through the imagination—thereby providing a solution to the South African impasse created by apartheid" (328). Of all the border-crossings that occur in this novel, I would argue that the most important in terms of the country's larger transformation is the novel's renegotiation of the divides between public and private and between past and present.

36. Mda articulates a similar view in his own voice when he writes, "We cannot just sweep [the past] under the carpet, and hope that all of a sudden we shall live in brotherly or sisterly love, in a state of blissful amnesia.... We must never forget, but of course this does not mean that we must cling to the past, and wrap it around us, and live with it, and be perpetual victims" ("Theater" 43).

Conclusion

1. That these resentments surfaced so explosively helps to explain the sensitivities toward xenophobia in *Welcome to Our Hillbrow* by Phaswane Mpe, a Pedi speaker who lived in Johannesburg: Mpe, too, would have experienced the discrimination and intimidation felt even more keenly by foreign African immigrants.
2. Titlestad notes that Deleuzean cartography "does not entail the dissection and representation of a plain of meaning but produces a sense of manifold manipulations of meaning from provisional positions" (14).
3. Huyssen, e.g., discusses "the obsession with memory itself as a significant symptom of our cultural present" (3).

Bibliography

Abrahams, Yvette. "Was Eva Raped? An Exercise in Speculative History." *Kronos* 23 (1996): 3–21.

Adam, Heribert, and Kanya Adam. "The Politics of Memory in Divided Societies." James and Van de Vijver 32–47.

Amin, Ash, and Nigel Thrift. *Cities: Reimagining the Urban*. Cambridge: Polity P, 2002.

Appadurai, Arjun. "Grassroots Globalization and the Research Imagination." *Globalization*. Ed. Arjun Appadurai. Durham, NC: Duke UP, 2001. 1–21.

Asmal, Kader, Louise Asmal, and Ronald Suresh Roberts. *Reconciliation through Truth: A Reckoning of Apartheid's Criminal Governance*. Cape Town: David Philip, 1997.

Attridge, Derek. "Zoë Wicomb's Home Truths: Place, Genealogy, and Identity in *David's Story*." *Journal of Postcolonial Writing* 41.2 (2005): 156–65.

Attridge, Derek, and Rosemary Jolly. *Writing South Africa: Literature, Apartheid, and Democracy, 1970–1995*. Cambridge: Cambridge UP, 1998.

Attwell, David. *Rewriting Modernity: Studies in Black South African Literary History*. Pietermaritzburg: U of KwaZulu-Natal P, 2005.

Bapela, Obed. TRC Human Rights Violations Hearing. Alexandra, Johannesburg. 29 October 1996. http://www.doj.gov.za/trc/hrvtrans/alex/bapela.htm.

Barnard, Rita. *Apartheid and Beyond: South African Writers and the Politics of Place*. Oxford: Oxford UP, 2007.

Barnett, Ursula A. "*Country of My Skull: Guilt, Sorrow, and the Limits of Forgiveness in the New South Africa* (Review)." *World Literature Today* 73.4 (1999): 802–03.

Beinart, William, and Saul Dubow, eds. *Segregation and Apartheid in Twentieth-Century South Africa*. London: Routledge, 1995.

Benjamin, Walter. *Reflections: Essays, Aphorisms, Autobiographical Writings*. Trans. Edmund Jephcott. New York: Harcourt Brace Jovanovich, 1978.

Bennett, Jill. *Empathic Vision: Affect, Trauma, and Contemporary Art*. Stanford: Stanford UP, 2005.

Benzien, Jeffery. TRC Amnesty Hearing. Cape Town. 14–16 July 1997. http://www.doj.gov.za/trc/amntrans/capetown/capetown_benzien.htm.

Bethlehem, Louise. *Skin Tight: Apartheid Literary Culture and Its Aftermath*. Pretoria/Leiden: UNISA P/Brill, 2006.

Bizos, George. *No One to Blame? In Pursuit of Justice in South Africa*. Cape Town: David Philip, 1998.

Bizos, George. "Why Prosecutions Are Necessary." Villa-Vicencio and Doxtader 5–9.

Blumberg, Marcia. "Re-Membering History, Staging Hybridity: *Ubu and the Truth Commission*." *Multiculturalism and Hybridity in African Literatures*. Ed. Hal Wylie and Bernth Lindfors. Trenton, NJ: Africa World P, 2000. 309–18.

Blunt, Alison, and Gillian Rose. "Introduction: Women's Colonial and Postcolonial Geographies." Blunt and Rose, *Writing Women and Space* 1–25.

———, eds. *Writing Women and Space: Colonial and Postcolonial Geographies*. New York/London: Guilford P, 1994.

Bond, Patrick. *Cities of Gold, Townships of Coal: Essays on South Africa's New Urban Crisis*. Trenton, NJ: Africa World P, 2000.

———. *Elite Transition: From Apartheid to Neoliberalism in South Africa*. Pietermaritzburg: U of Natal P, 2000.

———. *Talk Left, Walk Right: South Africa's Frustrated Global Reforms*. Pietermaritzburg: U of KwaZulu-Natal P, 2004.

Bonner, Philip, and Noor Nieftagodien. "The Truth and Reconciliation Commission and the Pursuit of 'Social Truth': The Case of Kathorus." Posel and Simpson, *Commissioning the Past* 173–203.

Boraine, Alex. *A Country Unmasked: Inside South Africa's Truth and Reconciliation Commission*. Oxford: Oxford UP, 2000.

Boraine, Alex, Janet Levy, and Ronel Scheffer, eds. *Dealing with the Past: Truth and Reconciliation in South Africa*. Cape Town: IDASA, 1997.

Borras Jr., Saturnino M. "Questioning Market-Led Agrarian Reform: Experiences from Brazil, Columbia and South Africa." *Journal of Agrarian Change* 3.3 (2003): 367–94.

Boyarin, Jonathan, ed. *Remapping Memory: The Politics of Timespace*. Minneapolis: U of Minnesota P, 1994.

———. "Space, Time, and the Politics of Memory." Boyarin, *Remapping Memory* 1–37.

Bozzoli, Belinda. *Theatres of Struggle and the End of Apartheid*. Johannesburg: Wits UP, 2004.

Braude, Claudia. "Elusive Truths." *Mail & Guardian* 12–18 June 1998: 9.

Bremner, Lindsay. "Crime and the Emerging Landscape of Post-Apartheid Johannesburg." Judin and Vladislavić 49–63.

———. *Johannesburg: One City Colliding Worlds*. Johannesburg: STE Publishers, 2004.

Brink, André. "Stories of History: Reimagining the Past in Post-Apartheid Narrative." Nuttall and Coetzee 29–42.

Brison, Susan J. *Aftermath: Violence and the Remaking of the Self*. Princeton, NJ: Princeton UP, 2002.

Brittain, Victoria, and Gillian Slovo. *Guantanamo: Honor Bound to Defend Freedom*. London: Oberon Books, 2005.

Brown, Alison. "Challenging Street Livelihoods." *Contested Space: Street Trading, Public Space, and Livelihoods in Developing Cities*. Ed. Alison Brown. Warwickshire/Cardiff: ITDG/Cardiff UP, 2006. 3–16.

Bundy, Colin. "The Beast of the Past: History and the TRC." James and Van de Vijver 9–20.

Bunn, David. "Comparative Barbarism: Game Reserves, Sugar Plantations, and the Modernization of South African Landscape." Darian-Smith, Gunner, and Nuttall 37–52.

———. "Whited Sepulchres: On the Reluctance of Monuments." Judin and Vladislavić 93–117.

Butler, Judith. "Afterword: After Loss, What Then?" Eng and Kazanjian 467–73.

Cameron, Dan. "An Interview with William Kentridge." *William Kentridge*. Ed. Neal Benezra, Staci Boris, and Dan Cameron. Chicago/New York: Museum of Contemporary Art/Abrams, 2001. 67–74.

Carklin, Michael. "Dramatic Excavations and Theatrical Explorations: *Faustus*, *Ubu* and Post-Apartheid South African Theatre." Emenyonu 23–33.

Caruth, Cathy. *Unclaimed Experience: Trauma, Narrative, and History*. Baltimore: Johns Hopkins UP, 1996.

Certeau, Michel de. *The Practice of Everyday Life*. Trans. Steven Rendall. Berkeley: U of California P, 1984.

Christie, Kenneth. *The South African Truth Commission*. London: Macmillan, 2000.

Clarkson, Carrol. "Locating Identity in Phaswane Mpe's *Welcome to Our Hillbrow*." *Third World Quarterly* 26.3 (2005): 451–59.

———. "Visible and Invisible: What Surfaces in Recent Johannesburg Novels?" *Moving Worlds* 5.1 (2005): 84–97.

Coetzee, Carli. "Krotoä Remembered: A Mother of Unity, a Mother of Sorrows?" Nuttall and Coetzee 112–19.

———. "'They Never Wept, the Men of My Race': Antjie Krog's *Country of My Skull*." *Journal of Southern African Studies* 27.4 (2001): 685–96.

Coetzee, J.M. *Disgrace*. London: Secker & Warburg, 1999.

Coetzee, Yvette. "Visibly Invisible: How Shifting the Conventions of the Traditionally Invisible Puppeteer Allows for More Dimensions in Both the Puppeteer-Puppet Relationship and the Creation of Theatrical Meaning in *Ubu and the Truth Commission*." *South African Theatre Journal* 12.1–2 (1998): 35–51.

Commey, Pusch. "South African Land: A Ticking Time Bomb." *New African* November 2002: 12+. http://search.ebscohost.com/login.aspx?direct=true&db=aph&AN=8560141&site=ehost-live.

Commin, Jane. "Review: *Terrestrial Things* by Ingrid de Kok." *New Contrast* 30.4 (2002): 64–67.

Coombes, Annie E. *History after Apartheid: Visual Culture and Public Memory in a Democratic South Africa*. Durham, NC: Duke UP, 2003.

Coullie, Judith Lütge. "The Incredible Whiteness of Being." *Alternation* 9.1 (2002): 226–37.

Culbertson, Roberta. "Embodied Memory, Transcendence, and Telling: Recounting Trauma, Re-Establishing the Self." *New Literary History* 26 (1995): 169–95.

Cullinan, Patrick. "Review: *Transfer* by Ingrid de Kok, *Departures* by Moira Lovell, *Solstice* by Don Maclennan." *English Academy Review* 14 (1997): 151–60.

Czeglédy, André. "Villas of the Highveld: A Cultural Perspective on Johannesburg and Its 'Northern Suburbs.'" Tomlinson et al. 21–42.

Dangor, Achmat. "Apartheid and the Death of South African Cities." Judin and Vladislavić 359–61.

———. "Being Short-Listed Is Brilliant—but It's Even Better to Be Read." *Sunday Times* 10 October 2004.

———. *Bitter Fruit*. Cape Town: Kwela Books, 2001.

———. *Kafka's Curse*. Cape Town: Kwela Books, 1997.

Darian-Smith, Kate, Liz Gunner, and Sarah Nuttall, eds. *Text, Theory, Space: Land, Literature and History in South Africa and Australia*. London: Routledge, 1996.

Dawson, Ashley, and Brent Hayes Edwards, eds. *Social Text* 81 (2004). Special issue: *Global Cities of the South*.

Daymond, Margaret J. "Bodies of Writing: Recovering the Past in Zoë Wicomb's *David's Story* and Elleke Boehmer's *Bloodlines*." *Kunapipi* 24.1–2 (2002): 25–38.

———. "Complementary Oral and Written Narrative Conventions: Sindiwe Magona's Autobiography and Short Story Sequence, 'Women at Work.'" *Journal of Southern African Studies* 28.2 (2002): 331–46.

De Beer, Diane. "Telling Our Untold Stories: The TRC Inspires Achmat Dangor's Latest Novel." *Pretoria News* 5 November 2001, sec. Interval.

De Kok, Ingrid. "Cracked Heirlooms: Memory on Exhibition." Nuttall and Coetzee 57–71.

———. *Seasonal Fires*. New York: Seven Stories P, 2006.

———. *Terrestrial Things*. Cape Town: Kwela/Snailpress, 2002.

———. *Transfer*. Cape Town: Snailpress, 1997.

Dear, Michael, and Steven Flusty. "The Postmodern Urban Condition." *Spaces of Culture: City-Nation-World*. Ed. Mike Featherstone and Scott Lash. London: Sage, 1999. 49–63.

Deleuze, Gilles, and Félix Guattari. *A Thousand Plateaus: Capitalism and Schizophrenia*. Trans. Brian Massumi. Minneapolis: U of Minnesota P, 1987.

Derrida, Jacques. *Archive Fever: A Freudian Impression*. Trans. Eric Prenowitz. Chicago: U of Chicago P, 1996.

Doxtader, Erik. "Easy to Forget or Never (Again) Hard to Remember?: History, Memory and the 'Publicity' of Amnesty." Villa-Vicencio and Doxtader 121–55.

Driver, Dorothy. "Afterword." *David's Story*. Zoë Wicomb. New York: Feminist P, 2000. 215–71.

Du Preez, Max. *Of Warriors, Lovers and Prophets: Unusual Stories from South Africa's Past*. Cape Town: Zebra P, 2004.

Dube, Pamela Sethunya. "The Story of Thandi Shezi." Posel and Simpson, *Commissioning the Past* 117–30.

Duiker, K. Sello. *The Quiet Violence of Dreams*. Cape Town: Kwela Books, 2001.

Durrant, Samuel. "Bearing Witness to Apartheid: J.M. Coetzee's Inconsolable Works of Mourning." *Contemporary Literature* 40.3 (1999): 430–63.

Eakin, Paul John. *Fictions in Autobiography: Studies in the Art of Self-Invention*. Princeton: Princeton UP, 1985.

Easton, Kai. "Travelling through History, 'New' South African Icons: The Narratives of Saartje Baartman and Krotoä-Eva in Zoë Wicomb's *David's Story*." *Kunapipi* 24.1–2 (2002): 237–66.

Emenyonu, Ernest, ed. *New Directions in African Literature. African Literature Today* 25. Oxford/Trenton/Ibadan: James Currey/Africa World P/HEB, 2006.

Eng, David, and David Kazanjian, eds. *Loss: The Politics of Mourning*. Berkeley: U of California P, 2003.

Episode 45. *Special Report*. 27 April 1997. SABC, Johannesburg. http://www.law.yale.edu/trc/episode_select.asp.

Eyerman, Ron. *Cultural Trauma: Slavery and the Formation of African American Identity*. Cambridge: Cambridge UP, 2001.

Facing Death... Facing Life. Dir. Ingrid Gavshon. Featuring Duma Kumalo. Angel Films, 2000.

Felman, Shoshana, and Dori Laub. *Testimony: Crises of Witnessing in Literature, Psychoanalysis, and History*. New York: Routledge, 1992.

Frenkel, Ronit. "Performing Race, Reconsidering History: Achmat Dangor's Recent Fiction." *Research in African Literatures* 39.1 (2008): 149–65.

Frescura, Franco. "The Spatial Geography of Urban Apartheid." Zegeye 99–125.

Gallagher, Susan VanZanten. *Truth and Reconciliation: The Confessional Mode in South African Literature*. Portsmouth, NH: Heinemann, 2002.

Gane, Gillian. "Unspeakable Injuries in *Disgrace* and *David's Story*." *Kunapipi* 24.1–2 (2002): 101–13.

Garman, Anthea. "Confession and Public Life in Post-Apartheid South Africa: A Foucauldian Reading of Antjie Krog's *Country of My Skull*." *Journal of Literary Studies* 22.3/4 (2006): 322–44.

"Gauteng Reels under Xenophobic Attacks." *Mail & Guardian Online* 19 May 2008. http://www.mg.co.za/article/2008–05–19-gauteng-reels-under-xenophobic-attacks.

Gaylard, Gerald, and Michael Titlestad. "Introduction: Controversial Interpretations: Ivan Vladislavić." *Scrutiny2* 11.2 (2006): 5–10.

Gbadamosi, Gabriel. "Clouds over the Rainbow Nation: *Bitter Fruit*, Achmat Dangor's Tortured Search for Human and Political Reckoning after Apartheid." *Guardian* 13 December 2003. http://www.guardian.co.uk/books/2003/dec/13/featuresreviews.guardianreview12

Gevisser, Mark. "From the Ruins: The Constitution Hill Project." *Public Culture* 16.3 (2004): 507–19.

Gibson, James L. *Overcoming Apartheid: Can Truth Reconcile a Divided Nation?* Cape Town: HSRC P, 2004.

Goebel, Allison. "Is Zimbabwe the Future of South Africa? The Implications for Land Reform in Southern Africa." *Journal of Contemporary African Studies* 23.3 (2005): 345–70.

Graham, Shane. "'I Was Those Thousands!': Memory, Identity and Space in John Kani's *Nothing But the Truth*." *Theatre Research International* 32.1 (2007): 68–84.

———. "Mapping Memory, Healing the Land: Zakes Mda's *The Bells of Amersfoort*." *Ways of Writing: Critical Essays on Zakes Mda*. Ed. J.U. Jacobs and David Bell. Pietermaritzburg: U of KwaZulu-Natal P, 2009 (forthcoming).

Graham, Shane. "Memory, Memorialization, and the Transformation of Johannesburg: Ivan Vladislavić's *Propaganda by Monuments* and *The Restless Supermarket*." *MFS: Modern Fiction Studies* 53.1 (2007): 70–96.

———. "The Truth Commission and Post-Apartheid Literature in South Africa." *Research in African Literatures* 34.1 (2003): 11–30.

Graybill, Lyn S. *Truth and Reconciliation in South Africa: Miracle or Model.* Boulder, CO: Lynne Rienner, 2002.

Gready, Paul. *Writing as Resistance: Life Stories of Imprisonment, Exile, and Homecoming from Apartheid South Africa.* Lanham, MD: Lexington Books, 2003.

Green, Michael. "Translating the Nation: Phaswane Mpe and the Fiction of Post-Apartheid." *Scrutiny2* 10.1 (2005): 3–16.

Hall, Saffron. "South African English in the Post-Apartheid Era: Hybridization in Zoë Wicomb's *David's Story* and Ivan Vladislavić's *The Restless Supermarket*." *postamble* 2.1 (2006): 13–29.

Hamilton, Carolyn, Verne Harris, Jane Taylor, Michele Pickover, Graeme Reid, and Razia Saleh, eds. *Refiguring the Archive.* Cape Town: David Philip, 2002.

Harris, Ashleigh. "Accountability, Acknowledgement and the Ethics of 'Quilting' in Antjie Krog's *Country of My Skull*." *Journal of Literary Studies* 22.1/2 (2006): 27–53.

Harris, Brent. "The Archive, Public History and the Essential Truth: The TRC Reading the Past." Hamilton et al. 161–77.

Harris, Verne. "The Archival Sliver: A Perspective on the Construction of Social Memory in Archives and the Transition from Apartheid to Democracy." Hamilton et al. 135–51.

———. "A Shaft of Darkness: Derrida in the Archive." Hamilton et al. 61–81.

Harrow, Kenneth. "The Marks Left on the Surface: Zoë Wicomb's *David's Story*." Emenyonu 53–66.

Hart, Gillian. *Disabling Globalization: Places of Power in Post-Apartheid South Africa.* Berkeley: U of California P, 2002.

Harvey, David. *The Condition of Postmodernity.* Cambridge, MA: Blackwell, 1990.

———. "Contested Cities: Social Process and Spatial Form." *Transforming Cities: Contested Governance and New Spatial Divisions.* Ed. Nick Jewson and Susanne MacGregor. London: Routledge, 1997. 19–27.

Hassim, Aziz. *The Lotus People.* Johannesburg: STE Publishers, 2002.

Hawley, John. " 'Archaic Ambivalence:' The Case of South Africa." *Critics and Writers Speak: Revisioning Post-Colonial Studies.* Ed. Igor Maver. Lanham, MD: Lexington Books, 2006. 67–84.

He Left Quietly. By Duma Kumalo and Yael Farber. National Arts Festival, Grahamstown, South Africa. 5 July 2002.

Helgesson, Stefan. "Johannesburg as Africa: A Postcolonial Reading of *The Exploded View* by Ivan Vladislavić." *Scrutiny2* 11.2 (2006): 27–35.

———. " 'Minor Disorders': Ivan Vladislavić and the Devolution of South African English." *Journal of Southern African Studies* 30.4 (2004): 777–87.

Henry, Yazir. "Where Healing Begins." Villa-Vicencio and Verwoerd, *Looking Back* 166–73.

Hlongwane, Gugu. "'Reader, Be Assured This Narrative Is No Fiction': The City and Its Discontents in Phaswane Mpe's *Welcome to Our Hillbrow*." *Ariel* 37.4 (2006): 69–82.

Hoad, Neville. *African Intimacies: Race, Homosexuality, and Globalization*. Minneapolis: U of Minnesota P, 2007.

Hobson, Janell. "The 'Batty' Politic: Toward an Aesthetic of the Black Female Body." *Hypatia* 18.4 (2003): 87–105.

Hunt, Emma. "Post-Apartheid Johannesburg and Global Mobility in Nadine Gordimer's *The Pickup* and Phaswane Mpe's *Welcome to Our Hillbrow*." *Ariel* 37.4 (2006): 103–23.

Huyssen, Andreas. *Present Pasts: Urban Palimpsests and the Politics of Memory*. Stanford, CA: Stanford UP, 2003.

Irlam, Shaun. "Unraveling the Rainbow: The Remission of Nation in Post-Apartheid Literature." *South Atlantic Quarterly* 103.4 (2004): 695–718.

Jacobs, J.U. "Cross-Cultural Translation in South African Autobiographical Writing: The Case of Sindiwe Magona." *Alternation* 7.1 (2000): 41–61.

———. "Reconciling Languages in Antjie Krog's *Country of My Skull*." *Current Writing: Text and Reception in Southern Africa* 12.2 (2000): 38–51.

———. "Zakes Mda's *The Heart of Redness*: The Novel as *Umngqokolo*." *Kunapipi* 24.1–2 (2002): 224–36.

James, Deborah. "Land for the Landless: Conflicting Images of Rural and Urban in South Africa's Land Reform Programme." *Journal of Contemporary African Studies* 19.1 (2001): 93–109.

James, Wilmot, and Linda van de Vijver, eds. *After the TRC: Reflections on Truth and Reconciliation in South Africa*. Athens/Cape Town: Ohio UP/David Philip, 2000.

Jameson, Fredric. *Postmodernism, or the Cultural Logic of Late Capitalism*. Durham, NC: Duke UP, 1991.

Jayawardane, M. Neelika. "The Museum and the Public: Memorial Building and Representing 'Unpronounceable' History in Zoë Wicomb's *David's Story*." *Scrutiny2* 12.2 (2007): 61–74.

Jeffery, Anthea. *The Truth about the Truth Commission*. Johannesburg: South African Institute of Race Relations, 1999.

Johnson, David. "Theorizing the Loss of Land: Griqua Land Claims in Southern Africa, 1874–1998." Eng and Kazanjian 278–99.

Jones, Basil, and Adrian Kohler. "Puppeteers' Note: The Crocodile's Mouth." Jane Taylor, *Ubu and the Truth Commission*. Cape Town: UCT P, 1998. xvi–xvii.

Judin, Hilton, and Ivan Vladislavić, eds. *Blank___: Architecture, Apartheid and After*. Rotterdam/Cape Town: Netherlands Architecture Institute/David Philip, 1998.

Kani, John. *Nothing But the Truth*. Johannesburg: Witwatersrand UP, 2002.

Kaplan, E. Ann. *Trauma Culture: The Politics of Terror and Loss in Media and Literature*. New Brunswick, NJ: Rutgers UP, 2005.

Keil, Roger, and Klaus Ronneberger. "The Globalization of Frankfurt Am Main: Core, Periphery and Social Conflict." Marcuse and Van Kempen, *Globalizing Cities* 228–48.

Keith, Michael, and Steve Pile, eds. *Place and the Politics of Identity*. London: Routledge, 1993.

Kelly, Erica. "Strangely Tender: An Interview with Ingrid de Kok." *Scrutiny2* 8.1 (2003): 34–38.

Kentridge, William. "Director's Note: The Crocodile's Mouth." Jane Taylor, *Ubu and the Truth Commission*. Cape Town: UCT P, 1998. viii–xv.

Khumalo, Duma. TRC Special Hearings on Prisons. Johannesburg. 22 July 1997. http://www.doj.gov.za/trc/special/prison/khumalo.htm.

Khumalo, Sibongile. "Displaced Foreigners 'Still Too Scared to Return.'" *Mail & Guardian Online* 3 July 2008. http://www.mg.co.za/article/2008-07-03-displaced-foreigners-still-too-scared-to-return.

Koyana, Siphokazi. "Qholorha and the Dialogism of Place in Zakes Mda's *The Heart of Redness*." *Current Writing* 15.1 (2003): 51–62.

———, ed. *Sindiwe Magona: The First Decade*. Pietermaritzburg: U of KwaZulu-Natal P, 2004.

———. "'Why Are You Carrying Books? Don't You Have Children?': Revisiting Motherhood in Sindiwe Magona's Autobiographies." *English Studies in Africa* 45.1 (2002): 45–55.

———. "Womanism and Nation-Building in Sindiwe Magona's Autobiographies." *Agenda* 50 (2001): 64–70.

Koyana, Siphokazi, and Rosemary Gray. "An Electronic Interview with Sindiwe Magona." *English in Africa* 29.1 (2002): 99–103.

Krog, Antjie. "The Choice for Amnesty: Did Political Necessity Trump Moral Duty?" Villa-Vicencio and Doxtader 115–20.

———. "The Cook, the Stew and the Taster: Writing from Inside, Editing from Outside." *Scrutiny2* 11.2 (2006): 91–96.

———. *Country of My Skull*. Johannesburg: Random House, 1998.

Kruger, Loren. "Making Sense of Sensation: Enlightenment, Embodiment, and the End(s) of Modern Drama." *Modern Drama* 43.4 (2000): 543–66.

LaCapra, Dominick. *Writing History, Writing Trauma*. Baltimore: Johns Hopkins UP, 2001.

"Land Ownership at Crisis Point." *New African* March 2003: 36+.

Landsman, Anne. *The Devil's Chimney*. Johannesburg: Jonathan Ball, 1997.

Langer, Lawrence. *Holocaust Testimonies: The Ruins of Memory*. New Haven, CT: Yale UP, 1991.

Le Roux, Hannah. "Hell/Whole: The Inversion of Constitution Hill." *Art South Africa* 2.4 (2004): 38–44.

Lefebvre, Henri. *The Production of Space*. Trans. Donald Nicholson-Smith. Oxford: Blackwell, 1991.

Legassick, Martin. "British Hegemony and the Origins of Segregation in South Africa, 1901–14." Beinart and Dubow 43–59.

Lewis, Simon. Review of Ingrid de Kok, *Terrestrial Things*. 2003. H-AfrLitCine, H-Net Reviews. http://www.h-net.msu.edu/reviews/showrev.cgi?path=175221048835719.

———. "Telling the Truth Commission: Representing the TRC at Home and Abroad." *Journal of Commonwealth and Postcolonial Studies* 9.2 (2002): 25–46.

Lyster, Richard. "Amnesty: The Burden of Victims." Villa-Vicencio and Verwoerd, *Looking Back* 184–92.

Maake, Nhlanhla. "Inscribing Identity on the Landscape: National Symbols in South Africa." Darian-Smith, Gunner, and Nuttall 145–55.

Magona, Sindiwe. *Mother to Mother.* Cape Town: David Philip, 1998.

Maier, Charles. "Doing History, Doing Justice: The Narrative of the Historian and of the Truth Commission." Rotberg and Thompson 261–78.

Mamdani, Mahmood. "A Diminished Truth." James and Van de Vijver 58–61.

———. "Reconciliation without Justice" (Review of *Reconciliation through Truth* and *The Healing of a Nation?*). *Southern African Review of Books* November/December 1996. http://www.uni-ulm.de/~rturrell/antho3html/Mamdani.html.

Manase, Irikidzayi. "Mapping the City Space in Current Zimbabwean and South African Fiction." *Transformation* 57 (2005): 88–105.

Marais, Mike. "Bastards and Bodies in Zoë Wicomb's *David's Story.*" *Journal of Commonwealth Literature* 40.3 (2005): 21–36.

———. "Visions of Excess: Closure, Irony, and the Thought of Community in Ivan Vladislavić's *The Restless Supermarket.*" *English in Africa* 29.2 (2002): 101–17.

Marcuse, Peter, and Ronald van Kempen. "Conclusion: A Changed Spatial Order." Marcuse and Van Kempen, *Globalizing Cities* 249–75.

———, eds. *Globalizing Cities: A New Spatial Order?* Oxford: Blackwell, 2000.

Marlin-Curiel, Stephanie. "A Little Too Close to the Truth: Anxieties of Testimony and Confession in *Ubu and the Truth Commission* and *The Story I Am about to Tell.*" *South African Theatre Journal* 15 (2001): 77–107.

Marston, Sallie A. "The Social Construction of Scale." *Progress in Human Geography* 24.2 (2000): 219–42.

Massey, Doreen. *Space, Place and Gender.* Cambridge: Polity, 1994.

Mather, Charles. "The Changing Face of Land Reform in Post-Apartheid South Africa." *Geography* 87.4 (2002): 345–54.

Matshoba, Mtutuzeli. "Nothing But the Truth: The Ordeal of Duma Khumalo." Posel and Simpson, *Commissioning the Past* 131–44.

Mbembe, Achille. "Aesthetics of Superfluity." *Public Culture* 16.3 (2004): 373–405.

———. "The Power of the Archive and Its Limits." Hamilton et al. 19–26.

Mbembe, Achille, and Sarah Nuttall. "Writing the World from an African Metropolis." *Public Culture* 16.3 (2004): 347–72.

McEachern, Charmaine. "Mapping the Memories: Politics, Place and Identity in the District Six Museum, Cape Town." Zegeye 223–47.

McGregor, Liz. "Kabelo Duiker: Young South African Novelist Scarred by a Childhood of Apartheid." Obituary. *Guardian* 7 February 2005. http://www.guardian.co.uk/news/2005/feb/07/guardianobituaries.booksobituaries.

Mda, Zakes. *The Bells of Amersfoort.* In: *Fools, Bells and the Habit of Eating: Three Satires.* Johannesburg: Witwatersrand UP, 2002. 111–61.

———. *The Heart of Redness.* Oxford: Oxford UP, 2000.

———. "Theater and Reconciliation in South Africa." *Theater* 25.3 (1995): 38–45.

———. *Ways of Dying.* Cape Town: Oxford UP, 1995.

Meiring, Piet. *Chronicle of the Truth Commission.* Vanderbijlpark, South Africa: Carpe Diem, 1999.

Meyer, Stephan, and Thomas Oliver. "Zoë Wicomb Interviewed on *Writing and Nation.*" *Journal of Literary Studies* 18.1–2 (2002): 182–98.

Miller, Andie. "Inside the Toolbox: Andie Miller in Conversation with Ivan Vladislavić." *Scrutiny2* 11.2 (2006): 117–24.

Mkhuanazi, M. TRC Human Rights Violation Hearing. Alexandra, Johannesburg, 30 October 1996. http://www.doj.gov.za/trc/hrvtrans/alex/mkhuanaz.htm.

Morrison, Toni. *Beloved.* New York: Plume, 1987.

Moss, Laura. "'Nice Audible Crying': Editions, Testimonies, and *Country of My Skull.*" *Research in African Literatures* 37.4 (2006): 85–104.

Mpe, Phaswane. *Welcome to Our Hillbrow.* Pietermaritzburg: U of Natal P, 2001.

Naidoo, Venu. "Interview with Zakes Mda." *Alternation* 4.1 (1997): 247–61.

Nash, Catherine. "Remapping the Body/Land: New Cartographies of Identity, Gender, and Landscape in Ireland." Blunt and Rose, *Writing Women and Space* 227–50.

Ndebele, Njabulo. "Of Lions and Rabbits: Thoughts on Democracy and Reconciliation." James and Van de Vijver 143–56.

Number Four: The Making of Constitution Hill. London: Penguin, 2006.

Nuttall, Sarah. "City Forms and Writing the 'Now' in South Africa." *Journal of Southern African Studies* 30.4 (2004): 731–48.

———. "Flatness and Fantasy: Representations of the Land in Two Recent South African Novels." Darian-Smith, Gunner, and Nuttall 219–30.

———. "Stylizing the Self: The Y Generation in Rosebank, Johannesburg." *Public Culture* 16.3 (2004): 430–52.

Nuttall, Sarah, and Carli Coetzee, eds. *Negotiating the Past: The Making of Memory in South Africa.* Cape Town: Oxford UP, 1998.

Nuttall, Sarah, and Cheryl-Ann Michael. "African Renaissance: Interviews with Sikhumbuzo Mngadi, Tony Parr, Rhoda Kadalie, Zakes Mda, and Darryl Accone." Nuttall and Michael, *Senses of Culture* 107–21.

———, eds. *Senses of Culture: South African Culture Studies.* Oxford: Oxford UP, 2000.

O'Brien, Anthony. *Against Normalization: Writing Radical Democracy in South Africa.* Durham, NC: Duke UP, 2001.

Oboe, Analisa. "The TRC Women's Hearings as Performance and Protest in the New South Africa." *Research in African Literatures* 38.3 (2007): 60–76.

Omar, Dullah. "Building a New Future." *The Healing of a Nation?* Ed. Alex Boraine and Janet Levy. Cape Town: Justice in Transition, 1995. 2–8.

Orr, Wendy. *From Biko to Basson: Search for the Soul of South Africa as a Commissioner of the TRC.* Johannesburg: Contra P, 2000.

Phelps, Teresa Godwin. *Shattered Voices: Language, Violence, and the Work of Truth Commissions.* Philadelphia: U of Pennsylvania P, 2004.

Posel, Deborah. "The Meaning of Apartheid before 1948: Conflicting Interests and Forces within the Afrikaner Nationalist Alliance." Beinart and Dubow 206–30.

———. "The TRC Report: What Kind of History? What Kind of Truth?" Posel and Simpson, *Commissioning the Past* 147–72.

Posel, Deborah, and Graeme Simpson, eds. *Commissioning the Past: Understanding South Africa's Truth and Reconciliation Commission*. Johannesburg: Witwatersrand UP, 2002.

———. "Introduction—the Power of Truth: South Africa's Truth and Reconciliation Commission in Context." Posel and Simpson, *Commissioning the Past* 1–13.

Quayson, Ato. *Calibrations: Reading for the Social*. Minneapolis: U of Minnesota P, 2003.

Qureshi, Sadiah. "Displaying Sara Baartman, the 'Hottentot Venus.'" *History of Science* 42 (2004): 233–57.

Rassool, Ciraj, Leslie Witz, and Gary Minkley. "Burying and Memorialising the Body of Truth: The TRC and National Heritage." James and Van de Vijver 115–27.

Rastogi, Pallavi. *Afrindian Fictions: Diaspora, Race, and National Desire in South Africa*. Columbus: Ohio State UP, 2008.

Rich, Susan. "Interview with Ingrid de Kok, December 1997." *South African Poets on Poetry: Interviews from New Coin 1992–2001*. Ed. Robert Berold. Pietermaritzburg: Gecko Poetry, 2003. 111–17.

Robins, Steven. "City Sites." Nuttall and Michael, *Senses of Culture* 408–25.

———. "Silence in My Father's House: Memory, Nationalism, and Narratives of the Body." Nuttall and Coetzee 120–40.

Robinson, Jennifer. "(Im)Mobilizing Space—Dreaming of Change." Judin and Vladislavić 163–71.

Robolin, Stéphane P.R. "Loose Memory in Toni Morrison's *Paradise* and Zoë Wicomb's *David's Story*." *Modern Fiction Studies* 52.2 (2006): 297–320.

Ross, Fiona C. *Bearing Witness: Women and the Truth and Reconciliation Commission in South Africa*. London: Pluto P, 2003.

Rotberg, Robert, and Dennis Thompson, eds. *Truth v. Justice: The Morality of Truth Commissions*. Princeton, NJ: Princeton UP, 2000.

Rothberg, Michael. *Traumatic Realism: The Demands of Holocaust Representation*. Minneapolis: U of Minnesota P, 2000.

Ruden, Sarah. "*Country of My Skull: Guilt and Sorrow and the Limits of Forgiveness in the New South Africa* (Review)." *Ariel* 30.1 (January 1999): 165–79.

Sachs, Albie. "His Name Was Henry." James and Van de Vijver 94–100.

———. "Personal Accounts." Boraine, Levy, and Scheffer 20–25.

Saks, D.Y. "Remembering Adam Kok: Griqua Nationalism in the Apartheid Era." *Quarterly Bulletin of the South African Library* 51.3 (1997): 109–15.

Samuelson, Meg. "The Mother as Witness: Reading *Mother to Mother* alongside South Africa's Truth and Reconciliation Commission." Koyana, *Sindiwe Magona* 127–44.

———. *Remembering the Nation, Dismembering Women? Stories of the South African Transition*. Pietermaritzburg: U of KwaZulu-Natal P, 2007.

Sanders, Mark. *Ambiguities of Witnessing: Law and Literature in the Time of a Truth Commission*. Stanford, CA: Stanford UP, 2007.

———. "Truth, Telling, Questioning: The Truth and Reconciliation Commission, Antjie Krog's *Country of My Skull*, and Literature after Apartheid." *MFS: Modern Fiction Studies* 46.1 (2000): 13–41.

SAPA. "Police Torturer Despises Himself, TRC Told." 20 October 1997. http://www.doj.gov.za/trc/media/1997/9710/s971020a.htm.

Sassen, Saskia. "Spatialities and Temporalities of the Global: Elements for a Theorization." *Globalization*. Ed. Arjun Appadurai. Durham, NC: Duke UP, 2001. 260–78.

Schaffer, Kay, and Sidonie Smith. "Human Rights, Storytelling, and the Position of the Beneficiary: Antjie Krog's *Country of My Skull*." *PMLA* 121.5 (2006): 1577–84.

Schatteman, Renée. "Interview with Sindiwe Magona." *Scrutiny2* 11.2 (2006): 154–64.

"Should Reform Be Faster or Steadier?" *Economist* 9 July 2005: 38–39.

Sihlongonyane, Mfaniseni Fana. "Land Occupations in South Africa." *Reclaiming the Land: The Resurgence of Rural Movements in Africa, Asia and Latin America*. Ed. Sam Moyo and Paris Yeros. London/Cape Town: Zed Books/David Philip, 2005. 142–64.

Simone, AbdouMaliq. *For the City Yet to Come: Changing African Life in Four Cities*. Durham: Duke UP, 2004.

———. "People as Infrastructure: Intersecting Fragments in Johannesburg." *Public Culture* 16.3 (2004): 407–29.

Simpson, Graeme. "Tell No Lies, Claim No Easy Victories: A Brief Evaluation of South Africa's Truth and Reconciliation Commission." Posel and Simpson, *Commissioning the Past* 220–51.

Skotnes, Pippa. "'Civilised Off the Face of the Earth': Museum Display and the Silencing of the /Xam." *Poetics Today* 22.2 (2001): 299–321.

Slovo, Gillian. *Red Dust*. London: Virago, 2000.

Smith, Neil. *Uneven Development: Nature, Capital, and the Production of Space*. Oxford: Blackwell, 1984.

Smith, Neil, and Cindi Katz. "Grounding Metaphor: Towards a Spatialized Politics." Keith and Pile 67–83.

Sommer, Doris. "'Not Just a Personal Story': Women's *Testimonios* and the Plural Self." *Life/Lines: Theorizing Women's Autobiography*. Ed. Bella Brodzki and Celeste Schenck. Ithaca: Cornell UP, 1988. 107–30.

Soyinka, Wole. *The Burden of Memory, the Muse of Forgiveness*. Oxford: Oxford UP, 1999.

Spearey, Susan. "Displacement, Dispossession and Conciliation: The Politics and Poetics of Homecoming in Antjie Krog's *Country of My Skull*." *Scrutiny2* 5.1 (2000): 64–77.

The Story I Am about to Tell. By the Khulumani Support Group, Bobby Rodwell, and Lesego Rampolokeng. Perf. Khulumani Support Group. Market Theatre, Johannesburg. 10 June 2000.

Taylor, Jane. "Truth or Reconciliation?" *Rhodes Journalism Review* May (1997): 3.

———. *Ubu and the Truth Commission*. Cape Town: UCT P, 1998.

———. "Writer's Note." *Ubu and the Truth Commission*. Cape Town: UCT P, 1998. ii–vii.

Titlestad, Michael. *Making the Changes: Jazz in South African Literature and Reportage*. Pretoria/Leiden: UNISA P/Brill, 2004.

Titlestad, Michael, and Michael Kissack. "'The Foot Does Not Sniff': Imagining the Post-*Anti*-Apartheid Intellectual." *Journal of Literary Studies* 19.3/4 (2003): 255–70.

———. "Secular Improvisations: The Poetics of Invention in Ivan Vladislavić's *The Exploded View*." *Scrutiny2* 11.2 (2006): 11–26.

Tomlinson, Richard, Robert A. Beauregard, Lindsay Bremner, and Xolela Mangcu, eds. *Emerging Johannesburg: Perspectives on the Postapartheid City*. New York: Routledge, 2003.

Truth and Reconciliation Commission. *Truth and Reconciliation Commission of South Africa Report*. 5 vols. Cape Town: TRC, 1998.

———. *Truth and Reconciliation Commission of South Africa Report*. Volumes 6 and 7. Cape Town: TRC, 2003.

Tutu, Desmond. "Foreword by Chairperson." *Truth and Reconciliation Commission of South Africa Report*. Cape Town: TRC, 1998. 1–23.

———. *No Future without Forgiveness*. New York: Doubleday Publishing, 2000.

Understanding Apartheid: A Supplement for Teachers and Learners. Apartheid Museum. http://www.apartheidmuseum.org/supplements/issue1/intro.html.

Van der Merwe, Chris N., and Pumla Gobodo-Madikizela. *Narrating Our Healing: Perspectives on Working through Trauma*. Newcastle, UK: Cambridge Scholars Publishing, 2007.

Van der Merwe, Hugo. "National Narratives versus Local Truths: The Truth and Reconciliation Commission's Engagement with Duduza." Posel and Simpson, *Commissioning the Past* 204–19.

Van Zyl Slabbert, Frederik. "Truth without Reconciliation, Reconciliation without Truth." James and Van de Vijver 62–72.

Van Zyl, Susan. "Skyhooks and Diagrams: The Signing of South Africa in Ivan Vladislavić's *The Exploded View*." *Scrutiny2* 11.2 (2006): 75–84.

Verwoerd, Wilhelm, and Mahlubi "Chief" Mabizela. "An Interview with Zapiro (Jonathan Shapiro)." *Truths Drawn in Jest: Commentary on the Truth and Reconciliation Commission through Cartoons*. Ed. Verwoerd and Mabizela. Cape Town: David Philip, 2000. 153–60.

Viljoen, Louise. "On Space and Identity in Antjie Krog's *Country of My Skull*." *Under Construction: Links for the Site of Literary Theory*. Ed. Dirk De Geest et al. Leuven, Belgium: Leuven UP, 2000. 39–59.

Viljoen, Shaun. "Non-Racialism Remains a Fiction: Richard Rive's '*Buckingham Palace*,' *District Six* and K. Sello Duiker's *The Quiet Violence of Dreams*." *English Academy Review* 18 (2001): 46–53.

Villa-Vicencio, Charles. "On the Limits of Academic History: The Quest for Truth Demands Both More and Less." James and Van de Vijver 21–31.

Villa-Vicencio, Charles, and Erik Doxtader, eds. *The Provocations of Amnesty: Memory, Justice and Impunity*. Trenton, NJ: Africa World P, 2003.

Villa-Vicencio, Charles, and Fanie du Toit, eds. *Truth & Reconciliation in South Africa: 10 Years On*. Cape Town: David Philip, 2006.

Villa-Vicencio, Charles, and Wilhelm Verwoerd. "Constructing a Report: Writing up the 'Truth.'" Rotberg and Thompson 279–94.

Villa-Vicencio, Charles, and Wilhelm Verwoerd, eds. *Looking Back Reaching Forward: Reflections on the Truth and Reconciliation Commission of South Africa*. Cape Town: UCT P/Zed Books, 2000.

Vladislavić, Ivan. *The Exploded View*. Johannesburg: Random House, 2004.

———. *Propaganda by Monuments & Other Stories*. Cape Town: David Philip, 1996.

———. *The Restless Supermarket*. Cape Town: David Philip, 2001.

Walaza, Nomfundo. "Insufficient Healing and Reparation." Villa-Vicencio and Verwoerd, *Looking Back* 250–55.

Walder, Dennis. "The Necessity of Error: Memory and Representation in the New Literatures." *Reading the "New" Literatures in a Postcolonial Era*. Ed. Susheila Nasta. Cambridge: D.S. Brewer, 2000. 149–70.

Walker, Cherryl. "The Limits to Land Reform: Rethinking 'the Land Question.'" *Journal of Southern African Studies* 31.4 (2005): 805–24.

Wallmach, Kim. "'Seizing the Surge of Language by Its Soft, Bare Skull': Simultaneous Interpreting, the Truth Commission and *Country of My Skull*." *Current Writing* 14.2 (2002): 64–82.

Warnes, Christopher. "Interview with Ivan Vladislavić." *MFS: Modern Fiction Studies* 46.1 (2000): 273–81.

———. "The Making and Unmaking of History in Ivan Vladislavić's *Propaganda by Monuments and Other Stories*." *MFS: Modern Fiction Studies* 46.1 (2000): 67–89.

Wasserman, Herman, and Sean Jacobs, eds. *Shifting Selves: Post-Apartheid Essays on Mass Media, Culture and Identity*. Cape Town: Kwela, 2003.

Watts, Michael. "Baudelaire over Berea, Simmel over Sandton?" *Public Culture* 17.1 (2005): 181–92.

Weideman, Marinda. "Who Shaped South Africa's Land Reform Policy?" *Politikon* 31.2 (2004): 219–38.

Wells, Julia C. "Eva's Men: Gender and Power in the Establishment of the Cape of Good Hope, 1652–74." *Journal of African History* 39 (1998): 417–37.

Wenzel, Marita. "Appropriating Space and Transcending Boundaries in *The Africa House* by Christina Lamb and *Ways of Dying* by Zakes Mda." *Journal of Literary Studies* 19.3/4 (2003): 316–30.

White, Hayden. "Historical Emplotment and the Problem of Truth." *Probing the Limits of Representation: Nazism and the "Final Solution."* Ed. Saul Friedlander. Cambridge, MA: Harvard UP, 1992. 37–53.

Wicomb, Zoë. *David's Story*. New York: Feminist P, 2000.

Willemse, Hein. "Zoë Wicomb in Conversation with Hein Willemse." *Research in African Literatures* 33.1 (2002): 144–52.

Winer, Stan. "Play Gives an Outlet to Collective Betrayal." *Reconstruct* 16 July 2000: 8.

Wittenberg, Hermann. "Race, Memory and Trauma" (Review of Sindiwe Magona's *Mother to Mother*). *English Academy Review* 15 (1998): 318–21.

Wolpe, Harold. "Capitalism and Cheap Labour Power in South Africa: From Segregation to Apartheid." Beinart and Dubow 60–90.

Wood, Felicity. "Taking Fun Seriously: The Potency of Play in Ivan Vladislavić's Short Stories." *English Academy Review* 18 (2001): 21–37.

Woods, Tim. *African Pasts: Memory and History in African Literatures*. Manchester: Manchester UP, 2007.

Woodward, Wendy. "Beyond Fixed Geographies of the Self: Counterhegemonic Selves and Symbolic Spaces in Achmat Dangor's 'Kafka's Curse' and Anne Landsman's *The Devil's Chimney*." *Current Writing* 12.2 (2000): 21–37.

———. " 'Jim Comes from Jo'burg': Regionalised Identities and Social Comedy in Zakes Mda's *The Heart of Redness*." *Current Writing* 15.2 (2003): 173–85.

———. "Laughing Back at the Kingfisher: Zakes Mda's *The Heart of Redness* and Postcolonial Humour." *Cheeky Fictions: Laughter and the Postcolonial*. Ed. Susanne Reichl and Mark Stein. Amsterdam: Rodopi, 2005. 287–99.

Young, Elaine. "Interview with Achmat Dangor." *Kunapipi* 24.1–2 (2002): 52–60.

———. " 'Or Is It Just the Angle?' Rivalling Realist Representation in Ivan Vladislavić's *Propaganda by Monuments and Other Stories*." *English Academy Review* 18 (2001): 38–45.

Zegeye, Abebe, ed. *Social Identities in the New South Africa*. Cape Town: Kwela, 2001.

Zerbst, Fiona. "A Poetry of Purgatory" (Review of *Transfer* by Ingrid de Kok). *New Contrast* 27.3 (1999): 62–64.

Index